LORD OF SHADOWS

LORD OF SHADOWS

MARY LENNOX

FIVE STAR

A part of Gale, Cengage Learning

Detroit • New York • San Francisco • New Haven, Conn • Waterville, Maine • London

GALE
CENGAGE Learning™

Copyright © 2008 by Mary Glazer.
Five Star Publishing, a part of Gale, Cengage Learning.

Set in 11 pt. Plantin.
Printed on permanent paper.

LIBRARY OF CONGRESS CATALOGING-IN-PUBLICATION DATA

Lennox, Mary, 1944–
    Lord of shadows / Mary Lennox. — 1st ed.
    p. cm.
    ISBN-13: 978-1-59414-697-8 (hardcover : alk. paper)
    ISBN-10: 1-59414-697-7 (hardcover : alk. paper)
    1. Aristocracy—Social Class—England—Fiction. 2. London (England)—Fiction. 3. Great Britian—History—19th century—Fiction. I. Title.
    PS3612.E55L77 2008
    813'.6—dc22   2008016370

First Edition. First Printing: August 2008.
Published in 2008 in conjunction with Tekno Books.

Printed in the United States of America
1 2 3 4 5 6 7 12 11 10 09 08

In Memoriam
Arthur Stix Glazer
Husband, Dearest Friend, Forever Love

ACKNOWLEDGMENTS

This has been a year when friendships and family have given me more than they could ever realize. So with love and gratitude, I thank Cassie and EJ, Phoebe and Dave, James and Jette, Carla and George for their love and protectiveness. Special love to my sister, Susan, and you, Mom.

To my critique partner, Amy Tolnitch, to all Five Corners—Jackie, Sarah, Jenn and Misti—hugs for friendships that brought back the joy of writing. And to Deni Dietz, brilliant editor and writer, a huge thank you for wrestling with a difficult format, and your unerring nose for the pink weeds so expertly eradicated from this book.

PROLOGUE

The Duke of Wimbley's Town house
London, May of 1843
In darkness and disguise, Devlin Ramsay Carmichael led a murderer toward his brother's chamber.

Jesus, I should be sweating in agony, Dev thought. But he felt nothing other than cold clarity. Actually, he hadn't recently felt much one way or another, unless a waking nightmare hit him.

The debacle in Afghanistan had been the last straw. Now, he trusted only logic and concentration to serve. For the most part, it kept him sane.

"Finally," Abdul Massad, heretofore trusted advisor to Dev's brother, King Ari of Zaranbad, whispered. "I'll wipe the Dassam dynasty from the earth."

As they navigated the dim corridors, Dev's thoughts centered on the one flaw in the plan he'd devised. Massad hadn't revealed whether he'd opted for a pistol, a knife, or poison. But the man was weaker and slower than Ari. It must be poison. Sternly, he subdued an unruly twinge of anxiety threatening his control.

They were almost at Ari's door when Massad grabbed Dev's arm. "Careful. Act normal. We must get away before the king's body is discovered. When the moment is ripe for me to act, slip outside and wait for me."

Dev nodded and rapped twice on the door—the signal he and Ari had devised.

The kohl and ochre mixture darkening his face, and his black

9

turban, jodhpurs and coat would hide his identity if Ari remembered to dim the lamps in his sitting room.

"Enter," Ari called from inside.

Dev lifted the latch, walked into the darkened study and threw his brother a tight smile of approval. Shadowy lamplight glimmered on a low table between Ari's wing chair and another, set opposite it. Dev made a servant's obeisance, right hand touching bowed forehead, then heart, then steepled against his left as he bowed.

Ari indolently waved a hand in acknowledgment from his seat at the table. One leg crossed elegantly over the other, the king was dressed in full European regalia, with the royal Badge of the Leopard displayed on a wide maroon ribbon crossed over his chest. His proud bearing clearly revealed his solid sense of his place in the world.

Whereas, Dev realized with a twinge of envy, *I belong nowhere.*

As Abdul Massad bowed to Ari, Dev retreated and stood against the wall directly behind the minister.

Massad shivered, moved a bit closer to the fire, and rubbed his hands together. "Your Majesty, I have news from Zaranbad from your esteemed grandfather, which I felt must take precedence over the festivities welcoming you to England."

"Please," Ari said, raising his hand in an unconsciously imperial gesture. "Sit opposite me, my dear Abdul, and relay to me this news."

He motioned to Dev, who, on cue, brought two delicate, etched crystal cups filled with tea and pomegranate juice to the low table between them. Then he bowed and backed toward the door, letting it close behind him without leaving the chamber, but slipping instead into the shadowed alcove beside it, where he had a good view of the room.

Massad's shoulders relaxed minutely as he assumed he was alone with Ari. Dev supposed he'd be more comfortable committing regicide without a witness.

"My grandfather is well?" Ari asked in a voice laced with concern. From reports by his own men, Dev knew the deeply loved old man was in fact quite well, and that Massad used the falsehood as a ploy to distract the king.

"There is a problem with his health," Massad said in a voice that seemed wracked with misery. Then he sat back, seemingly to await the impact of his words.

"What sort of problem?" Ari's voice shook.

"His heart is not good."

"This is very bad news, indeed." Ari stood and walked to the tall window overlooking the rose garden. The blazing reds and golds of the season's display were dimming in the growing twilight. He stared out, his hands clasped behind his back. Dev could see his shoulders trembling.

Oh, excellent, he thought. *Ari could tread the boards with that act.*

Quickly, Massad pulled the vial from his sash, and emptied a pinch of the contents into King Ari's glass. *Aconite, perhaps,* Dev thought, his fists clenching. One tenth of a grain would kill a rabbit. Two whole grains could easily wipe out a king. Massad carefully wiped his hands with the napkin beside his own glass and then rose.

"My king," he said quietly, coming up behind Ari.

Dev moved to the table, his feet silent on the deep carpet.

"I fear that if you wish to see your grandfather alive again you should return to Zaranbad in all haste. Come," Massad soothed. "Sit and take chai. It will revive you, and we can plan your return visit."

Ari drew out his imitation of grief long enough for Dev to do what he must and slip again into the shadowed alcove beside the door.

Finally, Ari returned to his seat and said, "But the treaties

11

with the British, the new embassy for Zaranbad—all this will not be accomplished if I return immediately."

"The decision is yours, of course. I would not for a moment assume to question your judgment," Massad said as he took his tea with eager, shaking hands and emptied it into his mouth. As soon as he swallowed, the little minister gasped and clutched his throat.

Dev raced to kneel beside Massad. "Quickly," he said. "What poison?"

"Nabee!" Massad gurgled the Indian name for the substance, clutching his heart and staring up at Dev with wild eyes. "My gods, you switched the glasses."

"Aconite. Just as I thought," Dev said as Ari leaned over Massad from the other side. Dev turned Massad's head as he cast up the contents of his stomach. He wiped Massad's mouth with a napkin.

"We don't have much time," he told Ari. "Quickly, get him down."

They laid Massad prone on the carpet as he began to convulse.

"Abdul, it is Prince Devlin," Dev said quietly. "I have an antidote here—digitalis. Take it and you will live. First you must tell me, who is your leader? The members of the United Band? You have only a moment before it's too late."

Massad's pulse was already thready and weak. His breath came in labored gasps. His gaze glittered as he stared up at Dev. "You double-damned chameleon," he rasped.

Dev snatched the antidote from his pocket. He needed this man alive, and he only had a minute left.

"Drink this while there's still time, then give us the names."

Massad turned his face away and clamped his lips shut. "Compared to facing the man who ordered this plot, death will be a blessing," he said hoarsely.

"Who did it?" Tension snaked through Dev. If Massad wasted any more time . . .

"Take the antidote! I can protect you from him!"

Abdul gasped, and grabbed his belly. "I do not know him. But we know he gutted a servant when in a rage. What would he do to me or my family?"

"Drink! I'll find him," Dev urged, pulling Abdul toward him. He pried Massad's jaw open, pouring the contents of the antidote into his mouth.

Massad spat it out. "He is clever and cruel as Satan. You will never find him." He doubled over, clutching his chest.

Another enemy of England dying at his feet.

What have I become? Dev wondered in bleak self-disgust. But it was as it was. Someday, he'd deal with it and all the other demons from the past. Not now. That way lay madness.

"If I betray this devil," Massad said in a weak whisper, "my wife and children will die." His body spasmed once, twice, then lay still. Color leached from his face, tingeing it with gray.

Dev choked down bile. He knelt beside Massad and gently wiped his face.

"Dev!" Ari's urgent voice cut through his despair and guilt. "Do something! We need his information."

"It's too late," Dev said.

"How in the name of God could you have let this happen? You're a doctor!"

Ignoring the question, Dev asked one of his own while examining the body. "Did Massad have any health problems? A heart condition, perhaps, of which I wasn't informed?"

"Christ," Ari muttered. "Yes."

Dev would have acted far differently had he known. However, once again, he was torn between two oaths as yet another man suffered and died before his eyes.

Dev slowly rose to his feet and took up the weary burden of

self-control. The shock and regret was all in a day's work in the shadow world he inhabited.

He straightened his shoulders, turned from the king, and opened the door to check the hallway. "You may leave me to deal with Abdul's body," he said in an expressionless voice. "Prepare yourself for the festivities."

Ari opened his mouth to say something, and abruptly shut it again. He strode to the door, opened it with fumbling hands, and closed it after him. Dev stood still, listening to Ari's footsteps as he almost ran down the hall toward his rooms.

Dev knelt beside the minister's body, gently rearranging his contorted limbs and shutting his eyes. Abdul Massad had helped him up onto the back of his first pony. He'd been a laughing, carefree man in those days, predisposed to tell thrilling tales about djinns and caverns of precious jewels.

Dev found a shawl draped across a chair and covered Massad's face. "Farewell, Abdul," he said softly. Then he walked to the tall window, opened it, and gave a low whistle. Two men appeared at the window and climbed into the room.

"My lord," one said as they both bowed.

The notes of a waltz wafted from the ballroom on the floor above. The ball had begun. Dev would enter that room soon, his usual cool and aloof mask in place, as though he hadn't just betrayed one sacred oath for another.

He pointed. "Over there," he said. "Take the minister's body to the East End. Remove his purse and leave him lying in an alley near one of the higher priced brothels. Then alert the authorities."

"My lord?" said one. "You'll be safer if we strip and dress him as a homeless drunk. If we alert the authorities, the United Band will know that we thwarted this attempt."

"Perhaps. Or perhaps they will think he needed a woman's comfort before carrying out his orders. This way, he will be buried according to Zaranbadian custom. Even a traitor deserves a proper burial."

The men nodded quietly and rolled the body in the Turkey carpet lying at the foot of his chair. They slipped out the window with the carpet, and disappeared into the night.

Dev picked up the delicate crystal glass holding the last drops of the poison. He stared at it for a moment, pressing his lips together. When the agony swamped him, he flung it with all his might against the back of the fireplace. It burst into thousands of tiny shards, melting away in the heat of the flames.

CHAPTER ONE:
A LADY'S REPUTATION

As she slipped out the French doors of the Duke of Wimbley's ballroom, Lady Caroline Berring wondered for the hundredth time when the next ship would be leaving for America. Or India. Or Timbuktu, for that matter. Anywhere would be preferable to being here, snubbed by ladies and lasciviously perused by those who called themselves gentlemen.

She sighed and tiptoed down the stone stairs into a small, secluded arbor beneath the balcony. The scent of tobacco smoke revealed the presence of others near her hideaway. Caroline crept farther back into the arbor and then heard a familiar voice just to the left. Maximillian Standridge, Earl of Nearing and a good friend of her brother William, spoke to someone unknown. His low voice reached her quite clearly.

"I'm going to dance with Lady Caroline Berring tonight," Nearing said, and immediately Caroline cheered up a little. Nearing was one of those men she occasionally danced with simply because he seemed to know how to talk to her without ogling.

"You wish to fix your interest with her?" the other man murmured.

There was a pause, then Nearing sighed. "Alas, I cannot marry her." His voice sounded so wistful that Caroline couldn't even bring herself to be hurt by the words. "Do you think she might agree to a liaison?"

"I shouldn't imagine she would consider anything of the

sort," came the terse reply. Caroline could almost feel the tension in the other man's tone. "And what stupid people suggested long ago about her is pure rubbish. Maxim, you cannot possibly think Society knows its arse from its elbow.

"Furthermore," the stranger went on in an ever-so-slightly heated voice, "I cannot believe that you contemplate propositioning a gently bred girl. She will most judiciously consider it a painful insult and you a blackguard for suggesting it."

Caroline's heart raced. Who was the man defending her so nobly when others would only have cheered Nearing on?

"I hate to consider such a thing," the earl said in a somber voice. "My heart would much prefer to offer her an honorable match. But you know my grandmother. Heaven forefend that I humiliate the family by less than a completely unexceptionable mate."

He cleared his throat and sighed. "I must confess that I find Caroline quite enchanting—so much so that I long to be with her in *some* way if not in the *right* way. It makes me furious that her prospects are so dismal, but I'm helpless to do anything about it. Unless something happens to raise her in the eyes of the ton, she'll have to take some country baronet or an untitled gentleman for a husband."

"The dowry doesn't tempt?" his companion asked. "I hear that she's got a fortune. Even that Hall shrew found herself a viscount with one, and she was a merchant's daughter."

"Unfortunately, in my case, the dowry's not enough to offset a man's duty to his family name," Nearing said. "When I mentioned my intention to wed her, Grandmama almost had apoplexy right there in the dining room. She spoke some gibberish about blemishing the line. You know how good she's been to me. I couldn't bear to disappoint her."

Caroline pressed her fist to her lips to keep back the sob that threatened to expose her. The urge to flee seized her. Picking up her skirts, she slipped from the arbor and raced for the formal garden beyond the balcony.

It's so unfair, she thought miserably as she ran down the darkened pathway toward the fountains. She had been born a respectable seven months after the death of her supposed father, the Earl of Eversleigh.

It would have been quite all right had she been a brunette like her mother and the earl, she thought as she slumped down onto a bench. But she had the auburn hair and deep blue eyes of the Duke of Hartford, rumored at that time to be a very good friend of her widowed mama.

She breathed in the cool night air, and relaxed her tight shoulders beneath the shawl that warmed her bare arms and décolletage. The moon rose cool and mysterious in the night sky.

She looked up at it, wishing that the pure, clear light would bring her peace.

But she seethed. Inside, she roared her fury. Perhaps it was hearing such hateful truths from Nearing's lips. Perhaps it was a culmination of all the nights like this, when, barely tolerated, she kept to the fringes of ballrooms, overhearing whispers about herself. She'd had more than enough, by God. It was time for something better to happen to her.

Suddenly, a new, startling thought entered her mind. Perhaps she'd had it all turned about wrong for the past year since her come out. Better things didn't just *happen.* Perhaps she would have to *make* them happen.

When a young woman dashed into the shadowed garden just beyond the balcony, Maxim Standridge, the Earl of Nearing, whipped round to his friend, Devlin Ramsay Carmichael, the Marquess of Headleymoor. "What was that?" he asked.

"You mean 'who was that.' That was Lady Caroline Berring."

"No!" Maxim groaned. "If so, she heard everything! You must be mistaken, Dev."

"I am not."

"How is that possible? You couldn't see her in the dark."

"The wind brought her scent to me as she ran off. She smells of wildflowers, and as far as I can tell, it's not from a particular perfume."

"Eh?" Nearing's voice took on a combative tone. "And how would you have gotten close enough to know her scent?"

"In the guise of Ram Dass, I've spoken to her several times."

"Jesus. My apologies for insulting you. I'm a bit undone. Of course you'd never act the cad with her," Nearing said, for once envying his friend's sangfroid. "Dev, how am I ever to make this right?"

"Go inside and pretend you haven't the slightest clue as to who that mysterious woman in the garden was. I'll think of something. Good thing I'm still in disguise."

Maxim shook his head in bald admiration. "A damn good one it is, too. I wouldn't have recognized you if I hadn't heard your voice. Please accept my thanks, old fellow."

"Thanks are not enough. If I fix this for you so that Lady Caroline does not think you a despicable lecher and your grandmother declares you a dutiful grandson, you will do me the favor of marrying Lady Caroline and treating her with the respect she deserves. Agreed?"

"If you could do all that for me, I'd crawl across the cold stones of the church and remain on my knees before her for the entire wedding ceremony."

"I might just hold you to that," Devlin Carmichael said, and, wrapping his turban over his hair, walked down the path into the garden without another word.

The scent of lilacs and fresh greenery in the recesses of the garden did not calm Caroline at all. She was—livid. Yes, that was the word. Nearing and all the men in that ballroom could go to the devil. No wonder she hated these balls. Why had she come tonight?

Her lips tugged in a wry smile. She couldn't hide from the facts. She'd come to get another glimpse of the enigmatic, aloof Devlin Carmichael, Marquess of Headleymoor, newly returned from exotic lands far to the east.

All the town was talking about him. He had an enormous fortune and stood to inherit a dukedom someday. These two facts outweighed his one flaw—he was the son of not just a duke, but a princess of Zaranbad, that small, but wealthy country that neighbored India to its west. And although the royal family of Zaranbad was Christian, it was not quite European in skin color. The prince's skin tone was a golden tan, which Caroline found quite attractive. But were it not for his wealth and position, Society might have given him the same treatment it gave her.

Perhaps his understanding of Society's prejudices had resulted in his stiff and mighty pride. For if she had ever seen a walking, breathing lesson for a woman to place character above beauty, it was the Marquess of Headleymoor.

The man was a study in the exotic—blond hair, with tip-tilted, deep, dark eyes beneath light brown brows, a straight, perfect nose, and sculpted lips. He looked like something wild and glorious and unpredictable that had stepped right out of nature into a tame English garden. But he acted like the most stiff-rumped peer in the nation. As there were rather a few of those strutting about Society, the dubious honor was hard won.

It was absurd to waste time thinking of someone whom she'd no doubt despise upon acquaintance. However, as she stood little chance of making this particular paragon of pride's acquaintance, it mattered little if she stared a bit.

Look where her foolhardy fascination had gotten her! She'd just faced rejection again for a peek at the top-lofty marquess.

There you have it, she thought. *I'm a simpering idiot.*

Well, to the devil with fleeing in shame from every social encounter. She would pack her trunks and tell Mama she was leaving for an adventure. She'd go to India, where people would only stare at her because she was a foreigner, and not the Duke of Hartford's bastard daughter.

She bowed her head. Something wet and cool dropped on her hand. It glittered in the moonlight. Fustian! Why should Nearing, miserable cur that he was, make her cry?

But at that thought, the dam broke. All fumbles, she tore off her shawl. Burying her face in it, she sobbed.

And realized that she wasn't alone when a man's gloved hand, holding a snowy white handkerchief, appeared in front of her face. Swamped by mortification, she took it and looked up to see a tall Indian dressed in a black jacket, jodhpurs, and turban bending over her.

"My lady, are you unwell?" a soft, musical voice asked.

The voice was familiar, and spoke of another evening when she had been hurt and alone and desperate for a kind word. "Yes—no—I don't know." She blew her nose and looked up. "Ram Dass?" she asked.

The Indian doctor who hovered in the background in the Duke of Wimbley's service was the only man who could have found her like this without humiliating her. Last year, at a particularly difficult house party, a woman of low station publicly cast aspersions on Mama and her. Magically, Ram Dass appeared by their side, and with tact and kindness, spirited them out of the room before Mama could burst into tears.

"Yes, my lady, it is I."

"Hullo," she said glumly and sighed.

"Lady Caroline," Ram Dass said in his deep, soft voice. "It is the wish of this servant to aid you. If you would tell me what is troubling you, perhaps I could do so."

Caroline tried to laugh, but it sounded more like a sob to her mortified ears. "I don't think anyone can help."

Ram Dass knelt on one knee and looked up at her. His face was dimly visible, giving her a greater sense of security, as if she were in the kindly presence of a celestial spirit, or in Ram Dass's case, a djinn.

"Perhaps I can help," he said. "A lady might say things to a stranger that she would not share with her own family. I am almost, but not quite, a stranger. I am also observant of this English Society which I serve. If nothing else, I can offer a fresh perspective."

The concern in his voice was terribly comforting. "If you could help, I would not wish a sympathetic pat on the shoulder," Caroline said. "I want action, pragmatic action that will change my life, and that of my mother, for the better."

Ram Dass cocked one dark brow in question, and then rose to sit beside her. "I apologize for this liberty, but if I am to hear of this wish for action, I must be close enough for softly spoken confidences."

His size and his proximity did not remind her of a spirit. His muscled arm almost touched her shoulder, and Caroline felt . . . enveloped in strength and warmth. She blew out a deep breath she'd been holding. Staring resolutely ahead, she stumbled through a halting recitation that picked up speed as she revealed everything—about overhearing Nearing's cruel words, about the snubs and the insults and the lure of America, far away from British Society.

"But it's not just I who feels each hurt, you know," she said. "Mama is so very sad. And she's always apologizing, as though this were all her fault, when in reality, it took two to make a scandal. I don't think I can leave her alone to endure it."

She tried to stop the flow of words pouring out in a rush, but it felt so good to tell someone she knew to be kind and trustworthy. Finally, after what seemed a torrent of words, she turned to face Ram Dass and stared into his wise, expressive face.

"Now, sir, tell me. Do you honestly know of a way to get what I wish, for myself, and my poor mother?"

Ram Dass smiled, and his whole face was transformed into something that Caroline wished she could study and paint—mischief, intelligence and beauty all at once.

"I do, in fact have an answer, my lady. It is my modest opinion that all societies will ever be cruel to those without a true place in them. If you wish to transform British Society's attitude toward you and your mother, you must appear to be above the rest, so one dares approach you only with extreme politesse."

Has the man not been listening to me at all? Caroline asked herself impatiently. "And how could I ever manage to do that, given my present position as a scandalous . . . lovechild?" she said through teeth gritted in frustration.

"Ah, but did I not say that I am unusually observant of this British ton? And I happen to work for the father of a man who has been hoping to make your acquaintance. Any attention from him would immediately raise you above the rest of the young ladies at this ball."

"The Marquess of Headleymoor—wishing to know me?" Caroline squeaked. "You must be bamming me, and that is not what I would have expected from you."

"I am not—how do you say it?—bamming—teasing you. I am perfectly serious, my lady."

"But the Marquess is actually rather a—a—" At the very thought of speaking to Headleymoor, Caroline's palms became damp with perspiration.

"A bit pompous? A bit aloof?"

She nodded slowly, staring up in the dim light of the torches at Ram Dass's amused expression beneath the dark turban.

"His demeanor is so cold it burns. I've heard ladies stutter their acceptance the few times he's deigned to ask them to dance.

"I do not have a nervous disposition," she went on hurriedly, "but at times, I believe he has—has looked at me, with those piercing eyes. It made me feel as though my insides were exposed, and all tangled in knots. I end by feeling furious with him."

There was a long pause, in which Ram Dass cleared his throat and Caroline slumped in gloomy disappointment. Even Ram Dass must realize how hopeless it all was.

"Lord Headleymoor is a very observant man," he finally said. "He is also a very serious man, which accounts for his expression when he might have glimpsed you on one occasion or another."

"I know that look of his, Ram Dass. One would not call it serious, but judgmental. And furthermore," Caroline said with more than a hint of the asperity she felt, "Headleymoor is a man of great wealth and position. He may have some excuse to be so proud and unpleasant, but from where I stand, it is a small one."

"It is this servant's opinion that he feels the weight of being a prince of Zaranbad as well as the heir to a dukedom." Ram Dass rose and lifted his face to the breeze as he spoke. "Of course, the British would never address him as 'prince,' for they would have to admit to themselves and the world that a peer of the realm could actually have the blood of Zaranbad in him, as well. That would be almost akin to having an Indian or Chinese marquess in their midst."

A rather long pause followed this impassioned speech. Then more mildly, Ram Dass said, "Please accept this servant's apology for such rudeness. My petty reflections upon British prejudices have no part in this discussion."

Caroline laughed. "I should say they're at the heart of it."

"Nevertheless." Ram Dass bowed his head, waved his hand, and began to pace. "As I was explaining, Lord Headleymoor has much to carry upon his shoulders. He learned early in life not to trust easily."

Several steps away from the bench, he turned with the military precision of a trained officer, and returned, his hands clasped behind his back.

"I must humbly emphasize that, above all, if you wish to take your rightful place in Society, you should accept the prince's request to dance with you. No matter what you think of him."

Caroline rolled her eyes. "Dance with a man whom I dislike in order to become more acceptable to other men."

"Rather their mothers, I believe," Ram Dass said.

"You are indeed a wise man," Caroline said with a grin.

"One or two dances with the prince would not be so terrible a fate, would it?" Ram Dass went on in a devastatingly persuasive tone. "He has no prejudice against ladies who think and read—I know you'll like that. Why, just the other day, he confided that he would give a great deal to speak with a lady about politics or literature, or life."

Caroline laughed, this time, an unbelieving sound of mirth. "Perhaps one without my highly questionable background."

"Lady Caroline," Ram Dass said rather sternly, "the prince has decided that most ladies in England bore him to tears. He does not count you among them. Now, is your conscience so rigid that it would stop you from dancing with a man whom you believe to be too proud—even if it saved a beloved mother from unhappiness?"

"No. No, *I* should be too proud to live, if that were the case. Still, I can't help but feel that you have overly ambitious plans for my position in Society. For to interest this prince—who has not seemed interested in any lady—would be a coup that even the most jaded among the ton would admire." A smile threatened to break forth at the thought of shocking those who regarded her with disdain.

"I see no reason why you could not interest a prince, my lady. You need only remain in one spot as he approaches you tonight. For I once watched you slip away before he had the pleasure of speaking to you."

"Were you there, then, at the musicale last week? I didn't see you."

He made a sound rather like a surprised cough, then straightened into his usual military stance. "We have no time for idle questions. I must again instruct you, Lady Caroline, to accept my advice on this matter. Dance with Lord Headleymoor."

Caroline felt a deep thrumming in her bones, as though the world had begun to turn backwards on its axis. And all because Ram Dass declared that the disdainful Marquess of Headleymoor might be interested in knowing her.

"Right." She took a deep breath and squared her shoulders. "Should the marquess approach me, I shall accept. I shall even try to think of him as another human being with his own problems, rather than an iceberg come to drip all over the ballroom floor."

Ram Dass smiled, a sweet, gentle curve of sculpted lips, and Caroline was struck anew with an appreciation of the man's beauty and warmth. "Then this humble servant asks that you return to Wimbley House and refresh yourself in the lady's retiring chamber. The prince will arrive with his brother soon. I would expect that you will prefer to appear before him—and Society—without tearstains."

Caroline accepted Ram Dass's arm as he led her back into the house and pointed the way down a long corridor to the lady's retiring room. He bowed gracefully over her hand, and she wondered for a moment what it would be like to simply be "sought out" by Ram Dass on his own behalf. He, too, was mysterious, but unlike his master, never daunting.

Impossible thought, she chided herself. What few friends her mama had now would totally ostracize her should Caroline run off to Gretna with an Indian servant, no matter how kind, how intelligent he was.

She'd better accept Ram Dass's advice and quit daydreaming about impossible adventures. And what would it mean to Mama if her reputation could rise from near shame to acceptability?

"Thank you," she said, and turned toward the retiring room. "I shall do as you suggest. Should Headleymoor deign to invite me to dance, I shall be properly grateful for his heroic condescension." She laughed, and waving good-bye over her shoulder, walked down the corridor to wash her face and prepare for a ludicrous campaign to catch a prince's eye.

Chapter Two:
To Dance with a Prince
(and/or a Marquess)

Dev took the long hallway at a run to meet Ari and his father. His time with Caroline Berring had made him unconscionably late. Still, it was worth enduring his father and Ari's exasperated frowns. Caroline's wit and honesty never ceased to surprise him. Somehow, just knowing he might be able to help her gave him the equilibrium to go on as he must, despite losing another chunk of his soul with the death of Abdul Massad.

Now, halfway down the hall, he gave an apologetic bow to his father and brother, who stood with their backs to the door leading down to the ballroom. Ari's best friend and Foreign Minister, Hossam Ali stood just behind them. The tall, dignified man winked, his dark eyes bright with warmth and good feeling.

"Hurry, my prince," he called with an ironic wave. "The flower of British aristocracy awaits." Hossam was the epitome of the perfect ambassador for Zaranbad. His charm and easy banter, as well as his brilliant mind, were legendary. Dev couldn't blame him for whatever ill feeling there was between Ari and himself. The blame for that rested solely on their shoulders.

It would have been better if it weren't so. But it was, and always had been. For the life of him, Dev never quite knew why.

"Wait, my lord!" Thurston, Dev's valet, gave a discreet squeak from behind, waving a snowy cravat that Dev had apparently forgotten.

"Sorry," he murmured to his father, whose love of punctuality knew no bounds. Dev was duly punished when the old fellow's lips tightened in disapproval.

"Almost done, my lord," Thurston said, and finished tying the stupid thing deftly. Dev hit the remaining space between himself and his family at top speed. As one, they turned and walked through the door. Then Hoynes, the butler, cleared his throat and a hush fell over the ballroom below.

"His Royal Majesty, King Ari of Zaranbad. His Excellency, Hossam Ali, Foreign Minister of Zaranbad. The Duke of Wimbley. The Marquess of Headlymoor," the butler intoned.

The crowd turned toward them silently, their bows and curtsies deep.

A bright burst of fanfare followed them down the wide marble stairway, the music turning first to the anthem of Zaranbad, and then that of England.

Ari looked every bit a monarch, Dev thought. His father was tall and straight, and looked every bit a duke of the realm. And he—well, he thought with an inner sneer—he looked a fraud torn between two worlds, as he did every night. No one seemed to notice, he realized, as several of those curtsies and bows were reserved for him—meaning his status as a duke's heir, of course.

If a fraud walks into a ballroom and nobody recognizes him, is he really a fraud?

"What you did today was brilliant, my lord prince," Hossam Ali said to him in an aside as they reached the bottom stair. "You saved your brother's life, and I told him this in, I am afraid, blunt speech. It is a shame that King Ari is at times so unwise as not to realize what a treasure he has in his brother."

"You are kind, Hossam. As always," Dev said, as Abdul's face, contorted in a rictus of death, rose before him.

Blinding color flashed before Dev's eyes. Blood.

Blood on the snow of a mountain pass. Abdul, groaning in

the library. And in the background, a small figure twisting against the rope around his neck. His dead, come to haunt him again. He stumbled to a stop.

Breathe, he thought fiercely. *Breathe.* He blinked, and the nightmare vision dissipated, leaving only the brilliantly lit ballroom and the crowd already clustering close. He breathed.

In Paris, Dev had worked with a brilliant professor, a student of Mesmer. He knew that trauma could produce demonic visions and waking hallucinations. Grimly, he buckled control about himself like armor and continued down the ballroom.

Think of Caroline Berring. That's right. Before, he'd always thought of her as a sweet and fragile damsel in distress. Unfortunately, he now knew she was also intelligent enough to rebel against her situation. Fragility and determination, he thought. A bad combination, that. She needed protection. The sooner Maxim married her, the better.

As though Hossam had intuited the flow of his thoughts, he asked, "Are there any fine ladies present who might pique the interest of the Marquess of Headleymoor?"

He managed a smile, cautious even with a man he should trust implicitly. "Look about you, Hossam. Are there any here who look as though they have a thought in their heads other than titles, land, and fortune?"

Hossam smiled. "It is the same in Zaranbad. Finding a jewel is a difficult task, but one that perhaps you should put your mind to. You spend too much time alone, my friend. Some lady in England must be more than just an advantageous match."

"Should you find one," Dev drawled, feigning boredom, "be certain to point her out to me."

Hossam laughed, and left him to return to Ari's side as he greeted the lords and ladies waiting in the queue to meet him.

And Dev was left with thoughts of Caroline, and what he could do for her. If even Hossam was curious about his romantic prospects, his ersatz courtship of Caroline might alert the United Band to her supposed importance to him, and thus the Dassam family. Was he putting Caroline in harm's way? He didn't wish to bring her into this mess.

Dear God. He must play out this sham courtship quickly and give her a place of honor in the ton without endangering her life.

A footman in formal dress and powdered wig offered him a glass of champagne. He took it and downed half of it, glancing round the ballroom for his elusive prey.

Finally, he saw Caroline Berring leaning against a column near the east corner. She was gowned tonight in quiet, golden brown satin trimmed with ivory lace at the heart-shaped bosom and bottom of the skirt. The color dulled the wonderful auburn highlights of her bright hair, while also dimming the roses in her cheeks. But nothing could hide the voluptuous lines of her figure. Nor could the camouflage subdue the liveliness of her expression.

He frowned. *She's for Maxim,* he reminded himself as he took a step in her direction. *That's the point of this exercise.*

"Headleymoor! Lovely do. Food's the best I've had this Season." Reggie Downs, Viscount Greenleigh, shook Dev's hand and waved vaguely in the direction of the chamber to the left of the ballroom, where a midnight buffet had been set up.

"Good to see you, Greenleigh," Dev said with a smile. Reggie was a rather dim and jolly fellow who'd been at Harrington with him.

"Didn't see you out riding to hounds this year," Reggie said. "A shame, that. My new pack is pulling together beautifully."

"I'll hope to be home next season," Dev said, remembering that Reggie was kind. And gullible. And a bit of a gossip. "Reg, what do you think? I wish to ask the little Berring to dance. Perhaps twice."

"Lady Caroline, twice? Not serious about her, are you? Like her myself, but you know it won't do, old sport." Reggie glanced about the ballroom and then poked a finger toward his head. "It's the hair," he mouthed.

"What about it? I like her hair."

"Well, I do, too. But that's the whole point, isn't it?"

"Can't see why. Her great-grandfather had even brighter hair."

"Great-grandfather?"

"Haven't you ever heard of Red Rupert Berring, the fifth earl?"

Reggie's eyes grew round. "I thought that was because of his violent temper."

"No, no. The hair," Dev said idly, gazing in Caroline's direction. "Of course," he went on in a lower voice as others gathered around him, eager for the latest *on dit,* "no one really remembers the hair. Red Rupert powdered, as they all did at that time. Also, apparently, he darkened his brows with paint. Well, must be off before they make up the next set."

He strolled toward Caroline, smiling in satisfaction as whispers sprang up behind him.

"Headleymoor, wonderful crush," a man said on his left. Dev murmured something vaguely appropriate, shook the man's hand and kept going.

Caroline had pushed off from the column and was standing straight and tall, like a brave prisoner before a firing squad. Their eyes met across the diminishing space between them. An indefinable heat rose in him, and his heart began to pound, slow and hard.

The reaction was so unusual that it startled him. He took a deep breath, attempting to scotch the bothersome feelings racing through him, but it seemed a losing battle. Particularly when she managed to look like a luscious doe about to bolt.

And so she should, when he felt like a randy buck with only one thing in mind.

Her eyes widened and her tongue peeked out, licking her lush bottom lip. The gesture had his groin aching, his steps hastening, and his tongue tying into knots. Damnation. After all the years of refusing any lure set out for him, he was racing forward without a thought of the consequences.

She's for *Maxim,* he reminded himself. He must accomplish this mock courtship quickly. Thank God he would only be forced to endure this loss of control for a few days, after which Caroline's success in the marriage mart would be assured.

He came to a halt just inches away from her. Her elusive wildflower scent wafted to him, and he breathed it in, savoring the clean, fresh fragrance.

Vague thoughts of protocol intervened. He turned first to her mother, the dowager countess of Ravenwood, hiding her youthful beauty behind a dark blue satin ball gown that barely revealed her collarbone. He made his bow.

"Lady Berring, how good of you to accept our invitation. I beg an introduction to your daughter."

Lady Berring jumped a little, as though she weren't accustomed to being addressed by gentlemen seeking an introduction to her daughter, and then smiled, a sad, sweet smile that filled him with a fierce urge to protect both of them.

"Lord Headleymoor, my daughter, Lady Caroline Berring."

Caroline's face went rosy with color. "My lord," she said, as she sank into a graceful curtsey. He took her hand and bowed over its softness, and a jolt went from his hand to his groin, startling him in its intensity.

He had a powerful, impulsive desire to throw Caroline over his shoulder and run up the stairway with her, claiming her in the most primitive manner a man could. He wouldn't stop, wouldn't let her down until they'd reached his bedchamber.

And his bed.

And along with this mad, amazing surge of lust, he felt something so odd he couldn't, at first, put a name to it. Peace, he thought in surprise. And a powerful sense of this moment, as the rest of the world and all its brutality slid away.

The orchestra struck up a waltz, and if he couldn't seize Caroline, he could at least seize the moment. "I am very happy to make your acquaintance," he murmured low. "My pleasure would be complete if you would give me this dance," he said, while heady anticipation rushed along his veins. How would it feel to hold her close?

All in the name of duty, of course. His lips curved in an uncustomary smile.

Caroline was reluctantly caught in the blaze of Headleymoor's presence. It was embarrassing to realize that even though she didn't trust him a whit, the man managed to affect her. She felt . . . short of breath. Dazed.

What a lobcock she was! She'd seen that look of shock on his face when he'd first touched her hand. She'd seen the disapproving frown that followed. The man was just as stiff rumped as she'd expected him to be.

Just look at that ramrod-straight back, that absurdly dignified mien. That smile.

Oh, dear heaven, when he smiled, he absolutely glittered. He looked beautiful, warm, predatory and amused all at the same time.

Internal alarm bells resounded through the reckless hum of pleasure rolling though her. Would Headleymoor, like Nearing, think to seduce her into becoming his mistress? She distinctly felt something very . . . sensual in Headleymoor, particularly when she looked straight into his deep gaze.

"My lady?" He bowed again, a jerk of his head and shoulders with something of impatience in it.

Caroline mentally shook herself. Oh, yes, his pompous lordship/highness had just asked her to dance.

"I should be honored," she said, trying to keep the note of irony out of her voice. But his brows went up, and she knew he'd caught the double meaning. *I should be honored—but I am not at all sure that I am.*

She took his proffered hand and walked to the floor of the ballroom.

He turned and faced her, not letting go of her right hand. His expression was serious, concentrated, his eyes full of intensity as he slowly, inexorably placed his hand on her waist and pulled her closer.

She found herself forgetting to breathe.

He took the first step and she fell into the waltz.

If there was one thing she knew she did well, it was dancing, even if the only person who had ever danced with her more than once was her dancing master.

She could not hold back the smile tugging at her lips. "How lovely," she said.

"Indeed," he replied, but he was gazing down at her as though he meant that she was lovely. She gazed back, self-consciousness overwhelmed by a start of recognition.

I know those eyes. How is that possible? We've just been introduced. Mooncalf, she thought, *this is your great social triumph of the Season. For pity's sake, pay attention and bask away. 'T'will be over soon enough!*

He was graceful and commanding as he swept her into turns and glides around the packed ballroom. She wanted to throw her head back and laugh at the fun of it all while the candles in the crystal chandeliers glittered overhead.

"You dance beautifully, Lady Caroline," he propounded.

So serious and proper, she thought. This won't do.

"Thank you," she said with a grin. "So do you." Then she

couldn't help it. The startled look on his face was just too much. She burst out laughing and did throw her head back, if just for a moment. The candles, the music, the warmth of his body so close, moving perfectly with her was just too delicious.

"Forgive me, my lord. Alas, I realize from your expression that it is not the done thing to return a man's compliment."

"I am only surprised by your modesty. You are far better than I at this particular exercise, and I am sure you have many other accomplishments, as well," he said.

"None that you would consider admirable," she said in a hushed voice as the grin threatened again. "I would expect you to perform with more élan than I at the pianoforte, and my old governess would no doubt judge your embroidery stitches to be smaller and straighter than mine, as she declared mine the worst she had ever seen."

"Whether you embroider beautifully or play the pianoforte with élan, your manner has always been that of a great lady." His eyes flashed with a protective glint out of keeping with her self-mockery.

She stared up at him in shock. "How noble, my lord, to defend me even from myself," she said, and then the smile tugged at her lips again.

They whirled about the room in silence for another moment, and then he cleared his throat, obviously preparing to make another foray into polite conversation.

"I hope that you find the Season enjoyable this year," he said. She then felt him wince, and her jaw tightened at his realization of his misstep. It was so painfully obvious that she had never enjoyed the two Seasons Mama insisted she endure.

"It is exactly as enjoyable as the last Season," she lied, gazing again at his left shoulder. These months in London were even worse because her only friend, Lilias Drelincourt, had eschewed town for a long stay in the country with her husband and new son.

"Yes, except for the weather," he continued quickly. "Much less rain this year so far."

Polite conversation was such a bore, Caroline decided. "Indeed," she said in mock solemnity. "I believe that this May has seen more sunshine than the three Mays previous to it. But before that as you might recall, April was exceptionally rainy. Too bad you weren't here in March to observe . . ."

He stared down at her and then slowly, like a prehistoric creature breaking out of a glacier, he smiled for the second time. A real, honest, broad, devastating grin.

"I am sorry for sounding so . . ."

"Stuffy?" she provided sweetly.

He sighed, raised his eyes as though seeking heavenly support in sparring with this unruly maiden. "Perhaps you will allow me to begin again, Lady Berring. You do dance divinely. I am delighted that you think I dance well. I would be very happy to speak with you on other, more interesting topics but at the moment, I cannot bring a single one to mind."

Goodness, an apology and an honest, self-effacing comment. She felt as though the ice in his veins was melting before her eyes.

"As it happens, having overheard many banal conversations, I am well equipped with them when duty calls," she said. She peeked up into those dark eyes again, and found them ever so slightly crinkled—in amusement, she hoped.

"Perhaps you would enlighten me on the subject of flowers—which flowers you particularly prefer and which you dislike. That should take us around the room at least twice."

"If you wish," she replied, relaxing a bit more. "Roses are, of course, quite beautiful, but I despise red roses. They have become a sad cliché. To my mind, pink roses tinged with gold as they open are the most delightful. They have a more subtle perfume."

"And they hide a mysterious secret within their petals, do they not?" he asked her in a voice like deep velvet. "While they're sleeping, at any rate."

Only by the most rigid self-control did she keep her jaw from dropping to the vicinity of the floor.

He could not have meant Tennyson's shocking poem from *The Princess.*

But once her dizzy mind had seized upon it, she couldn't seem to dismiss the possibility. The lovers waking in a natural bower. To love again . . .

Whatever that entailed. And about which details she was intensely curious.

An odd quickening thrilled through her belly. She cleared her throat and attempted to shake off the feeling of drowning in sensation. Now that she was no longer sparring with him at every beat of the music, she noticed that his arms were strong and firm around her, his tall, broad-shouldered body warm and close.

She had a moment of panic. Was he, by any chance, a cunning old soul who guessed Caroline was the type to sneak a peek into her brother's new book of Tennyson's outrageous poetry? A reprobate who thought to lure her into . . . whatever men lured ladies into with a poem?

No. He looked dreadfully solemn again, a sure sign that he couldn't have just shared a double entendre with her.

Then he pulled her closer. She could feel the heat of his body through his formal attire, the strength of his arm wrapped about her. As he bent his head to hers, she wondered if he could feel the heat on her cheeks and know what she was thinking. For a moment, they glided together, his legs shockingly close to her skirts, her heart beating a tattoo in her throat.

She had to stop this—this whatever it was—immediately. "I suggest we now, ah, do as others do and gossip with wit and venom about absent acquaintances," she whispered, pulling back a little from his arms.

"Indeed, that would be welcome," he said, and seemed to choke for a moment.

Was he swallowing a laugh? No. There was a distinct rose tinge beneath his tanned cheeks. Mortification was certainly heating her own cheeks. Was the man truly laying his snare for a . . . what did Nearing call it? A liaison? But would a rake blush? She couldn't be sure of anything.

As they circled, he glanced about at the rest of the dancers and cleared his throat. "Your mama is in fine looks tonight. I take it she is well?"

"Yes," she said with relief at the change to a less oversetting topic. "We shall go down to Eversleigh soon. She enjoys Kent and I find it as close to heaven as one can get, unless one counts Scotland." She peeked through half-lowered lids and saw the avid looks cast their way. Then she made the mistake of looking up into his deep eyes. At which point, she completely forgot what she was about to say.

A few beats passed, and he said in a stifled voice, "We were discussing Scotland?"

Ah, yes. She mustn't forget their audience. "My grandfather, Lord Holland, lives there. He is a wonderful gentleman, although a bit eccentric. And he has taught me all sorts of excellent skills."

There was a pause, as they circled again. She looked up at him, to find him watching her with a thoughtful expression on his handsome face. "What sorts of skills?"

How would he react if she answered honestly? If her reputation hadn't already done so, it would certainly destroy any idea of her as the consummate lady.

She felt a bubble of laughter tugging, tugging, tugging at her throat, and swallowed hard.

"Oh, this and that." She widened her eyes and gave him what she hoped was an angelically vague smile.

"This and that what?" he asked, smiling back at her.

"Rather dull stuff, actually," she lied. "Agricultural husbandry, etcetera, etcetera."

Thank heavens the orchestra chose that moment to end the waltz. Caroline stepped back out of the prince's arms and allowed him to lead her to her mother.

He bowed over her hand again, just as stiffly as he'd done before. "A pleasure, my lady. Would you care to save another for me later this evening?"

"Why?" The word slipped out before she could call it back.

"I beg your pardon?" he said, his brows lifted in surprise.

"Why would someone like you wish to dance with someone like me?" Oh, God, this was just what she'd feared. She'd forgotten herself, and blurted. She wanted to sink into the floor.

But he surprised her. Again. "You have just given me the answer to your question, Caroline," he said softly, with that intent look on his face. "I would prefer dancing with you over all the ladies at this ball, because with enough encouragement, you will sometimes say what you think."

Caroline snapped her mouth together before her jaw dropped to her clavicle. Fumbling for the card in her reticule, she handed it to him without being able to look him in the eye. She wished suddenly that the spaces weren't so woefully empty. With a flourish, he wrote his name down for another waltz, and bowed to both Caroline and her mother before walking away, his perfect back as straight and stiff as a parson's. Or a soldier's, she amended with a jolt of recognition—of another man's back, in the garden a short time ago.

★ ★ ★ ★ ★

Good God, Dev thought as he walked away from Caroline Berring. What was wrong with him? As soon as he'd touched her hand, he'd felt like a savage, wishing to slip her gown from her body, to take her down and bury himself inside her, and make her cry out at the peak, and—Christ! He had to stop this.

He'd thought it would be easy—Lord Headleymoor, cool and controlled, doing the noble thing to save a damsel in distress. And here he was, a randy, babbling idiot, feeling things he'd never felt before! How was he to act for the next week or two of this sham courtship? It would be a living hell, this lack of control, with no hope of release.

There was nothing to do but play the proud and unpleasant iceberg she'd called him in the garden. That's what she'd remember when Maxim and she were married—her husband's cold and stiff friend. She'd laugh at him, and be glad she'd not wed him.

And the bloody allusion to roses! What in hell was he thinking, to make reference to Tennyson's sensual poem while dancing with an innocent? He knew exactly what he'd been thinking of, damn his soul. It was sheer luck that she had not possibly understood him.

He must stop caring what she thought of him. His job was to make the way straight for a more deserving man. Maxim could give her the love she needed. Maxim was not haunted by the past. Maxim's uneventful life would protect her from all harm.

There was the other danger, as well. Caroline Berring *saw* people. Really saw them. Given her quick mind, if this mock courtship went on too long, she would easily recognize him in his guise as Ram Dass.

But at least, in his role as Ram Dass, it might be easier to dam up this deluge of lust. An Englishwoman would never think of Ram Dass in that way. It just wouldn't occur to her that an

Indian servant was also a red-blooded male. Whereas, with Lord Headleymoor, Caroline flushed and peeked at him from beneath her lashes, eliciting from him a flash of heat that nearly burned the ballroom to cinders. And that air of mystery about her drove him wild to discover her secrets.

What, for instance, had Lord Holland taught her, besides "this and that"? She was covering up—he just knew it. And it fascinated him.

Well, Maxim would have the pleasure of learning her secrets. Or would he even wonder if she had any?

Ballocks, he told himself, and caught the eye of a footman carrying a tray of champagne. Maxim was the best of men. Dev grabbed a glass and downed it in one gulp.

Caroline would be happy and secure with Maxim. Dev would make sure of that.

"I need to speak to you," King Ari said to his half brother. Dev stood with an empty champagne glass in his hand, staring at the opposite wall as though the secrets of the Universe were writ upon it. At Ari's words, he woke from his trance, nodded, and the two of them walked together toward a private study just off the ballroom. As soon as the door shut behind them, Ari turned on him.

"How could you have made such a mess of things?" Ari said in a hiss. Despite his realization that he'd not given Dev a pertinent piece of information about Massad's health, he was still furious. It was unfair of him, he knew, but the resentment he felt made it difficult to be logical.

Dev's head lifted, and his dark, expressionless eyes met Ari's. "Would you have preferred that I left the cup at your place after he put the aconite into it?" he asked in a cool voice.

"I am sorry about Abdul," he went on. "I wish that we'd foreseen his fear of this unknown leader. I wish we'd learned who the leader was, but at least we now know to look for a Zaranbadian aristocrat who is unconscionably cruel to his underlings."

Dev certainly had recovered quickly from his attack of conscience, Ari thought. "You speak of his death as though it were nothing! I knew the man for ten years. Are you really so hardened that all you can say is 'I'm sorry' in that disengaged manner that only proves you're not the least bit moved by what happened tonight?"

Dev's eyes narrowed. "You will think what you wish of me, Ari. It may comfort you to remember that Massad tried to kill you."

"Abdul was a close friend who betrayed me and died a terrible death. You've no right to lecture me, Englishman." Ari drew himself up to his full height, and he was still a few inches shorter than his brother, damn it! One fist closed into a tight weapon, and oh, how he'd love to punch it right in Dev's face.

Normally, he would not have allowed his resentment to overpower his general sense of decency. But in the aftermath of the last, terrifying memories, his nerves jangled and his head pounded.

Whom could he trust to help him walk that tightrope between holding his kingdom and bringing it into the nineteenth century? Dev was brilliant, daring, and charismatic. But he wasted his gifts on England, when Zaranbad needed him. For this, Ari could hate him, if not for the fact that their mother had loved this golden son of her second marriage more than she loved Ari.

"I'm damned if I'll allow you to preach at me," he said. "I shall consult with Hossam Ali, who understands the problems of a country you barely know."

He saw with satisfaction that he'd struck a blow, after all.

And why shouldn't he have said what he did? Dev cared

about nothing other than those crazed adventures on which he risked his neck. Always for England.

He, Ari, was the one who sacrificed everything for Zaranbad. Even his wife's health and happiness.

He glanced at Dev, expecting to see the maddeningly inscrutable expression he usually wore when they were together. Instead, for one instant, he saw vulnerability and pain beneath the usual cool surface of Dev's dark eyes.

"So be it," Dev said. Without another word, he turned and left Ari alone in the study.

Ari's satisfaction faded like the English fog on a sunny day. In its place was a sense of helpless regret.

Why should he feel so guilty? Everything he'd said to Dev was basically true. Even if he'd said it for one reason alone—to wound.

"Caroline," her mother said in an excited whisper. "I knew it. I just knew if we came tonight something wonderful would happen."

"Mama," she said, patting her mother's hand. "It was but a dance. Perhaps Headleymoor thinks it his duty to dance with all the unmarried ladies at his ball."

"He's not dancing now," Caroline's mother said, nudging her head in the direction where the prince had disappeared a moment before. "He just left the ballroom with King Ari of Zaranbad."

Caroline knew it was time to stop her mother's foolish expectations from running away with her. "Before you decide he's the answer to your prayers, Mama, you must understand that I found him . . . confusing and rather, ahem, pompous," she said, knowing she was desperately searching for an objection. "It must be a real coup to make him laugh. I only unearthed a smile."

Her mother nodded, but in that distracted way that made Caroline realize she hadn't taken one word she'd said seriously. "He's a prince, as well, my dear.

"I remember King Ari's and Headleymoor's mother," Mama continued, as if Caroline, fascinated by all things foreign, didn't know these salient facts. "The ton was agog with the news that the Duke of Wimbley had married the widowed princess of Zaranbad. Then she came to England and conquered their hearts. She was so beautiful and so very brilliant. She was received by the king with all honors.

"Tragically, she died when Headleymoor was only four years of age. The duke mourned her for years. Perhaps with his father so overset, young Headleymoor never had anyone to talk to during that sad time. It could make a man rather . . . taciturn. Perhaps he needs to be with someone who can teach him to enjoy communicating. And it would hardly be a waste of one's time, Caro. After all, a lady can simply rest her eyes on that face and physique as she gives polite conversation a ripping good try."

"Mama," she gasped, as a few young men approached.

"Well, he is quite handsome, isn't he?"

The men headed straight for them. For a quelling moment, she wondered if Nearing or Headleymoor had told some of the eligible men in the ton that she would make a fine mistress, or whether they'd come to that conclusion, themselves.

But three perfectly groomed bachelors bowed politely, presented themselves to her mother and then begged an introduction to her. By the time they had all left, she had a half-full dance card and a request for her company for supper. It was a miracle.

By the time the prince arrived to claim his waltz, Caroline felt her lips curve despite her misgivings about him. As he swept her into his arms, she looked him straight in the eye. Honesty, she felt, would serve them far better than the usual pleasantries.

"I thank you, my lord."

He gave her a surprised look. "For what, pray?"

"For a never-to-be-forgotten evening. You must realize that you can influence popular opinion. In this case, you have turned me into someone less exceptionable. I am very grateful."

For a moment, he looked a little . . . troubled. Then a slow smile, whose sweetness almost made her knees weak, formed on his perfect lips. "I did notice that you have been dancing more tonight. And I take it you were glad to do so?"

"I enjoyed it, but to be quite honest, I should be grateful to sit one dance out if I could." She peeked at her feet. "My slippers, you see. They're new, and I had not thought that I would be using them quite so energetically tonight."

"Your feet hurt?"

She felt a half-ironic smile tug at her lips. "Put rather baldly, my lord, but I'm afraid so."

"Come, then. I shall introduce you to my father and the King of Zaranbad. And then I shall find a seat for you so you may rest for a while."

"That is very kind of you. By the by, on such an occasion as this, do I call you my lord, or your highness?"

"For now," he said, "please call me Headleymoor."

Caroline stared. She couldn't help it. Was he intimating that she would, someday in future, call him by his given name? What game was he playing with her?

"This way," he murmured and placed her hand in the crook of his arm. Again, she had that strange sense of breathlessness and warmth his closeness seemed to engender. She could feel the play of muscle beneath the superfine evening coat. Her skirts and petticoats swished against his long legs as they walked through the ballroom. He must have patterned his strides to match hers, for it felt as though they were in perfect step.

Suddenly, he stopped short, and she found herself slightly off balance. He stood there, his arm seeming to turn to iron beneath her hand. She glanced up at his face, uncertain, and caught him looking daggers across the ballroom at a man of taller than average height, with hair so blond it was almost white, and light blue eyes. The combination made him look the way she'd always imagined a Viking would look, strong and Nordic and . . . interesting. The man gave her a melting smile, and it was all she could do to stop herself from smiling back at him, although they'd not been introduced.

For an instant, she saw something strained in Headleymoor's expression, a kind of helpless fury in his dark eyes. Then he looked down at her once again. His expression was so cool and arrogant that she must have imagined his reaction to the stranger.

Her gaze scanned the ballroom for the man, but he was gone.

"Terribly sorry to almost trip you up," Headleymoor said. "I stopped to search for our party."

He led her to the group surrounding the duke and the king. "Lady Caroline, may I make my father known to you?" he said quietly.

Caroline curtsied low as the duke took her hand. He was a handsome man with silver hair. His blue eyes seemed to question as they gazed from Headleymoor's face to hers and back again. A broad smile—one could almost call it a grin—spread on his face.

Then he bowed over her hand and murmured, "Enchanted, my dear. I knew your father. It was tragic—the illness and then his untimely death before he could hold you in his arms."

With an effort, Caroline contained her gasp. No one ever spoke in her presence of her supposed father. "Thank you for your kind words, your grace," she murmured. *I think.*

The King of Zaranbad stood ready to greet her. King Ari had the same dark eyes as Headleymoor, and a square jaw that betokened no nonsense from inferiors. Broad and strong, he lacked Headleymoor's tall, cat-like grace. Giving her a grave smile, King Ari bowed over her hand.

"I am very glad to meet you, Lady Caroline Berring," he said in an imperious voice. "Earlier today, I questioned my brother about what lady might suit my plans, and he mentioned your kindness and generosity to your friends."

"Very gracious of him to do so, your majesty," Caroline said. *What plans?* Her deep curtsey hid her curiosity as to where this abrupt monarch's words might lead, as they were given as a command rather than a pretty compliment.

"I have brought my wife to England, as well as my royal self and my ministers."

"Oh, how wonderful it must be for her to travel. I am afraid I have never been farther than Scotland," Caroline said.

"I do not think it so wonderful, Lady Caroline Berring. It is much too cold in England for my Janighar. Gatherings such as this one, with all the noise and the confusion, will exhaust her." He frowned, looking around at the ballroom as though it were but a step from here to an invalid's bed.

"I would not say this to just anyone, but as you are a lady to whom my half brother sees fit to introduce me and his father, I may speak clearly. Queen Janighar is very . . . fragile. She would not be happy with crowds. Yet she must appear at just such an event quite soon, as we must meet at a formal dinner and ball with the English Queen." King Ari cleared his throat and stared down into her eyes, his own as fierce as an eagle's.

"I shall not have her picked at and made unhappy by unkind remarks about her . . . difficulties. If you would be so kind," his voice swept on decisively, "you will visit her. You have a stillness that will comfort her. And those sympathetic eyes seem to

49

understand without words. Yes."

He nodded his head abruptly. "You will prepare her for the evening I am certain she is dreading, which is to arrive so soon. And you will accompany us to this event, in order to give my Janighar the strength she will need to sustain such a troubling situation."

"I . . . I . . ." Ever since Caroline had danced with Headleymoor, life had begun to spin faster than a runaway hoop. Now here she was in what seemed to be a comic opera, complete with a king who commanded rather than asked an Englishwoman to aid his shrinking violet of a wife.

But there was something behind that clear command that struck her as almost, well, profound and desperate worry.

Worry by a loving husband for his wife.

She cleared her throat. "I should be delighted to entertain the princess in our home, your majesty."

"No." King Ari's abrupt negation only added to the feeling that she'd left the real world behind for some odd farce. "You will come here, to Wimbley House. I cannot have her venture out on the London streets."

"I would never suggest such a thing, your majesty. She would naturally come in a carriage, accompanied by a woman she trusts, or perhaps one of your servants."

"You will come here in that carriage," King Ari said. "I believe tomorrow, at three o'clock in the afternoon will do very well. I shall send a servant for you, and—"

"Ram Dass will go," Headleymoor interrupted.

"Ram Dass may be busy tomorrow," King Ari said with a frown of displeasure.

Headleymoor placed her hand on his arm and pulled her closer to him. For the second time that night, she could feel the taut bunching of his muscles all the way through his evening coat and her glove. "Ram Dass will be most eager to ensure that

Lady Caroline both arrives and leaves Wimbley House in perfect safety and security."

The king glared at Headleymoor. "Yes, well, I suppose that if I ask for such a favor, I must accept whatever inconvenience occurs as a result."

"You are certainly correct in that supposition."

Caroline glanced from one proud brother to the other. Life had turned topsy-turvy in the matter of an hour. The perennial wallflower and scarlet maiden was now to be the advisor to a queen? Where was reality when a lady needed it?

Chapter Three:
To Take Tea with a Queen

Dev rode through St. James Park early the next morning, his head full of what needed to be done in order to make Caroline Berring's life better. He found it a hope-filled subject that took his mind from the troubled thoughts that had kept him up most of the night. Squeezing his chestnut stallion, Samson, into a canter, he felt the cool morning breeze on his cheeks and relaxed into the motion, calming his mind as Dr. Gupta, his mentor, had taught him to do when he was particularly disturbed by memories.

Shortly after he left the bridle path for the less traveled paths of the park, he saw Nearing trotting his mount toward him.

"What was so important that you pulled me out of bed at this ungodly hour?" Maxim asked him.

"What else? Lady Caroline Berring," he said, feeling peeved. "Your intended. Remember her?"

Instantly, he was ashamed. Nearing's prospects with Caroline should not have pricked his temper.

"Of course I remember her," Nearing said with a touch of asperity. "I also remember you dancing with her twice. And I could tell you enjoyed it."

"One always enjoys a turn about the room with a woman of sense as well as grace," Dev said in a cool voice. "And I was doing it for you, you idiot."

"I fail to see how you courting my wife-to-be is in any way charitable to me," Nearing retorted.

Dev sighed. Usually his friend was a good deal more cunning than he seemed this morning. Indeed, Dev owed him more than he could ever repay for aiding him through the horrors of the Afghan War. Caroline must have really gotten to him, if he was this blind to Dev's true motives. Or maybe not, he thought in chagrin.

"The purpose of last evening was to raise Caroline in the eyes of the ton. Seeing that Society for some strange reason deems me the pick of the Season, it was the obvious decision for me to show marked attention to her. Already, rumors are circulating that she is, in truth, the daughter of the late Lord Eversleigh. Another week of that and my supposed interest, and you can have her without fear of being disowned by your wealthy grandmother."

"It isn't the fear that the family fortune will slip through my hands, as you well know," Nearing said hotly. "It's Grandmama. She's all I've had for a very long time. I cannot disappoint her. You've always understood that."

Dev nodded. "I do know, Maxim. It is understandable that you want to make her proud, and I have reason to know that her prejudices are few. But will you truly care for Caroline? She's . . . vulnerable, you know. And she's been lonely for a long time."

"I swear to you, Dev. I'll make her happy."

"Well, then. Give me time to do what I can, and then take her. But Maxim—none of your precipitous moves. Have some patience. It won't be long."

"All right, old fellow. I bow to your superior understanding." They rode on in silence for a few moments. Then Nearing said quietly, "I saw Gerard Visigore at the ball last night. I hadn't realized he'd returned from India."

Dev's hands clenched on the reins and Samson jerked his head in protest. Instantly, Dev relaxed his grip and patted the chestnut's neck in apology. "I saw him, too."

"I'm sorry," Nearing said. "If there's anything that I can do . . ."

"You already did it, long ago," Dev said, attempting a smile. "Don't let Visigore bother you. It's been ages. We both know I'll have to deal with being in the same room with him if I'm to go about in Society at all."

"I heard he's made a fortune investing in the East India Company. Too bad he didn't get what he deserved while he was in India—there was an outbreak of cholera in Delhi just three months ago."

Dev managed a shrug. "Perhaps someday."

"No doubt," Nearing said, looking carefully away.

Dev assumed he was giving him time to recover.

"People like Visigore come to a bad end sooner or later," Nearing said.

For the sake of the world and his peace of mind, Dev sincerely hoped it would be sooner rather than later.

In the small, elegant town house at Twenty-five Berkeley Square, Caroline awoke the next morning to the sound of several maids bustling into her chambers. She peeked through the ecru silk bed curtains and watched in amazement as three bouquets of hothouse flowers took their uncustomary places on a desk, a bureau, and a chest.

"Sorry to disturb you, m'lady," Emma said, putting down a bouquet on her bedside table. "There are two more in the drawing room. Your brother just came in from Eversleigh House to breakfast with you and Lady Margery. He ordered the rest of the flowers upstairs. He said the scent was too cloying so early in the morning."

"Why?" Caroline asked, jumping out of bed and walking over to a large bouquet—her favorite pink roses with a hint of gold on the outer petals, just opening. With unsteady hands, she pulled out the card.

Thank you for the delightful waltz, she read. It was signed simply, *Headleymoor.*

She bent over the roses and their deep, sweet scent filled her nostrils. He'd managed to find her favorite roses this early in spring. She bit her lip to keep from smiling, but the smile escaped her, nonetheless.

He'd remembered.

"I'm afraid your brother has a bit of the headache," Emma said. "I suspect that a good cup of tea with his kippers will help his disposition."

"William was out late again, was he?"

"Aye. His valet told Sarah, the upstairs maid—they've been courting for a while, now—that Lord William left for his club and then stopped in at the ball last night."

Caroline felt a pang of hurt. He'd stopped at the ball and hadn't bothered to come over to say hello. It shouldn't have surprised her.

She knew he'd made a pact with himself. If any man disparaged his sister, he would defend her with his life, but he would keep away from her when she went into Society. That would limit the amount of damage he'd have to sustain.

She didn't blame him. She'd seen the black eye he'd come home with that first holiday from school, and never questioned his decision afterward. Privately, Will was kind, if rather blunt. Indeed, he had even seen to it that she and Mama could have this pretty town house, right next door to Everesleigh House, the family's mansion used during the London Season. It was a way of publicly distancing himself without thinking himself a snake.

" 'Tis the valet's opinion that Lord William tippled a bit more than usual, and he's right done in because of it. But I wouldn't let anyone bother you today, my lady, if I was you." Emma shook out a morning gown and laid it on the bed. "For Cook heard from the green grocer this morning that the ton is talking of nothing but you and the Marquess of Headleymoor, and how he introduced you to his papa and the king, and how you're going to take tea with a queen today."

Caroline felt her eyes widen. "The green grocer knew all that?"

"Oh, indeed. He'd been to several town houses before ours. And something about your hair, and how your poor dead papa's grandfather was a redhead, too, only nobody remembered it 'til now, because he went powdered all the time, as was the custom then."

All these years. Caroline swallowed hard. She wanted to run down the hallway and barge into her mother's bedroom and shout "is it true?" Yet it was a forbidden subject, no matter that it had stolen her happiness from the time she was old enough to understand the word "bastard."

She dressed and made her way down the long, circular stairway into the dining room. William was still sitting in the chair at the head of the table, his face buried in the latest issue of the *Times.* In his present mood, she had hoped to miss him completely.

"Good morning," she said as she placed some kippers, tomatoes and eggs on her plate. She dropped one of Cook's excellent scones beside them and walked to the long dining table.

William's reply was a groan. Then he snapped the paper shut and put his head in his arms. "What the devil are those bouquets doing on the tables in the drawing room and the hall? My nose can't take the scent this morning."

"I have no idea, as I haven't seen them yet. One of those in my chamber is from the prince."

Will squinted up with one eye. "What prince?"

She gulped. Had she actually said "the prince"? How embarrassing. "I meant the Marquess of Headleymoor," she said stiffly.

"The Marquess of Headleymoor sent you a bouquet of flowers," he said, slowly straightening and staring at her as though she'd grown another head. Then he sighed wearily and drew himself up even straighter, no doubt contemplating a duel.

"What's his game, I wonder?" Suspicion dripped from his voice.

"Two waltzes last night, William," her mother's cheerful words interrupted from the other end of the dining room as she sailed in. "And several other gentlemen followed suit. Apparently, the rest of the ton sees the marquess as a very powerful, very wealthy man, and the lady who arouses his interest is good enough for them. I should think that you would be congratulating Caroline upon her success last night at the duke's ball."

William stared at Mama in surprise, then reddened. His gaze slid down to his plate. "I beg your pardon," he said stiffly. "Didn't mean to insult you, Caro."

Caroline leaned over the table and patted his hand. "I know that."

A moment passed in silence as her mother filled a plate with a small repast and motioned for tea for herself and Caroline. "Last night marked the beginning of Caroline's true come out."

William's slow smile softened his angular features. "She drew a crowd of honest admirers, Mama?"

"Indeed. Headleymoor's interest in her encouraged other worthy suitors to believe that she is a rich prize on the marriage mart."

"Amazing that men are so easily led," Caroline murmured.

"In matters of reputation, they are," William said. "And apparently, from the blooms that have appeared this morning, you may expect that yours has undergone an advantageous change.

This is quite an excellent development, Caro. My advice would be to take advantage of it quickly and convince some decent fellow to pick up the handkerchief. I'll be happy to receive him at Eversleigh House when he's come up to scratch."

"I have no idea whether the men who sent bouquets will be to my liking," Caroline said. To her ears, her voice was as stiff as William's shirt collar, and that looked starched enough to choke him.

"Well, if the bees are buzzing round, please make haste to find one you can like. Knowing the ton, this could be a se'ennight's wonder, and after that . . . you know I want you happily settled in a home of your own," he said earnestly. "And we've had enough experience with what will happen if the prince no longer pays attention to you."

"William!" Mama cried. "That was cruel and unnecessary."

William tightened his lips. "I'm sorry, Mama. But Society is cruel. And rather necessary to one's future, unfortunately. Please, Caro. Make a quick and sensible choice in the next week, and your reputation will be secured for the rest of your life. By the by, Mama, did Nearing send a posy?"

"Yes, actually," her mother said in satisfaction.

"Good, good. Thought he might. Had a word and a brandy with him at the club last night after the ball."

Actually, several brandies, from the looks of Will, Caroline thought.

"Good man, Nearing. You could do worse."

Caroline gaped. What had that insulting clod discussed with William? Certainly not the truth. If so, William would have to call him out, poor fellow, and her brother was not a very good shot.

As Caroline pulled on her gloves in the large front hall a few hours later, she pondered what William had told her. The truth was that she would be a fool not to take advantage of Headleymoor's fleeting interest.

Even now word was getting out that she was to meet the Queen of Zaranbad for tea. That would certainly increase her mother's standing and her standing. But taking advantage of Headleymoor and his family felt . . . tawdry. Sad that tawdriness and necessity were often companions in the world of the ton.

A beautifully appointed chaise and four pulled to a halt in front of the town house. She peeked through the small leaded-glass window above the table that now held calling cards from the gentlemen who'd sent the bouquets. She was glad she didn't have to entertain them today. Tomorrow would be soon enough to deal with those who still exhibited any interest and called.

Ram Dass, tall and serene in a long blue jacket with jodhpurs and turban to match, took the walk and stairway quickly. Caroline drifted to the door just as Munson, the butler, opened it.

Ram Dass smiled. "You are quite prompt, Lady Caroline. My master will be impressed to learn of this very unusual occurrence."

"I am generally prompt. And I am also eager to meet the queen," Caroline said with a smile, as he handed her into the carriage and climbed in, himself, to sit opposite her. His long legs took up a great deal of space, coming rather close to her skirts. She didn't know whether to move or to remain where she was. A lady would move, but then, Ram Dass was used to people insulting him in any number of thoughtless ways.

She stayed where she was and cast a glance at him. "Is she really as fearful as King Ari believes her to be? Will she fret when she meets me? Is there any way I can put her at ease?"

Ram Dass smiled, his expression so gentle and reassuring that she didn't even need words to calm herself. But he gave them to her, anyway.

"Queen Janighar will be a delightful surprise for you. As you will be for her. I think you will like her very much, and she will find you fascinating."

She stared at him in surprise. "Fascinating? Hardly that."

"Oh, Lady Caroline," he said softly. "One day you will truly look at yourself in a mirror and you will find a vibrant and elegant lady staring back."

She didn't care to look at herself, she realized. She only wanted to look at Ram Dass at the moment. "You are kind, Ram Dass, but hardly truthful."

He just shook his head. His lips curved, and he looked wise and enigmatic. His face was such a lovely olive tone, very much like King Ari's complexion.

He really was quite a beautiful man. One could drown in those poetically dark eyes. His features were all as perfect as— well, actually as Headleymoor's. Straight nose, high, sculpted cheekbones, and a mouth so lush that one wondered whether it felt as soft as it looked. Caroline went hot all over and dropped her gaze to her hands, now clenched on her lap.

What a scandal that would make for Mama—a daughter who wished to steal a kiss from a servant.

"I hope you enjoyed my master's ball last night, Lady Caroline." Ram Dass's quiet voice broke through her embarrassment.

"It was everything delightful," she murmured.

"And did you also enjoy the roses Lord Headleymoor sent you?"

"They were lovely," Caroline said. Oh dear. Roses. She could feel the hot blush rising from her bosom to her cheeks. *Mental note: eschew all poetry.*

"Ahem." She sat straight and stopped her hands from wringing on her lap. "Ram Dass, have you known Lord Headleymoor for a long time?"

"Indeed. He worked in India on several . . . projects for the

British government. I know him very well."

"I, ah, I have a bit of a problem talking to him."

Ram Dass leaned forward in his seat, and he seemed very close, suddenly. Her heart, which had never succumbed to such foolishness as a flutter seemed to be doing an excellent impression of agitated butterfly wings. It was disconcerting that she had now twice had feminine palpitations in the presence of two different men.

She, who was always calm when men were in proximity! And why should she not be? After all, none of them had ever shown any interest in her. At least, she thought with a grimace as she recalled Nearing's words last night, no interest that could be deemed proper.

"Could you describe this problem?" Ram Dass asked, breaking into her thoughts and looking quite serious. She remembered that, in his country, he was known as a learned doctor, and a scholar of human emotion.

Her shoulders relaxed. She could trust him with her questions, no matter how foolish.

"He is not an easy man to . . . ah, converse with. One moment it seems as though he's saying one sort of thing, and the next, as though we are speaking of something entirely different. Ahem. Of perhaps a subject polite ladies and gentlemen do not discuss together, no matter how much they might think about such a subject.

"Then we grow silent. And I respond to silence by prattling. Worse, I am sometimes irreverent. He may have disapproved of my levity, or my—my curiosity. It's all very confusing. I can't tell where I am with him.

"For a moment, I thought he might understand," she rushed on, remembering her embarrassingly vulgar thoughts in response to his comment on rose petals. "And then, I hoped that he *didn't* understand. Or that I didn't, or, oh, I don't know how to put it."

She took a deep breath and huffed it back out in frustration. "What I mean to ask is this: Would Headleymoor find irreverent humor shocking?"

Ram Dass didn't seem to know what to do with his mouth for a moment. His lips pursed and then wobbled and then pursed again.

"I apologize for appearing . . . flummoxed? Is that the right word? It is just that you put things in such a candid manner. I am unused to candor. To give you an answer that you may well understand, the prince has not in recent years, lived exclusively in England, but also in India and Zaranbad, and most of his social congress was with the gentlemen of the diplomatic corps.

"He is unfamiliar with the niceties of conversation with ladies," Ram Dass continued. "He simply needs to become more at home with the variables of speaking to a lady."

"I see." She waved an airy hand, laughing. "You might tell him then, that if he is interested in learning how to converse with English ladies, he will only confuse himself if he continues to talk to me."

Ram Dass turned his head and stared out the window for a long moment. All she could see of his face was a tense jaw.

When he turned back, his gaze was narrowed, intense. "Lady Caroline," he said. "Be patient with Prince Devlin. If he cannot yet impress you with his wit and intelligence, he is a good man, and very kind to those he cares about."

"Oh, no!" Caroline put out her hand and laid it on Ram Dass's arm. It felt like forged steel, just as Headleymoor's had last night. She wondered vaguely whether the two of them engaged in athletic activities together in order to stay so fit. "I didn't mean to imply that Headleymoor was slow-witted. Only that he might find me improper. I merely wished to say that I will understand if he is uncomfortable in my presence."

"I see," Ram Dass said with a true smile this time. He was really quite devastating when he smiled. "At least I have the language barrier to explain my—how do you say it—clodpole reaction?"

Caroline laughed. "That is it exactly."

For the rest of the journey, Ram Dass regaled her with a view of last night's festivities from a servant's point of view. She learned how Lord Carnisby so enjoyed the goose at the supper table that he stuck a drumstick into his coat pocket. How Lady Trilby had too much punch and ended one set on the ballroom floor, having pulled her partner down on top of her. How Lord Eckensby and Mr. Lippet had almost come to a duel at Ecarte, in which Mr. Lippet accused his lordship of cheating. The scandal was only averted when Lady Eckensby calmly took over his lordship's next hand and lost a great sum of money to Mr. Lippet.

Evelyn, Lady Trilby, and Patricia, Lady Eckensby, had come out last year, and made marriages the ton thought magnificent. Yet their lives were filled with trouble and humiliation. Caroline wondered whether she misjudged the lives of these supposedly lucky and glittering people she barely knew.

"We have arrived, my lady." Ram Dass's soft voice broke into her musings. The carriage had stopped before Wimbley House, the great stone edifice even more imposing in daylight than at night.

He led her into the great hall. Alabaster vases holding grand bouquets still stood along the marble stairway, but the ribbons and streamers had already been removed. As she climbed the broad stairs, she looked up into the domed ceiling, where nymphs and satyrs danced around Persephone and her mother, Ceres.

"There is a very fine fresco in the drawing room to your left," Ram Dass said, "and a portrait of the prince's mother by the great painter, David. Perhaps some time soon, you will have time to see it."

"I have heard much of his work," Caroline said.

"This portrait is very simple, and very beautiful." Ram Dass stopped before a carved oak door and knocked. A footman in full livery with powder in his hair opened the door and bowed. "Here I shall leave you to meet the queen," Ram Dass said.

Caroline walked into a small, ornate drawing room. Despite the fine May weather, a fire crackled in the fireplace and every window was closed. The walls were covered in a rose silk material, and a gilt table beside the sofa held a Sevres tea set.

"Thank you, Frederick," a soft voice said from the other side of the ivory brocade, camelback sofa. "You may go."

As the door quietly shut behind Caroline, a young woman rose and turned toward her. She felt her way around the couch and stood very still. She was a tiny, beautiful woman, in a soft blue silk gown. A woolen shawl meticulously embroidered in blue flowers encased her shoulders. Her black hair lay free in a straight, silken fall down her back.

She had a flawless face, with a small, slightly upturned nose, high cheekbones, a sweet and generous mouth the color of a deep pink rose, and a diagonal scar running from the middle of her right brow to her temple. She smiled a little uncertainly, her dark eyes gazing almost in Caroline's direction. Then she put her hands together in a gesture akin to prayer and bowed her head.

"I am very glad to meet you, Lady Caroline. My name is Janighar."

She held out her hand and Caroline, with a feeling of intense sympathy moved forward quickly to take it. "I am delighted, your majesty," she said. "Are you familiar with the room, or shall I help you to your seat?"

The queen smiled, and Caroline could see why the king had

been so protective of his beautiful young wife last night. In addition to being blind, Queen Janighar's expression was quite definitely the sweetest Caroline had ever seen.

"I can manage," Janighar said. "I have spent the last days learning this room and my bedchamber. I am now ready to go on to the other chambers. At this rate, it will take me only a hundred years to traverse the entire house. And then there is the country estate, as well."

"Do you know the palace in Zaranbad well?"

"Better than some who serve me," she said with a smile, as she made her way back to the sofa and sat down and waved to a chair beside the table holding the tea tray. "But it is not necessary. In Zaranbad, I am always accompanied by servants. Here, I would prefer the liberty to learn my way."

Caroline said nothing, but she wondered just who was fearful in this royal family and who brave.

The queen indicated the tea set. "Would you mind pouring for me?"

"I would be delighted. Cream and sugar or lemon?"

Janighar shed her shawl and threw it over the back of the sofa. "I prefer it with lemon, thank you, as I take it at home."

Caroline surreptitiously unbuttoned two of her top buttons. The room really was over warm.

She poured and put the china cup and saucer down on the table. She poured another for herself and added lemon to it. The princess felt along the tabletop until she found it, and raised the cup to her lips.

"There are some lovely tarts and scones here, as well. Would you care for some?" Caroline asked.

"Lemon or strawberry?"

"Strawberry."

"Oh, good. I dislike the lemon tarts. They are so sweet, and they should be tart. Tart tarts, no?"

"Yes," Caroline said, and the smile must have been in her voice, as well as on her lips, for Janighar smiled back and carefully took the plate Caroline offered.

"Lady Caroline, my brother-in-law told me that I can trust you implicitly."

Why? Caroline wanted to ask for the second time in less than twenty-four hours.

"You learned from my husband that I must soon meet the queen?"

"Last night. Yes. And," Caroline said in a rush, "the king said that you might find the occasion a bit daunting."

"Bah! I am determined to make a good impression. Ari is so eager to bring Zaranbad into the world of western nations—as an equal, not a lesser country. Great Britain is a very important ally. I tell him that I am happy to do my part, but he worries. Does he fear I will disgrace him, or become overset by the experience? I do not know. But I shall do neither. And I am very happy that you are here, for you will know just how to act in any situation involving the British aristocracy."

Caroline burst out laughing. "Forgive me," she said, raising a hand limply in the air as she tried to quell the fit of mirth. "I've been foisted off on you by a series of unfortunate miscommunications. Some poor soul must truly think that I know something about Society and how it works. I must warn you, I watch much of Society from the fringes. Until Headleymoor danced with me last night, there was some doubt as to whether I belonged in the ton, at all."

"Oh, dear," Janighar said slowly. "What are we to do then?"

"Find someone who does know something about all this. We shall learn together, I think, for there's a good deal more fun in this sort of nonsense if we do. Are you game to try?"

"A game? Is it a game?" Janighar asked her, puzzled.

Caroline laughed. "Just an English figure of speech. I meant 'are you willing to try'? And yes, it will be a kind of game."

"Whom shall we find to play this game with us and teach us the rules?"

"We shall find him here in Wimbley House. We must ask Ram Dass to teach us everything he knows. For I am convinced that he knows it all."

Janighar clapped her hands and then clasped them over her mouth, like a little girl who knew she was about to say something she oughtn't. "Excellent! Most excellent. I shall ask Ram Dass tonight. And will you come again?"

"If you wish. I should be glad to learn as much as I can, myself," Caroline said.

The queen smiled and took a bite of her tart with all the regal grace of a, well, a queen. "Now, tell me as much as you can about Society, and its expectations."

"I suppose we could start with Debrett's Peerage," Caroline said.

Janighar pulled the bell hanging close to her chair, and a silent footman entered a moment later. Shortly after that, he re-appeared with the large, leather-bound book.

"Very well," Caroline said, warming to her subject. "We'll start with titles. One calls the dukes 'your grace.' Next come the marquesses. At times, this can be an honorary title, as in Head-leymoor's case, because he is the heir of a duke."

"I understand. It is much the same in Zaranbad. But we call the children of our nobility Lords of the Sun, and Ladies of the Moon."

"I like that," Caroline said. "Very poetic."

Janighar had an excellent memory. They had already finished the list all the way through the viscounts when she raised the back of her hand to her forehead. "Lady Caroline, do you think it is rather warm in here?"

"Yes, actually, I do."

Janighar sighed. "I passed an open door on my way to this drawing room. There was a lovely breeze, and it seems very reasonable outside today. Warm enough, perhaps, for a walk." Her voice had a wistful note to it that touched Caroline's heart.

"It is lovely outside, your majesty. The sun is shining. And the garden behind the house is full of blooming roses."

"Roses. Do you suppose that we might . . . leave a bit of our lesson for later?"

Caroline grinned. "Indeed. Too much study will only make it more difficult to memorize what we need to know. If you take my arm, we shall find a way to slip out into the garden."

A short time later, Caroline found the ballroom in which she'd danced with Headleymoor the night before. She tried the double doors that opened onto the garden and found them unlocked.

"Success!" she cried, and led the queen down the semicircle of stairs into the gravel walks of the formal rose garden.

Janighar lifted her face to the sun with a look of delight. "I can hear everything! Birds calling to each other, and insects or mice, perhaps. And there is a small building a hundred paces to our left, with a high roof, where sleeping bats stir in their sanctuary."

"I can't hear all that. Do you suppose your other senses have become stronger now that you've lost your sight?"

"Oh, yes. I can smell the scent on a man as he walks by, and several other unpleasant ones he's hiding beneath that scent," Janighar said. "And I can feel tiny irregularities in cloth and in wood. I've half a mind to wonder whether I could take up a life of crime, given my new awareness."

Caroline choked back a laugh. "Well, if the Home Office has need of a criminal mind, I shall recommend you."

But as she looked up at Janighar, ready to ask more questions, she saw the queen's smile fade and her dark, beautiful eyes gaze sadly at nothing. She felt for Caroline's arm and grabbed her hand. "It is what I need, Lady Caroline. Some work, or an adventure—to make me feel that I have value. To make my husband understand that I have not lost—lost everything that made me what I was to him before this unfortunate happening."

"Well, I, ah, I . . ."

Caroline usually prided herself in coming up with pragmatic suggestions in times of trouble. She'd seen enough of those times to understand that feeling in control of a situation made a deal of difference in how one viewed it. But now, she felt an inept interloper, treading into an unknown cycle of misunderstandings and hurts between two people who so obviously cared the world for each other.

She led Janighar farther into the garden and said, "I don't quite know how I can help you. I am not very wise when it comes to men and love and, and all that."

"If you were my friend," Janighar said in a low voice, "you could listen and laugh with me, and perhaps, just in the talking, there would be comfort and even a few good ideas."

Caroline cleared her throat and swallowed a little lump. She had one dear friend, far away. Otherwise, there was no one for her, until now. "I should be honored to be your friend, your majesty."

"Then you must call me Janighar, Lady Caroline."

"And you must call me Caroline." They continued down the garden walk, Janighar guessing the color of a particular rose from its scent.

"Janighar!" A deep, masculine voice boomed from the terrace.

"Oh, dear," the queen murmured. "Caught like a thief in the night."

King Ari strode toward them, a look of concern and thunder

on his face. "What are you doing out in the open breeze? And without your shawl?"

Janighar sighed, then straightened her shoulders. "I am blind, my lord king. Not sickly. I cannot remain cooped up in that huge old house with nothing to do. I am learning of the peerage in preparation for the Queen's ball. And as every school child knows, exercise is a good antidote for too much learning. Now, with your permission, Lady Caroline and I shall continue our walk."

"My dear," the king said gently, taking her hand. "I came to tell you that Lady Caroline's time with us is at an end today. Imagine my fear when I could not find either of you in the drawing room. I searched half the house until I came to the ballroom and saw you walking here."

"I should have notified a servant," Janighar said with a bow of her head. "Please forgive me, my lord. But I am perfectly safe, and the day was so beautiful."

"Perfectly safe," Ari muttered. "Dear Heaven, would that it were so."

He took his wife's hand, tucked it into the crook of his arm, and brought her close to his side. His face starkly revealed his love and his helpless fear for her. "My sweet Janighar, I shall compromise with you. If you wish to walk through the garden, you must do so with a phalanx of several guards. Will you promise me that?"

Janighar nodded, her head bent to Ari's shoulder. "I will. Is it still dangerous?"

"Yes, my love. I am sorry, but we must be very careful."

He turned to Caroline. "We have enemies, my lady. Perhaps, under the circumstances, it would be wise of you to eschew future visits to Wimbley House."

A tear slipped down Janighar's cheek.

An offer of friendship—the second of two in her entire life—

set against a dangerous situation. "Would you abandon a friend in his time of danger, my lord king?"

"Of course not. But I am a man."

"And you believe that a woman has less of a sense of honor than a man?"

"Well, yes—I mean no, of course not," King Ari said as Janighar stiffened beside him and Caroline's eyes flashed. "But I would not expect you to feel you must remain at the queen's side until the danger is over."

"Well, so much for faith in womankind," Caroline said. "I shall be honored to visit the queen whenever she wishes to see me, and I hope that she will soon be able to return my visits, as well." Caroline dropped into as graceful a court curtsey as she could manage. "Will that suit, your majesty?"

Janighar straightened herself to her full height of five feet, and replied in a voice that could have easily have come from Queen Victoria. "Excellent, Lady Caroline. I shall expect to see you often, either here, or in Berkeley Square."

Dev stood dressed in what he considered his special operations clothing—black coat loaded with pistols and knives, black shirt, trousers and boots, black knit cap to hide his blond hair. His look-out position was a narrow, filthy alley in the East End, where he and Tom Jarvis, the newest recruit, waited for a sign from Felix Kendall.

Kendall, the youngest son of a viscount, had worked with the Home Office for several years, and was well versed in the latest Zaranbadian crisis.

It seemed just yesterday that he and Kendall, fresh out of Oxford, had been as eager as young Tom for a chance to defend England against her enemies. They'd been sure that the day would soon come when England would be safe. But it seemed that enemies were always in abundance.

Now Zaranbad, that small, wealthy kingdom, was threatened by a mad army of extremist zealots, disrupting the prosperity and peace the country had known for generations.

Running footsteps hammered against cobblestones in the distance.

"What's that?" Tom Jarvis whispered. Dev could hear the tightness in the boy's voice and feel the bunching of his own muscles in readiness.

"Prepare yourself," he said low, as he pulled two pistols from his coat pocket.

Kendall rounded the corner, racing toward them, breathless. Three men ran after him, shouting curses in Zaranbadian.

Kendall raced by them, trying, no doubt to protect his companions by leading the blackguards past them. But the men halted a few feet from Dev's hiding place. Dev fired, and one dropped like a stone. The last two hesitated, then came on fast, screaming imprecations.

Tom fired and missed, cursing.

Dev shoved Tom down as a pistol flared and cracked in the darkness. He fired again, hitting another assailant in the shoulder. The man cried out and fell heavily. The third kept coming, fast and low. Dev crouched, elbowed the ruffian in the groin, and rolled him onto his belly. The conspirator slithered on the wet cobbles, cursing as a knife flew from his hand. Dev slammed his knee into the man's back and pulled his hands up behind him, lashing them together. He could smell sweat as well as the garlic on the fellow's breath—an eastern custom, that, to protect one's health against miasmas like the cold, yellow London fog.

He hauled the insurgent to his feet and signaled with three sharp whistles. Dobbins came round with the coach, and Dev threw the trussed villain inside.

Kendall appeared, breathless and limping, holding his side.

"Did you take a bullet?" Dev asked him, reaching into the coach for his doctor's bag.

Kendall shook his head. "Just a stitch in my side." He took a look at the third assailant, still lying on the cobbles. Kneeling over him, he obstructed Dev's view of the man. In the darkness Dev could hardly see Kendall, who made some movement with his hands.

"What are you doing?" Dev asked.

"Checking his pulse," Kendall said. A moment later, he limped back to Dev's side. "He's dead," Kendall said, still breathless from the run.

Dev frowned. "I thought I hit him in the shoulder."

"You did. But it seems he broke his neck falling on the cobbles. Sorry. My fault. I thought they'd never see you in the darkness."

"No matter this time," Dev said. "Next time, have a care for young Tom here. He has a wife and new baby to go home to tonight."

"I'll do my best, Headleymoor. I always have," Kendall said stiffly.

"I know you will," Dev said and slapped him on the shoulder. "Let's get this fellow to gaol and we'll see what we can do about an interrogation tonight."

"I'll do it," Kendall said. "You've done enough, and if I'm not mistaken, you've got to do the pretty tonight at Ayres House."

"As I've no doubt you got an invitation, as well, I'll take him."

"But I've got a tin ear. And if I'm not mistaken, I don't have Nearing sniffing around my present romantic interest." Kendall's grin flashed in the light of the carriage lamps.

"Nearing? What have you heard that I haven't?" Dev said, with what he hoped sounded like perturbation in his voice.

Actually, it seemed to slide in on its own.

"Spoke to Eversleigh today. Nearing sent flowers to Lady Caroline, who, if I'm not mistaken, danced with you twice last night at the ball. He left his card today and plans to attend the musicale tonight. Word is that if she's acceptable to you, she'll do as a bride for him. Just thought I ought to warn you to arrive on time and get the seat you want."

"Nearing." It seemed that Maxim was losing little time to secure Caroline's affections, which meant that Dev wouldn't need to carry on the charade of the infatuated swain much longer. He ought to feel relieved, but instead, Kendall's words brought about an odd, flat reaction in him.

He didn't know what was wrong with him. Caroline's happiness was all but assured. Will Berring would accept Maxim's suit immediately and dance a jig of relief at her wedding. A question nagged at him. Would Maxim truly appreciate her originality, her humor, her refreshing honesty?

First things first. He must ensure that Maxim had no trouble with his grandmother when he announced his engagement to Caroline. "I suppose I'd better get going," Dev said. "Send me word if you get anything out of our friend tonight." Dev jerked his head toward the carriage, and Kendall nodded. In the dull light of the carriage lamps, Kendall's usually jovial expression was grim.

But Dev barely registered the change in Kendall. Caroline's fate and his role as her suitor took up all of his thoughts. He needed to bathe and dress before his performance tonight.

He jumped into the carriage, hauling the prisoner into the opposite seat. Kendall and young Tom leaped in behind him and Dev rapped on the ceiling of the coach. It rumbled forward over the cobbles and threaded its way through the warrens of London until they reached Newgate.

Kendall jumped down and pulled the prisoner out of the

coach. "I'll take it from here," he said with an easy smile.

"Sir," Tom said as he poked his head out the coach door. "I'll come with you. Just in case there are others who want him back."

"Good idea, Tom," Dev said. "Go with them and keep a sharp eye out for trouble."

Kendall's frown was followed by an expression of light amusement, as though black night gave way to bright dawn. "Enjoy the music, old fellow," he told Dev. "Let me know which of the ladies shone tonight."

"I'll see you tomorrow, after you've had a chance to learn as much as you can," Dev said. As the carriage pulled away, he leaned back against the squabs, deep in thought concerning Lady Caroline Berring.

If he was truly to give her happiness, then his first job was to get rid of every brown gown Caroline owned and replace them all with colors. Emerald green velvets, shimmering blue silks, even mauve—perhaps mauve, among all colors, would bring out those wonderful glints of sunset in her hair. And those high, girlish bodices would have to go, as well.

She had been blessed with the physical attributes of a goddess. There was no reason on earth why, in polite company, her gowns couldn't at least hint of the treasures beneath.

The carriage pulled up to Wimbley House and Dev stepped down, waving Nobbins on to the stables. As he slowly climbed the stairs, he thought of young Tom Jarvis's small town house on the outskirts of Mayfair. It was a neat, pretty little treasure of a house, two stories high with bright blue shutters and the brick painted white. Tom took great pride in it, having worked very hard to achieve this much for his adored Mary and their little Anna. Dev had taken tea there, with a very shy Mary and Tom bursting with pride that a marquess would accept the invitation.

Tom had given up time with his wife and child to safely secure the scoundrel they'd captured in Newgate Prison tonight. His wife would be so glad to see him when he arrived home. She was the type to wait up for him.

Jealousy pricked at Dev, only to be clamped down deep in the recesses of his mind, forbidden to rise again any time soon. He was quite all right just as he was, and someday, perhaps he'd find someone whom even he could wed.

CHAPTER FOUR:
MUSIC AND HONOR

If there was one stately home in England where Caroline felt comfortable, it was Ayres House. The mansion stood back from Grosvenor Square behind a tall wrought-iron fence, and its beautiful grounds were in a riot of bloom this May evening. She entered beside her mother and walked toward her host with a little bounce of pleasure at seeing him so fit and happy.

The Duke of Ayres greeted her with a warm buss to her cheek, as did Lady Edith, his daughter. After an exchange of the latest news of his granddaughter and Caroline's friend, Lilias Drclincourt, the duke patted her hand.

"All strings tonight, my dear," his grace said. "You must tell me how they fare compared to the last musicians."

"I am waiting for you to give us an example of excellent musicianship at the pianoforte, your grace," Caroline said.

He patted her hand and colored a little at her compliment. "If I were to do such a thing, I would expect you in the front row, Lady Caroline, rather than your usual seat in the back. And you must certainly make an example for the rest of the audience by applauding loudly and long, before I attempt to publicly match professional musicians. For tonight, I only ask that you enjoy the evening."

"I shall do my best, your grace," she said with a laugh and a curtsey, and made her way into the already crowded music room. The small quartet was warming up as she looked for a seat near the back of the room, as far from notice as she could.

But her gaze seemed to have a mind of its own, or perhaps it was the sudden, lithe movement from the front row that caught her eye. Lord Headleymoor stood there, looking at her. In the glow of lamplight, he looked like a young Apollo, serious and proud.

He began to thread his way past people taking their places in the front rows. He paused occasionally to bow to one of the loftier matrons of the ton, or to exchange greetings with a peer. Always he kept that same cool and distant mien.

Before she was ready, he was standing before her, that slight, almost indiscernible smile on his face. Yet his eyes seemed to speak. Heavy lidded, mysterious, intense, they conveyed a danger that made her legs slightly weak. He took her hand and bent to kiss it, something perfectly unexceptionable, except for the delicious manner in which his kiss lingered. Its whisper of warmth went straight through her glove. She wished there was no glove at all between them. Good lord, what was wrong with her?

Warmth flooded her body. Her breasts seemed to swell and tingle at the same time. She realized with a shock that he was staring down at her, his dark eyes almost black with—could that be desire?

He was taking forever to greet her, she realized, startled. As warm as she had been before, she froze now, in fear. They might become objects of scandal while they stood hands clasped for this length of time. She peeked to the left and right. Although interested glances darted their way, people seemed more impressed than shocked.

He cleared his throat. Turning slightly, he placed her hand in the crook of his elbow. "I hoped that you would sit beside me," he said. "There's an excellent quartet by Mozart and then one by Beethoven to follow. I believe the front row would be a proper place to observe the hands of the musicians as they play."

And, she noted, a very good place for the ton to observe them.

Without asking whether she agreed, he led her to the front row, stopped before two seats in the very middle, and removed the programs he'd apparently placed on them. He handed her into her seat and bowed to Lady Farraday on his left before taking his own.

"Do you enjoy these musicales?" he asked. His head bent toward Caroline as he spoke, as though he wanted to be as close as he could to her. But there was something a bit theatrical about his motion that aroused her caution.

"I enjoy them a great deal." She pretended to read her program while her mind busily pondered what Headleymoor was about and why. Rustles around and behind them revealed the audience craning their necks toward her. From the side, she caught the flash of lamplight on a quizzing glass raised to an inquisitive eye.

"But I recall your words of last night." His tone cut into her thoughts, part commanding, part entreating, as though she were an actress who'd forgotten her lines. "You do not play an instrument, Lady Caroline."

"Not at all," she said, falling into her part with a smile. "Nor do I sing particularly well. Do you play, my lord?"

He shook his head. "My mother was musical, and she had great dreams for me, but I disappointed all her hopes. I think I admire those who can play more because I have no talent for it, myself."

Well, Caroline thought, he is not mean spirited, nor envious. The man was everything a woman could want and he seemed to be interested in her. Why did she not trust him? *With Headleymoor, the only time I feel like myself is when I'm feeling something I ought not,* she thought, and felt the warmth steal up her cheeks.

"But you enjoy riding, I've heard," he said, valiantly pulling her out of her thoughts as Society stared.

"Very much."

"I have seen you in the park with your mount. He's every bit of sixteen hands and seemed high spirited. Yet your hands are quite small."

He was staring at her hands again. Oh, dear. "A rider usually needs strength to control such a horse," he went on.

Hmm. Reverting to being a nosy parker, was he? "Please do not worry about my horsemanship. I am always in control of my Firestorm," she said. "Besides, he wouldn't hurt a fly."

"I beg your pardon," he said. "I only asked because . . . ah, because Ram Dass was a bit concerned."

She frowned. "Ram Dass need not worry, as well."

The string quartet's musicians were seated now, and tuning their instruments.

"You don't like his concern?" he asked her, over the cacophony.

"I like Ram Dass very well, but I am a bit insulted by his assumption that I cannot take care of myself on horseback. I am quite competent at what I choose to do."

He raised a brow at this, and for a fleeting moment, Caroline thought she spotted a twinge of hurt in his eyes. "You surprise me, Lady Caroline," he said. "I would have thought that you would be touched that he cares for your welfare."

"I do like knowing that," she objected, suddenly feeling small and mean. "I just wish that he would trust me to do things well, or not do them at all if they are dangerous."

Headleymoor pressed his lips together. In the pause, Caroline began to wonder what exactly was going on behind his cool mask.

"Ram does trust you, but he, like all men, would place your safety first."

This time, she realized, his face was alight with expression.

When they discussed his servant's ideas about her, why did Headleymoor shed his celebrated calm?

"I am reasonable, my lord," she said earnestly. "I do not take unnecessary risks. Unless circumstances demand it."

"And what would be a necessary risk?" he asked, a hint of exasperation threading itself through his voice.

"I would put myself in danger to save a friend. Or a member of my family. Or," she said with a smile, "Ram Dass."

"But not me," Headleymoor said with a rueful grin..

"Should we become friends, I would also include you in the list," she said.

"Then for my safety, as well as the pleasure of being with you, I shall hope that we become friends," he told her, and then the music began. It drifted in and out of her thoughts. The music and the silence between them seemed almost a living thing—an inchoate communication of emotion. Her self-consciousness and the caution melted, making her even more aware of the man sitting beside her.

His shoulder was very close to hers. The scent of him, clean, warm, male, with a hint of sandalwood, radiated to her in waves of feeling. She shut her eyes and let him fill all her senses, more alive and open than she'd been in a long time. She felt as though she were standing on a precipice, poised to either fly or fall.

In the pause between the second and third movements of the Beethoven, the strings tuned their instruments. She heard a rustle of paper to her left, and watched Lady Farraday's program drift to the floor. Headleymoor scooped it up before it could hit the carpet, and turned to the older woman.

"Thank you, Headleymoor," Lady Farraday said coolly.

"It is my pleasure to have done you a service, no matter how small," he said softly, with a smile that lit up his dark eyes. have always considered you one of the finest ladies of the to despite your rather incisive comments concerning several of t

younger members of Society. Or perhaps because of them."

That was the longest and most amusing string of words Caroline had heard coming from him since the beginning of their acquaintance. She watched in fascination as Lady Farraday gently rapped her fan against his arm.

"You have a great deal of cheek, young man. It is a good thing that I admire honesty in my friends. Come call on me soon, and bring your young lady with you," she said with a nod and smile toward Caroline.

"Oh, but I'm not . . ."

"Lady Caroline," Lady Farraday barked. "I believe your role in such conversations is to stare down at your lap and blush. See if you can undertake that task."

"We will both look forward to calling upon you with a great deal of relish," Headleymoor said. "And suspense."

Lady Farraday gave him a good poke with her fan and a broad smile.

As the last movement began, Caroline actually did stare at her lap. She felt like laughing helplessly, and she felt like running from the room screaming.

Headleymoor was most definitely not himself—at least not the self she had watched and studied from a distance. He had bent that famous pride of his to act the charming wit with Lady Farraday. Wrangling an invitation from her was a coup, not for him, but for Caroline. Why had he done it? Why all the worry about her safety in the saddle? Why did his awareness of their audience seem uppermost in his mind through much of their last two conversations? How could she trust him when he transformed himself as swiftly as a chameleon? Was he showering her with attention for some knotted, Byzantine design?

After the last movement, she could finally excuse herself to go to the ladies' retiring room and ponder the question. When she entered the corridor off the chamber, she still hadn't solved

the puzzle. The library stood just to her left. She could give herself a little time in there to find the answers to her questions.

Caroline pushed the heavy oak door open and walked in. A few candles burned in candelabra on either side of a long library table, and a few others stood in candlesticks beside some comfortable leather chairs.

Books rose to the ceiling, but in the dim light, only the bottom half of the shelves were truly visible. Caroline approached the tall, leaded windows and drew back the curtain to look out into the night. She leaned her forehead against the cool glass and shut her eyes. She knew why she questioned Headleymoor's every word and deed.

She wished, above all, not to be hurt. Not again, after all the other slights. Further down the hall, she could hear the hum of voices as people strolled about in the other rooms thrown open for the musicale.

Then the latch on the library door clicked and the door swung open.

"Caroline?" A man's deep voice. Not Headleymoor. Footsteps came closer, and she heard an amused laugh.

"Come out, my lady. On my honor, I shan't trouble you in any way. I pray you, trust me."

Her eyes widened and she stepped from the alcove by the window. "Nearing?" she asked in surprise.

"None other. I needed to see you, Caroline, to apologize, to make you understand . . . I know you heard me last night."

She narrowed her eyes and felt her hands tightening into fists at her side. "Oh, I understood exactly what you meant last night, my lord. Now if you'll excuse me, I shall leave you dominion over the library." She strode toward the door, eager to quit this small space while her enemy stood too close.

His hand shot out and clasped her elbow. It didn't hurt, but there was no way she could unlatch it from her arm, and her skirts would muffle any kick she might be able to attempt at this distance.

"How dare you, sir? Unhand me now!" She frowned. "Listen to me. I sound like the insipid heroine of a bad gothic novel."

The candlelight revealed Nearing's dark, handsome countenance. His deep blue eyes appeared distraught and miserable. "You don't understand, Caroline. I've wanted you these two years, since you made your bow. And I could do nothing—the family name, all of it, depended upon my marrying someone unexceptionable. So I thought perhaps, given that I couldn't offer what I should, I might gain your love anyway, and we might have something so good together that it would offset the misery I'd go through in my life."

She laughed. "Your misery? What about mine? Did you believe that I would actually deign to be any man's mistress? Watch him make a marriage with another woman? Have children by her? Refuse to recognize any child I might have?"

She pulled away from him and began to pace. "Dear Lord, can you believe I'm actually treating this as hypothetical? It will never happen, my lord. Not ever."

"Caroline, I have watched you so long, overheard your laughter and recognized your wicked sense of humor. Is it any wonder that I would find other women dull and insipid? And that was to be my fate, whether you would deign to love me or not."

To her shock, he went down on one knee. "But all that's changed, now. Since Headleymoor and his family have shown you such favor, Society has turned one-hundred-eighty degrees about. Even my grandmother has heard the news, and I don't need to wait for anything or anyone to help us."

"Help us? What do you mean?" This night was taking on the confusing turmoil of a fever dream.

"The circumstances of your birth have changed utterly. Two

or three of Society's dragons are my grandmother's close friends. They have suddenly remembered your great grandfather definitely had ginger hair. They say that the thought had slipped their minds all these years because of powder and wigs back then. My dear, you are suddenly an Incomparable."

He threw his head back, his arms flung wide as he knelt before her, looking at her with eyes that shone like deep blue sapphires. "It's possible now, my dear, dear Caroline. Don't you see? We can marry, we can have our children together and love them together. We're free."

He rose so quickly she nearly spun from the motion, but he wouldn't drop her hand. Instead, he pulled her to his chest, and bent his head to her. "Marry me, Caroline," he whispered in her ear. "Make me the happiest man on earth."

She was torn between laughter and scorn. His shining eyes told her he really believed himself to be a man in love, while his actions were those of an actor who suddenly believed his part to be real, rather than a play. "Let me go, Nearing."

"I spoke to your brother last night," he said, ignoring her command. "I hinted that I would ask for your hand, and he's already approved the match." His arms clasped her tighter, and his lips descended. His kiss was hard, passionate, and just a bit theatrical.

Caroline was being dragged into a Cheltenham melodrama. She would not have it. She struggled, pummeling his chest with everything she had, kicking despite the smothering crinolines and skirts. She shoved her head sideways and reached up to his cheek, her fingers clawed beneath her gloves.

"Get off, get off at once!" she screamed.

The door slammed open. Nearing thrust her behind him, but she sidled as far away from him as she could and peered into the hall. The light from the candle sconces shone on the golden hair and broad shoulders of a very tall, very enraged marquess.

He strode into the library and slammed the door behind him. Several tomes from the upper shelves hit the floor with a loud slap of leather against wood.

"Hell, Maxim," he said with a sigh. "Now I have to call you out."

Headleymoor's soft voice was much scarier than a shout would have been. "Damnation, man," he said. "You can't encroach upon the solitude of a gentle lady in order to treat her like a dockyard sailor would a . . . well, you know what I mean." He glanced Caroline's way.

Then he moved, graceful, deadly, panther-like, until he and Nearing faced each other with a distance of two feet between them. Headleymoor kept shaking his head, hands on hips, like an exasperated schoolmaster. At that moment, Caroline realized that Nearing must be Headleymoor's very good friend.

"Pistols or swords?" Headleymoor asked quietly.

Caroline closed her eyes in horror. That was all she needed—two close friends fighting a duel over her. She could never live with the guilt. Nor actually, now that she thought of it, the scandal that would throw her right back into the role of an untouchable.

"Pistols," Nearing said clearly and concisely.

Nearing was an excellent shot. Almost as good as she was, to hear her brother brag about him. And for once, she could read Headleymoor's expression clearly. He looked heartbroken.

If they were to go out into some lonely field right now, he wouldn't stand a chance. And despite her recent ascension to acceptability, she'd lived before with being damned in Society's eyes. She sighed, and quickly pulled off her long kid glove. Buttons popped and scattered across the carpet.

But what was her favorite pair of gloves compared to a man's life?

She walked up to the two of them. Their faces were within

inches of each other and they stared each other down with fire in their eyes. With a wiggle and a shove of her elbow into someone's hard stomach, she inserted herself between them. Then she slapped Nearing sharply on the left cheek with the glove.

"Huh?" he said and rubbed the offended cheek.

"Excellent choice, Nearing," she said. "Pistols it is, at dawn. Where are these sorts of things usually conducted? Just tell me that, and name your second."

"Just a moment, Caroline," Headleymoor said, pulling her gently around to face him. "The glove bit was mine to do."

She raised one eyebrow at him in a superior look she'd learned from watching his father the night before. "I'm the injured party, and I'm challenging him. It's my honor, and I'll defend it, thank you very much."

"With a pistol?"

Behind her, Nearing cleared his throat. "I'm afraid she's a crack shot. As fine as Lord Holland, actually, from what her brother told me."

"Will told you? How many others has he told?" She would now die. Right here in the library. The coroner would call it Death by Mortification.

"Lord Holland, eh?" Headleymoor looked down at her through narrowed eyes. "And in *The Ladies' Journal of Accomplishments* does shooting belong in the category of 'Animal Husbandry' or 'This and That'?"

She scowled right back at him. "A lady does not brag of her accomplishments, no matter how . . . odd they might be."

"Nonsense. You simply wished me to know as little about you as possible," Headleymoor said in a low mutter.

"I refuse to feel guilty for taking a virtual stranger into my confidences. What might be considered a bit eccentric in another woman would be seen as proof of unacceptable proclivities in me. Now, let's get on with my duel," she said.

Nearing turned her round gently. "No, no, Caroline. Can you really believe that I would stand across from the woman I love and shoot her?"

"I wouldn't have believed you would follow the woman you love into a dark room and force your attentions on her when she demanded you stop. But you were perfectly happy to do that." Twisting with a shimmy that pulled her crinolines and skirts after her in the small space she still occupied between the two men, she faced Headleymoor.

"I need Ram Dass," she said. "Tell him I need him as my second."

Headleymoor pursed his lips into a thin line. "Ram Dass, and not me."

Frustration caused her stomach to clamp. Neither Headleymoor nor Nearing had promised to eschew the duel. They might very well appease her with lies and then secretly agree to kill each other at dawn. She bit back a sob. "I trust him," she said. "I need him."

"I'm trustworthy. I should be your second," Headleymoor said hotly. Then he started in confusion and frowned. "What am I saying? I absolutely forbid this duel."

Nearing groaned. "I am an idiot—an impetuous dolt. I apologize for everything I've done, Caroline. And yet, my punishment will be just. I have lost your regard, and there will be no other woman for me."

Nonsense, Caroline thought. But that rejoinder wouldn't get them all out of this farce. She poked Headleymoor in the stomach. Her finger met hard muscle. But he must have finally realized she needed a bit more space, for he stepped back. She turned again, nodding regally at Nearing.

"Then I declare that enough of a punishment to satisfy my honor. You may remove yourself from this room immediately.

Headleymoor and I shall leave in another minute. Your final penance will be to determine that no one, and I do mean no one sees us depart the library. I am determined to become respectable, do you hear? And that means no more gossip."

"As you wish." He walked toward the door and turned at the last moment before opening it. "Caroline, I don't suppose there's any hope that I might redeem myself in your eyes?" Nearing gave her such a blue deviled look that she was tempted to comfort him, until she realized that he'd only take that for encouragement.

"None whatever," she said.

"I understand how angry, how insulted you feel right now," he murmured. "But I shall hope that sometime, something I do will soften your heart toward me. Meanwhile, I shall do my best to deserve your respect." He opened the heavy door. Glancing both ways down the hall, he quietly departed the chamber.

She turned to Headleymoor, who was eyeing her with the fascination of a child with a new species of butterfly.

That bit sharply. She'd hoped to see a little respect in his eyes.

"I thought you were a gentle soul, but you really can be a bit frightening," he said meditatively.

She shrugged. "When one grows up without companions, one becomes what one wishes to become. The only difficulty is in hiding it from those who would be horrified."

"I'm not horrified," he said softly, walking toward her. "Have you other talents that have not come to Society's attention?"

Something grew warm in the vicinity of her heart. She couldn't stop her smile. "Grandfather taught me how to find edible berries and roots. I can set a snare, and I am decent enough with a bow and a knife. But I cannot use a sword very well at all. I suppose I just wasn't interested in learning how. I might begin lessons now, in the event of another duel."

"Ah. Your grandfather would be proud of how you handled that," he said, with a look of approval she had never expected to see from him.

She nodded. "He thought that women's lives were worth more than sitting in corners at Society balls. Particularly my life. I have thought that exploring the world with him would be far preferable to balls, even those in which I danced every dance."

She looked away from him. It must be the darkness of the library or the lunacy of the past half hour that made her tongue refuse to quit wagging.

"And now do you still think that?" His eyes, those deep, mysterious pools seemed to open on his soul. They drew her toward him, made her forget where they were.

"I would so like to see India and Zaranbad and the Pyramids, too." She shook her head. "After tonight, leaving England sounds more and more alluring. What a disappointing waste." She laughed, then shrugged. "My first kiss, I mean," she explained.

A small gust of wind wafted through the open window. The candles guttered. The room was plunged into darkness.

He was there, right before her, his hand slipping around her back, pulling her close.

"Care to try a second?" he whispered low.

"Erp," she squeaked in surprise. His scent was so wonderful, masculine and clean and slightly exotic.

He lowered his head. His lips brushed hers, soft, coaxing, a mere touch, nothing at all like Nearing's brand of possession on her lips.. There was nothing in her world but that soft, teasing contact. Her lips tingled from it. All the layers between them—her gown and chemise, the crisp linen of his evening shirt and his embroidered waistcoat were not enough to mask the hard strength of his chest against her breasts. Immediately, her nipples tightened, and her breasts felt heavy and full. She had an overwhelming urge to rub them against his chest.

He pulled her closer, and kissed the side of her mouth, the sensitive spot beneath her ear, the place where her jaw met her neck.

"Caroline," he murmured. "You're so soft. Everywhere."

His mouth covered hers again, his tongue licking lightly, learning the contour of her bottom lip. Then his teeth gently bit down on it, making her gasp. He took advantage, his tongue plunging into her mouth, stroking, while his hands molded her body, sliding up, up toward the fullness at the sides of her breast.

There was nothing in the world but his hands, his lips, the beauty with which he played her like an instrument.

A voice murmured outside the door. She jerked her head away, stifling a gasp. The footsteps receded down the hall.

"Oh, God. I'm sorry," he said, putting her away from him. He cleared his throat. "Lady Caroline, would you do me the honor of—"

"Nonsense," she interrupted, stumbling away from him. What had just happened here? How had she fallen so enthusiastically into his arms?

They knew nothing about each other. He was beautiful and exciting. But she didn't trust him, not really. A whole lifetime with a man one couldn't trust? She had to stop this—this declaration before they were both in trouble.

"Nothing happened," she whispered. "Not really. We must forget all about this. Put it out of our minds. Get out of here as quickly as possible. Shall you check the hall, my lord?"

Dr. Gupta, a tall, gentle stork of a man with whom Dev had studied medicine in Zaranbad, gave him a long look when he returned from the musicale. "You seem to have a great deal on your mind," Dr. Gupta said. "Has this to do with the threats against your family, or the young lady you so assiduously court?"

Court? Hah! Grabbed and kissed and would have done much more had the young lady not come to her senses, saving both of them from a terrible mistake. Of course it was a terrible mistake.

"I am concerned about the young lady," he said. He was a cur, a scoundrel, the worst sort of villain. He'd betrayed his best friend, and taken advantage of an innocent young girl.

Barely out of the schoolroom.

Who smelled like wildflowers and woman.

Oh God, she smelled good.

"I've been a cad, and I don't wish to talk about it. If I am very careful, no real harm may come of it."

"You want this woman—the one your friend wants as well?"

Dev sighed. "Do you have second sight, or spies who skulk in libraries at musicales?"

"Neither, my lord. I am merely guessing at the cause of your consternation, and delighted if it is so."

"Delighted? I am the lowest of men, a craven sensualist, a rake who should never be invited to dine with decent folk."

"In other words, you kissed the young lady in a library."

"The young lady my best friend wishes to wed."

"And the young lady slapped your face and ran from the room, no doubt," Dr. Gupta said, looking at him intently.

He shut his eyes in mortification. "It was too dark for her to see where to run."

"Ah. Then she must have screamed for help."

"Actually," Dev said as he began to pace the room, "she whispered. She's not the screaming type."

"A levelheaded Englishwoman," Dr. Gupta said. "Better and better."

Dev rounded on him. "Don't you see? I betrayed my best friend!"

"Well, where was he? Why did he not kiss the young lady in

the library?"

Dev stopped pacing. "He tried. She would have none of it."

Dr. Gupta smiled benignly. "But she would have some of you, apparently."

"She's an innocent," Dev almost barked at the man. "Don't make her out to be anything else."

"An innocent with a good head on her shoulders, I would venture. She chose you to kiss. Better and better and better."

Dev threw up his hands. "You don't understand the cultural intricacies. I did a terrible thing tonight and I don't know how to fix it. Thank God Ram Dass will see her tomorrow. Perhaps he will convince her to give Maxim another try."

"You could visit her tomorrow. She might prefer that."

"No. She will prefer Ram Dass to me every time. She will tell him how she really feels."

"Ah. She's not aware of the masquerade?"

Dev stared down at his boots. "State secrets and all that. I met her last year as Ram Dass, and she seemed to trust him. Actually, I shouldn't be so aggravated that she prefers Ram Dass. He'll give her as much of a push in Maxim's direction as he can."

Dr. Gupta frowned and rose to his feet. "Your Highness, listen to yourself! Despite your so-called motives and your so-called guilt, you are courting this woman as two men in proxy for a third man. It's gotten to the point of absurdity, for one of you is jealous of the other two—and I'm not speaking of Ram Dass!"

Dev frowned. "I am not jealous of Maxim. And certainly not of Ram Dass. I am merely . . . upset because I have been a fool with Lady Caroline and she will hate me for it. And she will never hate Ram Dass."

That was because an Indian servant would never imagine taking an Englishwoman in his arms. But Lord Headleymoor, the Englishman, spent way too much time imagining just that with this particular Englishwoman.

He certainly dreamed about doing so—and in colorful detail that left him heavy and aching. He blamed everything that happened in the library on that dream.

Caroline lay naked beneath him, all soft, glowing skin, her slender legs wrapped about his waist, her head thrown back in abandon just as it had been when they waltzed. He'd bent his head to the peaked nipple of her lush breast, licking, suckling, and she'd moaned. Not a ladylike moan either, but the deep, eager sound of a woman who wanted him beyond anything to come to her. A woman in the throes of passion.

Not passion for Maxim. Nor for Ram Dass. For him. Only for him. And in the darkness of that library, he'd seized the chance, and found out how much better the reality was than the dream. Now what the hell was he going to do?

Dr. Gupta put his fists on his hips and rolled his eyes. "Englishmen! Mad every one of you. I ask you, what will this Lady Caroline Berring do when she discovers that you and Ram Dass are one and the same man? How will you ever explain yourself? If you fear she thinks less of you now, just wait until that moment."

She must never know, he thought. Then she'd hate both of him. "Can't tell her yet. Not until this business with Ari is over. Then. I'll tell her then."

Dr. Gupta sighed. "You have ever had difficulties learning to trust to your karma. I wish you very good fortune, my prince. You are going to need it."

The next afternoon, Caroline was trying very hard not to tap her toes in impatience. All morning, gentlemen and their mamas had called. The large blue drawing room had been so full of babbling humanity and servants bringing tea and cakes that

Caroline had found it difficult to breathe. She wasn't used to being with so many people at once and found the need to contribute to the drone of conversation exhausting.

Headleymoor did not come to call. After the thrill of his kiss last night, she had thought he might stop by, just to be polite, if nothing else. It was insulting that he hadn't come to call. By God, she'd been right to stop him before he declared himself. He so obviously didn't care a rat's tail for her.

After all, he'd kissed her in the darkness, and he'd touched her in places that a man should never touch a woman unless she was his wife. And he'd made her not care about anything but his hands on her body, his mouth covering hers, his tongue mating with hers . . .

Someone said something to her right, and she smiled automatically, turning to grasp at the straws of the conversation. It was the Dowager Countess Darby's eldest son reciting a poem in praise of Caroline's eyes—something about the soft blue of the evening sky.

Yes. Far better to pay attention to honorable men who called upon her in daylight than moon away for men who kissed one in the dark and were never heard from again.

Mr. Epsom came in and sat beside her, discussing his country house and its many rooms in need of a woman's touch before rising and bowing himself off.

Reggie Downs, Lord Greenleigh, a rather sweet and muzzy-headed man—unless one was speaking of hounds and hunting—told her about the kennels he was certain she'd enjoy seeing and the fine new mare he'd just bought.

"Wide enough through the chest, good lungs, I'd vow, and strong legs for a mare—thick canon bone and a kind eye. The sort you'd probably love to hunt. Why not come down soon with your mama? I could mount you easily." This enthusiastic dialogue came to a sudden halt as Reggie turned beet red.

Caroline knew enough about horses and mating to recognize a huge faux pas when she heard one. But Reggie had always been kind to her, long before anyone would recognize her.

She stifled her desire to laugh and said solemnly, "I should love to see the mare. How fast is she?"

Reggie was off again and running.

Munson entered the drawing room, followed by Ram Dass, who bowed to the company assembled. "Lady Eversleigh, my mistress the Queen of Zaranbad requests the presence of Lady Caroline Berring at Wimbley House."

Finally! Caroline thought. The oohs and ahhs from impressed matrons were not nearly as satisfying as this blessed reprieve from the Afternoon Call.

"With your permission, Lady Eversleigh," Ram Dass said.

"Yes. Of course," Mama said, regally inclining her head.

Caroline rose with a rustle of skirts and curtsied on her way out. Despite her destination—after all, Wimbley House was where *he* lived—she felt like a child let free from lessons to run outside and play.

Once down the walk, Ram Dass took her hand and helped her into the large and comfortable closed carriage with the Wimbley crest emblazoned on the door. He leaped inside and closed the door, shutting the world out. After the last two hours, it was like going from the howling desert winds into a calm, green, shaded oasis. She could almost hear the water playing in the fountains.

She settled against the squabs with a sigh of relief and smiled at him, as he gracefully stretched his long legs across the space between the seats.

"You seem weary, Lady Caroline."

She laughed. "It's because of our newly elevated station. My mother and I are now at home to young men and their mamas on a daily basis. I find it exhausting, but she looks ten years younger, and her pleasure is palpable. I don't dare ask that we have a day of rest from all this yet."

Ram Dass stared out at the street. "That ritual can also be revealing for you. Have you found any particular . . . callers who have struck your fancy?"

Caroline's heart hitched, then continued on in its beating. Silly to think that Ram Dass actually felt jealous of the men who now seemed to be courting her. And yet . . .

His lips formed a grim line and the nostrils in his straight, fine nose flared like a stallion scenting a rival. When he looked like this, the resemblance to Headleymoor was almost uncanny. Other than the dark brows and olive skin tone, Ram Dass could be Headleymoor's brother.

"No one in particular," she answered him, attempting a casual tone.

"I see. Perhaps you will dance again with Lord Headleymoor at the Queen's ball," he said.

"Perhaps."

Ram Dass's posture lost some its stiffness. Of course, she thought as pieces of the puzzle fit together. He must not be Indian, at all, but a son of the prince's grandfather. Not by a woman in the harem, for the Dassams did not have a harem. No, it would have been a servant, or perhaps, a lady married to another man. And recently widowed.

Her heart clenched in empathy. They had a great deal in common. Born on the wrong side of the blanket, tolerated but kept apart from their families, allowed some but not all of the rights and privileges of nobility.

"I am sure that he will enjoy that, Lady Caroline."

She was certain Headleymoor wouldn't care one way or the other. But the puzzle that was Ram Dass now made so much sense, and she understood why she was so happy in his presence. And why, with just the touch of his hand, he could take away her weariness and ennui. Or, she realized in dismay, make her wonder what would happen if she didn't have to protect Mama from Society's censure. Of course, Ram Dass would probably be shocked and horrified that an Englishwoman would be so bold as to wish to become more . . . than a sort of friend to him.

She glanced in Ram Dass's direction, saw the straight, proud way in which he sat—like a prince of the blood.

Poor lost souls, she thought. We are so much alike.

And worlds apart.

An hour later, she stood, hands on hips, and watched Queen Janighar walk slowly up and down the library in Wimbley House while the most popular mantuamaker in London, Madame Millefleur, nodded her approval.

"The gown is ravissant, your majesty. All eyes will be upon you."

"What a frightening thought," Janighar said with a little moue.

"It's beautiful," Caroline said. "And since everyone will be watching you anyway, why not look your best?"

If a kitten could growl, Janighar's little sound would have been just that. "I am beginning to wonder what there was about a sanguine disposition that so attracted me to you in the first place. Can you not say something doom-filled about the Queen's ball?"

Caroline stood up and walked over to the mirror before which Janighar stood, but couldn't see herself.

"I will instead describe the gown. Here. Run your fingers over the lace at the shoulder. Very fine—a soft, cream color. And the brocade is ice blue. And then feel here, to the waist. They've sewn dark blue velvet cording down each panel along your stays. And here, right below the waist, before the gown bells out? A vee of the same dark blue cording, and more down the skirt, all the way around."

Charlotte knelt before the princess, and lifted up the skirt. "Feel here, at the bottom. The same lace, cream colored, and ruffled, again, around the back and the small train. Madame is correct, Janighar. You look ravishing."

"I do, don't I?" Janighar said in a hushed voice. "I shall be beautiful, Caroline. And you must be beautiful, too. What color will you wear?"

"I have a very serviceable golden brown silk that will do quite well," Caroline said, looking longingly at the ice blue confection before her.

"Lady Caroline wears a great deal of brown," Ram Dass said from a corner where he stood.

"Brown?" Janighar said in horror. "No, no, that will not do for such a fine occasion. Madame, is there a chance that you and your staff can put together a gown for Lady Caroline in time for the ball?"

The modiste pondered the question for a short moment. "It will be a rush, of course, but for you, your majesty, there should be no problem."

"Ram Dass decided what color I should wear, and he did well, did he not?" Janighar said. "Now it's your turn, Caroline. Ram Dass?"

Ram Dass bowed from his place across the chamber. "Yes, Majesty?"

"Lady Caroline needs something magical for the ball. Will you choose her colors?"

"I would be oh-so-very honored. This servant declares that there is no question," Ram Dass said in his soft, musical tones as he placed himself before Caroline. "Lady Caroline must wear a gown of rose silk, always changing in the light, as does the color of her hair. The trim must be rose-gold, in the lace on the elbows and the skirt. No lace at the top. And a line at the bodice like so." He pulled out a fashion plate with a sweetheart neckline that dipped shockingly low.

Caroline's eyes widened. That fashion plate must have been made for a member of the demimonde. Never could she walk into a ballroom, particularly the Queen's ballroom, so boldly . . . on display. "Oh, no. That neckline is far too low," she said.

Ram Dass smiled. "Lady Caroline. You are courageous enough to dance with a prince. And this line of the bodice top, it is—how do you say?—*de rigeur.*"

"Oh, yes," Madame Millefleur added, nodding sagely. "It is not so very low, my lady. With your measurements, it will look exactly right."

"But . . . wait!"

The co-conspirators had turned to the library table, where Ram Dass dipped a quill into an inkpot and applied it to a piece of foolscap.

Caroline tapped her foot and cleared her throat, but the only one who seemed aware of her reactions was Janighar, who stood in her lovely gown with a faint, knowing smile on her face.

"I say," Caroline began, but Ram Dass and Madame Millefleur were bent over the table, off in their own little world, completely ignoring her and her objections.

"I see exactly what you mean," Madame Millefleur said, looking over Ram Dass's shoulder as he sketched his ideas with a quill.

"I don't wish a new gown," Caroline muttered.

"And twined in her hair, roses the same color as the silk. There are some at Wimbley House. The prince will know where to find the finest," Ram Dass added, handing Madame Millefleur a quick sketch of the gown he envisioned.

"I never wear roses. Or a rose gown," Caroline said faintly as her hand rose automatically to cover her hair.

"Well, you should," Madame said, with a shrewd look at her. "The effect will be *magnifique.* Come, Ram Dass, you will help me find the correct fabric for such a gown."

Caroline was left in the middle of the floor, staring at herself in the cheval glass that the modiste had set up and growing more and more irritated by the moment. What she wore was her choice, not Ram Dass's!

After Ram Dass and Madame had left the room, a maid helped Janighar out of her ball gown.

"I'll take it, your majesty," a young, cheerful dressmaker said. "I'll fold it properly so that no creases appear in the material."

The girl was back shortly, helping Caroline out of her gown and petticoats. "And you, my lady," she said as she deftly took measurements. "May I say that the servant was right about the color? You'll look right beautiful in the gown, I promise. I'll do most of the last stitching and the trim. I promise you, it will look ever so fine."

She was gone in a whirl of skirts. Caroline was left staring at herself in the mirror. Shivering in only a corset, chemise, crinolines, stockings and slippers, she wondered just how, in the last week, her life had been thrust completely out of her hands and into those of the House of Dassam.

"Is my mother in the pink drawing room, Munson?" Caroline asked as she strode into the hall at Twenty-five Berkeley Square.

"Yes, my lady," Munson said. "But she's . . ."

Caroline heard no more as she ran up the stairs and turned left. "Mama," she called, stepping through the double doors and turning to close them. "I'm to wear a very bright gown to dinner with the queen, and it's going to be cut fearfully low."

She turned to face the room again, and wished she hadn't. Her mother was in the process of disentangling herself from a tall, auburn-haired man with bright blue eyes.

Mama stared down at the turkey carpet, red-faced as a dairy maid caught with the stable boy. The man was—well, she might as well call him what he really was—her father, the Duke of Wellsingham.

Caroline stared from one to the other, feeling as though she'd been turned to stone. Hard, cold stone, impervious to any more misery or betrayal or lies.

"How long?" she asked in a voice that seemed to come from far away. "How long have you been with him, while making me face down ridicule and disdain in order to convince the world that *this* never really happened?"

"Caroline." Her mother held out a hand in a pleading gesture. Her voice was laced with tears. "You don't understand."

Caroline straightened her back and cast a look of fury in her father's direction. "I understand perfectly. I was given to comprehend not two nights ago that if I wished to ever love, your course might be the only one open to me. And then—and then, a man spoke to me kindly—a man who knew of a way to change my fate. But now, if the two of you continue to . . . to . . ."

She steadied her trembling hands and tried to control the tremor in her voice. "That will no longer be a possibility for me, will it? Think, Mother. Your friends, whom you missed so much. They will brand you again. Because of him!"

Before, she had told herself it didn't matter what Society thought. It was so much easier than wishing for acceptance when there was no hope of it.

Then Headleymoor had come into her life and she'd begun to think perhaps she, too, could have a future. Real friends. A husband. Children to love.

And now, just when that hope had become a possibility, these two people—who should have been the first to protect her—shattered that dream, not only for herself, but for Mama as well.

She whirled away and reached for the double doors. She felt

the hard imprint of brass crushed against her palms.

The fire of resentment burned deep in her stomach and lungs, so that it seemed the very air was about to explode in a conflagration of wrath. Slowly, she straightened and faced them again.

"Did you think what this would do to me, Mama? It wasn't so bad, until now, when I've had a taste of what I—what you might have."

She paused and turned to the man who stood beside her mother now, his arm around her shoulders, protecting her from her daughter, as though he had a right to do so. As though he had any rights before her.

"Did you think of her or me for minute, *your grace?* After a few days of acceptance, we shall be outcasts again. You are cruel and selfish, and I am ashamed to be your child." She opened the doors. "Just as I've been all my life," she said softly, and ran from the room.

CHAPTER FIVE:
BUCKINGHAM PALACE

In the upstairs rooms of a rat-infested tenement near the docks, Felix Kendall, dressed entirely in black, threw his greatcoat down and took a seat opposite his present superior. He had not been told who headed this operation to overthrow King Ari Dassam when he accepted the job, nor had he expected to be informed. It was enough that Kendall's gaming debts had been settled and his father need never discover how endangered his estates had been.

With that shameful act, he'd gotten a code name—Jackal. He felt it was quite apt for the way he now felt about himself. The powerful leader who had given him his orders was called Wolf. On Kendall's first visit to this den of thieves, it was with shock that he discovered "Wolf" was not Zaranbadian. He could have been from any Northern European country, but though he spoke like a foreigner, Kendall had his suspicions. Wolf was an Englishman pretending a Scandinavian accent.

Kendall cursed the day he'd accepted the desperately needed lucre that had pulled him into this man's orbit.

However, with the unpredictable United Band, Kendall always came prepared. There were three pistols and two knives hidden in various pockets and his boots. The Home Office had taught him well.

As was his custom, Wolf's face was half covered by the tail of his turban, which also covered his hair and neck. Above this mask, his eyes glittered with malevolence kept barely under control. That was what gave Kendall a queer, nauseating lurch of fear inside. If the control slipped, he didn't know what this man would do.

"I hear the man Headleymoor took tonight is in Newgate. I thought you told me he would be easy to snatch back without any repercussions."

"Headleymoor said our other agent should come to Newgate as well. There was nothing I could do—no way to eliminate a captive right in front of the new recruit. He is too full of honor and patriotism to have witnessed the situation without reporting it."

"Why the hell didn't you simply eliminate him?" Wolf said in a calm, cold voice of ice.

Kill Tom? Kendall shoved his hand beneath the table to hide the tremor. He reminded himself that he was armed, and that reassured him enough to regain his voice. "I couldn't kill him, too. It would only place suspicion on me, and at this point, neither you nor I can afford to have that happen."

What he could see of Wolf's face grew dark with frustration.

It was enough impetus to encourage Kendall's hands to slowly move toward his hip, where one of the pistols lay in his breeches pocket. "Don't worry. I've thought of a way to solve this little problem."

Wolf lifted a brow and nodded. "Tell me your plan."

Kendall smothered his sigh of relief. It was no good showing weakness to Wolf. Like his code name, he could rip one's throat open and enjoy tasting the blood.

"The Dassam dynasty has one weakness," Kendall said. "They allow themselves to love. All we need to do is take one of their women and hold her for a prisoner exchange. They will give up our man very quickly—you'll see. Within twenty-four hours, he will be among his friends again. Furthermore, the United Band trains its men to endure interrogation. Put that together with the humane treatment the prisoner will get from King Ari, and we can be certain that he will not break in the meantime."

"What you say has merit. I will discuss your ideas with my Zaranbadian friend. He knows whether King Ari will trade a man he can eventually break for his woman. He and I will think of a plan and you will help us to execute it. Are we agreed?"

Kendall bowed his head and rose. "Completely. Let me discover where they go and when, and I shall find a way to make this happen. I can promise you that it will be done quickly, and in a way to make the Crown wonder whether the East India Company's supervision of Zaranbad isn't more important than the independent monarchy they've promised King Ari in the past."

After the nasty scene in the drawing room on Berkeley Square, Caroline spent every afternoon at Wimbley House in Janighar's company. Caroline and her mother treated each other with courtesy, but Mama refused to discuss the duke. Caroline's dismay about her own prospects for happiness was overshadowed by her fears for her mother. Yet Mama demanded time and quiet, instead of open discussion.

Wimbley House provided a magnificent refuge from the confusion and resentment clouding Caroline's mind. Today, she and Janighar explored its endless corridors, huge drawing rooms, and ancient bedchambers. Suddenly, Caroline stared up at the ceiling and giggled, then clapped her hand over her mouth.

"What is it?" Janighar said as they stood arm in arm.

"The ceiling. It has a painting of cherubs and extremely plump ladies."

"And?" Janighar demanded.

"They're draped in little more than their long hair."

"Oh."

"Indeed."

Caroline had never been accepted in the company of respectable girls until Lady Lilias Drelincourt had insisted upon a friendship that lit Caroline's days with happiness.

Just as Lilias had to leave her for a happy life in the country, Janighar would leave England someday soon. The thought made Caroline ache in anticipated loneliness. But the chance to laugh and talk and share confidences with Janighar was even more precious to her for its impermanence.

"In the palace, there are many books a lady should not read," Janighar said as they walked slowly about the room.

Caroline glanced at her. "You look like a satisfied cat with a very large mouse."

Janighar's smile became even more mysterious and smug, if that could be possible.

Caroline stopped dead. "You've read them."

Janighar majestically inclined her head. "Indeeed."

"Well?"

"Well," Janighar began and described one of the pictures.

"Sounds like the way mares and stallions mate," Caroline told her in what she thought was a rather worldly tone. She so wished to cover her shock at the description.

"I think so. Have you seen that?"

"At my grandfather's. He didn't think that I should be kept from understanding all aspects of life."

"You ride?"

"Oh, yes."

Janighar's face lit in a bright smile. "Ah, my very favorite thing to do growing up. My friends and I used to run to the stables barefoot and leap on the horses. We'd ride like the wind through the encampment of my father, who is, among other, grander things, a sheik of the desert. You have stirrups, have you not, in England?"

"We do." Caroline felt her lips widening in a great grin. Whether with forbidden books or horses, Janighar seemed as irredeemable as she was.

"As we were barefoot, we could not use stirrups properly. But we didn't wish to be proper at all. We wrapped our legs around the leathers and used the metal stirrups as spurs, banging them against our ponies' flanks. Poor things. They seemed to enjoy the speed more than they hated our drumming."

"Oh, it sounds a wonderful way to grow up."

"Unfortunately, it did not last long. I should not share this with an innocent maiden. The topic is not proper."

Caroline laughed. "And the books were?"

"That is true," Janighar said in a lofty voice. "I shall tell you because you do not shock easily." She took a deep breath. "My mother came to me one night, looking terribly concerned. She told me that if a girl rode astride, she could, ahem, lose her innocence. She feared that my husband would be very upset if I did not prove a virgin on my wedding night."

Caroline's cheeks grew very red, but not from the forbidden topic being discussed. That only interested her enormously, that such a thing could happen to a woman. But after the description of the forbidden picture book, she didn't quite understand how one could lose her virginity while riding astride a pony.

She sighed. If Mama decided to end her affair, Caroline might have a husband someday. As a child, she'd ridden astride whenever she could, and often without a saddle. It seemed that she was headed for a difficult scene on her wedding night, if she ever had one.

She thought about it that night as she dressed for the ball at Buckingham Palace. "Ah, well," she whispered to her reflection in cheval glass, noting her high color and narrowed eyes. She really was seething with resentment against the duke and her mother.

"One must accept the inevitable," she warned herself. "In all probability, Mama will continue this affair with the duke. Society will chew on that tasty bit of gossip and I shall not have to beg my husband's forgiveness and explain anything. The problem is moot."

She turned from the mirror and threw on her cloak. What did she care, anyway? She was going to America.

The antechamber of Buckingham Palace was warm with a good, hot fire in the fireplace. As he entered with Janighar and Ari, Dev wondered whether his brother had warned the palace that his queen was a fragile flower in need of warmth to keep her constitution strong enough to brave the English spring. Whereas Dev knew that Janighar was healthy as a horse—actually a good deal healthier, when one thought of the many equine diseases that could bring a good mount down.

"The Earl of Eversleigh, Alicia, Dowager Countess of Eversleigh, Lady Caroline Berring," the powdered footman announced with grave intonation, and Caroline moved forward into the blue drawing room in a shimmer of rose silk and gold lace, graceful as a nymph. The flowers, the same deep rose color as the gown, brought out the magnificent fire of her upswept hair. Dev hoped that each time she caught their scent in the warm room, she would think of him—well, of Ram Dass, anyway.

But she didn't look like a nymph, languidly lying in the sun on the bank of some woodland stream. She looked more like a goddess, burning with a flame too bright for mortals to bear. Or a brilliant, glittering jewel. Whatever emotion she felt, it gave her cheeks a high gloss of color to match her gown, and her eyes were the brightness of sapphires. Was it excitement or anger? He could not tell.

He regretted his promise to Nearing, made this morning after his friend had pleaded with him. But sometime tonight, he would have to fulfill it. He would have to beg Caroline to give Nearing another chance. And Caroline would know that Dev's courtship was a sham. She would never speak to him again.

"The King and Queen of Zaranbad, the Marquess of Headleymoor," the footman intoned.

Dev walked into the drawing room, already filled with a select group of the aristocracy who had come to the more intimate dinner before the ball. He spotted Robert Epsom and Reggie Downes, Viscount Greenleigh among the guests. Nearing was absent tonight, having gone to the country, a disastrous decision, Dev thought in concern, given that he ought to be crawling on his knees and begging for Caroline's forgiveness himself. Thus sparing Dev Caroline's eternal mistrust and anger.

Queen Victoria was a small woman, with a sweet face. She was not particularly beautiful, but really, in her own way, she charmed the eye. As Dev entered the drawing room, Queen Victoria and her prince were chatting with the Eversleigh party.

"It is so good to see you out among us," Victoria was saying quietly to Caroline as Dev approached them. "Prince Albert and I wish you to know that it is past time for us to become better acquainted. If you had not already been presented last year at Court, I would insist upon it now, and this time, I would give you the kiss you deserve as the daughter of a peer."

Caroline's face never lost its expression of modest affability, but Dev could see that beneath her polite smile was a devastation he could not understand, given that the queen had been very discreet in her comment.

A powerful, hot burst of protectiveness flashed through him. It set him afire to bundle Caroline off from the dinner to a haven where old rumors had no place, and only security and contentment abided.

"Delightful gown," Victoria continued. "The roses do your lovely hair justice."

"Your majesty is very kind," Caroline said with a smile that seemed to fool all but him.

"Ah," Albert said, looking up with a smile. "Headleymoor, excellent of you to come tonight. And" the prince consort continued, "we are delighted that you have brought us his most beneficent majesty, King Ari, and his dear queen, Janighar."

Dev bowed and took his cue to take a step backward.

"I am very pleased that you accepted our invitation to come to England and speak with us," Victoria said to Ari. "Your ministers' talks with Sir Robert Peel have gone well, I hear. But we have long desired to speak with you on grave concerns for both our countries. Thus far, our prime minister and our trade representatives have wished to control our talks, but it is time for the two of us to discuss such matters of importance. If you could spare a few moments alone with me tonight, perhaps some of our problems could be easily solved."

"As long as it is clear that Zaranbad will remain totally independent of England, I will be delighted to speak with you alone, your majesty," Ari replied. "I believe too in honest and open negotiations between kings and queens."

"Oh, well put, Sire! During the ball, it will be possible for us to disappear for a few moments. And now, Queen Janighar, could you tell me what you have found in England that has pleased you the most so far?"

Janighar's smile lit her lovely face. Her hand reached to the side and unerringly came to rest on Caroline's arm. "Friendship, your majesty. It is a rare and precious gift."

"I am very glad to hear that," Queen Victoria said. "Royalty is a lonely position. One is fortunate to have a friend to speak with, and share one's problems and joys." She looked up at

Prince Albert, who beamed down on her, and Dev began to wonder whether the royal couple's love match was all palaver or whether such things existed, no matter what the rank or position.

"Shall we go in to dinner?" the queen suggested, and took Ari's arm. Prince Albert ushered Janighar into the cavernous state dining room.

As Eversleigh gave his arm to the dowager countess, Dev reached Caroline's side and bowed. "May I, my lady?"

Robert Epsom poked at his shoulder. "Forgotten your precedence, my lord?" he said with a smile, holding out his arm to Caroline. "Lady Farraday, as the daughter of the Duke of Isley, is waiting for you to lead her in. As the heir to an earl, it is right and fitting that I sit beside Lady Caroline, the daughter of an earl."

There was nothing Dev could do but bow to Epsom, the cur, and offer his arm to Lady Farraday, whom he had already sparred with at the musicale. Good thing that she had little respect for polite conversation and a good deal of acerbic wit. And he just knew that, after that musicale, she was watching him with a great deal of amusement tonight.

"I say," Lady Farraday said with a rather sly grin, after Dev had stared down the table at Caroline and Epsom for too long and lost the train of conversation. "Epsom is stealing a march on someone, I believe. Seems to be putting himself out handsomely for the little Berring. She could do worse. Of course, if she wished a less traditional life, she could do better."

"I am sure that whoever Lady Caroline chooses will be a very lucky man," Dev said, after making a concerted effort to unclench his teeth.

"Then you do expect her to choose?" Lady Farraday pulled out her lorgnette and studied him through it. "You, I suspect, have little interest in becoming one of those upon her list?"

"I would never presume to reveal my thoughts on that subject to you, dear Lady Farraday," Dev said, pushing himself to appear polite and urbane. "It would imply an unseemly amount of interest in such gossip on your part."

Lady Farraday gave a humph and thumped him on the foot with her cane. "You already have revealed them, my boy. It was plain as day at the musicale that you and she were destined." She narrowed her eyes at him. "Don't shrug it off so easily, Devlin. I saw your face when you looked for her and found her. Transparent as glass, you are, to the right pair of eyes. And mine are still as sharp as a hawk's."

"As ever, my lady, you have original opinions," Dev managed with what he hoped was an amused smile. "When the time comes for me to pick up the handkerchief, I shall ask you to again predict whom I shall choose. But for now, I fear, I shall remain my lonely and unattached self."

"Humph," Lady Farraday said again, giving him a gimlet eye over her lobster bisque. "You may fool others, dear boy, but you do not fool me. You know, Devlin," she said in a softer voice, "your papa I can tolerate, but I loved your mama. She was a treasure. Like that one speaking so politely to Epsom. You may spend the rest of this interminable dinner contemplating life with and then without that gel. And if you don't keep a watch out, Epsom's not the only one in this room who will attempt to grab her up before you get the courage to do so yourself.

"Meanwhile," she announced in stentorian tones, "I shall babble to you about dogs. Droning conversations concerning one's dogs are always a good background for deep and serious thought, unless," she said with a nod toward Queen Victoria, "one is speaking to another intelligent soul who adores dogs."

Dinner was excruciating. Dev had to sit and attempt polite conversation with Lady Farraday, who made up for her shockingly intimate remarks by monopolizing the conversation with a long, involved panegyric to her five Corgis, their loyalty, honor, sweet huge ears and doe-like eyes. Dev heard all he ever wanted to hear—at several decibels louder than a roar—about those dogs.

All the while, Epsom truly was stealing a march on Nearing, while Dev could do nothing but fume at Caroline's delighted smiles and Epsom's obvious pleasure in discussing whatever fascinating subject they might be discussing down and across from him, their voices muffled completely by the countess's enthusiastic bellows.

It wasn't fair. Epsom was certainly intelligent and honorable and rather handsome, but Caroline deserved someone better. Would he understand and appreciate her wit, her strength, her admirable lack of interest in the good opinion of fools? No, he would probably insist that she court the idiots who had so callously judged her in the past, because he could not imagine a woman desiring anything other than acceptance into the inner circles of the ton.

When the gentlemen were left alone with their port, Ari leaned over and said, "I have not yet had a chance to speak with Mr. Robert Epsom, Lady Caroline's dinner companion. Please introduce me immediately. I would like to know what sort of man shows such a marked preference for Janighar's very good friend."

Thus, Dev had to introduce Epsom to his brother, and hear the two of them engage in pleasant conversation concerning problems with the East India Company. Prince Albert joined in the conversation, and it soon became apparent that both men were listening carefully to Epsom's concern that the Company was too corrupt to hold so much power in India. The worst of it was that Dev agreed wholeheartedly with Epsom. Still, there had to be something wrong with the man.

Ah yes. He was too old for Caroline. At three and thirty, he would never do for a young woman nearing twenty. He, or Ram Dass, rather, must speak to Caroline of this tomorrow, when he brought her to Wimbley House to visit with Janighar.

When, some time later, he entered the glittering ballroom alight with thousands of candles in the huge chandeliers, he easily spotted Caroline across the room.

Epsom was leaning over her hand. By the time Dev had taken a step, Epsom had already positioned himself for the first dance. At least they'd begin with a quadrille, Dev thought. It would not do to have her waltz with Epsom.

The stately steps of the quadrille seemed to take a very long time, but when at last it was done, Dev found himself exactly where Epsom had left Caroline, having bowed over her hand for quite a bit longer than he should have.

Dev stood just behind her, again indulging in the scent of roses, and beneath that the clear, pure scent of Caroline, sweet and green like spring shoots and sunshine. Inhaling with a deep sense of delight, he turned her round to face him and bowed. "May I have the waltz?" he asked her, as the orchestra began the first strains.

She nodded silently and gave him her hand. He took her hand and curled his arm about her waist, pulling her a bit closer than propriety found exceptionable. He didn't give a damn.

He would never get any closer to her. And he was in the mood to take every quarter meter he could.

The music lilted through the ballroom and they swayed to it, circling slowly, smiling at nothing, making desultory conversation while their bodies seemed to speak together much more clearly. He turned, and she was right there in his arms, never behind in a step. Her movements were willing and light, as though they'd made up the steps together and learned them in some faraway place, an otherworld where he could be reliable and keep her safe, and she might find him as eligible as any other man.

He couldn't push back the dream, not while they were so close that he could scent the elusive, clean, essence of her, like fresh meadow flowers warmed by the sun. It was only halfway through the dance that he remembered with a pang of misery that he had to apologize for Nearing's behavior.

He looked down at her face, upturned to the chandelier lights and the flowers wreathed across the ceiling in swaths. Her blue eyes were darker in this candlelit ballroom. They sparkled like stars in a twilight firmament. And her smile was soft and open, without caution or her usually vaunted self-control.

It was unfair, he thought. Damnably unfair to break the spell enclosing them both in its warmth and promise.

It was his own bloody fault. If, as Ram Dass, he'd pushed Nearing's suit with her earlier, he wouldn't have to jerk them both out of this bubble of delight. He had to do it. He did, after all, understand the meaning of the word, honor. He took a deep breath.

"I must apologize for the other night, my lady," he said softly.

She looked up at him with a wry twist on those beautiful lips. "No need, my lord. I told you at the time to put it from your mind."

"I cannot do so," he said.

Her gaze seemed to melt as she looked up at him. For a moment, he lost himself in those sweet, clear eyes. Then he remembered and plunged ahead, trying to make it all come right for them both.

"I mean that I betrayed my friend, who is a good man, a man who would adore you all of your life."

For one second he thought he saw dismay in her blue eyes, but no, that was impossible. She must know by now that they . . . that he . . . that her happiness did not depend upon his selfish wishes.

He began again. "He has a true desire—"

He choked on the noun because it was, unfortunately, the correct one. "He wishes to wed you and to treat you with all the respect and honor you deserve. No one could have been more mortified than he was. I hope you will not remove him from your list of eligible suitors, but let him show you himself what he feels for you, and what kind of a man he is."

"I find it interesting that you are so involved in pleading another man's case, my lord, particularly after your own actions last night." She said it lightly, as though she had these little flirtations all the time. He felt himself bristle at the thought.

"I suppose you know Nearing very well?" she asked.

He nodded. "I have known him since early days at Harrington, when he was a brave and valiant friend. He also has a warm and open heart, and will protect those weaker than he no matter whether he will be hurt in the end or not.

"That is the man who wishes to marry you," he said gently, hating every word that passed his lips, even though they were all true.

The music stopped, and Caroline stepped immediately out of Dev's arms. The last time they'd separated in a dance, her retreat from his arms had been slow, almost dream-like. Now she cut the contact as sharply as a razor slitting delicate skin.

Something deep inside him twisted and ached.

She backed another step and raised her head. Unsmiling blue eyes froze him in a stare of disdain. "It is commendable that you can wax poetic in the defense of your friend's cause. I will accept his calling card again, should he wish to proffer it." She curtsied quickly and, while in the act of turning away, said "Thank you for that waltz. I can see my way from here, my lord. Don't bother to accompany me."

Good God, she'd almost cut him on the dance floor! Society

must be madly whispering about this already. He glanced to the left and the right, and indeed, found people in small groups looking at him and speaking rapidly to each other in low voices. He'd wanted to fulfill his pledge to his friend, the best man he could think of to win her, and as a reward, became tomorrow's *on dit.*

Wonderful.

Caroline stood on the balcony overlooking the green park that ran down the length of the palace walls and hoped the breeze would cool her cheeks. She was ashamed of the welter of feelings roiling through her. What a heyday those people out there must be having with her behavior right now.

It didn't make sense. She'd known Headleymoor for less than a week and yet she felt . . . insulted that his interest in her had nothing to do with his own desire for her, but all to do with Nearing's.

Oh, yes, she'd been suspicious at first, but when she was with him, she'd gotten the feeling that beneath that cool and proper exterior beat the heart of a man who wanted adventure and excitement and perhaps, just perhaps *her.* She'd gone over that kiss in the library a hundred times as she dressed for tonight. She'd wondered if he would look at her in her new gown and want to kiss her all over again.

And she'd wondered what fires burned in the depths of his dark eyes, and whether she was the woman to make them roar to life. It was embarrassing to realize that such sensual thoughts inhabited her fevered imagination. How fitting for the bastard daughter of a duke! And she had acted upon those forbidden thoughts just the other night.

She should go home. Home to Eversleigh, in the country, where she could ride away her frustration and loneliness. Yes, tomorrow, she would begin to pack and—

A dark shadow moved across the balcony. She smelled him, rank sweat and excitement. A shudder of awareness shook her, and she wheeled to run back inside, calling an alarm.

She gasped as a hand clamped around her mouth, hard, and a knife lay across her throat.

"Do not speak. Do not move," a voice said in accented English. "Show me that you understand my orders."

She nodded slowly, her heart drumming in her throat so close to that sharp steel pressed against her. She could feel the man's fingers digging into her flesh, feel the sickness roil through her stomach. She tried to breathe, but could only manage faint, short gasps. Her legs felt like sodden leaves, with no strength to stand, much less move.

The blackguard glanced down toward the garden beneath the balcony and softly whistled. A man stepped out of the shadows, gave a tug on a rope attached to the balcony rail, and began to climb upward. A moment later, he appeared on the balcony and slipped into the shadows near the doorway to the palace.

"Psst!" the villain holding her hissed in her ear. "You will go to that door and call a footman. You will say that you are faint and ask that Queen Janighar come to you here. I will tell you when."

A moment passed, then another, while the music and the babble of conversation went on inside, as though the world weren't about to end.

"Now!" the man hissed.

She stumbled, fearing the slice of the knife, knowing that when she got to the door, she would shout to the footman that the palace was under siege.

A sob lodged in her throat as thoughts flashed through her brain. She thought of her mother, and wished they'd spoken more these last weeks. She reminded herself that although she would die, Janighar and the others would live. She just wished that she was braver, or that she could think of something—anything to save herself. The villain must have sensed her thoughts, for he held her to the knife with a painful grip across her chest. Roughly, he pulled her along with him.

Two seconds more to the door. One second. They were visible now, if anyone was watching. But the orchestra played on, unheeding. Couples circled, wove carefully across the floor, concentrated only upon the waltz.

Trembling, she prayed that her voice would be strong enough to sound the alert. That the knife wouldn't silence her before she could.

"Now, or I kill you," the blackguard growled in her ear. It was over. A preternatural calm filled her as she opened her mouth and screamed her warning.

CHAPTER SIX:
ESCAPE

Dev's shout split the air. "Caroline, DROP!"

At that sound, Caroline obeyed instantly. The thug's knife flashed outward as she fell. She rolled hard, and landed near the stone balustrade before she could catch herself. Slowly, she pushed to her feet, fighting the weight and constraints of her jumbled petticoats and gown.

The killer lay on his stomach across the balcony floor. Dev's arm locked around his throat, and his knee jammed into the small of his back.

A second later, Felix Kendall ran to the balcony and shouted for more help. Footmen immediately raced after the second man and hauled him back from the edge of the balcony, his arms pinned beneath his back. Others grabbed Caroline's captor and began to drag him away.

As he helped Caroline rise, Dev caught the brigand's black stare. It was leveled straight at Kendall, and Kendall rather than sneer, turned away from him. A chill ran up his spine. These two knew each other, and the brigand felt betrayed. Kendall, a man Dev had known for years, suddenly seemed another person altogether. A person who deserved careful watching.

Somehow, the brigand broke free of the guards. "For Zaranbad!" he shouted, and slipped a knife from his sleeve. With a flourish of his knife hand, he intimidated the footmen, who pulled back from him. "Down with Dassam!" the brigand cried.

Dev pulled Caroline with him behind a pillar. The knife glittered in the light as the man raised it to throw. But as his eyes shot from side to side, he found no one unprotected. With another unintelligible shout, the ruffian sliced his own throat. Caroline gagged and shoved her face against Dev's chest.

"Call for the guards! Search the palace!" Victoria's imperious voice rose above the babble and confusion.

Dev swept Caroline up and ran into the ballroom. He knew how long it would take to defend this palace from such a threat, and he didn't have the time. More traitors might strike at any moment.

Ari and Janighar were huddled against the far wall—good. They could get out from there. He whistled, and his brother looked up. Dev jerked his head sideways and Ari took Janighar's hand, slipped out the double doors on that side leading out from the ballroom.

"Put me down, Headleymoor," Caroline whispered. "I can run. Fast."

He didn't wish to let go of her—ever. It had been so close a thing. If he had been but a moment later, Caroline would have been too far away to save from kidnapping. And those bastards would have demanded what Ari couldn't give them. Caroline would have . . . he couldn't think about it now, or he would go mad. His arms tightened around her, and he ran even faster after his brother.

"Headleymoor," she said. "I'll slow you down."

"Nonsense," he said softly. "You're light as eiderdown."

"Put me down," she said between clenched teeth. "Now!"

He bent as he ran and eased her down quickly. She hit the floor on both feet and took off beside him, fleet and strong for all her delicacy.

"My brave girl! Must you always argue?" Dev said with a fierce grin, looking about for more of the villains, terrified that they'd find her an easy target in her bright gown. He was exhilarated by her speed, her strength, the feel of her hand in his.

Oh, why had he insisted on her wearing rose? Brown would have blended so well into the shadows.

"Caroline," he said as they sped through an anteroom. "Stay with me. Run as though the hound of hell has caught your scent." They raced across the floor, dodging couples who were also wildly trying to find an exit. Reaching the stairs, they clattered down after Ari and Janighar.

The coach was already at the door, with Janighar inside and Ari leaping in, as Dev and Caroline raced across the cobbles to get to it. The horses were restless, pawing. The leader, hearing screams and shouts from the palace, reared. As the coachman fought to hold the horses, Dev flung Caroline inside the coach.

A shot rang out in the darkness. "Headleymoor!" Caroline cried and he could hear the terror in her voice. For herself?

No, the foolish girl was thinking of him, for her head poked out the open coach door to ascertain if he was all right.

The team bolted forward. With a running leap, Dev made it into the coach and slammed the door shut.

"Wimbley House!" he shouted out the window to Dobbin. He pulled Caroline close and held on to her for dear life. She was alive. She was going to be all right. He never wanted to let her go.

They flew through Grosvenor Place, barely missing the barriers being erected for Ari and the Queen's parade from the palace tomorrow.

Caroline felt her heart slow from a gallop to a canter as they approached Wimbley House. The night had taken on the aspects of a fever dream. While danger threatened from every corner, Headleymoor had become calmer and more in charge. It made her wonder what other dangers he'd faced, as he appeared so completely at home with tonight's tumultuous madness.

When the carriage pulled into the drive, Headleymoor slid his arm from her shoulders with seeming reluctance. He told Dobbins to stop at the side rather than the regal front entrance. Ari, Janighar and Caroline slipped from the shadows and into the house, as Headleymoor remained behind, speaking softly to Dobbins.

Silently, they waited for him in the hallway. "We must plan what to do," he said, and led them into the small library on the second floor. The butler laid a fire there immediately and brought brandy and four glasses.

Caroline stared at hers for a long time and then took a sip. The liquid burned, but the warmth soothed. Headleymoor and Ari were in the corner, discussing something that they obviously didn't wish Caroline or Janighar to know. Ari was arguing vehemently with Dev in whispery hisses that could not be overheard. A moment later, they both went out into the hall and shut the door firmly behind them.

Janighar and Caroline sat very still, straining their ears. Dev said something indiscernible in a very low voice.

"Bullocks!" At that roar from the king, Caroline and Janighar started.

"My husband never curses in my presence," she whispered to Caroline.

"Janighar and I shall take the royal coach to Newcastle tonight. And that's the end of it. I shall not have her endangered in this England again."

"Absolutely not," Dev shouted back.

"I. Am. The. King," Ari shouted.

"Very well. If you insist upon leaving," Dev said in a tight voice, "there is nothing I can do about it. I shall see you outside at half midnight."

Ari nodded. The door opened and he poked his head inside the library. "Janighar, my love. Go to your room and bid farewell to Lady Caroline Berring. I shall order the servants to pack."

"As you wish, my lord." Janighar grabbed Caroline's hand and walked slowly up the stairs with her in silence. When they entered Janighar's chambers, she shut the door and flung herself into Caroline's arms.

"I had not thought we would part so soon," Janighar said. Her cheek against Caroline's was wet.

Caroline sighed. "Neither had I, but I knew that sometime you would have to go home."

"It is just that home . . . it is lonely there for me. The court is a rather solemn place right now. My ladies in waiting are still so . . . well, since I became blind, they do not know how to speak with me. Even before that, it was difficult. You see, their families were depending upon them to make a good impression on the Queen of Zaranbad. Not one lady would laugh or talk freely with me, for fear I would disapprove of something she'd said."

Janighar slumped into a chair, while tears ran down her face. "I dread going back to that. I wish . . ."

With that, she turned toward Caroline. Through her tears, her face shone like a Renaissance saint's in the midst of a vision. But Janighar, Caroline knew, was more a mischievous little devil contemplating an outlandish scheme. Immediately, she became intrigued.

"What are you dreaming up?" she asked.

"You said once that you would love to see Zaranbad." She grabbed Caroline's hand. "I'll have you know that Zaranbad is not nearly as dangerous as this England. That is why Ari is demanding that we leave now, before anyone can arrange another attempt to kill him or kidnap me."

It was so tempting. It was what she'd dreamed about almost every night. Adventure, friendship . . . When again would she ever get a chance like this one? Still, to just leave England in the middle of the night . . .

"I don't know, Janighar," she said.

"Piffle. You wish adventure as much as I do." Janighar pulled Caroline to her desk. "You could write your mama right now to tell her that you will be gone for a few months at my royal request. As for your clothing—I have several robes that will fit you, with the hem let down."

"But Mama, without me . . ." Caroline thought of the strained silences between them in this last week. Mama needed time and peace to make decisions about her life.

The ladies still called. Kind and honorable men did, too. Without the friction of Caroline's presence, there was a chance that Mama might find one of them more admirable than the duke.

"You have told me yourself that she is happier now than she has been for many years. And you will return soon."

It would be good for Mama to drop the burden of worrying over a troublesome child who had no place in the world.

Especially if that child were the honored friend of a queen off on an adventure.

Caroline smiled. "I suppose Mama would be delighted to have some time to herself."

"Then quickly! Write to her."

Caroline dipped the quill and set it to paper, with Janighar fussing over her to hurry. She didn't do as good a job as she wished, but the letter said everything that needed saying, especially the bit about Caroline's love and fervent wishes for Mama's happiness.

Janighar called a servant to take the message to Berkeley Square. "Let us think of a feasible way to bring you along without Devlin's or Ari's knowledge."

"Oh, no, Janighar." Caroline backed up, holding her hands

out, palms up in a gesture of negation. "I shall not be a party to untruths."

Janighar drew herself up and stuck her chin in the air. "That is only because Ari would inform him that we are taking you with us. Devlin would be furious that you even contemplated this journey. He does not wish even us to leave England tonight. Ari, on the other hand, will be delighted that I bring my dearest friend with us. He's told me how pleased he is with our friendship, and how much happier I seem now that you and I know each other. He is king, and I am queen. If he gets his way, I get mine. Devlin is not going to spoil this for me."

Caroline shivered. A scene popped up in her imagination— Ari furious at not being informed of her presence until they reached Newcastle. Caroline alone on the streets of Newcastle, in the middle of the night. In a flimsy ball gown. She wondered if she had enough coin to hire a coach, or find a respectable inn.

So many things could go wrong. Then she glanced at Janighar's face and winced at the combination of determination and tear stains. She didn't think she could bear that look for long.

Besides, she had already surmised something her friend had not. Despite King Ari's certainty that their men were the equals of any brigands on the road, she was not so sure.

Brutal villains had breached the very walls of Buckingham Palace. One of them had held a knife to her throat. They had put two queens in danger.

Caroline numbered among the few of her fine qualities the gift of an unerring eye and a steady hand. If her friend needed defending, it would come from an unexpected corner, and the unexpected often made the difference between life and death.

The clock chimed the quarter hour. "Call your maid, Janighar," Caroline said. "Quickly."

Janighar's brows furrowed as she tugged the bellpull. "What exactly are you planning, Caroline?"

"I'll tell you as I dress," she said.

"In what?" Janighar asked.

A quiet knock on the door announced the maid, who entered and curtsied. Quickly, Caroline explained what she needed, and the maid, eyes wide, ran out the door and returned shortly afterward with a stable boy holding an armful of folded clothing.

"You're the lad to help with the king's carriage tonight?"

"Aye m'lady," the boy said, clutching his hat. "Lord Headleymoor just gave me my orders."

A Cornish lad, Caroline thought. An accent to hide behind, and she'd always been a good mimic. "The plan's been changed. Go along with you, now." She reached into her reticule and held out two crowns. "This ought to be enough to make it all right."

The boy's eyes widened. "More than enough, m'lady. I'll bring you the difference in the morning."

"Keep it," she said. "His lordship wished it."

The boy bowed and turned to race out the door.

Janighar's hands went to her hips. "His lordship wished it? Caroline, you go too far."

"Nonsense. A few moments only to fool Headleymoor. Then we can stop the coach and I shall travel inside with you and King Ari."

"You begin to frighten me, Caroline. You are more devious than I."

"I doubt that," Caroline said with a laugh.

"What else do you need?" Janighar asked her a few moments later, when she was ready.

"Pistols and shot," Caroline replied. "One should never go anywhere at night without them."

"In the library," Janighar said. She grabbed Caroline's hand and they hurried down the corridor, tiptoeing past the drawing room from which serious and deep male voices issued.

Caroline grabbed two pistols and checked them quickly. "They'll do." Janighar fumbled in a drawer and drew out a leather pouch full of shot and powder. Caroline packed both pistols, put them in the stable boy's coat, grabbed a third and loaded it, then stuffed it into her reticule.

"I'm having second thoughts. If Devlin discovers that we've taken you, he'll be furious," Janighar said with a shudder. "I should not like to cross Devlin when he's furious."

"Nonsense. He's completely controlled at all times," Caroline replied. "If he's going to upbraid me, he'll do it in a quiet, cool voice."

Janighar gave a great sigh. "I am not so certain of that."

Inside Caroline, excitement and anticipation welled up. She felt a grin tug at her lips. All her life, she'd been a victim of Society's censure, kept in her place.

And a shameful, mean little place it was.

She'd writhed against that inequity. Now, she had a chance to act with honor if there was need, and to embark upon the adventure of a lifetime. She couldn't wait to begin.

The crunch of carriage wheels and the jingle of harness sounded outside the window. "Let us go," she said softly.

The two of them crept down the back stairs.

"I shall see you once we're underway," Janighar whispered, hugging her.

After watching Janighar feel her way along the corridor wall toward the front hall, Caroline took a deep breath and slipped out the side door. The coach stood beneath the portico, its horses restive, jangling their metal bits and harness.

A wind was up, chilling the night. Clouds slid over the moon, turning the land black around her. There was nothing but the lit house at her back and in front, the dark carriage, the lamps the only beacon against the misty darkness. Lowering her voice and imitating the young Cornish lad, Caroline called softly up to the coachman. "I'm to ride beside ye tonight. Lord Headleymoor's orders."

"Come on then, lad. We've a long way to go."

She took a big step up, feeling light and free without the constraints of crinolines and corset.

Climbing up beside the coachman, she took her seat.

Dev stood at the library desk, quickly folding a piece of stationery. "Simmons," he said as the door opened and a footman hurried in, bowing. "Take this message to Sir Horace at the Home Office. Tell him I am perfectly serious—twenty men in Newhaven, waiting at the outskirts of town. Send them immediately. And tell him it is most important to detain Kendall—make up some other mission."

"Kendall, my lord?" asked Simmons, a brawny ex–Bow Street Runner turned servant in the last month to aid Dev.

"Indeed."

"Yes, my lord. I'll go at once." Clutching the wafer, Simmons strode from the room.

"Send Roderick in," Dev called.

The footman, another ex-runner, hastened in a moment later.

"This goes to Tom Jarvis," Dev said, handing another note to Roderick. "See that he knows exactly where the men must rendezvous with us outside London."

Roderick listened intently as Dev delineated the plan.

"Aye, my lord," he said when Dev had finished. "I'll tell him."

Caroline huddled in the stable boy's coat, missing her own warm, fur-lined cloak. The door opened to the portico, shedding light on the coach. King Ari, still dressed in his court

130

grandeur, stood in the light with Janighar and Headleymoor. The butler shut the door and darkness cloaked them. Caroline could just discern their shadow-like figures approaching.

"Are you certain that I cannot convince you to do otherwise?" Headleymoor asked the king.

"Absolutely. We shall be out of England by first light and far out to sea on the morrow."

"So be it." A sigh from Headleymoor, then a crack that sounded suspiciously like a fist to a very solid jaw. Ari's broad shoulders slumped and he fell backwards in slow motion. With a clink, something landed beside Ari's body.

"Devlin, what have you done?" Janighar screeched.

"What had to be done, my dear."

A tall shadow bent to the tiny one and Caroline could see Headleymoor's dark silhouette as his lips touched Janighar's forehead. Footmen quickly lit the rest of the royal coach lamps and lifted King Ari.

"These men will take you to your destination." Headleymoor stooped and lifted the metal object that had fallen from Ari when the king had been coldcocked by his own brother, Caroline realized with a shock.

As Headleymoor placed the object on his head and slipped into the carriage, Caroline's stomach clenched in sick understanding. He wore the crown of Zaranbad. Another coach approached, and the footmen lifted Ari, carrying him to it and placing him inside. Another took Janighar and placed her beside her husband. "No, Devlin!" she shouted.

"Wait!" Caroline took the first step down from the coachman's seat just as the crack of the coachman's whip drowned her voice. The coach jerked forward and she clung to the metal handrail for dear life. The hooves of the horses sounded like thunder in her ears. Fingers grabbing hold in desperation, she swung herself back into her seat as the coach veered round the drive and raced down the street.

Caroline's pulse raced with it. She shuddered, heart pumping like a steam engine in her chest. Straining a look over her shoulder toward Wimbley House, she saw the second coach carrying an unconscious King Ari, along with Janighar, racing off in the other direction.

Had Headleymoor just kidnapped his brother and usurped the throne? Was the hero who'd rescued her tonight a villain who had just stolen a kingdom?

"No," she said aloud. It wasn't possible.

But as the carriage careened through the darkness, Caroline wondered what in God's name she had gotten herself into. Then she just held on and willed her stomach not to leap into her throat as they zigzagged in sickening lurches through the dark streets. Finally, the carriage slowed to a trot.

"All's ready, Dobbins?" Headleymoor called from the coach, and Caroline shivered at the icy calm in his voice. What with the noise of wind and horses' hooves against cobbles, she hadn't heard him lower the window.

"All set my lord," Dobbins called softly back.

"Our men are in the closed carriage behind?"

"Aye. As you've arranged, they'll take the first wave of gunfire, but from what you say, there'll be another after that. So the rest was done accordin' to your orders."

"Mercury and Apollo are being ponied to the meet down the Newhaven road?"

"Aye, my lord, and Samson, too."

Caroline heard the chink of metal. In the dim light of the carriage lamps, Dobbins handed her the reins and took out his pistols, checking the powder. Thank heavens Grandfather Holland had taught her to drive. Dobbins must have been satisfied with the pistols, for he put them both into his greatcoat pockets and took over the reins.

"Ah," Headleymoor called, his head still out the coach window. "If one of the horses slackens, we'll have a fresh mount. Excellent idea. They'll be following, but not too closely, I think. Keep the lamps glowing until we reach the Newhaven road. Then we'll go hell for leather. Understood?"

"They're your best boys, my lord. They'll run well for you tonight. I could tell when I bridled Samson that he knew you were in for some excitement. He thrust up his head twice, just like he did when you raced him at Ascot last year."

"He won, then, didn't he? If he's ready, the others will follow. Well, Dobbins, we may as well get on with it. The United Band will hit us as soon as we enter the city."

Although his words froze Caroline's blood, a huge sense of relief rolled through her. She sat straighter in the darkness. Of course Headleymoor was no villain. He was risking his life to give his brother a chance to escape while he led King Ari's erstwhile killers astray. And he expected trouble with the ruffians. Atop the coach, she relaxed against the wooden back of her seat. Her hands automatically searched for the pistols secreted on her person. In this fight, Headleymoor would need every able-bodied man.

And woman.

Dev leaned back against the squabs of the carriage and closed his eyes. He would never forget the terror of seeing Caroline stumbling beside that cursed member of the double damned United Band, a knife at her throat. It had weakened him, almost made his hand tremble before he threw the blade that sank into the ruffian's knife arm. Never before, in all the years of clandestine battles, had he hesitated for a split second.

He wondered if she had a knack for getting into trouble, or whether it was just a bad combination of Caroline and the Dassams that had led to tonight's near fiasco. He had a sneaking feeling that Caroline might be capable of attracting trouble all by herself. Witness the peril she and her friend, Lilias, courted last year by racing ahead of their grooms in St. James Park.

It was a good thing that Nearing was taking Caroline on. Dev didn't think his heart could stand the strain.

The horses kept up a fine pace as the carriage wound out of Belgrave Square and down the road to the Vauxhall Bridge. As they crossed the Thames, Dev glanced back to see that three men followed, not four blocks behind, on horseback. He sat back and readied his pistol, taking care to keep his profile outlined in the glow of the carriage lamps, with the bloody royal crown of Zaranbad on his head. Three men here, and more to meet him in Newhaven, no doubt, just in case these three couldn't bring him and Dobbins down.

Dobbins flicked his whip and the horses kept up the pace. They weren't really pushing themselves—they'd have enough left if there was trouble up ahead. As they reached the outskirts of London, more horsemen approached from the side street. The coach filled with Dev's men halted, and the agents jumped out into the street. Shots rang out and Dev looked back. Three of the traitors fell, but there were others on horseback, rounding the skirmish and racing after his carriage.

Dev grabbed his first pistol as one of the blackguards gained on the coach. He threw the crown to the seat beside him, knelt on the floor of the coach, and prayed that the springs were very, very good. He steadied his arm on the sill of the open window and waited.

The man drew alongside, his face half covered by the extra cloth of his black turban. Dev shot and saw the man tilt, his eyes wide with shock in the light of the carriage lamp. He fell at the side of the road, his horse galloping off into the darkness.

Dobbins picked up the pace, moving out now, as they came into the village of East Grimstead. Round the corner they turned, neat as a needle through fine embroidery. Dev felt a grin of admiration curve his lips. His coachman was truly the best whip in three counties.

Silently but for the jingle of leather, five riders swung alongside the carriage, and doused the lamps.

"Just us, my lord," Tom Jarvis called at the window. "We got the rest of 'em."

Dobbins reined in the horses. Dev jumped out and took Samson's reins from Tom Jarvis, clapping him on the back. "You'll be careful, Tom," he said. "Remember all I told you."

"I'll remember my lord—steady arm, stay in the shadows, and let them come to me on a dark night."

"Right. They won't be expecting any of you, so all should go well. Dobbins," he called softly. "Keep your head down, will you?"

"I alus does, my lord. Ned," the coachman said, turning to the stable boy. "You take the other two horses for his lordship."

The boy froze for a moment. He looked at the two horses, at Headleymoor, and at the men he had to protect him on this journey. He took a deep breath and leaped down from the coachman's box.

Ned was a game one, Dev thought in admiration. He hated to use him tonight, but he needed those horses fresh enough for the last gallop, and the lad weighed far less than Dobbins.

"My lord?" Tom asked in a troubled voice. Dev turned at the sound and only caught the shadow of Ned, the stable boy, swinging up on Apollo and clasping Mercury's reins in his right hand.

"What is it, Tom?"

"Why isn't Lord Kendall in on tonight's work?"

"It wasn't possible," Dev said vaguely. He wasn't quite ready to voice his suspicions. Kendall had been a good friend and a good soldier for a long time. But that quick glance between him and the Zaranbadian who'd held Caroline at knifepoint had been enough to make Dev suspicious.

At the sound of hoofbeats, he tightened the reins and pulled a pistol from his pocket. "Ready, Ned?" he asked the small boy beside him on Apollo.

"Aye, my lord," the boy answered in a gruff voice. There was something vaguely familiar about the voice, but Dev had already squeezed his leg against Samson's side and they were off like a shot. Dev glanced over and saw the lad's shadow beside him. He kept up easily, his body rising slightly from the saddle into a two point position, seeming to float in tandem with and just above the horse's back, his left hand light on Apollo's reins. His right hand was just as steady leading Mercury on the near side of his horse. Mercury was sometimes a bit skittish under a new hand, but he cantered on beside the boy as though he understood his every silent command.

Perhaps, if he lived through tonight, he would let the lad train some of his cattle. He obviously had the touch for it.

And the stamina, as it turned out. They rode fast, going cross country to make up the time, pressing toward Newhaven faster than Dev had ever ridden before. He figured that the traitors had at least half an hour on them, as they'd probably known for days where the king's yacht would be moored, and sent their men ahead to meet them as they rode into the port town. If only the clouds held.

They did more than hold. About an hour after Dev and the boy had begun riding, the skies opened and rain pelted them hard. Then the wind rose with it, and despite the warm spring night, a chill crept into the air.

The horses' sides were slick with rainwater, the steam rising from them as they kept up the pace, sometimes a canter, sometimes a trot. Dev's cloak, good Melton wool just for such a night as this, kept off some of the rain, but the lad's cloak, surely cheaper and thinner, must be soaked by now.

The boy made not a sound, but rode steadily on, and Dev's concern mounted until he almost forgot that they both might be lying dead on the Newmarket road in another half hour.

"Take my cloak, boy," he said.

"Nay, m'lord. It'll slow us down, and we've not got much farther to go." Despite the strong Cornwall accent, the boy's gruff voice held a definitely familiar note. But as Dev realized the lad was right, his mind turned to how they could quicken the pace without injuring the horses. All might well be lost if they stopped to rest for even a moment.

Another stretch on the road, then a detour through a hay field to escape a dark blot of what might be men ahead, and Dev saw the lights of Newhaven in the distance. He and the boy rode the horses hard, then, straight toward the town, Dev's hand on his pistol as they pulled into the outskirts.

At that moment, the wind blew up and the clouds parted just enough for the moon to streak the streets with a ghostly light.

The shots came at once. Samson gave a sharp whinny and stumbled.

"My lord," shouted the lad—no accent this time, Dev noted dizzily as Samson tried to run on three legs. The boy had brought Mercury up beside him. Dev leaped from one horse to the other, barely making it as Samson went down. His throat closed on a lump of sorrow for his brave horse—all that glory, courage, and breeding, brought low by these brigands!

And then, as Dev scrambled with the reins, the lad fired, steady and quick and neat. Another villain cried out and Dev heard a crash. He had his balance then, and his pistol in his hand. As a third shadow raised an arm, Dev shot, and the man fell without a sound. Then he and the boy were free, and racing down the cobbles for a ship whose sails were already beginning to billow out.

"My lord," came a soft cry from the right. Men closed in behind them, Dev's men, guarding them on either side, and one even brought up the rear with a horse, still running on three legs. They were almost to the quay when gunfire erupted from the left, to be answered by their own shots, and then they were there, he and the lad leaping from their mounts and running, the lad pausing, firing once more as they raced for the yacht, the sails now full in the wind, and the men aboard lowering a rope to swing them up.

He pulled the rope toward him, grasped the lad by the waist, and held hard as the men tugged them up, up, dangling from the side as the waves rolled the ship like a metronome, and then higher over the sea churning below them in the storm.

Dev's men on the dock were still firing, and then surrounding a few of those bastards still alive. And Dev took a deep breath of relief and smelled sea and wind, and . . . wildflowers. He stared, in horror and shock, at the lad in his arms, just as a gust of wind tugged off the boy's sodden cap. A fall of soft curls flowed down to the middle of a feminine back. Soft breasts pressed against Dev's chest. The pair of legs in wet, clinging breeches were long, slender and muscled from doing all the things a lady should never do.

The men gave a last heave and they landed together on deck, in a jumble of arms and legs. Dev rose, trembling slightly at the memory of the feel of her, soft and supple against him, all curves and muscle together.

His devious little Amazon.

He helped her to her feet with all the courtesy of two worlds, drilled into him by his father and his grandfather. As she rose, chest heaving with the effort, and, he suspected darkly, excitement, he scowled down at her.

"By God, Caroline," he said in a voice tight with anxiety and exasperation. "If we get out of this alive, I'm going to kill you."

The next morning in the fog-filled hour before dawn, Felix Kendall rode his bay gelding toward Wolf on one of the riding paths in St. James Park. Wolf's message had demanded that they meet here now, before any of the ton would take their exercise. He was armed, but there was always the possibility that Wolf would shoot first. He cursed the day he'd made that Faustian bargain with the United Band.

Kendall froze. A tall man on a blood bay trotted toward him. As he came closer, all Kendall could see was a dark cloak, its hood raised so that it shadowed Wolf's face completely. But the voice was chillingly familiar.

"Your men bungled the job," Wolf said, the menace in his voice making Kendall squirm with burgeoning terror.

His horse jerked his head, and for a moment he had all he could do to keep the bay from bolting. Did the animal sense danger, or just Kendall's panic?

"That's due to the foreigners who attacked the palace," he replied. "Lady Berring would have made as good a hostage as the Queen of Zaranbad. Headleymoor's over the moon for her. If they'd taken her, the marquess would have turned over our man in the blink of an eye. They shouldn't have panicked. Wogs," Kendall muttered. "You can't trust 'em with even the simplest task."

Wolf nodded. "The real culprit's Headleymoor. Apparently, he got the King and Queen of Zaranbad away last night."

"Yes. They've left no trace."

Wolf paused, stroking his chin. "I'll speak to the man who leads the United Band. He knows the family well enough, and he ought to be able to take appropriate action to rid us of this problem."

"Good idea," Kendall said, while all that was left of his

conscience screamed no. "What appropriate action are you contemplating?" he asked, desperately trying to think of a way to succeed without bringing about Dev's death. They were friends, damn it—comrades on so many dangerous missions.

"When it is time, I shall tell you," Wolf said. Without a farewell, he wheeled his horse and galloped off, a figure dark as death.

Kendall turned his own mount toward home. For the nonce, he thought he was safe. All the same, he galloped the whole way back to his town house, and, throwing the reins to the stable master, made for the door in a run.

Chapter Seven:
Chateau Valoir

Caroline gazed listlessly out the carriage window at field after field of green meadow and yellow flowers. They had been traveling south from Dieppe for several days. Despite her pleas that she was only slowing him down—that he must leave her and find sanctuary in his chateau, Headleymoor rcfused to listen. So they traveled by coach, where all could see them as they passed, through Normandy down into the Loire Valley.

It was then that she grew even more feverish. Even though she was too weary to think, she could feel the change. Headleymoor seemed half out of his mind with worry, furious that there weren't the herbs and the medicines he needed when they stopped at one of several village apothecaries along the way. He bathed her face in water that felt cold as ice, and held her when the chills wracked her body.

It was only when they reached the River Cher, and the verdant land of the Dukes of Wimbley, that he heaved a sigh of relief.

"Caroline," he said in a voice filled at once with a softness she'd never heard from him and a note of fear. "We're almost there. Soon I shall be able to give you what you need to make you well. Just hold on. Please hold on!"

She heard his voice, but in her dreaming state, the words didn't register. No matter, whatever he'd said had been good. At least she thought that was right.

She must have fainted, because the next she knew, she was

lying in his arms, as he carried her up, up a circular stone staircase toward light and air and oh, it was beautiful, and she wondered if she had actually died, because heaven must look like this—all open to so much light.

After a moment, she whimpered, because the light hurt, and so did everything else. He put her down gently on something soft, but her limbs ached and cramped, and she tossed, trying to get away from the pain.

"Cara," he said.

Headleymoor is talking to someone else, she thought. Someone dear—isn't that what cara means?

His hand came close to her face and he held out a spoon of something for her. She tried to drink it, but it tasted vile, like radishes and garlic and onions and ack—ground up seeds in the bottom that hurt her throat. She turned her head away from the offending spoon.

Headleymoor began to argue with the person he called Cara. Caroline couldn't understand what he was saying, but he was very fierce about it while he turned her head again toward him. She shut her mouth against the disgusting stuff in the spoon and let him talk and talk and argue with the wench.

The next wave of pain sliced through her head like a jolt of lightning. It ached dreadfully, and she wanted to get away from it. Ram Dass, she thought. And must have said it aloud, for he bent over her, blessedly blocking the light, and she said again, "Ram Dass," in a voice that sounded like that of a fretful child—so high and frightened she didn't recognize it as her own.

"My very dear, tell me," he said, and she thought, he isn't even paying attention to me, he's still busy wooing that Cara person while attempting to cram swill down my throat.

So she said with a croak of demand, "I want Ram Dass. I need Ram Dass." Ram Dass would care about her enough to know she was sick and she needed help. Ram Dass was trustworthy, not like a certain very beautiful and powerful man flirting with some unknown light o' love he kept in his chateau.

"I'm important, too," she whispered aloud, her own sense of insult hidden inside the frog-like croak of her voice.

The next time she surfaced, there was Ram Dass, gently shaking her awake. His dark, sweet eyes gazed down at her, and he bent over her like a guardian angel, his white turban a nimbus in the light on a bedside table behind him.

"You're here," she said. Somehow, she managed to move her heavy hand and found his. She held on for dear life.

"I'm here, and now you will get well, Lady Caroline," he said in that mellifluous, dark voice, and she knew she was safe.

He made her drink the same vile stuff on the spoon, but it was Ram Dass, so it must be necessary, and she drank it down. "Eugh. What was that?"

"Radish juice, ground radish seeds, leeks, garlic, onions, special mushrooms."

"A witch's brew," she whispered.

"Indeed. Magic to make you well."

As her lids began to drift shut, she tried to hold on tight to his hand. "Don't go away!" she thought she said.

And she must have, for he smiled so sweetly her heart swelled, and he said, "I shall be here as long as you need me."

Always, she thought, and sailed on calm, gentle waves, into a half sleep.

Dev watched Caroline drift off looking so comforted that he wanted to shout out an objection. He knew there was something ridiculous about being resentful of . . . himself. But why must it be Ram Dass alone whom she trusted? Why not him?

He called Mimi into the room. "I have sent for hot water. Could you bathe Lady Caroline when she awakens? I've brought her a few of my things. They should suffice while I send to Le Mans for clothing."

Mimi stared at the man's nightshirt. "These are soft and fine linen," she said approvingly. "I can cut and stitch the sleeves and she will be quite comfortable."

"Very good, Mimi." He walked out of the room and strode to the gardens, pacing past rows of peonies and Chinese forget-me-nots. He was sick of two identities. Sick of Devlin Carmichael being the public face for Ram Dass, an agent for Her Majesty's government. As though Devlin Carmichael was the disguise and therefore did not exist.

If it were anyone but Caroline he would be laughing, but seeing that she would take nothing from him—not concern, not the medicine he'd tried to pour down her throat—it suddenly didn't seem fair that only a shadow man got the trust that he wished she could give him.

After they'd finally arrived, he'd been like a man possessed. His hands had literally shaken as he ran down into his laboratory to find the herbs to make rafinin to fight the disease, and willow bark to fight the fever and the pain. Only to realize that his patient was fighting him, and refusing to take any of it.

Had Ram Dass not taken over, he'd have had to hold her nose and shove the stuff down her throat, or simply tube her like a horse. He supposed he should be grateful.

After a time, he looked up to see Mimi coming toward him in the dusk. With a shock, he realized he'd been fighting this dark mood for at least two hours.

"I have bathed Lady Caroline, m'lor'," Mimi said. "She is sleeping comfortably now. Perhaps you would like to see her."

"I would."

Mimi looked pointedly at his turban. "Would you care to bathe first, m'lor'?"

He stared down at his darkened hands and shook his head.

"No. I shall go up to her now." After all, being Ram Dass was the only way she would permit him to remain beside her night and day.

Well, that wasn't such a terrible fate, was it? Dev thought later as he carefully climbed into bed and settled against the headboard, turning the lamp down so shadows played on the walls in the dim light.

He realized with shock that he had lifted Caroline and drawn her close so that her head rested against his shoulder and his arms closed around her.

For a moment, he held her close, feeling peace steal through him. The comfort of her trust had him relaxing for the first time since the escape. His lids drooped and shut. He drifted between sleeping and waking.

An instant later, he woke, stifling a cry of terror and pain. A horrifying scene had arisen before his mind's eye.

Blood on the snow in Afghanistan. Blood in a school room. Caroline's tortured body hanging from the rafters, as the poor, young student, Jonathan Dinsmore, had hanged so many years ago.

Caroline moaned and he looked down at her. His arms were locked about her, as tightly as a vice. Still shaking, he carefully lightened his grip. Trustingly, sweetly, she burrowed against him seeking his warmth and comfort.

He shut his eyes and quelled the shudders still wracking his body.

"You'll be safe, by God," he whispered, a vow as much to himself as to her. He must be very careful not to let her see how much, how very much he felt for her. She might just return his affection in some foolish burst of gratitude.

Gently disengaging himself from her, Dev drew the quilt over her, and took a seat in the wing chair beside the bed, where the servant Ram Dass could sit each night to watch over her and bathe her neck and face in cool water.

In the dim light, he gazed at her pale face. She had always been such a combination of strength and vulnerability. Now she just looked fragile and ethereal. He had done this to her.

From a young age, Dev had understood that his enemies could destroy those whom he tried to protect. "Not you, Cara," he vowed. "Never you."

"There, milady. You begin to look *très belle,* with this new *robe de chambre,* and color has returned a bit to your face," the young maid Mimi said after she'd brushed out Caroline's hair. Mimi, with her sparkling brown eyes and trim figure, looked *très jolie,* herself as she carefully drew the sleeves of another fine linen shirt down to her wrists. The shirt was comfortable, but it only covered her thighs. Somehow, though, she didn't mind too much that Ram Dass saw her like this.

But once, Headleymoor had walked into the bedchamber to enquire as to her health, only to find her standing in one of these men's shirts at the washstand, attempting to wash her face. She'd felt the cool air on her calves and a mortifying heat rise to her face. Headleymoor, with a stammer of apology, had whisked himself immediately from the chamber.

"I am so happy to see you recovering," Mimi added, helping her into the large feather bed and smoothing the counterpane over her. "His lordship was like a madman during those first days, when we weren't at all certain . . ." Mimi reddened and swallowed, and turned away.

"Was I really that ill?"

"Well, I caught his lordship praying by your bedside on the first night," Mimi said.

"That seems quite out of character," Caroline said with laugh.

"He was on his knees, milady," Mimi insisted.

"Probably looking for a lost button," Caroline said. "Besides,

I was never that sick."

Mimi's brows rose. "We were very concerned for you—all of us below stairs. And M'sieur Remy looks forward to the day when you will be well enough to come down to dinner and taste some of his excellent cuisine."

A very loud and prolonged rap sounded on the door.

When Mimi called out, Headleymoor's head poked around the door in a most tentative manner, Caroline thought drowsily.

"How are you feeling, Lady Caroline?"

"Rather well, thank you." The dreadful pain in her head and throat had receded, leaving a manageable ache and an unaccustomed lack of energy. That would normally unnerve her, but as new and interesting things were happening each day, she barely had time to think about herself.

Lord Headleymoor had come this morning to read the most exciting book to her about a woman who had married a king. Each night, she had to tell the king stories that would hold his interest, or he'd lop off her head.

Mimi, leaped up and curtsied to Headleymoor. "I shall leave, mi'lor'?"

"No, not quite yet, if you please. I shall need help."

As he walked into the room, Caroline realized that his arms were full of what looked to be a rainbow of gowns, and another maid followed with unmentionables and stockings of silk, not just in black and white, she saw, but in rainbow colors, too. Oh, my, France really was a different country. So she was content to lie abed like a lazy princess and watch what new surprises Lord Headleymoor would offer up for her amusement.

"They're the best I could do," he said. "They came from Le Mans."

A third maid hurried in with a tea tray. Placing it on the table near the wing chair, she took some of the gowns from Headleymoor and helped Mimi, who already had quite a few in her arms, to open the wardrobe.

Mimi smoothed a silk sky blue gown with the reverence, Caroline mused, of a priest with a prayer book.

"This one, mi'lor'. I think it is quite acceptable," she said, turning it this way and that. "Milady will look like a princess— the blue matches the blue of her eyes."

Headleymoor's lips quirked. "So I thought, Mimi."

"Yes, mi'lor'. It is my opinion that you have chosen very well," Mimi said, nodding in obvious approval at a rose tea gown.

Quickly and efficiently she took each gown from the other maid and placed it inside the armoire, while the maid with the lingerie opened a cupboard and began carefully setting the delicate silks on different shelves. And then, with a curtsey accomplished in unison and three faces rosy with smiles, Mimi and the other two maids whisked themselves out the door.

"It would be great fun if I could take you to Paris to buy gowns when you are feeling more the thing," Headleymoor said, sitting beside the table. "I have cousins there who could serve as chaperones. But for the nonce, we must hide until I get word that all the villains are caught. Cream and sugar?" he asked.

"Yes, please." Then she laughed. She could not help it.

"What?" he asked with a smile, handing her a cup of tea.

"Oh, it's you, really," she said. "You come in with treats and stories, as though I were some spoiled child on her birthday, and then you dream up excursions even more exciting, when in reality, we are fugitives from a gang of thugs."

"Actually, the thugs were easier to suppress than this bunch," he said. "Thugs in India, at least."

"Were they a terrible lot?"

"The worst," he said with a rueful expression. "They dressed like travelers and strangled the unfortunate people who traveled with them. They did their gory deeds in the name of Kali, a cruel goddess. But that was in Bentick's time, and he got rid of them."

Caroline traced the pattern of a leaf on the damask tablecloth. "Have you noticed, my lord, how many of the worst deeds are done in the name of religion? What a dreadful corruption of our highest ideals. Is all India that frightening?"

Headleymoor shook his head and smiled. "Oh, no. It's much like England. Wonderful and terrible at the same time. Men beg in the streets while others, decked in the finest silks, gold, and precious stones, are carried in tongas past them, barely noticing."

Caroline placed her elbow on the arm of her chair and leaned forward to catch every word, every nuance.

"But I have met saints in India and in Zaranbad, too, living examples of what men should be. They're wise and compassionate. I think my grandfather might be one of those men, with his dream of making Zaranbad into a modern democratic society. And Dr. Gupta is another saint. He is the man who taught me, among other things, all he knew about medicine."

"My grandfather seemed that sort of man to me." She smiled, remembering. "Mama sent me to him in the lowlands of Scotland every summer. I learned ever so much from him. He was very taken by the Americans, and admired their constitution and their laws. At the same time, he despised their attempt to compromise on the Slavery issue. He could be a bit irascible, for of course, even saints have flaws."

He smiled. "And did you wish to live in Scotland?"

"No. I thought perhaps I'd like to go to America—into the west, where everyone is new, as I would be. Lately, I have been thinking of it a great deal. But tell me about Zaranbad."

Headleymoor sat back in his chair, his gaze thoughtful and his long fingers stroking his wineglass. They were long and graceful. Caroline shivered, thinking of those fingers on her.

"Zaranbad is a land coming out of the dark ages into this new age. My grandfather began it all by giving the poor the right to decent wages. Now, many of them own the land they worked as tenants for centuries.

"It is for this reason that the United Band sprang up. They are agents of the wealthy nobility in Zaranbad who want their land back, despite the fact that the former tenants paid a reasonable sum of rupees for it."

"And you fight this United Band for Zaranbad?"

Four days later, Dev left his workshop carrying a concoction of yogurt mixed with Indian herbs he had learned from the Ayurveda, a reposit of ancient Indian medical practice. It was for Caroline. Thank the angels who watched over foolishly courageous young ladies, she improved more each day.

One of his men raced in from the battlements of the chateau.

"*Une voiture, mi'lor',*" he said. "*Avec un—*a crest. *C'est Anglais, je pense.*"

"*Oui,*" Dev said, handing the man the concoction. "Take this to my lady and I will look at this carriage." He took the narrow stairway to the battlements and gazed down across the Cher, to see a black closed carriage racing across the bridge. One look at the crest and he knew who it was. "Let him pass," he shouted down to his men at the portcullis. "And send him into the ivory drawing room."

Looking out the window overlooking the courtyard, he watched the carriage rattle over the cobbles. Nearing waved away a footman and threw open the door himself, leaping out before the vehicle had stopped rocking on its springs.

"Your master, at once," he shouted.

"This way, mi'lor'," one of Dev's men said.

Dev hurried into the ivory drawing room and ordered tea

before the door slammed open with enough force to hit the wall.

"Dev, you'll not believe what's happened! Caroline's missing. You've got to help me find her! I say." Nearing paused to take in Dev's turban, jodhpurs, and darkened face. "What are you doing in costume? Isn't that Home Office kit?"

"It's all right, Maxim," Dev said, ignoring that last because it was just too humiliating to explain that Caroline preferred him as the servant, not the master. "Caroline's here, and she's much better."

Maxim's eyes widened. "What do you mean, she's here? How can she be here, without anyone knowing where she's been this past week? Here," he repeated. "With you."

"It's a long story. Sit down and have something to drink."

Maxim's eyes narrowed to blue shards. "What the hell have you been about? The King and Queen of Zaranbad have disappeared, and Caroline along with them. Her mother's half out of her mind with fear, and her brother has hired detectives to find her." He strode forward until he and Dev were almost nose to nose. "All this time, my future wife is here. With *you?*"

He clenched his fist and shook it. "Give me one reason I shouldn't tear your heart right out of your chest."

"Maxim—"

"Don't Maxim me, you—you, prune-mouthed, hypocritical lecher. 'Just give me a little time with her before you plead your case, again, Maxim,' " Nearing mimicked as he brandished his fist at Dev. " 'Have some patience and let me ease the way.' Damn you, Headleymoor, I bet you eased the way—right into her—"

"Don't say it. Don't even think it," Dev said low in warning.

"Into her bloody heart, then!" Maxim roared. "What else do I need to know, other than you've got her here, you damned turncoat!"

"Maxim, wait," Dev said, holding up a hand.

"Pistols or swords, you snake!"

"I'll explain everything while I change out of this disguise. Then I'll take you up to her. You'll see for yourself just what's been going on here. And you'll not let her know that Ram Dass is anyone but the servant she thinks him to be."

"Why the hell shouldn't I expose you?"

Dev shook his head in exasperated frustration. "Because the only man she trusts around here—and that includes you, by the way—is Ram Dass."

Caroline slowly opened her eyes at the knock on her bedchamber door. She'd tired herself earlier by composing a note to her mother to alleviate her fears. It hadn't been easy to reveal so little to her and at the same time reassure her, but Caroline thought she'd done the best she could, considering the impossible situation.

"Hullo," she told the little ruby-throated hummingbird hovering over his miniature nest, which lay right outside one of her windows. She'd been watching him since she'd awakened from her feverish stupor, and his jeweled feathers, tiny body, and wonderful, buzzing wings fascinated her.

The knock sounded again, a bit louder. Perhaps Ram Dass would come soon with that lovely concoction he'd make for her. Always, he was a warm and caring presence in the room. She needed to thank him for helping her through this.

She called out softly, so as not to hurt her already raw throat.

Lord Headleymoor bowed as he entered. His lordship was so very different from Ram Dass. He made her heart quicken and her head ache when he came into the room to see how she was.

He was too exciting. Too cunning. His thoughts seemed too intricate to follow sometimes. Occasionally, during her illness, she became aware of him standing beside the bed, gazing at her, his dark eyes lit with some emotion that made her blood race. She thought he might live on a more intense plane than normal humans, and burn more brightly.

"I see you are indeed beginning your recovery, my lady," Headleymoor said. "I must ask your indulgence, for as you well know, the last week has not seen an ordinary series of events for us. Lord Nearing has come to me because I have . . . certain talents, one of which is to locate missing people. You may not be aware of the fact that you have been missing for the last—"

"Seven days," she concluded, quickly interrupting him. "But I left a letter behind for my mother."

Headleymoor grimaced. "Apparently, in the excitement, it was never delivered."

"Oh, God." Caroline shut her eyes in misery. "She must be mad with fear by now."

"Indeed. That sorry occurrence is what happens when one goes off on an adventure, no matter how compassionate the motive for doing so."

"One usually doesn't think one will end up ill in France, rather than safely on the road, writing letters home," she said heatedly and ended by coughing.

Headleymoor coolly poured a glass of water from her bedside pitcher and handed it to her. "I believe a mustard plaster is in order," he said as she sipped. "I shall order one at once, along with some soothing herbal tea."

"Ram Dass will determine whether I need one or not," Caroline replied.

"He already has done so," Headleymoor said curtly, then turned to a footman hovering in the doorway and nodded. The man bowed and ran off.

It occurred to Caroline that Headleymoor, if married to the wrong woman, might well become insufferably dictatorial. She arched a brow at him and noticed with satisfaction that he blinked. When he cleared his throat and turned away, she also noted that his ears were a bit red. With well-deserved embarrassment?

She smiled and settled back against the pillows.

"To return to the topic at hand," Headleymoor said, "Nearing is here. He was gravely concerned when your brother reported to him that you were missing. He wished my help in finding you, but as you are already found, and, I was quite thankful to report, on the mend, he wishes to see you. He will take whatever messages you have for your mother with him when he leaves Valoir."

"Oh, dear," she said aloud without meaning to.

"You don't wish to see him?" Headleymoor's face brightened. Or was that just the sun breaking through the clouds outside the window?

"Do I look as though I am yet fit to challenge the man to another duel?" she asked with a laugh that turned into another cough.

"That mustard plaster ought to be here any minute," muttered Lord Headleymoor as he handed her the water glass again.

His prediction came true, for Elise, the nursemaid Lord Headleymoor had hired for her, appeared at that moment and shooed Headleymoor out of the room.

"I shall return with Nearing," he called through the shut door, as Elise applied the plaster to Caroline's chest. When she had finished, she pulled a large shawl over Caroline's shoulders and poured her a cup of tea. Caroline put the cup to her lips and breathed in the soothing scent of rose hips and mint.

Lord Headleymoor entered a moment later. Behind him, Caroline spotted Nearing, his brow wrinkled in a look of grave concern.

"How are you faring?" he asked her, crossing the bedchamber and bowing over her hand.

Headleymoor remained at the door, gazing at the two of them, his eyes unreadable.

"Far better now, thank you," she said. "If you would be so kind as to post this letter to my mother, I would be even better, my lord."

"I am relieved to hear that. Dev tells me that it was a complete surprise to him when he discovered you on board the ship. Is this true?"

Headleymoor's gaze seemed to burn. There was a tension about him that fairly hummed across his shoulders, as though someone had plucked a harp string wound much too tightly.

She nodded. "I'm afraid I had visions of glory, sir. I took the stable boy's place in that night's adventure, and never realized how it would all come out—me here, so far from Mama, and my note to reassure her never sent."

"My dear Caroline, you must be very careful not to allow your kind heart to get in the way of your health again, not to mention your reputation."

Caroline glanced at Headleymoor. Nothing about his posture or his expression had changed, but she sensed an even tighter coiling of his muscles.

"Therefore," Nearing went on, "you must realize that if this gets out—and I must assure you that someone will pick up the threads of your last week's absence—it will spell ruination, not only for you but for your whole family."

"I have faced such before, sir," Caroline said, and would have tossed her head for good measure except that it was beginning to hurt. Dreadfully.

"Have a care, Maxim, that you do not undo all Ram Dass's good work," Headleymoor said from the doorway. Caroline felt a chill run up her spine, and it had nothing to do with fever.

"I am only stating the situation boldly so Caroline may make proper decisions," Nearing said through clenched teeth.

Caroline didn't quite understand what was going on, seeing that she was rather muzzy-headed at the moment with her wretched nose and throat, but she had a feeling that these two friends were, for some reason, imitating two very strong, angry dogs in one of those dreadful fights upon which men of low character wagered.

Looking from one to the other, she thought she just might put her money on Headleymoor. The heat vibrating off him seemed to rival that of her mustard plaster.

Nearing ignored Headleymoor and looked deeply into her eyes. "Caroline, no one must discover that you have been living without chaperonage in the house of an unmarried man of, I might add, somewhat questionable character. The only solution is for you to marry, very quickly. I present myself as a viable option."

"That's impossible. I've been too ill for men of questionable character to compromise," Caroline said and then coughed.

Headleymoor silently crossed the room, refilled her glass of water, handed it to her, then returned to his customary skulk in the doorway.

"I think that we could go on very well together," Nearing continued, as though he had not heard her. "I admire you enormously for your courage, no matter how misplaced it was. You know how badly I want you. And I believe that you will find me a kind and caring husband. Once I've made my vows, I shall take them very seriously, Caroline. I shall not stray."

"Why do I have to make this decision now?" she asked, but her gaze flew to Headleymoor.

"Nearing is right, Lady Caroline," Headleymoor said. "Society is cruel and quick to condemn. Many people will believe the worst because they will know themselves capable of doing such a thing. Many will simply enjoy the pain they cause, the quick crash of a lady whom others began to consider with respect and interest. Then there are those who fear that if they do not condemn along with the rest, they too will become grist for the gossip mills."

"Dev, you needn't let your own experiences so darken Caroline's view of those whom she will call friends in a year or so as my wife."

"Oh, no, Maxim. Let us not allow the truth to destroy the lovely portrait of Society that you're painting," Headleymoor said with a cool, cutting edge to his voice.

"I need time," Caroline said.

Nearing bowed and kissed her hand. "Of course. I shall give you until tomorrow to think about this. But if you decide to wed me, we shall do it soon. I will put it about that you and I went to visit my grandmother, as she had given her blessing for the match.

"And your maid," he continued, pacing the chamber, "was rushing to pack your trunk and accompany you. She forgot to deliver your letter to your mama, until several days had passed, at which point she came to you in tears and you immediately sent a messenger with another letter."

"Extremely clever, Maxim," Dev said. "I congratulate you."

"Congratulations are not yet in order," Caroline croaked. "If you could leave me, gentlemen, I should like time alone to ponder this problem and its possible solution."

"Of course. Until tomorrow," Nearing said and left the room. His footsteps echoed from the stairway as he made his way down.

Headleymoor remained, gazing gravely at her. Silence filled the room for a moment.

"Oh, could I have been more stupid—more arrogant?" Caroline said in misery.

"You saved my life, Caroline. I shall never forget that."

"I did, didn't I?" She stared at her hands, feeling a bit better as she remembered that.

Headleymoor cleared his throat. "You do not seem over-whelmed with joy at the proposition of marriage to Nearing."

"I am afraid that any marriage made in haste under such a cloud is doomed to failure," she said in a voice that cracked a little.

"I understand." Headleymoor shut the door and took two steps into the room. He stared, not at her, but at the window beyond her bed. His mouth was set in a bleak line, but the rest of his face was unreadable. He looked down at his hands. They were clenched tightly together.

She sat up against the pillows, stiff with nervous anticipation.

He took a breath. Another. The ormolu clock ticked away the time like an inexorable sentence.

"I have killed," he said.

She shuddered. "I know. I think I killed one of them, too. I see his masked face in dreams. When I awake, I tell myself it was a terrible thing to do, but it seemed the only thing at the time. Did it not to you, as well?" she asked him in an uncertain voice.

"I am not referring to the men who would have killed us that night, Caroline." His voice was without expression, just like his face. But his eyes looked desolate.

"I am speaking of others—a man whom I poisoned, a short time ago. I watched him die before me, when I had the antidote in my hand. I misjudged his condition. When I realized that, I was too late to save him."

Her hand flew to her throat. "How did it happen?" she whispered.

"He had slipped the poison into my brother's glass of tea. I simply switched the glasses while his attention was elsewhere."

"Was he part of this plot against Zaranbad?"

He nodded.

"I see. You killed to save your brother. Why did you not give him the antidote and keep him prisoner?"

"I told him if he revealed the names of the plotters, I would give it to him. But he refused. So I gave it to him, anyway, and it was too late. I let him die."

Caroline thought for a moment. "How long did it take him?"

Headleymoor's head shot up in obvious surprise at her question. He probably thought she was a bloodthirsty witch. "It seemed almost immediate."

"You had no time to react, then."

Headleymoor nodded, but his eyes still held despair. She put her hand over her chest, trying to ease the hurt she felt for him. She knew now, herself, how horrible it was not to be able to forgive oneself for acts that one was forced to do.

"I tell you this because you have the right to know what sort of man I am. Because of the work I do. You've guessed at that, have you not?"

She nodded, wordless.

"There have been others," he said low, still staring past her into his own private hell.

Something became suddenly clear to her. This man, who appeared so brilliant, so certain, lived with constant self-recrimination. She dared not breathe for fear he would stop speaking. If he talked about it now, the poison might leach from his soul.

"I have done things that . . . I am not a good man. I am not an easy man to live with. But if you feel that you cannot bear a marriage to Nearing, I will give you the protection of my name, such as it is. If you hate the idea of living with me, you may live separately."

"You are offering marriage?" she asked in stupefaction. She put her head in her hands. The ache seemed to have left with Nearing, but it certainly buzzed with the absurdity of the situation. She had hoped that Headleymoor might find some solace in confiding his feelings to her. Instead, he had just proposed—a blooming marriage of convenience.

Here she was, the troublesome Caroline Berring, with a red nose and disheveled hair, who had received two marriage proposals from men who offered themselves as the sacrificial lambs on the altar of her disgrace. It was enough to confuse a philosopher and humiliate a maiden, even one so practical as she.

"I will give you the freedom to do whatever you wish to do," he went on. "You may read anything that strikes your fancy, ride to hounds, visit foreign lands, live with the Indian tribes in America. You will be free to do anything but indulge in an open affair that will insult my name. That is my proposal of marriage. It's the alternative to marrying Nearing."

"Why would you give me such freedom, when you get nothing, especially if I leave you immediately after the ceremony? There will be no consummation of the marriage, no child if I choose to do that."

The very things, she thought, *that I have wished for ever since you asked me to dance and changed my life.*

He shrugged. "You would be safe this way."

"What does that mean—safe?"

He gave her a long look. "You realize that I have enemies. I would not wish you caught in the cross fire." He walked toward the window and looked out, his back to her. "As to traveling, and . . . the rest, you told me once that you had a difficult time with Society's restrictions. Marriage to me will free you from them."

Caroline stared at him. "You think me a debauched coward," she whispered. "You allow me to run from danger and to take a lover, as long as I am discreet. Your proposal is an insult."

He froze, and she saw in the stillness of his stance something of defeat and misery. It made her suddenly wish to say yes, if only to take away the aura of loneliness that seemed to engulf him.

He lifted his chin and gave her a tight smile. "It's Nearing then, I take it? Shall I tell him you wish to speak with him?"

"I wish to speak with Ram Dass," she said.

He sighed. "I shall call him." And with that, he turned and left the room as silently as a ghost.

CHAPTER EIGHT:
DECISIONS

Dev took the stairs to his chambers two at a time. He'd botched it, and it was lucky he had. Still . . .

She'd called his proposal an insult. He hadn't meant for it to turn out that way. But what the hell had he been thinking with that promise to allow her the sort of freedom only a selfish hussy would enjoy? Did he have some childish hope that compromising with fate would give him everything? That she would stay with him and allow him to do the things he dreamed of doing to her?

It was too dangerous. If she stayed, his enemies would realize how much he . . . wanted her. Yes, that was the word. He wanted her. Nothing more.

He couldn't understand what had gotten into him. Nearing would be a good husband, at least in those terms that the ton held dear. He obviously lusted after her, dammit.

But when Nearing had offered for her, Dev's mind had gone absolutely still but for one thought. Nearing would never know how strong she was. How she looked when she was free of all constraints—riding against the wind and rain, the lightning illuminating her face, filled with fierce determination. Dev thought of her, laughing at the world around her in the midst of a dance at the ball. Nearing wouldn't see her indomitable courage, despite a soft inner core that hurt and cared too deeply.

Nearing would cage her, make her into the perfect wife and mother, without ever knowing the best of her was dying inside.

Yet Nearing would keep her safe.

Dev stopped dead on the stairway. His head dropped in defeat. All he needed was the thought of poor, dead Jonathan Dinsmore to quell whatever selfish impulses pushed him toward that course he could not take.

Slowly, he began to climb again, plunging deeply into his motivations and his desires in an attempt to understand and then quell the needs that had almost overpowered his sense of honor.

What a fool he was! How would he feel, sending her an ocean away from him, to be safe from his enemies? He sighed, recognizing the last ironic twist of fate. He, himself, would seal his own bitter destiny.

Ram Dass would counsel her to marry Nearing. It would at least be a typical marriage, not a sham or worse, living with the painful denial of everything he desired most in this world.

"Well?" Nearing leaped to his feet as Dev entered the drawing room. "Did you convince her?"

"I?" Dev barked out a laugh. "She wants Ram Dass, of course."

"Well, on with it, man. Go change into that turban and talk her into it."

Dev gave his friend a long look. "Are you sure, Maxim? Do you really care for her?"

"Of course I do," Nearing said hotly. "She's lovely and kind, and she'll make a wonderful mother. I shall be faithful to my vows, Dev. What more could a lady ask of her husband-to-be?"

Love, Dev wanted to say. *Passion. Companionship, and not just at table or at a soiree or a play. Delight, laughter, a man's joy at seeing a woman waiting for him when he comes home, the light in her eyes filling the whole world with brilliant color.*

He had seen that, as a very young child, when his mother

greeted his father. Many a night before he was taken to bed, he had seen them together, on a sofa, wrapped in each other's arms, and making room for him to crawl up on the sofa with them, safe and utterly content within the overhanging protection of their love. It was something he knew he'd never have, but he wished it for Caroline.

Maxim would be a good husband. As good as any aristocrat in England could be.

"I'll go dress. If she wishes to see you afterward, I'll be sure to let you know, but I have a feeling she'll take all night to decide what to do. If so, I suggest we have an excellent dinner and several bottles of a very fine burgundy I've in the cellar."

"Yes. Several bottles, if you please," Maxim said with an ironic rise of one brow. "It's going to be a rather long night."

"Milady, you should be abed." Mimi shook her head as she entered the room with a tray of hot chocolate, and tsked disapprovingly.

"I cannot keep still," Caroline said. She'd thrown on the dressing gown she found in the wardrobe and slowly walked the room. Now she stared out the window. The River Cher rolled by, flush with the late spring rains. At the quiet rap on the door, Mimi walked toward it and opened it.

Ram Dass frowned down at Caroline, and for a moment he looked rather like his half nephew, Headleymoor.

Mimi gave him a curtsey, which made Caroline like her even more than she already did. "I shall leave you alone with your patient, Ram Dass," Mimi said and swept out the door.

"Lady Caroline, please sit if you cannot remain in bed. It is most important that you recover and for that, you need all the strength in your body to work undisturbed."

"I'm sorry," she said meekly, allowing him to lead her to a chaise and plump pillows behind her head. He gently placed an afghan over her reclining form, and she secretly smiled at the thought of how delicate a rose he must think her, when in reality she was as strong as a thick-stemmed sunflower. "I couldn't bear to sit. I have a difficult decision to make and I badly need your advice." Without further ado, she told him everything.

"I see," Ram Dass said, when her rushed monologue came to an end. "And you do not know which man to accept?" He glanced up at her and for a moment, she felt Headleymoor's intensity in that glance. Then he rose and paced the room.

"You must tell me how you feel about these two men, Lady Caroline," he said. "I have often believed that the mind and the emotions have a good deal to do with the health of the body. So it is important, given that this is your future, that you understand your feelings in the matter."

She nodded. "Lord Nearing is a good man. I am convinced of that. He may have originally been . . . um . . . insufferable," she said because there was no other way to put it, "but he has shown a real interest in marriage to me. I believe he means it when he says he will not stray, that he will respect and honor me."

"I see," Ram Dass said, and his face seemed for another moment as impassive as Headleymoor's. "Those are very good reasons for choosing Lord Nearing. And what do you feel as you discuss those very good reasons with me?"

"I—I have a tightness that goes about my head and my chest like a clamp."

"Visualize that tightness and tell me what you think it symbolizes."

Caroline shut her eyes and simply let her body . . . feel.

"I feel as though I were in a cage, and there is barely room to turn around."

Ram Dass's voice was soft and soothing. "I see. And will you tell this servant what you feel when you think of life with Lord

Headleymoor?"

She shut her eyes again and relaxed against the chaise. "He gave me choices, but he doesn't want, nor will he offer warmth or caring. I feel free, but alone and confused and—and unwanted.

"He is a very private man, Ram Dass," she rushed on. "You know this to be true, do not try to make him into what he is not. And I think he is both aloof and too hard on himself, and I feel as though he needs understanding and—and love. But I do not believe that he will allow me to give him any. I truly think that if he could, he would wed me and then exile me to Siberia. I think he only proposed out of unreasonable guilt that he somehow caused this situation I find myself in, when in reality, I did this to myself."

She opened her eyes and saw him watching her with the sweetest, most loving expression. And she couldn't help it—she leaned into that warmth, into that sweetness.

"Do you know what I wish?" she whispered without thinking. "I wish I could marry a servant, and live with him and help him in his work. I wish he could leave his post in England and we could go to Zaranbad where he is much needed as a doctor, and we could both help that country find its rightful place in the world."

Ram Dass's face slowly changed. She registered shock, then something akin to consternation and dismay. She didn't see anything else, for her gaze fled from his face and dropped to her hands, twisting in the folds of the afghan. She wished she could run to the window and leap out into another world entirely, where the humiliation she felt wouldn't follow her.

"Lady Caroline," Ram Dass said softly, "you do me great honor, but this is an impossible wish. We are from two different worlds. I think you are like a child, dreaming of a way out of your present conundrum, and childlike, you pick this poor servant as a possible path. But you are, in reality, wiser than that child. When you are not wishing for a way to hide from the choice you must make, you realize that a union between a lady of the British Empire and a servant of another race is impossible."

"Of course," she murmured. "You would see it that way, having been treated as you have in England."

Then her head shot up and in a flash of temper and steel, she narrowed her eyes at him. "I do know that there is a certain sphere of this world in which reality reigns. It decrees that we are worlds apart.

"Whereas," she continued defiantly, "in the world of the spirit, I think we are very much alike. I think we have both been hurt and carried on despite that hurt. I think we observe the world with the same sense of irony and impatience and affection. I think we are loyal to a fault, and perhaps it would do us good to think, not of others in this matter, but for ourselves."

Silence greeted her magnificent oration.

She felt the heat of mortification stain her cheeks, but she had been right to say what she had just said. Hadn't she? Because it was truth—elemental, and essential, on the deepest level of human understanding.

Ram Dass stood where he was, straight and tall and duty-bound, looking at her with a world of compassion and something like reverence in his dark gaze.

The fire of certainty slid from her bones, leaving her weak and trapped.

She gave a long sigh before turning away so he couldn't see the heavy sense of doom descending. "As you pointed out so properly, we are worlds apart. Please, then, as a last service to me, do advise me," she managed to conclude. "Whom shall I marry?"

Ram Dass looked at her for a long time, but she had no

trouble holding his gaze. After all, she had to marry one of them, and Ram Dass, for all his self-abnegation, was an excellent judge of character.

Finally, he shook his head and laughed, a painful, self-mocking sound. "I suggest you take Lord Headleymoor," he said. "I am afraid you would be wasted on Lord Nearing, for he would never understand what he had in you."

Caroline waited for the door to shut quietly behind Ram Dass. She rose and waited for his footsteps to echo down the long corridor and be swallowed by the turkey carpeting of the stairs. She waited two beats longer.

Then she grabbed the vase of flowers sitting on the table beside her and flung them at the door with all her might. The vase shattered. Water seeped most satisfactorily from the crushed and twisted stems of the lilacs in the vase.

"Well, that was certainly mature," she said through clenched teeth. A sob escaped her throat, and another. She covered her face in her hands and gave in to the fierce tears. It just seemed like the right thing to do, given the impossibility of her position and the embarrassing things she'd allowed herself to say to one of the best men she knew—a man whose good opinion was worth its weight in gold.

Worst of all, she had only herself to blame. "Five days ago I had a chance to be happy with . . . with . . ." She flung her hands in the air and then covered her face again. "With *somebody*. But no, I had to go play hero and ruin my whole life."

Her restless feet began to pace, despite Ram Dass's warning. To perdition with Ram Dass.

"From the time I was a baby, I've been healthy as a horse," she muttered. "And considering horses' delicate digestive systems and seemingly constant lameness problems, healthier than a horse. Besides, I could always die a tragic death, and then he'll be sorry."

But whom did she blame for her misery? Ram Dass for refusing her proposal? Lord Nearing for bringing the subject up and loosing this tempest in the first place? Or—or—or, oh she knew whom to blame.

A soft, buzzing hum came from outside the closed window where the hummingbird hovered, his jeweled feathers glowing in the fiery light of the setting sun.

"It's all Headleymoor's fault," she told the bird. "If he hadn't been at the queen's reception, I wouldn't have been there. Of course, if he hadn't danced with me at his ball, I would still be the same tongue-tied, unhappy girl I was but two weeks ago. I wouldn't have the Queen of Zaranbad as a friend. I wouldn't have two marriage proposals—and one rejection—for that matter."

And she wouldn't have ridden through a dark and cloud-torn night, her heart beating wildly in excitement and delight at the pace and the danger and the hope that maybe, just maybe, they would prevail.

She walked toward the window, but the hummingbird didn't seem to mind the intrusion of her gigantic self into his world. She leaned against the glass, and he continued to sip from the nectar of the wisterias from the vine that clung to the white stone wall outside her window.

That was what marriage to Headleymoor offered. A chance to do things she would never be able to do otherwise. A chance to live fully in the moment, without fear that she was being judged.

Freedom to do as she wished, to believe what she wished, to read what she wished. Freedom, after years of restriction. She had heard that Headleymoor had mistresses. That women of a certain age and experience adored him and hoped he would choose them to take to his bed.

She would have to live with that knowledge and that shame—that he wanted other women. But apparently he didn't want her enough to even demand that she stay with him. However, did she really believe that Nearing would not stray when so many men did? And Nearing would expect her to be just as every other man's wife was—sweet, accepting, not very curious about matters that didn't concern her. The clamp of constriction tightened about her head and rib cage again, as confining as the corset she wasn't wearing.

And that was another thing. She strode over to the bellpull and tugged. At a soft knock, Mimi entered and curtsied. "Yes, milady?"

"Please ask Lord Headleymoor and Lord Nearing to join me," she told Mimi. "And please bring a few more pieces of foolscap and another quill."

"That maid, Mimi, just popped in. She says Caroline's d'cided," Nearing slurred. "Can't go to her, Dev. I'm castaway."

He dangled the empty brandy bottle from his fingers with his usual grace, but there was no question but that Maxim was too foxed to go to a lady and hear her accept his proposal of marriage.

This was the irony of a cruel fate—to go in Maxim's stead and accept by proxy her agreement to marry his friend. Dev sighed and rose from the wing chair by the fire, placing his glass on the table. "I'll go," he said.

"Good fellow, al'ays there when a man needs a hand," Nearing said. The brandy bottle fell with a thunk onto the carpet.

As Dev left the room, he heard his friend's first snore.

The door to Caroline's chamber was wide open and the lamps were lit high. He walked in to find her seated at the writing desk in the corner, dressed in the simple skirt and full-sleeved white blouse that he'd bought for her in the village of Blere.

She was bent over something she was writing, her quill racing across the page. Her cheeks were somewhat flushed. But, his doctor's eye noticed, it seemed to be the result of emotion, not fever, which would have left two bright red spots of color on an otherwise pale face. Still, after their last encounter, he approached warily.

She finished her work and signed it with a flourish, then rose. "Ah, Headleymoor, I see you got my message. I assume Lord Nearing will be coming quite soon?"

"Lord Nearing is feeling a bit . . . under the weather tonight. Perhaps it is the result of his hasty journey here."

She smiled and raised a brow. "From what my brother has told me about Lord Nearing, I am more of the opinion that his indisposition is the result of a copious amount of after-dinner brandy. However, that is beside the point."

Taking up the foolscap, she held it out to him. Dev took it from her and glanced down. One side was filled with small, neat handwriting. He glanced at her quizzically.

She drew herself up fully, and suddenly, she seemed the very image of a queen. "If you were at all serious about your proposal earlier, these are the demands that I would make upon you before agreeing to such an arrangement between the two of us."

Dev had a difficult time keeping his jaw from dropping to his neck. She actually was considering him as a husband? Over Nearing?

"I see that I had better read your terms, my lady," he said, and to cover the confusion and the spike of giddiness that raced through his chest, he crossed to the window and read the missive.

He saw it was a list—of what she planned to do and what he would allow, if he wished to marry her. The list was long and varied. "You will travel to America and live in an Indian teepee?"

She nodded.

"You expect me to buy whatever books you might want to read that are banned from the Ladies' bookstores?"

"I do expect that," she said in a cool voice.

"You will find friends where you wish regardless of their status and Society's condemnation. You name artists, writers, musicians, philosophers, and opera stars as possible acquaintances."

"I have decided to refuse Nearing, no matter what happens between us. After the proposal you offered, I expect that you are not interested in giving me children. If I were so lucky as to have children, I would wish them to be acceptable to the ton and curb my behavior. But you have intimated that this possibility is remote, to say the least. Still, Society will show its shock and disapproval of friends such as those I mention, and you will have to deal with that."

He felt his mouth drop open in amazement. "What's this about children? Why do you think I wouldn't wish to have them with you?"

She gave him a look that clearly conveyed the message that she must be talking to an idiot. "You don't even want me to stay in the same country, my lord. I may be unwed, but I am not stupid. One does not get a child by post."

She walked toward him, her face absolutely calm, despite her high color. "You may be at peace, my lord. I do not expect you to marry me. But I realize now that I am so far from the pale, I am free to do all these things. It would be easier for my mother if I had the protection of your name and your position, but that is not a consideration that should sway your decision."

Dev stared at the bottom of the list. It was a demand he could not imagine ever seeing on a contract of betrothal, and it set the blood beating heavy and hot in his veins. "I see there is one more line to your list of demands," he said and his mouth turned up slightly to one side. He gave her a look beneath his lashes, and she realized just how long and thick they were.

"Yes," she said, and lifted her chin. "I have realized these past days how very comfortable I am in the clothing you have given me. I do not believe that any woman, given the choice, would not demand to eschew a corset." By Jove, she'd even spoken the word aloud, when ladies usually vaguely referred to underclothing as "unmentionables."

Dear God, he thought. If Caroline can be so open about this, what will she be like in our bed? The prospects were dizzying, fueling his already burning lust into bonfire proportions.

Dev nodded and bent over the desk. With a flourish, he pulled the quill from the inkwell, signed the paper, sanded the signature, and handed it to her. "I am honored that you have accepted my proposal, Caroline. I believe that it is a good thing to understand each other. By the way, I shall be delighted to make a child with you, and not by post."

It was too much, and he had been tempted for too long. He wouldn't stay for more than a moment, or he would lose control of the raging flames this unexpected conversation had fanned. But they were alone, and thoughts of what she was not wearing beneath that pristine, high-necked blouse and full skirt were beginning to drive him mad.

Slowly, using every ounce of control he had, he pulled her close. She came to him easily, like a flower just picked, fresh and sweet-scented, supple but soft, leaning toward him as though he were the light of the sun; as though she, too, wanted the closeness, wanted the heat of his body pressed to hers.

His arms slipped around her, drawing her even closer, savoring the feel of excitement that coursed through his body. He could tell she felt the same, for her eyes sparkled and she slid her hands up his chest—what a feeling to have her touch him so intimately.

He pressed her into him, so his chest felt the glorious softness of her breasts—free of any constraint, no corset, no stays, just warm, yielding woman, making his heart beat wild and fast with the drugged, heady urgency.

He bent his head and gently, so very carefully, rubbed his lips against hers. Once, twice, and he knew he should step back, but she took that moment to sigh and raise her arms and slip them around his neck. She clung to him as he kissed her shut eyes, her cheeks, soft and sweet, and then, his hand wandered up to that unprotected, lovely curve of her breast, and he cupped it, and that sweet plump globe in his hand was all that the fire inside needed to roar higher.

His mouth plunged on hers and she gasped, and into that gasp he stroked his tongue, and tasted the sweetness of her mouth, while his hand stroked, learning the swelling curve and softness of her breast through the thin linen blouse. He could feel the hard nubbin of her nipple through the cloth. What color were they? It was suddenly of the utmost importance that he find out. How would it be if he took her down, and covered her with his body, all over, and kissed her, all over, and filled her with himself, and stroked her and stroked her and stroked her, as his tongue was doing, learning all of her, burying himself to the hilt, taking what he wanted, groaning, as he was doing now as he was—

Dear God, what was he doing? He froze in horror. To take her like a randy eighteen-year-old with no gentleness, no care! Gently, he disengaged himself, but he couldn't seem to grab the composure necessary to behave as a normal gentleman would, as though nothing too excessive had just happened. He suddenly realized that everything he felt when she was near could be labeled excessive.

"One more thing," he whispered. "Never doubt my readiness, nay my eagerness to devote myself to the goal of giving you those children you mentioned. Several children. I shall see you tomorrow, Caroline, when my blood cools enough for me to act the gentleman." He pulled her into his arms again and kissed her hard. Then he strode out the door and ran like a madman, before he went about the business of begetting right here, right now.

In the rose drawing room of Twenty-five Berkeley Square, Lady Margery Berring rose quickly as Robert Chantley, the Duke of Welsingham strode into the room. As soon as the door closed behind Munson, she flew into his arms.

"Oh, Robert! Thank heavens you've come. I need your help so badly, I can barely shape a thought for myself. Here, read this!" She fairly shoved a letter into his hand and sobbed on his shoulder as he read it.

"What's to be done, Robert? Oh tell me, what *can* we do, given the situation?"

The duke led her to the pink and ivory petit point sofa and sat down beside her. "There, there, my darling. I shall think of something to save our brave girl."

"Brave! Robert, when I think that we might have lost her on that terrible night. And she makes so little of it!"

"She's a regular Spartan, isn't she? Never fear, Margery. Headleymoor is an honorable man. But I promise you this. If my daughter doesn't wish to marry him, she will not do so. We'll find another way."

"I wish . . ." Lady Margery bit her lip and stared down at her hands.

Robert took them in his and lifted her chin. "What do you wish, my darling?"

"I wish that we had been able to marry all those years ago.

That we had been able to watch her grow, and help her to understand the world and life . . . together."

"As have I, all these years. But I'm here now, and I promise you that she will never lack for a father's love again. Even," he said with a quiet note of sorrow, "if she cannot return it."

Maxim Standhope, the Earl of Nearing, rose from his favorite dark blue wing chair in the study of Nearing House to greet Hossam Ali, the Foreign Minister of Zaranbad. Maxim had been back for only twenty-four hours, and the note he'd received this morning from King Ari's very good friend and counselor had disturbed him. He'd sent a footman in his own carriage to bring Hossam Ali to Nearing House as soon as could be, to hear what news there was of the king and his queen.

"I am so grateful that you could see me immediately, my lord," Hossam Ali said with a bow. "Particularly after your return just last night. It is very important that I speak to you, and then to Lord Headleymoor concerning the situation in Zaranbad."

"It is my honor to serve the king in any capacity I may," Maxim replied formally with a bow. "How may I serve him?"

"King Ari has received disturbing news from Zaranbad, news that he must share with his brother. It concerns the stability of the throne in the capital. I must get word to Lord Headleymoor that his brother and grandfather need him as soon as possible. But King Ari has no idea where Lord Headleymoor has gone. After that terrible night at Buckingham Palace, King Ari and Queen Janighar have not heard from him."

Hossam Ali rubbed his eyes wearily. "We must find Lord Headleymoor. The fate of Zaranbad depends upon King Ari speaking with him and gaining his help. I have tried to find him, but even his father does not know where he is. Then I thought of you, and how you have been friends since you were boys.

And I thought perhaps you would know where he is. If you do not know, then I am afraid that all is lost!"

Maxim felt truly sick. He'd been furious with Dev for stealing Caroline right from under his nose. He'd stormed away from Chateau Valoir, promising himself he'd never speak to Dev again.

But this terrible matter put things into perspective for him. Maxim had been to Zaranbad with Dev at a time when he was missing his own father, who'd died that winter.

He'd met Dev's grandfather, the kindly and wise old king, Varem, who had given up the throne in Ari's favor so he could counsel the boy and help him learn to be a true leader.

"Dev shared his grandfather with me," Maxim said slowly. "I had just lost my own father, and needed to feel . . . part of a family, I suppose. Dev and King Varem made me feel that."

He'd wanted to be Caroline's husband, but even more, he was Dev's friend. And a surrogate son of King Varem. There were some things more important than one's broken heart.

He turned to Hossam Ali and nodded. "I know where he is," he said. "Please keep this secret from all but the king, and for God's sake, go immediately to find Lord Headleymoor." Maxim turned to the desk, grabbed up a piece of vellum, and quickly wrote Headleymoor's direction upon it.

"Good luck," he said, handing it over and shaking Hossam's hand. "Tell Headleymoor I said to take care of himself."

Hossam Ali's expressive eyes filled with tears, and he bowed low to Maxim, fingers touching head and heart. "You may have saved Zaranbad and its people. May the good God who looks down upon us all protect and preserve you, my lord."

"And you," Maxim answered, walking beside Hossam Ali through the hallway. As Scrubs, the butler, opened the great double doors of the house, Maxim added, "Hurry as quickly as you can, Lord Minister."

"I shall, Lord Nearing. Good-bye, and with all my heart, I thank you."

CHAPTER NINE:
PATERNAL CONCERN

Dev sat opposite Caroline at one end of a huge dinner table in the echoing dining chamber with the candles in the chandeliers ablaze. His bride-to-be was smiling at his last remark and it occurred to him that he was, for the first time in a long time, having fun.

Caroline was impossibly alluring in a sky blue gown that matched her eyes. If he kept his gaze from wandering too close to the top of the gown, revealing a tantalizing hint of the most beautiful breasts in God's sweet world, he could get through this meal without throwing her across the table and ravishing her. At least he hoped so.

Inwardly, he groaned. While she was sick, he had been able to control the lust that thundered through him. He'd wanted only to protect her and to heal her.

But now, with her strength returned and her delight in Valoir's gardens, staff, and all the new dishes Remy set before her, she bloomed into a sensual, alluring siren. He found himself in a lather of need.

It didn't help that their conversations, touching on topics as varied as politics, travel, philosophers and the length of time it took to ready oneself for a ball, made it even more difficult to shut her out of his mind, his heart, and his straining sexual awareness.

He shifted in his seat and surreptitiously straightened his evening trousers.

She sat up a bit, glancing at him with those limpid eyes of hers. With the slight straightening of her shoulders, her breasts lifted, showing a miniscule amount more of that lush softness within the tight bodice. "Are you uncomfortable, my lord?"

"Not at all." *Don't look. Don't look.*

"You just seem a bit warm. We could certainly ask for a fire screen, if that would help."

He looked, and resisted the urge to groan aloud.

"I'm quite comfortable," he said, with just enough self-control to resist dumping the cut flowers from the huge epergne in the middle of the table and pouring the cold water over his head.

Oh, God, ever since he'd seen her list—actually, he'd taken it with him to read and re-read that night—the thought of her body free of restraint was more arousing than the most explicit art from the Kama Sutra.

She leaned forward in her seat, with a look of concern on her face. Not that he looked very long at her face. His gaze swerved downward to the gorgeous cleavage her position revealed and remained riveted there.

"I'm sorry to disagree with you, but your face is quite the color of a boiled lobster, sir. I wonder if I've given you my illness."

"Kindly sit back, Caroline."

She frowned. "You are normally never in a temper, Lord Headleymoor. You must be feverish."

He wrenched his gaze from the sensual feast sitting opposite him, and cursed the idiotic bargain that he had made with her in order to keep her from marrying Nearing. Go to America, indeed! Certainly not without him.

"I shall be cooler the moment you sit back in your chair."

Slowly, she sat back, a narrow-eyed look on her face that spoke of mistrust that she'd heard him aright.

But all he could think of now was his earlier vision and the empty expanse of table between them. How easy it would be to dismiss the footman, scoop her up and lay her down on that wide, sturdy table. It would be the perfect height, he thought, eyeing it. All he needed to do was to bend a bit, and she would be there, laid out like a feast beneath him, all of her skirts up about her waist, and her legs—oh, those long legs he'd seen in a stable lad's breeches, wrapped around his waist. Yes, it would be perfect.

He would expire from spontaneous combustion if they had to live in this proximity for many more days. He thought longingly of a special license.

"I suppose you will wish a wedding with bridesmaids, flowers, a large trousseau and a gathering of nosy parkers at Eversleigh?" He knew he sounded like a bear, but a man could only deal with so much temptation.

"I haven't actually thought about it," she said in a musing tone. "I never really considered the possibility, I suppose."

Oh, Caroline, he thought with a protective pang. It wasn't fair—how she'd been made to suffer the scorn of Society.

"You deserve a proper wedding, with all the jealous tabbies of the ton bowing and scraping before you," he said.

He would just have to wait patiently for word from Ari, so that Caroline and he could return to England and get this marriage underway.

He'd have to try to avoid her even more than he had, which was more and more each day as his hunger for her grew. Dinner was their only time together now. Perhaps he'd suggest that she don sackcloth for the next meal.

At first, she had seemed confused and hurt by his prolonged absence, and his heart ached that he had to make her unhappy to keep her safe from his lust. But her natural humor and curiosity soon had her asking him about Valoir and the tenants who farmed the land, and the crop of bright yellow flowers that he told her were for cooking oil and fodder.

Of course, it was possible that the excellent Burgundy they drank might have had something to do with their growing ease and pleasure in each other's company. He nodded to the footman to refill both their glasses.

"Antoine, who cooked this extraordinary boeuf Bourgonionne?" she asked in prettily accented French. Obviously, while he moped and burned for her, Caroline had spent her time learning more about the language.

"It's Monsieur Remy, m'lady," the footman said with a broad smile, completely forgetting his place in his delight that "m'lady" had enjoyed the meal.

"If you could ask him to come to the dining room for a moment after coffee and dessert, I should be honored to tell him how delighted I am with all of his cuisine," she said.

"Oh, m'lady, you would be honored? I must tell Remy at once, my lord."

And bowing, Antoine strode out of the dining room. Dev shifted in his seat, attempting once again to ease his discomfort, but no use. Antoine had left Caroline alone with a man who wanted nothing more than to forget he'd ever been a gentleman.

Marcel Remy appeared directly, a short, plump fellow in a spotless white chef's coat. He carried a tray of crème brule and Dev noticed that his smile beamed even broader than when he'd described his recipe for Calvados and apple crepes with a dash of lemon rind, a dish that had made Napoleon swoon many years ago.

"M'lady does me great honor," Remy said, bowing before Caroline as though she were Queen Victoria, herself.

"No, Monsieur Remy," Caroline said. "You do us honor every time you wield your brilliant talent and create such artistry as you have tonight."

"M'lady, I am overwhelmed that you are recovered, so now I can give you my best," he said. "This one—" he pointed to Dev, who had known Remy from boyhood, "is not at all a patron of haute cuisine. It is a delight and a boon to have such a one as you here, and I can only hope that m'lord will bring you often after the . . ." He coughed discreetly. "The Blessed Union, to inspire me to greater heights of creation."

Dev caught the tug at Caroline's lips and the sparkle in her eyes. "I should like that above all things," she said, covering her smile with her napkin as Remy carefully poured coffee for her with his own hands and stood guardian over her place as she tasted the crème brule. He seemed to quiver in expectation like a pointer about to flush a grouse.

Caroline's limpid gaze lifted to the chef's expectant face. "Superb," she said.

Remy clasped his hands in a gesture both ecstatic and relieved. "I now go to create tomorrow's petit dejuener. Antoine!" Remy snapped his fingers at the footman. "The port, if you please. And a little of that delightful brandy for m'lady. She is in France, now, and a true daughter of our country, if I am to be the judge, which, of course, I am in this household." After which he left the dining room, his chest puffed out like a pouter pigeon.

Antoine bowed and poured Caroline her first full glass of brandy. Once he'd left, she looked down at the glass and up at Dev, her lips quivering much like Remy's whole body had.

He loved seeing her like this—so free and full of life. Dev raised his glass in a toast. "To the true daughter of France," he said solemnly.

Caroline burst into a fit of giggles, and, trying to quell them, sipped a bit of brandy. The stuff must have gone down like fire, for she coughed, snorting in the most unladylike manner.

"I wonder," she managed finally, and then laughter got the

better of her.

Dev grinned. She was obviously not used to strong spirits and the combination of wine and brandy had gone slightly to her head.

"I wonder," she tried again, "whether a true daughter of France is permitted a cigar, as well."

Dev couldn't resist. He reached into the pocket of his dinner jacket and pulled out a long brown object, cut the end for her, and lit it. *"Alors, ma fille de France,"* he said, rising and bowing to her as he handed the cigar to her with a flourish. *"Tu es la belle reine dans cette pays.* And a queen's wishes, or even her whims, must be obeyed."

Lord, he was becoming a gallant. Just to please her. Caroline possessed him, no matter how few hours he'd spent with her. She was a part of his conscious and unconscious thoughts—his dreams, even, no matter how hard he tried to ignore her.

"I'd much prefer a kiss," Caroline said in a breathy voice. Then, like a child, she popped her hand over her mouth, her eyes wide and a blush stealing up her cheeks as she stared up at him.

Dev's hand shot out of its own accord. The cigar landed in the fireplace. He eyed the tabletop longingly, then pulled himself together. "A kiss for the Queen of Valoir."

His heart skipped in his chest. He raised her slowly to her feet, looking down into her face. It was flushed and filled with an excitement that heated his blood. Her eyes sparkled like sapphires reflecting candlelight, and she looked as though she were about to take a very high jump at a fast gallop—and as though the prospect thrilled, rather than terrified her. She ought to be scared. If she knew what he wanted to do to her, she would be.

He lowered his head, the brandy and the liquid heat flowing through him, making it all seem not awkward at all, but like a leap into space, into something mysterious and free from the fetters of the past.

He laughed, helpless against the tug of the tide in his blood, beating, beating, pulling him into the turbulent depths where he wished to be. "Caroline, the things we shall do together," he whispered, and bent his head.

Her lips were sweet from the brandy and her mouth was even sweeter with the last taste of the crème brule. And he wanted to taste all of her. He dove deep, his lips, his tongue, thrusting as he wanted to with his body, showing her what would be, if only . . . if only . . . if only . . .

His fingers danced up her side, along the smooth, slippery silk of her gown, and he was holding the soft weight of her breast cupped in his hand. Beneath the thin silk, her taut nipple peaked, and hosannas burst inside him, that she so obviously enjoyed him touching her.

"I love your breasts," he said. "They are so soft and plump. And so responsive." He brushed his thumb across her nipple, took it between finger and thumb and rolled it, while she cried out and gasped. "Look down. You are beautiful."

She bent her head and saw what he saw—his hand, large and dark against the whiteness of her, the swell of her, the puckered bud just begging for his mouth. He lifted the sweet globe of her breast from her bodice and lowered his head, licking across the nipple.

"Oh, my God," she cried softly.

"Say my name," he demanded, and took the nipple into his mouth, biting gently, suckling, mad to arouse her to the point of madness, so they would be in this tempest of passion together.

"Devlin!" she cried.

He lifted his gaze and in that instant, saw that her head was flung back in abandon, her graceful neck arched. He buried his head in the valley between her breasts and breathed in the scent of woman and wildflowers, his one hand stroking her breast, his arm holding her arched against the side of the table, his cock on fire as it pressed against her belly, his blood beating with triumph. His beautiful betrothed took to this pleasure like a child eating her first iced cake.

A knock on the dining room door awoke him from the delirium, to discover that his hand was cupping her breast, that he had her just where he'd wanted her earlier this evening, that he was on the verge of doing exactly what he'd told himself he must not do.

"My lord," Caroline whispered, straightening and motioning to the door, at which he heard a loud banging.

Carefully, he straightened her clothing. "Oh, God," he said, and dipped his forehead, placing it against hers and stroking her cheek. "I shall go mad, I think," he said softly, and released her. "The passion—you don't understand, Caroline."

"I think I should like to understand."

He laughed and bent his head, rubbing his lips lightly against the swell of her breast above the cleavage of the gown. "One day. I'll show you one day soon." Reluctantly, he stepped back from her.

She raised her hands to her flushed cheeks and turned away from the door as he called "enter," then returned quickly to the head of the table and seated himself.

"His excellency, Hossam Ali, on the King of Zaranbad's business," Antoine said hastily. "I am sorry to disturb you, m'lord."

Ari! Dev rose from the table so quickly that the glass of brandy rattled and a bit of the golden liquid sloshed over the edge. "I shall meet him in the study, Antoine. Please remain and escort Lady Caroline to her chamber as soon as she wishes to go."

Caroline ran to him and placed her hand on his arm. "Dev," she said quietly. "I will pray that the news is not . . . not . . ."

She seemed unable to go further.

"As will I," he said, giving her hand a squeeze. "I shall tell you as soon as I can," he added, turning for the door in haste.

"I shall wait in my chamber for you. Will you come and tell me, no matter what?"

He nodded and looked back as he left the room, at the open-hearted warmth in her gaze, buoying him up when every fiber of his being wanted to crumble. For if Ari had sent Hossam Ali here, to a place that no one knew existed, then something was terribly, terribly wrong.

Dev found himself running up the stairway and schooled himself not to crash the door open as he entered the study.

Hossam stood by the window, his back to Dev as he walked quietly into the chamber. What would be in Ari's letter? Had Zaranbad fallen to the traitors? Had they managed to get Janighar? The thought of her in the hands of such scum made his blood run cold.

"Hossam," he said, keeping his voice low and calm. "What has happened?"

Hearing the prince's strained voice, Hossam turned, wringing his hands, his eyes filled with tears. "Perilous danger everywhere, my lord prince! My news is so sensitive that I must talk to you away from the palace, where no one can hear what I say. I cannot even trust the guards that I came with, nor yours, for that matter. The United Band have bought everyone, it seems, and treachery is all around us."

Prince Devlin went very still, Hossam saw, and the prince's face grew so pale that the only spot of color in it was the dark brown of his eyes, suddenly void of all expression. "Have you a letter from my brother?" he asked in the quiet, dull voice of a man expecting a blow. And he would receive one, Hossam knew with sorrow, for he truly cared for Prince Devlin and badly wished he did not have to kill him.

"He was afraid to write anything that might be taken from me and used against all of you."

"I see," Prince Devlin said, and his eyes, if one could tell in this dim light, seemed to darken even more with foreboding. "Tell me, Hossam, is he alive? And Janighar? And my father?"

"It is your grandfather I worry for. There is rebellion in Zaranbad," Hossam said, watching Devlin's face carefully.

"I must walk, and think. Come with me to the garden," Prince Devlin said, his lips pressed like a man determined to endure deep pain as stoically as possible. The footman came forward, but the prince waved him off with a quick flick of his wrist.

They traveled down stairways and across halls with patterned marble floors and ceilings covered in carvings. Hossam was, as he had been since arriving in England, amazed at the wealth of the Carmichaels, and their power, not only in England, but in France, as well.

It was a terrible tragedy that they would not be able to wield it much longer, but Hossam had an eastern respect for fate and its vicissitudes, and this had to be accepted, along with the fate of King Ari and his grandfather. Prince Devlin was too tied to them all, and he was more clever than his brother.

Hossam hoped that he could spare the young lady he knew to be residing here, but if she saw and heard too much, he wasn't even sure of that.

The moon had slipped behind a cloud, and the garden, as they entered it, sank into darkness. It was all for the better that way.

As they walked along a gravel path, he could smell the scent of new roses and hear the musical lilt of a fountain playing. He sincerely hoped that Prince Devlin was soothed by the scents and sounds around him. Hossam wanted the prince's death to be swift and painless.

"King Ari received a message from a courier three days ago that the country is being torn apart by violence," Hossam said. "He immediately sent for me to come to his place of hiding."

"You mean in Bath?" Prince Devlin asked.

"Yes." Hossam tucked away that fact with delight. He would use it later to find King Ari after he'd dispensed with the prince.

"And," Hossam continued, "the United Band have attacked the capital city of Ranipur. The messenger said they were at the gates when he slipped out of the city. By now, who knows who is in charge of Zaranbad?"

"Oh, God," Prince Devlin said, and sat down on a bench, putting his head in his hands. It was perfect. He was unhinged by grief, unarmed, and above all, he trusted the closest friend of the king to be his friend, as well.

Would that it could have been so, but Hossam Ali had worked too hard for the great families' return to power to stop now.

"I am truly sorry, my prince," he said from behind Prince Devlin's back.

The prince didn't stir as Hossam pulled out his curved knife and took the necessary step to put the man's heart beneath his blade.

He raised the knife, only to feel the hard grasp of a hand on his wrist. The pain was excruciating as his wrist twisted. The knife slid from his hand to the gravel. A blinding light flared, and he saw a silent circle of men, all dressed in the powdered wigs of English footmen, but standing like soldiers around him.

He felt his knees wobble as he stared at the men surrounding him. How could it all have gone so wrong in the blink of an eye?

"How did you know?" he asked, squinting up at Prince Devlin as he stood above him, legs wide, arms crossed at his chest.

"The letter, Hossam. Ari and I knew there had to be another

traitor from the delegation. Neither he nor I would have sent a man, no matter how close to us, without a coded letter. You went to Maxim, didn't you? No one else in England could tell you where I was."

"The rebellion will happen anyway, without me," Hossam said calmly.

"Perhaps. But you will tell me who is the leader of this filthy lot, Hossam. And you will tell me who is the Englishman who has helped you."

Hossam drew himself up and forced his legs to stop shaking. He would stand and fight like a man before he met his end. It would be a particularly good death if he could yet kill Prince Devlin. The challenge was great, but he was almost as clever as the young prince was and he was burlier. Hossam was in fate's hands, and he would try once more to gain at least half of his goal.

"Why kill me?" the prince asked.

"Of the two Dassam brothers, you are more dangerous." He must keep talking, and wait for the opportunity to lunge. "Even though I failed, others will come after me," he said, watching the prince carefully. "You cannot have your democracy in the east, no matter how honorable it seems. The people will not understand it. They are like children who will grow willful and self-indulgent without the strict authority and control of a ruling class."

His right hand slipped into his sleeve, slowly, so the prince would not notice. "I warn you, it is not over. In the end you will lose. Tell Ari that I loved him, and if he had only listened to me and not to his grandfather, I would have been his loyal friend and servant until the end of my days."

It was there, that slight emotional twitch that told him the time was now. He lunged at Prince Devlin. The small, straight knife flashed, the second one that he carried. But somehow, the prince was waiting for him, one hand grasping his wrist, the other going for the knife. He cracked his head against Devlin's and they went down, rolling on the ground, over and over. Devlin somehow pinned him, but his knife hand broke free of the hold.

Hossam looked up at the man crouched over him, his eyes intent, cold as the icy British winter. Hossam got the blade up, almost to the prince's heart. His blood beat strong and triumphant. He would finish it now, before the men gathered could grab him.

Devlin's hand clamped again on his wrist, halting the blade just short of its target. But Hossam's blood lust was hot and insistent. He grasped the prince's throat with his left hand and tried to pull free of the steel grasp on his knife hand.

He could not fail. He must not fail. They rolled again, Devlin beneath him now, he realized in triumph.

As he tried to slash the blade downward, Devlin lunged to the side, elbowed him in the gut, and twisted his knife hand. He screamed at the crunch of bone. The knife came free into Devlin's hand.

He had to get the knife. With his good hand out, he lunged after it, and felt the icy blade slide between his ribs. The pain came seconds later, piercing enough to make him scream and collapse.

"Hossam!" He heard the pain in Devlin's voice.

The lights coming closer seemed to slither across his vision. "It was always Zaranbad," he explained to the shadowy figure of Prince Devlin hovering over him. His only regret was the look of pain and regret in Devlin's eyes, as the prince, mindless of the blood soaking his coat, knelt before him. Just before the spark of life fled his body, he felt Devlin close his eyes for him this last time.

★ ★ ★ ★ ★

Caroline stared out the wide window of her bedchamber. At the end of the formal gardens, just where the fountain played, a circle of torches lit the night sky. Figures fanned out, and other shadowy figures grappled with them. The torches landed in the flowerbeds, fizzing from the mist. The whole scene began to look like the entrance to hell. In that red and black-tinged darkness, she heard the bloodcurdling shouts and shrieks of men in battle.

Headleymoor must be in the thick of the fray—she knew him well enough by now to know he'd risk himself for his men.

She ran to the armoire where she'd placed her pistols and took them both out. They were already cleaned and primed— she'd seen to that herself, after she'd regained her strength. She raced down the stairs, past the statues on the landing, through the kitchen, where Remy and the scullery boys gathered knives, cleavers and the heavy steel hammers they used to tenderize meat. One of the bigger boys picked up an iron spit and ran for the door, holding it like a lance.

"*Allons*," Remy shouted, his plump legs pumping in a run. Caroline outstripped him and got to the door first, leaping over a low bench and cauldron set outside for soaking and plucking fowl.

Her heart in her throat, she ran between flailing bodies and tripped over someone's fallen wig as she searched for Headleymoor. The tumult all around her began to quiet when she saw him, kneeling, his white shirt dark with blood in the red glow of the fallen torches.

"Headleymoor!" she cried, and ran to him. He looked up from the ground and gave her a dull, weary look.

"Are you hurt?" she asked.

He shook his head and rose slowly, like an old man. She looked down. There were three men dead at his feet. Two were dressed in black, and the third—the third—oh, God, it was Hossam Ali.

So much blood. Even with her eyes shut, she could not stop from smelling the metallic reek of it in the air. She turned away, fighting the urge to gag.

The footmen were lifting their brands again, dragging the villainous foreigners who still lived, roping their hands behind their backs. She saw Remy, a cut on his forehead, binding a wound on one of the kitchen lads.

"I don't understand," she said.

And Headleymoor said in a voice of hurt and confusion, "Neither do I."

He looked down at himself, at Hossam Ali lying at his feet. As his gaze rose to meet hers, Caroline stood still and stiff as stone.

His dark gaze locked on her, his lips pressed together hard. He looked like a man suffering a wound and refusing to cry out. He stared at her clean silken gown and then he gazed down at his blood-soaked shirt, coat and trousers. With a stifled cry, he held his arms out from his side in a bitter mockery of offering and said, "This is what I am, Caroline. This is why, despite the circumstances, you must not wed me."

He came to her chamber late in the night. He'd washed all the blood from his body. His hair, she noted, was still wet from his bathing, and even though the night was unseasonably warm, he wore a formal and spotless coat, waistcoat, shirt, cravat and trousers. Servants came in and lit the tapers on all the candelabra, and the room gleamed, eradicating any fearsome shadows in the corners. But looking at the set of his mouth, the tension in his shoulders, she wondered if he carried that darkness within him, however brightly the room was lit.

For a moment, he looked at her in silence, and his dark eyes wore the weary look of a man slogging through a never-ending marshland, afraid that each step would suck him under.

"I feel I owe you an explanation," he finally said.

"Did you kill Hossam Ali?"

"Yes."

"Did he attack you?"

Dev nodded, his gaze still holding hers, but his face was white with the struggle not to—what? Not to look away? As though he were ashamed and looking straight into her eyes was his penance? She was filled with the desperate confusion she felt so often in his presence. But tonight was a night to push—to make him tell her the truth.

"Was he the leader of the United Band?"

"Yes. If he had not come at me, I believe I might have broken his neck. I know how to do that, you see. In one quick, vicious twist. I've been trained to do it, along with many other unsavory things."

"He wanted to kill you. And then he would have killed King Ari and Queen Janighar, wouldn't he?"

"Yes. He loved them, and yet his cause came before that love."

She rubbed her arms against the chill, despite the warmth of the room. "You think you are very much like him, don't you?"

"Yes. I would do anything to keep Ari and Janighar and my grandfather safe. Anything, Caroline."

In the silence, she heard the tap-tap of a moth on the windowpane, and the quiet voices of the men outside, tidying up the garden, even in the darkness, trying to get rid of all the blood and charred flowers.

Headleymoor looked infinitely weary, as though he had trudged through a wasteland for hundreds and hundreds of miles and had many more to go.

"I knew you must never wed me before, and I tried to make

194

a life for you that would make you happy. Now you see why I did so. After tonight I must withdraw my proposal. You need someone better, someone clean and straight in his thoughts, not the Byzantine warren that is my mind and my soul. I tell you this because it is the truth. I can never give you a whole and clean heart to love you. And worst of all, you will never be safe as my wife."

"What if I don't wish to be safe? What then?"

He gave her a look of such kindness, where pity and frustration intermingled. "I should still refuse to wed you. The life you would lead with me is not good enough for you."

"So you would deny me any real happiness in life and take yourself away because you believe yourself not good enough? This from a man who just managed to prevent himself and probably me from dying?"

He held his hand out to her, a look of struggle and misery on his face. "Caroline, think! Since you've been with me, you've almost died twice in twenty-four hours. Tonight, instead of fleeing at the sounds and sights of battle, you ran right into the thick of it. You exposed yourself to death for the third time. Because of me."

"Men!" she raged. "Why is it all right for you to die, and not for me?"

He came closer, his eyes narrowed in anger. "By God, woman, it's a matter of my duty!"

She stood her ground, blasting him with her own glare. "And it's a matter of my honor," she said, and turned away so she wouldn't have to see his face. He could lie so well, even with his expression. Another thing they'd trained him to do.

"How can I believe what you say?" she asked him. "How can I still hope that you're telling me the truth? I do not know you and yet I feel such . . . such things for you."

She shook her head in misery and frustration. "I have never

lied to you, or twisted the truth in such a way as to pretend to be anything other than what I am. And you have hidden yourself from me at every step. That is why I do not believe your very convenient excuse for breaking off our engagement, no matter how difficult a marriage it might have been."

She wanted to scream, to run to him and beat his chest, or tug his head down to kiss her and remind him of what they had shared, just hours before. But that was gone now, it seemed. Had it ever been real? Wasn't he just like all the others? She was good enough to dally with, to kiss and fondle. But not good enough to wed.

"You're lying to me. I know, because there's something you've hidden from me since the first moment you asked me to dance. What are you behind that mask you wear so well?"

His gaze filled with something that looked like dismay. And, she realized with a sinking feeling in the pit of her stomach, guilt. Then the curtain came down over his face, and he was Headleymoor again, aloof and expressionless.

"Please believe me," he said. "I respect and honor you. But I cannot put you in danger anymore."

She trembled, and it wasn't from fear. Backing to the wall, she wished there were more space to get away from him. A fine Ming vase stood upon the mantel. She'd admired it for some time. Most deliberately, she picked it up. It really wasn't so heavy, nor was it so far to the fireplace. She drew back her arm and threw it with all her might. It made a lovely sound—a crashing, splintering, loud sound.

Two vases in a very short time, she thought. If she had been reduced to the role of outcast shrew, she might as well make it as satisfying as possible. She whipped around to face Headleymoor, her rage filling her with a courage she'd never known she had before.

"Perhaps you made your proposal never expecting that I

would accept it. How horrified you must have been when I did! I hope that soon I learn to hate you, for I cannot bear to feel this way for long. Kindly get out and stay out."

He gave her a long, grave look. "Good-bye, Cara," he said, and walked out of her life, shutting the door so that there was no sound.

No color, she thought. No joy. No hope. Why had she ever thought it could be different? Hadn't she learned enough from the slights and the slurs she'd borne all her life?

Five days after the attack on Chateau Valoir, a grand carriage pulled up at the portcullis and a tall man was ushered in. Caroline heard voices in the front hall, but paid no attention to them. After giving orders to his men, Headleymoor had quit the castle, leaving a letter for her. After reading it through, she had thrown it into the fire.

In it, he had, in very gentlemanly language, asked her forgiveness, and told her again that he meant it—he wasn't good enough for her. That he'd already contacted Nearing, who would be more than happy to marry her, and that he'd also made certain that her reputation was not tarnished by the events of the past two weeks.

"Stuff!" she'd shouted, and watched the letter slowly curl and blacken and flame.

Not good enough for her! Whatever words he used, she knew the truth.

He wanted to bed her, but he didn't really want to wed her. Just as her father hadn't wanted her as his daughter, just as her brother didn't want her as his sister. Just as his own servant, Ram Dass, had not wanted her.

She would not cry. She would think of America. That was where she'd go, out to the great western lands, where it didn't matter whose daughter she was. She would build a house and live in it, with dogs and horses, and friends she made who wanted her just the way she was, no matter what any man in England thought.

A gentle knock on her door interrupted her thoughts. "Enter," she said, and a tall, handsome man stood in the doorway, the sun shining on his auburn hair. She looked into eyes the exact color of hers.

"My dearest child," the Duke of Hartford said. "I've come to take you home."

Chapter Ten:
Eversleigh

It was a strange journey to Dieppe. The closed carriage was well-sprung and comfortable, and there was time to talk to this man who seemed to know when to speak and when to be silent. He didn't ask her whether Headleymoor had taken advantage of her. His voice was reassuring and kind, and above all, he spoke without censure or pity.

"Your mother and I have put it about that you were overset by the events of that night in Buckingham Palace, and that your family took you to the country to recover. So many of the people we spoke with knew of the event. So many were there and saw that blackguard with a knife at your throat. It was the easiest thing in the world to convince them of your terror."

The duke smiled ruefully. "Would that you had been truly terrified, my dear. But I've known for years that you were much too courageous for the vapors."

"How could you possibly know anything of me?" she asked him, surprised and flustered.

He reddened, and she realized that he blushed as easily as she did. Another thing they had in common. Odd and disconcerting and interesting all at once, she realized.

"I will let your mama tell you how and why," the duke said. "And I have something to ask you, Caroline." He cleared his throat and looked very grave. "I should like to have your permission to marry your mother. Please do not give me your answer right away. If you could but wait a few days, until you see her and understand more about me, I should be grateful for an opportunity to speak about this again.

"In the meantime," he continued, "I wish you to know that several gentlemen have asked after your health in the last weeks, and among them, Gerard Visigore, Viscount Fortbras. He's the son of the Earl of Latham. It's an old family, one with great wealth and land, and Visigore has added to that wealth with his investments in India.

"He spoke to your brother several days ago," the duke went on, "and asked if he could court you. Seems he saw you across the ballroom the night of the Wimbley ball, and was immediately smitten. William is terribly amused, for Fortbras is famous for avoiding the parson's mousetrap, and here you have conquered him with one glance."

The duke gave her a reassuring smile. "You will find upon your return that Latham is among those gentlemen who wish to court you. If you find him to your liking, I think it would be an advantageous match. But Caroline," he cautioned, suddenly serious, after his attempts to help her bruised self-image. "Do not ever, ever agree to marry without love."

She nodded, unable to speak for fear of simply breaking down and sobbing. It was too late for that, she realized. She could never marry for love, because the man with whom she'd fallen hopelessly in love refused to marry her. Now, it was only a matter of hiding the truth from everyone who cared about her, including this stranger, her father.

Several days later, Caroline arrived at Eversleigh exhausted and disheartened. But as she approached the large Palladian house, standing majestically on a rise with the verdant hills behind it, she felt a sense of peace that had been missing from her life for the last weeks. It would be a good thing to remain in the country for the rest of the Season. To ride, to walk out and feel the warmth of the sun on her head, to listen to robins fighting over worms in the walled gardens seemed the best way to get over this ill-conceived notion that Headleymoor had felt something for her. Oh, not anything as much as she felt for him, but . . . something.

As soon as she alighted from the carriage, the great oak doors flung wide and Munson stepped aside as Caroline's mother ran out of the house and wrapped her arms around her.

"My darling girl, home at last, and safe! Thank heaven that you are back with us."

Her mother's tears felt warm on her cheek, and Caroline hugged her back, grateful for the love that her wounded heart needed so badly. Mama smiled through her tears and said softly to the duke, "I can never thank you enough for this, Robert."

"Not at all, my dear," the duke said, and gave her mother a look of such adoration that Caroline's heart ached. Still, she was home, and loved.

But Mama's love came with questions, and it was not fifteen minutes later that she sat down opposite Caroline in the rose drawing room, pouring a cup of tea and handing her a plate of Cook's extraordinary scones.

"You have not been eating, have you, darling?" Mama's hand caressed her cheek. "I've been so worried about you. I can see you're not fully recovered—you're pale and thinner. And your old *joie de vivre* seems to have slipped away from you. Did something happen at Valoir? Talking about it might make it easier for you."

"There is nothing really to discuss," Caroline said, pasting a look of reassurance on her face. "I was ill, that's all."

"Well, we have you back again, thank God. We shall make sure that you have rest and nourishing food. Then we shall provide pleasant company, to help you forget your ordeal. I've invited a few of my friends to Eversleigh for a house party in a fortnight. They will bring their children along. I think it will cheer you to have young people about."

Caroline could think of nothing more unpleasant than having young people about. In the past, it had always been a trial by fire to stand on the edges of Society and see the pitying looks or the smirks on the faces of women her age. The prospect of a house party seemed much more oversetting than riding through a freezing downpour beside Headleymoor.

"Your brother William has invited a few of his friends, as well, so there will be a rather large group," Mama went on as the drawing room door swung open. "Ah, there you are, William. I'll leave you two alone for a while. Cook is in a dither about feeding so many guests, and I must reassure her that she is quite up to the task."

Caroline's brother strode over to the ivory sofa upon which she sat and knelt before her. His brown gaze was softer than she'd ever seen it. Could it be that he was actually concerned about her?

He took her hand and patted it awkwardly. "His grace gave us Headleymoor's letter as soon as he received it. You're a brave girl, Caro. I didn't know you had it in you—to ride like that through the night and cold and rain, what a brick you were! Nonetheless, I'm glad you didn't accept Headleymoor's proposal. For all his wealth and title, he's not quite the thing, you know. The blood's not all English. No telling what he's got from the other side."

Caroline stiffened in affront. "Poorly done, William. Lord Headleymoor is every inch a gentleman, in any society."

William frowned, suddenly intense. "That's doing it a bit strong, my girl. Not sweet on him, are you? If so, he'll either wed you or face me. And I've been practicing while you were gone. I'm getting to be a fair shot. Not as good as you are, but not bad, either."

Oh, God. That was all she needed—pistols at dawn between

Headleymoor and her brother. What was it with men that they had to settle their scores by killing each other?

"Of course I don't care about the man," Caroline said quickly.

William gave her a smile and hopped up to sit beside her. "Good. Because there's a fine fellow, a buck of the first head. Just back from Italy, and he's eager to be introduced. Wishes to court you, my dear. Saw you at some ball—did his grace tell you?"

She nodded. "But William, I do admire Headleymoor, and all of England should thank him because he saved his brother from a dastardly plot. After all, King Ari's death while in England would have been a great embarrassment to the Crown."

"That is indeed true, my dear. I will say the fellow was quick to sniff out treason, and a good friend to have in a fight. But you know, with his background—and I'm not talking about his mother's race —he's a bit, well, a bit odd."

"What background?" Caroline asked. Even now, when it broke her heart to speak of him, she couldn't help but wish to know more about him.

"Caro, you will never repeat this, will you?"

"I know how to keep secrets."

"All that traveling back and forth between England and India," William said. "I've been thinking about it since we heard from him. No one really knows a thing about his trips. They're all hush-hush. I'm thinking cloak and dagger stuff, if you take my meaning. It would explain a lot about him."

"He's a spy?"

"I believe so," William said. "For England, of course. But still, it makes him quite unsuitable for you."

"A spy," Caroline whispered, and a chill went down her spine. In India. For some reason, Ram Dass appeared in her thoughts, his dark, mysterious eyes, his proud stance, his sculpted lips and high cheekbones, the nobility of his gaze fixed on her face, the gentle, mellifluous tones of his accented English.

Ram Dass the outsider. Just as she had been an outsider.

But Caroline, it seemed, was no longer an outsider, and Ram Dass, who looked so like Headleymoor . . . Was it possible? Had he played that game for years, to extract secrets for England?

Had the man played two roles with her all this time? Had he manipulated her, first in one glittering guise and then in another, softer one? Had he laughed about using her thus for weeks?

She tried to still the shaking, but could not. She thought of her proposing a match with Ram Dass, and closed her eyes in mortification. If it were true that Headleymoor and Ram Dass were one and the same, if he had hidden his identity from her all those times, then whatever she'd felt for him had to be a lie.

Oh, she would hate him for the rest of her life.

She clenched her hands together and managed a smile. "I should be delighted to meet your friend, William. Who is this man who wishes to court me?"

"Name's Gerard Visigore—Viscount Fortbras. He'll be the Earl of Latham when his papa puts his spoon in the wall. Seems that after one look at you, he was as love-struck as a young chit. Well, not that you're a young chit—you've much too much sense to be led by the heart, Caro.

"He's asked almost every day how you fare," William went on with a huge smile. "He's been that eager for your recovery—that's what we've put about, you know—so he can present himself. He's an important man, Caro. Wealth, presence, just ask Mama. And if you don't find him to your liking, several of my friends will be down with him at this to-do Mama has arranged. You'll have your pick, old girl, and won't that show all the matrons who've been such bi—pardon me, Caro—such busybodies forever."

He leaned over and gave her an awkward hug. "They're all

singing a different tune now, and everyone wants to know you. I'm so glad for you, Caro. I've always known you'd shine if only—well, there's no more trouble now, and this last adventure is just known among the four of us. His grace has been a regular out and outer about it all, and he's to be here, as well, if you will agree to it."

Caroline thought about the duke—her father, for heaven's sake—and how he'd seemed to know when she needed quiet and when to just talk about nothing of note without expecting that she speak.

For years, she had wondered what he'd thought when he learned that Mama was with child. Had he been relieved that he would never have to acknowledge her? Had he ever wondered about her? For now, it seemed that Mama and William were content to be in his company after all the rumors and hurtful slights.

Caroline wasn't so sure. She was too angry, too hurt by—by someone other than the duke, but then, the duke was a man too, was he not? She would withhold trust in that quarter, as well.

"I shall look forward to the house party, William. And to meeting the Viscount Fortbras."

Mama walked in on this last. "William's convinced you that this house party will be delightful, hasn't he?" She clapped her hands. "This is just what you need, my love. I'll send for Madame Millefleur. She will know just what gowns will look the most charming on you. I must say, Caroline, I never saw you in better looks than the night of that terrible attack in Buckingham Palace. Madame's choice of color for your gown was exquisite."

Only, Caroline thought as a band of steel clamped about her heart, it was not Madame Millefleur who had chosen the rose material of her gown.

"We shall dispel all memories of that terrifying night with the pleasures to come," Mama said with a smile.

Caroline managed a smile to reassure her mother that all was well.

If only that were true.

Two weeks later, Caroline stood beside her mother and her brother as they welcomed guests to Eversleigh. The house was filled with late spring flowers. Stone urns of pink and blue hydrangea graced the wide staircase leading up to bedchambers, and in each guest's chamber were vases of fragrant English roses from the gardens, where forget-me-nots of blue and pink grew side by side with giant pink snapdragons.

Their scent filled the whole house, and Caroline took deep breaths in between the enthusiastic compliments of ladies who had so recently pretended they didn't know her mother and her. But Mama looked ten years younger and her smile glowed with delight and real happiness.

This restoration of her mother's proper place in Society and the happiness that Mama now enjoyed with the duke was something that only Headleymoor, through his former attentions, could have given her, and for that, at least, Caroline couldn't truly hate him. She could resent, mistrust and be furious with him, of course. That was still more than possible.

The wheels of an elegant black barouche crunched on the gravel, and a man with blond hair so light it seemed to shimmer white in the sun, and eyes that crinkled with warmth and amusement, leaped out of the carriage, throwing the reins of his team to his tiger, still sitting in the open carriage. A footman ran down to the barouche and, bowing to the gentleman, took his trunk.

"That's the fellow who's mooning over you, Caro," William whispered, leaning toward her. "He's a fine whip, one of the best, and his horses have won at Ascot."

The man's smile deepened as he took the stairway. He was of average height, but his legs and shoulders were heavily muscled, she could see, as he strode toward her in his caped driving coat.

When he reached them, he bowed over her mother's hand. "What pleasure it gives me to see your daughter recovered at last, Lady Eversleigh," he said with a broad smile. "If you would be so kind as to introduce me, I should like to tell her myself how concerned all of Society has been for her health and her peace of mind."

"Of course, my lord. And may I say how very much we've enjoyed the bouquets of roses and lilies you've sent for the last week. I am sure Caroline will wish to thank you, herself. Caroline, my dear, this is Gerard Visigore, Lord Fortbras. Lord Fortbras, my daughter, Lady Caroline Berring."

Caroline curtsied as the viscount bent over her gloved hand. He seemed to spend a great deal of time pressing his lips against her hand, but his touch was not repulsive to her. Was that the best she could do—marry a man whose touch was not repulsive?

She mentally shook herself. She was not about to marry anyone. But if this man wished to flatter her, there was nothing she'd rather have at the moment. Her sore heart and the old feelings of inadequacy that had sprung up again at Headley-moor's rejection prompted her to manage a smile.

Fortbras straightened, his answering smile emanating good humor. "If I may be so bold, you are in delightfully fine looks, my lady. I was concerned that your ordeal would leave you wan and fearful, but I can see that you have recovered admirably."

It was really the gown that Madame Millefleur had designed, Caroline knew. The sky blue color complimented her eyes, and hair. That was what she got for finally freeing herself from wearing brown. But then, it had been Ram Dass who had freed her. Or perhaps his alter ego, Lord Headleymoor. For the last two weeks, there had been no word of the man. It was as though he'd disappeared from the universe.

And then, yesterday she'd learned from the duke that he was truly preparing to disappear.

He had written the duke a letter to inform him—or Caroline, should the duke choose to show her the missive—that he would leave England in a few days, for India and Zaranbad. He would be gone for several years, the letter said. He regretted Caroline's enforced stay at Valoir and asked pardon of her for any inconveniences that time might have caused her.

As if one could call the dull weight of misery she carried on her shoulders an inconvenience!

But Gerard Visigore, the Viking viscount as she'd dubbed him, stood before her now, all sunny nature and compliments, and why should she even think of Valoir for another moment?

"I hear you love to ride, Lady Caroline," Lord Fortbras' strong voice cut across her thoughts. "I would be delighted to see your stables. Perhaps tomorrow morning we could ride out together for an hour? Would that suit, Lady Margery?"

"If Caroline takes her groom along with her, I am certain that would suit perfectly."

"I shall look forward to it," the viscount said. "And may I say again how relieved we all are that after such an ordeal as you suffered, you are looking as lovely as you did that night I first saw you, at the Wimbley ball?"

"You flatter me, my lord," Caroline said with a self-conscious laugh.

"I but tell the truth, my lady, and if it flatters, it is only a mirror I hold up for you to see yourself as I see you."

Before Caroline could think of what to say to such a public wooing, Fortbras bowed and walked into the house, with a leisurely stride that signified complete self-assurance bordering on arrogance. Caroline began to wonder what she would think of him after a few days of association. Perhaps she would become used to such intensity and flattery.

"Caroline, by God, I swear. If we get out of this alive, I'm going to kill you."

The shocked, exasperated, ironic words of another man and another time gripped her.

What did it matter? At least Lord Fortbras seemed to be genuine, if a bit overwhelming in his style of wooing.

Another carriage stopped at the front walk and a man stepped down from it, dressed in relaxed country clothing—light woolen trousers and a heather-brown tweed jacket with a light brown waistcoat and cravat. His dark blue eyes crinkled as he surveyed her standing at the top of the stairs. A very handsome, tall man with a certain military bearing about him. Nearing, she thought in dismay. Here to right the wrong his friend had done her.

The wild plains of America looked better all the time.

"Eversleigh, Lady Eversleigh, Lady Caroline." Nearing bowed over her hand, his eyes kind and merry at the same time. This was a man she could like, she realized, as a friend. A true friend. Impulsive, overbearing, and wise, Nearing was exactly the sort of man she could depend upon . . . but never love.

"How are you?" he asked without preliminaries, without flattery, without guile. Refreshing, that.

"I am, as you see, somewhat recovered," she said.

"Only somewhat?" he asked, gazing down at her with narrowed eyes.

"Never fear, Nearing. The experience seems to have left me with a *determination* to recover, but it might take a little time."

"I see," he said. "Lady Eversleigh, might I borrow your daughter for a stroll in the garden?"

"Borrow away, dear boy," Mama said. "I know she'll come to no harm with *you*." Her subtle underscoring of the pronoun made Caroline realize just how much Mama disliked Headley-moor.

Nearing placed her hand on his arm and they walked around the house toward the garden. As soon as they'd gotten away from the crowd, Nearing bent over her with a look of grave concern.

"Caroline, are you still bruised from the events of that night?"

She stifled the urge to shriek or cackle like a madwoman. "Which events, my lord? Witnessing a battle with much blood and anguish in it? Or being virtually left at the altar by Head-leymoor?"

"Which was worse?" he asked with his usual bluntness. How grateful she was for that.

"The latter, I assure you," she said. There was no reason to dissemble with Nearing. After all, she would not wish him to be in the same position in which Headleymoor had placed her—confused and hopeful and in tumult every moment.

"I see. Did the blackguard break your heart?"

She nodded with a smile that didn't quite come off as well as she'd hoped it would. There was no need to hide from Nearing what she'd hidden from Mama and William these past weeks.

"I'm afraid so," she said. "But I'm strong, Maxim. Stronger than I ever thought I could be. I shall recover. It will take time, but I shall do so. And apparently, there are others who would take my mind from such memories. William has been talking to one of them, and I should like to know your feelings about the man."

"Which one, my dear?" Nearing said, bless him. He seemed to have recovered a little, himself, from the mad and sudden infatuation he'd had for her. Caroline was glad that it was only infatuation. This was a good man, one she would not wish to hurt.

"Gerard Visigore, Lord Fortbras. I'm to ride with him tomorrow."

Nearing's hand had clutched hers hard, and he was looking at her with a fierce expression.

"Maxim? What is it?" she asked him.

"Anyone but Fortbras, Caroline. I cannot tell you why, but you must not ever think of marriage with that man. Do you understand?"

"Does this have something to do with Headleymoor?"

Nearing's expression gave him away before he could answer. "I am not at liberty to say, but you must not encourage him. You should not ever be alone with him."

She was shocked at the intensity of his tone. They walked on for a moment, beneath a trellised archway festooned with blushing pink climbing roses. And in that moment, it came to Caroline that Headleymoor and Fortbras were enemies.

"Headleymoor hates him, doesn't he?"

Nearing nodded.

"Good."

"Caroline!"

She stuck her fists on her hips. "Don't act the shocked vicar. I do as I please, Maxim. And it pleases me to ride with Visigore tomorrow. Headleymoor no longer has any say as to what I do or don't do."

Nearing swiveled about until he stood in front of her, his lips set in a stubborn line. Caroline suddenly thought of the woman he'd eventually marry, and hoped to heaven he'd meet his match. "I shall tell William to lock you in your chambers."

She tossed her head. "William will just laugh at you. He admires Visigore."

"He's dangerous, Caroline. I swear to you."

Nearing looked so somber that she relented. "Pax," she said, and laid her hand on his arm. "I promise you, I shall take my groom. If there is any sign of trouble, Henry won't let anything happen to me."

"Don't let it go too far, Caroline. Promise me that, too."

"I judge character fairly well, Maxim," she said with a smile. "I've had a good amount of time to observe. I am not a fool, and I do not believe that anyone, at this point, can misrepresent himself again to me and get away with it."

"Remember, my dear, the old words about pride."

"The only fall I'll take will be from Firefly, if he's not been exercised in a while. I'm rusty after a few weeks out of the saddle and looking forward to a good gallop."

"This worries me, Caroline. I am glad that I am here to look after you a little. And my dear, should you change your mind and feel that you are indeed recovered, I would be honored if you would again consider my proposal."

"Honored, I am sure," Caroline said, and squeezed his arm. "But not quite as ecstatic as you might have been a few weeks ago."

Nearing frowned darkly. "Are you implying that I am a shallow man, incapable of feelings that last?"

She patted his arm, sorry that propriety would not allow her to give him a hug. He was so dear and unaffectedly complimentary in his sense of affront.

"Not at all. You are capable of the noblest, deepest love. Just not for me, Maxim. And aren't we glad that we've discovered it before it was too late?"

"What do you believe it was, then?"

"A charming infatuation, brought about by a very flattering feeling of lust."

"Caroline! The things you say." Nearing actually blushed, right up to the dark lock of hair that curled over his brow.

"Why? I heard you say the same thing that night so long ago—was it only a month?—in the garden at Wimbley House."

212

Nearing's hand rose and covered his eyes. "God, I'd almost forgotten that."

"I'm a different person from the girl I was that night. And I am flattered that you desired me, Maxim. I truly am."

Nearing just shook his head and put his hands on his hips. "Your brother must be going through hell worrying about where you left your maidenly sense of shame."

She laughed and took his arm again. For a moment, they walked on together in silence. And all she could think was: *Headleymoor would not look at me like that if I'd spoken so to him. He would have understood that, after all that happened, honesty is the only way to deal with such things as serious as tying oneself to another for the rest of one's life.*

She looked up to see Nearing's face take on a look of absolute doom.

"Tell me honestly, Caroline," he said carefully. "Did Headleymoor do anything to you while you were under his protection? Did he in any way do things that made you unhappy or shocked you?"

She shook her head. "No. And he gave me to know that when we married, he would not do so then, if I did not wish it."

Nearing stared hard at her. "He offered a marriage devoid of intimacy? Dear God, he must have cared a good deal."

"I believe it was his lack of interest in the prospective bride that prompted his relinquishment of his—what does one call them?—his conjugal rights. But yes, with me, that is perhaps what he wished."

"I see." Nearing strode on so fast she had to almost run to keep up with him.

"Maxim," she finally said. "If you wish to set a fast pace, please do so alone, before I get a stitch in my side."

He turned to face her, and she slipped her hand from his arm. "Did he say anything at any time about why he offered a sham marriage to you?"

"Oh, dear," she said. "I must tell you everything, and you will see me for the real Caroline at last. The best he could come up with was the statement that he didn't wish to put me in danger."

She shrugged. "Now, thinking about it, I would imagine that he was horrified when I not only accepted his proposal but also told him I would accept him in my bed."

Maxim made a choked sound, but Caroline was working something out aloud, and she was not at all concerned about shocking him. "When he seemed to find me . . . attractive, I assumed that he was interested in that aspect of our relationship, as well. But then, that last night, he found another way to release himself from his promise. A story that Mama and William could spread about London as to my fragile health and overset emotions. His relief must have been prodigious. He thought he could use the same excuse he's used before—that his very presence put me in danger—and I would believe it."

She turned to Maxim and said with all her grieving, wrath-filled heart, "Only I've changed, Maxim. Through these last weeks, I've become less malleable. I shall never allow a man to hurt me like that again, nor will I conform to Society's ideas of frail womanhood. If I choose to marry, it will be to a man who accepts me as an equal. I shall stand beside him and fight beside him. I shall not be manipulated and I shall not accept pretty lies."

She sighed and kept very still for a moment. She wanted to say it all for once and have it out and over without tears. "Head-leymoor never really wanted me as his wife. His desire was much more . . . of the moment. So you see, Maxim," she said, trying very hard to smile at him, "why I was so flattered by your . . . interest. Was that a more maidenly word?"

"I think I do see, my dear. Poor old Dev," he said almost to himself. "All this time I thought that he'd got caught up in his own scheme. But now I'm afraid that he's made the worst mistake of his life."

"It's no longer my concern, is it?" she said. *What mistake?*

"Caroline!" William waved from across the lawn, and she waved back.

"Come along, Maxim," she said. "I believe there is tea by the lake now."

But Caroline had little time to think about Nearing's words. The next day brought a beautiful, cool morning, and Caroline met Gerard Visigore, Lord Fortbras, at the stables, where Henry was already bridling Firefly for her.

"My dear Lady Caroline," Visigore said with a broad smile, bending over her hand again and casting an admiring look at the tight jacket and long skirt of her blue riding habit. She felt the heat of his glance all the way through her. Why did it not ease the loneliness within her? She was a fool not to enjoy this man's obvious admiration. It would be good for her to bask in it for a while. Wouldn't it?

"You look the picture of summer today," he continued. "That lovely riding habit echoes the blue of the sky. Only your eyes are brighter. I should like to keep them that bright and merry."

She smiled at him. "We are lucky to have such a clear sky and a cool breeze. We can really let the horses free for a good run."

A frown etched the lines in Visigore's face, and for some reason Caroline shivered. "Perhaps we shall go a bit slower than a run today, my dear, until we see how well your horse goes beneath you and how easily you can control him. He is rather large."

"Only sixteen hands, sir. I shall do very well upon him," she said, and watched his lips rearrange themselves into an apologetic smile. At that moment, he looked only handsome and charming, and she wondered at her sudden fear.

"I am taking liberties with you. Please forgive me, for I have no right." He paused for a moment with a meaningful glance at her. "Yet. But if that happy circumstance were to arise, I would be very, very careful with your person. Never would I wish any harm to come to you from actions that you might, without thought, engage in."

"I see. You seem a very careful sort of man," Caroline said. *With your possessions,* she added silently to herself. "Come, let us mount while the dew is still on the grass. And I shall take the meadow very carefully, my lord. To please you."

Oh, dear. She was beginning to dissemble with the best of them. Headleymoor would be pleased with how quickly she caught on to the process.

Fortbras lifted her into the saddle and she forced herself to smile down at him as his hands lingered on her waist. "Henry," she called as they walked from the stable yard. "Stay close today. I do not wish to have a bit of trouble. Lord Fortbras would be very unhappy if I did."

"Aye, milady," Henry said from right beside her in a voice laced with irony. "We wouldn't want to worry his lordship, would we?"

Dev threw the last of his books into the trunk and nodded to Alfred, the footman, to carry it downstairs. He had already taken leave of his father and sent a message to Ari and Janighar. He'd be in Zaranbad before they were and he'd have a chance to see that all was well with Grandfather and the city of Raniphur. When Ari came, they'd travel the land together at the head of the army and make certain that the United Band did not prey on any of their people.

He rather thought it might be a good thing to spend a few years in Zaranbad. He'd been excessively restless these past weeks. Sleep, when he found it, came only after intense athletic exercise and a heavy workload, and even then he didn't sleep well.

His dreams were haunted by visions of Caroline. Sometimes she sat nursing a child in her arms, and smiled up at some shadowy figure whose hand lay on her shoulder in a possessive caress. In others, she was crying, huddled in a corner of a miserable, crumbling cottage in the middle of a forest. As the door to the ramshackle hut opened, a large, forbidding shadow fell over her and she cringed. The shadow became a hulking, brutish monster. She screamed, cowering before a raised whip.

He woke with a start, the sheets wrapped around his body like a noose, his skin clammy and cold from sweat and terror for her. There was only one way to both protect her from his demons and begin to find a sort of sanity, Dev told himself. He had to go away.

For a very long time.

"Will that be all, my lord?" Alfred stuck his head into the doorway and Dev nodded.

His father would be waiting in the large drawing room of Wimbley House to say a last good-bye. That in itself would be painful, for the duke was very proud of title and very insistent upon duty. Dev would have to stand there and bear a lecture before he could take the carriage to Newhaven to board ship.

He sighed and took the long stairway down to the second floor. The doors were open to the drawing room and on this rainy summer day a small fire was lit in the grate, tinting the blues and ivories of the silk wall coverings into a rainbow of color.

Dev paused at the doorway. The duke stood in front of the blaze, his back to Dev. He didn't turn, although Dev cleared his throat as he entered.

"I am so very sorry that you must go," his father said without turning. "Having you here these last months meant the world, you know."

Dev's eyes stung and he blinked away the unruly emotion his father's words caused him. "It meant a lot to me as well, sir," he said.

The duke turned and Dev could see the bleakness in his gaze. "When your mother died, I became the sort of father a boy would never wish. I've known that and regretted it for years. Perhaps that is why you leave me now. After all, why would you agree to honor my dearest wish—to remain home with me, safe and happy, while I still have the strength and health to be a part of your life?" His smile trembled, but it was a brave attempt. "I do not deserve to ask for such a thing, for I was not there when you needed me."

Instantly Dev flashed on childhood memories. *How could you know? God, Father, do not bring that up!* he thought in sorrow. *What purpose would it serve now?*

His father gave him a look of love and guilt. Dev's throat closed on words he might have once said those many years ago, words about his guilt and the sense that life would never be right again. If only there had been a chance long ago to tell his father about what had happened.

"I heard rumors afterward—rumors that I couldn't believe would be true. After all, Harrington had been my school. The fellows had all been rowdy, but not cruel. I—I learned later how many times you had to fight, the names they called you. I left you to face that alone. There is no excuse for it, but I wish you to know that I was trying to get as far as I could from England, with its memories of your mother and the misery of her death.

"I can only be grateful that you had Aubrey and Maximilian to fight at your side. As I should have done. It is a father's duty to protect his child. I failed in mine, and I can only pray that someday you will come back to me and forgive me for not doing so when you needed me."

Dev cleared his throat. His father had always seemed so proud and remote. Dev had no idea that he'd meant something to his father, other than the heir who would follow in his footsteps and not muck it up too badly.

"It's over, Papa," he said, and stepping forward, pulled his father into an awkward hug. "I shall write often and in a few years, once all is calm in Zaranbad, I shall return."

His father hugged him fiercely and then patted him on the back and stepped away, turning to the fire and taking out a handkerchief. Dev waited until he'd blown his nose and tucked the linen back into his coat sleeve.

The duke turned back and nodded. "Well, then," he said in a fair imitation of briskness. "Got enough letters of credit, I suppose? Be sure to see your great aunt in Paris, should you decide to make a stop there."

"I shall, Papa."

The duke smiled at the old name from nursery days. "Keep yourself safe, my boy," he said, and shook Dev's hand.

"Yes, sir." Dev bowed and took the stairs quickly.

In the hall, Simms, the butler, was just opening the door. Before he could step aside, a tall, very familiar figure burst into the hall, turning his head to the butler. "His lordship is where, Simms?"

"Right behind you, Maxim," Dev managed to drawl, despite the tension creeping through his bones and muscles. "I thought you were rusticating in Kent this week."

Maxim nodded, breathless. "Thank God I caught you in time."

Dev grabbed Maxim's arm and pulled him into the library, shutting the door. "What the hell is wrong? Is Caroline ill?"

Maxim gave him a slow, intent look and then nodded imperceptibly. "Worse than that. Gerard Visigore is there. Word has it that he's quite eager to marry her. Plans to ask her any moment."

"Visigore? Christ!" Dev's fists clenched. "Dammit, Maxim, you said you would take care of her."

"Believe me," Maxim said in a voice that Dev knew was every bit as bitter as he felt. "I wanted to. I asked to." Maxim turned his full gaze on Dev and with it, all the power of hundreds of years of aristocratic sangfroid.

"She didn't want me, Dev. She wanted you. And when you so rudely insulted her, I fear she decided that she would do as she pleased. I told her not to ride with Visigore, but she insisted. As we speak, he's paying court to her with those disgustingly extreme compliments that women seem to love. Told her she was like the goddess of spring, and other fustian. She seemed to find him amusing, perhaps more than that."

Caroline, beneath the fist of Visigore? Dev's head pounded. His whole world tilted, thrusting him into that crazed, dangerous tide that would carry him to the one woman he craved and should not have. But it was the only way. Never would he allow Visigore to destroy Caroline as he had done poor, defenseless Jonathan Dinsmore. He swept the thought from his head and concentrated on speed. He needed sense now, not twenty-year-old terror to guide him. He had heard the vague rumors that crept about the ton, and knew that Visigore was just as ruthless today as he'd been at school.

He glared at Maxim. "Which is the fastest route to Eversleigh?" he asked, and ran up the stairs to pack his things.

CHAPTER ELEVEN:
REVELATIONS

Two mornings after her ride with Gerard Visigore, Caroline found herself hiding in a cozy nook on the second floor of Eversleigh. She was unused to talking so much with so many people, and needed a brief respite from all the sound and activity of a country house party.

Still, despite the melancholy she hoped she hid well, she found many of the people she'd talked with sensible and kind. It was almost as though they were relieved to finally be able to speak with her.

As the season for hunting was over, the men organized games that could be played with the ladies in the afternoon—archery and croquet and, on one rainy day, charades.

They made time for more masculine sports, as well. The men all enjoyed shooting, a mounted Point to Point across country from one church steeple to another, and an unplanned bout of games on horseback. They played tag like children, with much laughter and, at William's instigation, an old jousting game, using sticks for lances to catch rings hanging from posts down a long, straight run in the meadow.

William had caught her looking with longing at the game and trotted up to her. Bending from his horse, he whispered, "Sorry, Caro. I know you could top any of these fellows, but the scandal of a girl riding astride would spread through the ton. Visigore would be furious."

She sighed, and off he rode with a backward wave. Gerard

Visigore was a problem she had yet to solve. He'd been at her side constantly since their ride, appropriating the seat next to hers at tea each day, suggesting which sweets would be to her liking. How could he have no realization that she knew exactly which of Cook's pastries were her favorites?

He was insistent that he understood what she needed. For instance, she needed to be "protected" from speaking to too many of the young gentlemen who wished to sit with her, or dance with her.

She couldn't imagine why he'd appointed himself her "protector," given that she very much liked speaking with the others.

If Gerard Visigore was courting her, his courtship was beginning to feel both absurd and stifling.

It was only yesterday that she had begun to understand why he felt it his right to keep her from the others. She'd come back to the stables shortly after dawn, having slipped from the house to ride across fields and streams. The joy of that freedom was still thrumming through her when she spied Visigore sitting astride a steaming horse, his blue eyes alight with admiration and something that made her shudder as well.

"Originally, I had thought you a lady like all others, my dear Lady Caroline. But as I've made your acquaintance, I began to understand the glowing and sometimes rather overly adventuresome spirit within you. And when I saw you run for the stables this early in the morning, I had to follow."

He smiled and gazed at her with a moue that appeared falsely apologetic to Caroline. "Forgive me for seeming to intrude," he said, "but I am very glad I was here to warn you against doing such foolish things again as riding out without a companion alongside. I would be happy in future to ride with you any time you wish. You need but to ask."

He gave her a look of reproach. "That four-foot jump, for

instance," he went on. "As one grows older, one gains an understanding that such things are foolhardy."

Good God, the man had been watching her throughout her whole ride. While she thought herself alone, he had invaded her privacy, sneaking behind bushes and trees to watch her unawares! She felt soiled and sick.

"In my opinion, Lady Caroline," Visigore went on in a maddeningly calm, superior tone, "I realize that you must not assay more than an occasional log across a trail in future, and certainly not at a gallop. I tell you this for your sake. You must have guessed what sentiments provoke me to assure myself of your safety."

She kept herself from placing a hand over her queasy stomach and straightened her shoulders. "Good heavens, sir. I have taken higher jumps that that, and always come through in ripping good form," she said, and Henry appeared at her side, quietly taking the reins from her. "I am flattered that you take such trouble to give me your opinion on these matters, but I assure you, I shall not follow your advice."

"Perhaps not today, my dear," Visigore said with a grim smile. "But someday soon, I expect that your brother and I shall agree that I am the perfect man to advise you on all aspects of your life."

A chill rose up her neck, but she controlled the trembling in her voice as she nodded up at him and smiled. "My brother may think so, but as long as I am determined to remain the mistress of my own destiny, the point is moot. Good day, my lord."

She motioned to Henry to help her down, so that Visigore could not so much as touch the hem of her gown.

I can't wait until he leaves, she thought now in her perfect hiding place, sitting back and closing the curtain drawn over the alcove even tighter. She just hoped that he didn't importune her with an embarrassing offer that she would indeed refuse. She shuddered thinking of the discomfort that occasion would bring her.

Today, in her secret alcove, she could escape from all of this and read Mr. Dickens's *A Christmas Carol* for an hour. She was almost at the end and was terribly worried about Tiny Tim.

At a noise from the corridor on her left, she surfaced from the dreadful vision the Ghost of Christmas Yet to Come pointed out to Scrooge. Someone was coming down the hallway. She peeked round the curtain of the alcove and when she saw who it was, scrunched deeper behind it. Gerard Visigore strode toward her, dressed in breeches, coat and boots, with a whip in his hand. Other footsteps walked by her hiding place and she quietly took another peek.

It was a slender young man named Peeps, Visigore's valet. He stopped mid-stride a little beyond the alcove, and let out a small sound, like the screech of a rabbit caught in the jaws of a wolf.

Caroline peeked again to see what he'd found—had a bat flown in a window?

But all he saw was Visigore, evidently. The viscount gave his valet a narrow-eyed look that had Caroline covering the gasp that almost escaped her lips.

"I am very displeased, Peeps," Visigore said in a voice of soft menace. He pointed to his boot, where a bit of the blacking had not been polished to as high a sheen as the rest of the boot.

"I am so very sorry, my lord," Peeps said in a trembling voice.

"You should be. There is no one so inept as you are, Peeps. It is a wonder I keep you on, but I suppose it is in your interest to remain in my service and try yet again for a small degree of competence. For I could never give you a reference, should you decide that another master would be easier to fool."

"I did not see the spot, my lord. Honestly, I did not. Please,

please do not be angry with me. There wasn't much light and—"

"Are you saying that I have denied you enough candles to do your job properly? Do you dare to accuse me?"

"Oh, no, my lord. I wouldn't do that. You know I wouldn't."

"I know nothing of the sort. I know you are a disobedient sneak and that you deserve to be punished. On your knees now."

Caroline clutched the curtains together. Mesmerized and horrified, she peered through the slit. The valet sank to his knees and bent until his head pressed the floor. His shoulders trembled and she could hear the stifled sobs as he remained in that dreadful, subservient position.

Then she caught sight of Visigore's eyes. They glittered with anticipation and something else that made her nauseous.

The whip rose. She cringed back in the alcove, shuddering and shaking as she heard the first crack.

"Admit it, Peeps," Visigore said in a purr. "You are a vile, worthless piece of offal, not fit to lick my boots. Say it!" The whip cracked again, and again, and the servant whimpered.

Again it came, and again, and sobbing, the man cried out, "I am . . . a vile . . ."

"Say it all, Peeps," Visigore said softly, and Caroline could hear a smile in his voice.

"Worthless," Peeps shrieked as the whip cracked again. Caroline gagged.

Somehow, the valet got the rest of it out.

"Very good, Peeps," Visigore said in a croon. "You may now kiss my boot. Later, I shall tell you what else you may do for me."

Caroline heard the soft sound of a body collapsing on the floor. A moment later Visigore strode past her hiding place, whistling a tune and slapping the whip against his boots in time. She sank against the wall and held her breath as he passed, cursing herself for being such a coward. But she was sick to her stomach with fear.

Had she not sensed something in Visigore that repelled her, the person writhing and sobbing on the floor outside her alcove could very well have been her.

Not even on the night of the Queen's ball, when she felt the sharp, cold steel at her neck had she been as afraid as she was now. She waited a moment, trying to still the shaking that wracked her body. And then she crept out of the alcove.

The servant Peeps lay where he had presumably collapsed. She could hear sobs coming from the man and see his shoulders heaving. His black coat was ripped and through the severed strips of cloth, she could see blood.

She knelt and put her hand on his shoulder. He stiffened and flung himself away, his eyes wild with terror.

"Peeps, I am the lady in whose home you find yourself. Are you dissatisfied with your master?"

"Oh, my lady," Peeps moaned, and he hid his face in his arms.

"You needn't say a word. But if you would like employment in this house, I offer it to you. Without need of a reference. Do you understand?"

Peeps nodded, his head still hidden from her.

"I will take you to Munson, our butler. He and Cook will help to clean your wounds and when you are healed, you will take up your duties here. Is that all right with you?"

Peeps nodded again.

"Good," she said, sick at heart for him and what he must have experienced in service to Visigore. "When you are ready, Peeps. Until then, I shall sit beside you, very quietly." She gave him a few more minutes to cry in that silent, heartrending way.

Then she said, very softly, "Many times, when I've felt sad, I've found that a story will take me away from that sadness. Would you like me to tell you the story I've been reading?"

He nodded, and she began. For a short time, she told him all about the ghosts of Christmas present and past and still to be. And he slowly sat up, and then, stiffly, stood. Together, they made their way down the back stairs, and Caroline introduced Peeps to Munson as the new footman who'd just been hired to help at Eversleigh.

A few moments later, she climbed the stairway, feeling ancient as a crone, the horror of what she'd seen and heard still roiling in her stomach.

Visigore was mad. What he could do to those beneath him was a horror that must be stopped. But how?

While she thought and planned, she would avoid him at all costs. And she had already made it plain to all those below stairs that no one, *no one* was to reply to the summoning of his bell but Bridge, who weighed at least fourteen stone and wrestled any takers in the village. She made her way to the meadow, where William and two footmen were setting up targets for shooting practice.

"I'm sorry, Caro. Men only, you know," he said with a smile of regret for her.

"Will, I must talk to you. Immediately," she said. As she told him, the line of his mouth grew set and grim.

"It was horrifying, Will," she whispered.

William's eyes narrowed. "One can only wonder what else Visigore has done to that poor man. What else he's done to others who were in his thrall." William turned to her, his gaze full of fire and intensity. "Bridge is to answer his bell?"

She nodded.

"Good. I'll be sure to put it about that I trust Bridge implicitly. Visigore will not dare to touch him."

Caroline shuddered. "I can't think of anything worse than being within a hand's breadth of that man."

"Just one more night and he will be gone, Caro. But in the

meantime, you must never, ever see the man alone. Do you understand?"

She nodded. "I was a coward, Will. I could have run out into the hall and stopped it. But I was afraid."

He put his arms around her. "I'm so glad you didn't. God, to have you that close to him, alone, unprotected! It makes me furious and sick at the same time just to think of it. He might well have taken the whip to you, too. And when I think that I gave him permission to ride out with you. Thank God Henry was there. Henry's strong and wiry, but small all the same."

William did shudder at that. "Visigore will be busy this afternoon. We've arranged an informal steeplechase from Eversleigh to Maidstone. Stay here, away from him. And tonight, at the ball, say your dance card is full. I'll have one of the fellows take you in to supper. We'll keep you safe from him, Caro."

He stared down at his shoes then up into her eyes with a rueful smile. "I've not been much of a brother, I know. But I promise you on my life. You will be safe."

Later that afternoon, Caroline, deep in thought, left the little cottage where Peeps rested. Before the party had left for the steeplechase, she'd been careful to leave a message for her brother as to where she was going, and had slipped from the house without further notice. She needed fresh air and sunshine and the feel of life around her to dispel the sense of horror she'd felt earlier today.

The thing about safety, she thought as she walked back home, was that only the lucky ones could be assured of it. If one had wealth, a title, and a caring family, one was protected from villains like Gerard Visigore. But there were a great many more Peeps in the world than Lady Caroline Berrings.

It wasn't fair. And she was determined to do something about it. Just what she could do she hadn't discovered yet, but a problem was something that needed a solution. It didn't matter how small a difference she could personally make in solving it— she had to do something.

She trod the path past the lake toward a little creek that burbled over rocks and down in little falls as it meandered its way through the wood. Birdsong filled the late spring air. Not five feet from her, a robin fought with a worm, and she stopped to admire his tenacity. She held back a laugh, enjoying the sunshine and the wind soughing through the trees. Tomorrow all the guests would be gone and she could ride however she wished across the fields and meadows of Eversleigh.

How she longed for tomorrow and the end of this masquerade. She needed more time to forget everything that had happened since the first night Headleymoor had asked her to dance.

She stopped beside the brook and knelt to cup her hands and drink from the icy, pure water. She was bent in that position when she felt the sudden cold of a shadow blocking the sun. A chill rose on the back of her neck. She turned swiftly to see behind her, straining to look up.

Gerard Visigore smiled down at her, looming just as he'd done over poor Peeps. And she, kneeling beneath him, was in the exact position of servility as Peeps had been when Visigore had so brutally beaten him. In haste, she rose and wheeled to face him. Her fists clenched and she stared at him, doing her best to keep all expression from her face.

"My dear," Visigore said with a smile that held a gruesome, glittering anticipation. "I am delighted to meet you in this quiet, romantic spot where no one could possibly disturb our tête-à-tête."

Dev leaped from the carriage and ran up the stone stairway of Eversleigh. He banged loudly on the lion's head knocker. After what seemed an eternity, a tall man with thinning hair opened the door and stared at him with that supercilious air that immediately identified him as the butler.

"I must speak with Lady Caroline immediately," Dev said in his most commanding voice. "Be kind enough to tell her that Lord Headleymoor begs to attend her as soon as may be."

The butler's eyes grew wide and then narrowed to a piercing lance. "Lady Caroline may well not be at home to *you*, my lord."

"Tell her it is of the greatest urgency that I speak to her. Tell her that her safety is in jeopardy. She will speak to me then."

"I shall ask her, my lord." The butler disappeared up the grand stairway.

Dev stood in the hall, hearing nothing but the usual bustle of servants. Where were the other house party guests? Where was the family? A sound behind one of the doors leading into the large, open hallway had him turning to see two maidservants, staring at him with wide eyes. Immediately, the door slammed shut and he heard the sound of light, running footsteps away from him. What terrible things did they think of him in this household?

A few moments later by his pocket watch, the butler returned, followed by a burly footman with a troubled look on his face.

"Lady Caroline left the house an hour ago, my lord," the butler said. "No one has seen her since. And Lady Margery and Lord William are gone with the guests."

The footman cleared his throat. "You the man wot took Lady Caroline from the palace, 'ent ye, m'lord?"

"I am he," Dev said.

"And you ken how to fight?" the footman asked.

"I do." The sense of foreboding that had begun upon his entrance into Eversleigh increased in intensity.

The footman nodded to the butler. "Mr. Munson, ye' can trust him."

"I do not know what to do, my lord," the butler said. "We were given instructions to keep Lady Caroline safe from a certain member of the party. We had thought him gone to join in the steeplechase with the other gentlemen. But one of the maids saw him walking out about a half hour ago. Can you help us?"

The butler, so proud and scornful earlier, looked distraught now.

Dev badly wished to shout and rave at whatever wicked gods had kept him late by an hour. "Summon the servants," he said. "Quickly, man. One of them will know where she went."

He took the back stairway to the kitchen two steps at a time, and gathered them all round the huge wooden table. They sat, staring up at him, their eyes wide with fear and concern.

"I can see you all care about Lady Caroline. If anyone knows where she went, you must tell me immediately," he said.

The servant grapevine must have been at work here, for a kitchen maid slowly raised her hand and stood, trembling. First she looked to the butler. "Mr. Munson, is it all right to tell the secret?"

"It is all right to tell anything, Megan, if it will keep our lady safe."

"She took a basket from the kitchen before she left, and she put a book in it. She didn't tell me where she was going, but we all know of the poor man who is hiding in Granny Sophie's cottage. I think she went there, to help him."

"She has a kind heart, my lord, and would help all the world if she could," another maid said, turning to Dev, her tone a plea. "If you could but bring her back safe, we'd be ever so grateful."

"Tell me the way to this cottage and I shall do my best," Dev said, and in a moment, he had the direction he needed.

A lad ran from the kitchen, tugging on his cap as he slammed the door behind him.

"He's one of the grooms, my lord. He'll get you a mount. The best in the stable. If you would come wi' me now," the stable master said.

"Send men after me. Two will do."

The footman stepped forward at once, and another man, a tall gardener with broad shoulders.

Once outside the house, Dev ran toward the stable, the stable master and the two men following. When they reached the large stone building, a groom poked his head from the huge doorway, a horse already saddled—a glorious bay.

"Hullo," Dev said, patting the bay's neck.

"Jem told me to have one ready," he said, throwing Dev up into the saddle. "We're following directly. But this 'un's the best we've got. Name's Firefly. Take care of him, my lord."

"I'll be careful with him, never fear." Dev turned the horse and cantered him out of the yard.

He cut across rolling fields of timothy hay, something he'd never have done on his own estates, or any other. But he could hear it in the horse's hoofbeats. Time, rolling inexorably forward, faster, faster, until he was almost frantic with urgency.

"Dear God, let her be safe," he whispered, straining forward in the saddle, bent over the bay, turning in a quick angle toward the forest where he knew the cottage stood.

As he rode through the trees, he caught site of a brook babbling over stones and a clearing far ahead streaked in sunlight.

Dev squeezed his legs tight against Firefly's flanks and the bay responded magnificently. Muscled hindquarters bunched, and they flew over the brook, landing in stride, galloping now, weaving in and out around trees, over fallen logs, faster than the wind. To his right, a branch hung low over the path, half broken from the tree. Dev grabbed at it, and it broke into his hand.

CHAPTER TWELVE:
TRIAL BY COMBAT

Caroline backed away, her gaze fixed on Visigore's face. His blue eyes glittered like shards of ice. The smile on his face reminded her of a cougar she'd once seen in a portrait by an American artist. It was ready to spring on a small doe, cornered against a high rock wall.

She could not give way to fear. She'd seen what fear had done for poor Peeps.

Visigore smiled and bowed at the waist, and Caroline wondered how she could ever have thought this man handsome.

"My dear Lady Caroline, I must tell you the secrets of my heart," he said in a warm, caring voice.

I'd rather not know any more of your secrets, she thought. "I do not believe that we know each other so well as yet, my lord, for you to be opening your soul to me," she said with what she prayed was a believably carefree laugh.

"Yet I must, my lady. I took one look at you and knew that you were destined to be mine forever. It is early, I realize, for you to think of me as your affianced husband, but I have had longer to muse upon how very much I have come to care for you. To depend upon you for my happiness. Surely your brother has recently given me every reason to hope," he said with a smile that Caroline might have accepted as open and honest before recent events showed her his stained soul. "I believe that today, in this private sylvan spot, I shall be able to convince you of the reasons why you must make me the happiest man alive

233

and marry me."

Caroline madly attempted to discover some decent phrases that would put him off long enough to return to the house.

"I am indeed mindful of the great, no the *very* great honor you do me, my lord. I am only sorry that I must refuse your suit. After my, ah, ordeal at Buckingham Palace, I am too over-set to wed anyone at this time. But I must tell you how grateful I am for your kindness and, ah, gentleman-like manner."

"Oh, come now, Caroline," Visigore said with the first hint of impatience in his voice. "I am just the sort of man you need to protect you from the cruelty of the world."

Caroline knew exactly how Visigore "protected" those who depended upon him. With effort, she quelled the urge to laugh hysterically.

However, the moment passed as Visigore continued with his argument. "Had I been invited to the palace that night, I would have fought those villains so that you never would have been at-tacked. You do not understand these things yet. You are just a girl, really."

He took a step toward her, his smile almost carnivorous. She stepped backward, and then stopped and straightened her shoulders. With Visigore, she instinctively realized, one must never show weakness. It only spurred him to do his worst.

"You cannot really know how these things work, my dear. Often, a man simply has to take charge and show his beloved that he and she are meant to be together. Today I shall make your own desires clear to you, and by the time we have finished our private . . . discourse, you will realize that there is only one choice for you, and that is to accept my offer, and become my wife as soon as may be."

A horrifying glitter emanated from his eyes, and his move-ments were steady and slow as he walked closer. She realized with a gag of real terror that he was mad.

"Come," he said with another step. "I shall make it easy for you to accept my proposal. You will love it, Caroline. Everyone does, you see. In the end, you will beg for it."

His voice came to her through the thundering of panic in her ears. Speak. She had to speak and buy time. But how did one convince a madman of anything?

"I appreciate your . . . sentiments. However, I find myself suffering from the heat of the day. Come, let us go back to the house and discuss your terribly flattering offer together in the coolness of the drawing room," she began.

Visigore came on with that same twisted smile. "There is nothing to discuss. Now you will see how it will be between us, and there will be no turning back."

She was vaguely aware of the sound of hoofbeats quite close. She looked up. A shadow rider sprang from the forest like a vengeful god, leaping the brook and galloping toward them, his hand raised, some sort of weapon in it.

Visigore had barely time to turn before the hand swung down, hard, and the weapon hit him in the skull. He let out a gulp of surprise and fell like a rock. The rider came on, leaned over and swept her up, never breaking stride.

She screamed, flailing, punching, struggling.

"For God's sake, Caroline," Dev said in a voice as tight as a hunter's trap. "I'm saving you from a fate worse than death. Be so kind as to let me get on with it."

Caroline did not say another word on the way back to Eversleigh, Dev thought glumly. Bridges and the stable master galloped toward them a couple of moments after he'd turned the horse toward home.

"She's safe?" Bridges shouted.

Dev nodded and pointed to the grove behind. "There's some trash to pick up back by the cottage. Can you do that, Bridges?"

"Gladly, milord."

"Very good." Dev squeezed the bay's sides and Firefly sprang forward, cantering the path toward the stable.

Caroline sat before him on the saddle with her arms stubbornly crossed over her chest to keep from touching him. He could tell that she was trying very hard to control the little shudders that coursed through her. She needed comfort, but due to her damned pride, she wouldn't accept it from him.

Exasperated, he pulled her back into his body. "Did he hurt you?" His voice sounded strained to his own ears.

"No," she said, and he wanted to cry his gratitude to heaven.

His arm wrapped round her waist, his hand spreading across stays and starched linen. "I thought you weren't going to wear these things anymore."

"That was before you rejected our bargain and me," she said with a sniff.

"I did not reject you. I gave you a way to walk out on me without suffering any consequences, and you know it!"

"You did reject me! And left me prey to the likes of that monster, while you were at it."

He was just about to say, "did not" again, when the absurdity of the situation came crashing down upon him. The stable appeared around the next bend of the trail, with Henry running toward them.

Caroline noted that Henry looked dreadfully worried. "All's well, my lady?" he shouted across the distance.

"I'm fine," Caroline told him.

To Caroline's way of thinking, Headleymoor leaped from the horse and pulled her down rather too unceremoniously. She landed half across his chest, with one foot on the ground, but he was already tugging her toward the house, calling to Henry, who had the horse's reins in his fist.

"Send some men to set the horses to Visigore's carriage while

Bridges brings him back for disposal. If he comes to, tell him you've orders from Lord William to ask him to leave immediately. Do not allow him entry into the house. And tell him not to worry about packing. His trunk will arrive after him by wagon."

"Yes, my lord," Henry called back, astounding Caroline. Henry never followed orders unless he approved of the man making them.

Munson held the great doors open to the hall as Headleymoor tugged Caroline around the path to the front of the great house. "We need a place that is absolutely private, Munson," Headleymoor said.

"This way, my lord," Munson said with a low bow. "And from the staff, may I thank you for bringing our lady, home? I can see from the scowl on her face that she is safe and sound."

"You're quite welcome," Headleymoor said. If his jaw were any tighter, Caroline thought, his teeth would probably disintegrate beneath the pressure. Yet he held her wrist with firm gentleness that had her rebellious heart melting.

Headleymoor hurried up the wide marble stairway to the second floor and Munson, footsteps pattering behind them, called out, "To your right and two doors down, my lord."

"Thank you, Munson. Your men will return shortly with Gerard Visigore. I doubt he will be too aware of his surroundings. Be so kind as to put him into his carriage and send him home. I should also like tea and brandy as soon as may be."

"Immediately, my lord."

Headleymoor nodded and shoved open the door to a small study, done in cream and sky blue colors. He pulled her gently in behind him and shut the door with a firm click. Then he let her go and looked about. Sketches and watercolors lined the walls.

"These are quite good," he said. "Who did them?"

"I did," she said shortly. In the ensuing silence, she sank into the ivory brocade sofa, knowing that her legs would have given out in another moment. She had just enough time to breathe, and not nearly enough to quell her unruly emotions.

He turned and smiled, and the whole world seemed to glow from his face. How she hated him—and herself for still yearning to be the center upon which that warmth fixed itself.

"You have an astute eye," he said, "and a talent with line and color."

"Thank you." She didn't know what else to say, and then realized that she had something far more important for which to thank him. "I appreciate what you did today. The situation was not a comfortable one."

For the first time, the shudder she had held in check escaped. "Oh, drat. Drat, drat, drat!" She couldn't hold back the tears. They flowed like rivulets down, down, and she was sobbing, helpless to stop.

He was beside her in an instant, and then, somehow, she was on his lap and his arms were around her and she held on for dear life, sobbing into his chest while he rocked her and kissed her forehead, her cheeks, her lips, even as she sobbed and sniffled.

"When I heard that he was after you, my heart literally stopped in my chest," he said fiercely. "How dare he—how *dare* he attempt you?"

She looked up at him through her tears, at his beautiful face with its dark eyes, so kind, so caring. Could it be that he actually did care a little?

"He is a horrible man," she said. "He . . . he hurts people. To be alone with him is to be in hell."

Those eyes grew black with intense emotion that swirled in their depths—emotion that she could not understand. "I know, Cara. I know. He has been this way for a long time."

She rubbed her head back and forth against his shoulder, instinctively snuggling closer into the warmth and strength of him. "Were you at school with him, then?"

He nodded once, sharply, but said no more.

"You must have heard terrible things. Why did they not do something—send him down, tell his parents what they had in him?"

"His family was powerful and the scandal would have caused an uproar in the highest ranks. He left two years later. We arranged it so that he must."

Then she shuddered, remembering poor Peeps and how close a thing it had been for her. She raised her face, praying Headleymoor could give her an answer that would chase the goblins away. "Do you think he might leave England?"

He held her tighter. "I think so. I shall keep watch, as will others."

She blushed, seeming to awaken to the fact that she was sitting on his lap. She made to rise.

He held on. In the fear of what might have happened to her and the memories of his own bitter years, he could not let her go.

"Please, Cara. Not yet," he said softly. "Trust me. Just once more, trust me as you did. It was so close, you see. If I'd been just a little later getting here, he might have . . . oh, God. I need to feel you here, safe and warm beside me. I need to touch you."

He'd called her Cara. Dear one. He'd called her that once before, and then told her that he would not wed her.

She looked into those expressive eyes. He looked sad, and desperate, as though only her touch would make it better.

She realized that, no matter whether he would ever admit it to himself or her, there was an elemental part of him that called to her—in need. And that same part of her answered with an eagerness that overwhelmed her.

"Touch me," she whispered. "Please. I need to feel clean again."

His head bent to her, his lips touched hers. Careful at first, their gentle, inexpressibly sweet pressure caused her to sigh. The moment her lips opened, his tongue entered, delicately taking her mouth in a heady possession, stroking slowly. He groaned, searched the contours of her mouth, as though learning them was the most important thing in the world.

She moved restlessly, the same eager excitement rising in her belly and breasts and between her thighs. She shifted on his lap and he moved beneath her bottom, until she felt a hard ridge of desire pressed against her.

When she'd been nothing but an embarrassment that Society overlooked, she'd listened from corners and heard women talking of such things. She knew some liked the act of joining and some did not. She knew some men were adept at it and some were not even interested.

From all the information she'd gleaned, one thing was clear. Once again, they were alone together, and once again Headleymoor wished to engage in that act. She felt it in the strength of his embrace, the sounds torn from his mouth as he bent her back, kissing and licking the sensitive curve of her neck, the quick fumbling of his hands as he unbuttoned her bodice and reached inside.

She felt it in the catch of his breath as he cupped her breast and said, "I never thought I'd be able to touch you here, and here. I have to see you, Cara." And the look in his eyes as he loosed the ribbon of her chemise and freed her breasts was one of—worship.

This was what she needed. The open, clean presence of desire, to wash away the taint of Visigore's twisted brutality. The fire built in her with Headleymoor's touch, his look that spoke of reverence.

"Do you know your nipples are blush rose, just like the ones you wore in your hair the night of the Queen's ball? And your skin is dusted in gold," he murmured. "How very beautiful you are." His head bent and her back arched and somehow she was lying across his lap, and he was lapping at her nipple and his breath was warm against it, and his lips covered it and he began to suckle and she whimpered and moved against him, hips thrusting, wanting more and she felt his hand on her ankle, and it stroked up her calf, and it was beneath her skirts and petticoats, and her legs opened to give him better access, and she whimpered as he touched her there, where she hadn't ever touched herself, except in her bath, and she said, "Oh, yes . . ."

The door burst open. "Caro," William said from the hall just beyond the doorway. "Munson said you were up here and not to disturb you, but I was too scared not to check on you. That bas—blighter didn't harm you, did he? Willowby and I came back as soon as we realized he wasn't at the steeple."

In the stillness, Caroline shut her eyes in humiliation, while Headleymoor, lightning quick, brought his hand from beneath her skirt and closed her bodice and turned her in his arms, hiding her face in his shoulder.

From the doorway, William cleared his throat and turned to speak to someone behind him. "Not now, Willowby. Very overset by the business of the day."

William's friend mumbled something, and footsteps receded down the hall.

The door to Caroline's study clicked shut, but she could tell there was another presence in the chamber. She dared a quick peek, to see William's face frozen in a lobster-red stare of conflicting fury and shock.

She felt Headleymoor lift her in his arms as he slowly stood to face her brother.

241

Finally, she heard William's sigh of resignation. "I assume that congratulations are in order?"

"Caroline, I think you should go now," Dev said, as he lowered her to her feet and affixed the last button at the neck of her gown.

"But . . ." Caroline stood, looking from her brother to Dev and back again. He realized with a surge of warmth that she didn't wish to leave him alone, as though she could protect him from the unpleasantness to come with her mere presence.

"It will be all right," he said, squeezing her hand. "We shall not come to blows, but an agreement. Go, now. I shall speak to you presently."

She nodded and slipped from the room. He turned and faced William Berring, whom he knew only slightly, as the man was a few years older than he.

"I am sorry that you came in upon that scene, Eversleigh. However, it does not signify. I shall wed Caroline as soon as may be."

"You didn't seem very eager to do so a few weeks ago," William said, and his mouth was grim.

"There was a reason for my refusal. You know that Zaranbadian traitors have jeopardized my family. I sent her away so she could be safe from the blackguards. However, Gerard Visigore has made that problem seem minor compared to what he will do if he can get to her now."

William drew himself up. "Her family will protect her."

"As it did today?"

William had the grace to redden and lower his gaze to the carpet.

"It occurs to me that due to her adventuresome spirit and her bloody inconvenient sense of honor, Caroline gets into the thick of things whether one wills it or not. I may not be everything a man would hope for in a spouse for his sister. But as she seems to attract a shocking amount of trouble on her own, I insist upon being at her side in order to get her out of it."

Eversleigh's jaw had dropped to his stock tie. Then it slammed shut and he glared. Dev reckoned that William wished nothing better than to call him out for his outrageous behavior and his assessment of Caroline. But he'd wager that William was actually furious because he'd been hearing nothing more than the truth.

"If you wish," Dev said. "I shall be happy to prove my worth to her."

Eversleigh arched a brow. "Will you? Then come with me and let us see your proof."

Caroline ran up to her chamber, her body still on fire from Headleymoor's touch and her mind racing with worried questions. What were Headleymoor and William discussing in her study? Why hadn't she insisted upon staying? How could Headleymoor possibly protect himself against William's charges without her there to explain what had happened and why?

She slammed into her chamber and ran to the washstand. The act of pouring water from the pitcher and soaping a washcloth didn't banish the infernal questions racketing round her mind. Staring at her face in the mirror, she gave a low moan.

Would William make Headleymoor marry her, in spite of his unwillingness to do so? Would she have to go through with it, because of what William had just seen? What would she do if Headleymoor agreed to marry her because he pitied her and wished to save her reputation? He would feel like her prisoner, and she, his jailor. She would far prefer a wasting sickness and death to that humiliation.

Moving quickly, she yanked the bellpull and began unbuttoning the top of her riding habit. It was one of her favorites, but in the course of the last hours, she'd gone from wishing to burn it to thinking that it would forever remind her of Headleymoor's strong, warm fingers and his mouth, and his hands everywhere! Even now, just remembering caused a little thrill to wring through her from her still sensitive breasts to her belly, and below, where he had lightly touched her, leaving her damp and aching.

If she were to keep her sanity, she'd better get out of this riding habit quickly.

At a knock on her door, she called out, "Enter."

Megan bustled in, the ribbons on her maid's cap flying. "My lady, you won't believe what they're setting up in the meadow. Such a show as you've never seen in Eversleigh, I warrant. Look!" She pointed excitedly to the window and Caroline, holding the loose bodice to her chest, crossed the bedchamber to look out.

William and a group of the young men who had obviously just returned from the steeplechase were placing pistols out on a table and priming them. Headleymoor stood, silent and dignified, in the midst of all this movement.

Dear Lord, were they about to perform a duel?

"Megan, please help me dress immediately," she said, ripping fabric as she shimmied out of the habit and threw off her boots.

"Here, my lady. Wait and I'll help. Which will you wear, your new rose afternoon gown or the blue silk?"

"I don't care," Caroline said, gazing worriedly out the window. "Whichever is easier to fasten. Hurry. Oh, please hurry!"

"It's the rose, then," Megan said. "I like it the best, anyway."

Like blush roses, Headleymoor had said, and Caroline remembered it all with another wave of liquid heat.

Megan threw the gown over Caroline's head and, settling the

flounced skirt over petticoats, she began to fasten the tiny back buttons of the bodice.

Caroline ran to the window as soon as she was decently clad again. Several servants carrying targets bustled from the formal flower garden to the right of the house. They kept running to the meadow beyond, and set the straw targets down side-by-side.

The shooting began with William and Headleymoor each shooting the first shot together at two different targets. The young men ran to the table, grabbing up the pistols and handing them over to William and Headleymoor, as quickly as they could. The pace quickened as more servants arrived, carrying more loaded pistols. The crack of the guns resounded and echoed through the valley.

Caroline could see from her window exactly when William's arm began to waver. If he'd wished to win, he should have pitted her against Headleymoor, whose aim continued to be rock solid with each shot. Having seen him in action when it counted, she wasn't surprised. Finally, William called out, "Enough!"

Headleymoor lowered his arm slowly, placed the unused pistol into Munson's hand, and stepped back. The servants walked across the meadow and paced off a closer distance. They removed the foolscap targets from the straw backing and put up new ones of canvass.

Then they brought the used targets to the group of young men and held the targets up for perusal. William's shots began in the center and moved outward, spattering the edge of the circles.

On the other hand, Headleymoor had only one hole, albeit a rather large one, in the center of the bull's-eye, where each and every shot had landed.

William nodded and opened his mouth to say something.

Caroline pushed her window open and leaned out in order to

hear his words.

"Knives," William said in a grim voice.

Headleymoor nodded abruptly.

The pistols were taken from the table and several wicked-looking stilettos appeared in their place. The men watching Headleymoor and William set up a cheer.

"Don't let him win too easily!" one of them shouted.

Caroline shut her eyes in mortification.

William threw and the knife landed in the second ring. Thwap! Headleymoor's knife landed in the very center of the bull's-eye. Caroline turned away from the window and paced the room.

Thwap! Thwap! Came from below, and more, and more, until she heard Headleymoor say, "Enough?"

And William said, "Enough of *this*."

Of this? There was to be more? Caroline choked down a scream.

The servants marched out of the house again, this time with four sturdy posts that the head gardener used to stake the climbing pea vines. They hammered the posts into the ground until there were four corners, and then one of the footmen carried a length of rope to the posts and wrapped it round them in two parallel lines to make a square arena. Caroline heard the cheers outside.

"Look, my lady," Megan said leaning out the window. "They're putting up a boxing arena. I've never seen a match. This'll be something to tell my mother about next half day!"

"That is the last straw!" Caroline shouted.

William must have heard her, for he looked up at her window and shouted back, "Caroline, stay where you are. This is a necessary process."

"Fustian!" Caroline shouted. "I shall not have the two of you battering each other's heads today or any other day!"

"I shall not partake of the sport," William shouted back.

With horror, Caroline watched young Edward Willowby unbutton his shirt and hand it to a footman before entering the makeshift ring.

"I mean it, Caroline. Keep out of this," William called up.

Caroline slammed the window so hard that the panes rattled.

"Keep out, indeed. This is the nineteenth century. We are not barbarians," Caroline muttered as she strode out of her bed-chamber. She was furious, and not at all sure if she wished to send William or Headleymoor to blazes.

A moment or two ago, she had felt the greatest sense of con-nection with that man in the ring. But because of the outra-geous things that seemed to happen around him, she was once again becoming an object of ridicule.

She took the stairs quickly, running and sliding across the waxed parquet floor of the ballroom, where several of the ladies of the party were gathered at the large French doors, giggling and pointing toward the garden.

"Headleymoor strips beautifully, does he not?" one of the younger ladies sighed.

"What a lovely chest, and those arms," another said. "Good-ness, there goes Farthinghurst."

"That makes three in as many minutes," Helene Cooperthwait-Dinkens, one of the newlywed women said.

Hussies! How dare they look and gawp? That chest was hers! Caroline pushed through them and ran out the French doors.

Headleymoor stood in the center of the ring, his muscular torso bare, golden, and lightly glossed with sweat. Caroline gawped a bit herself, and found her hands itching to smooth away the sweat, to rub against the hard contours. To feel each inch of him.

What in God's name was she thinking? There sat Lord Far-thinghurst on his rump, leaning heavily back on his arms, his legs out flat in front of him. He shook his head slowly, as though to return his vision from double to single. Other men lined up for their turn at Headleymoor. Sooner or later, that golden god's strength would flag, and someone would hurt him.

Caroline shoved Lord Masterson out of her way. The man staggered a bit in surprise, but that could also be a residual of the blow to the jaw he was covering with that large piece of raw beef.

She walked to the ring and climbed inside, mindless of any petticoats or ankle that might show. Headleymoor stood silent and watchful as a wild wolf, with a quiescent power shimmering through him. She stood next to him and put her hands on her hips.

"What next, William? Swords?" She narrowed her eyes at her brother. "Anyone coming after Farthinghurst fights me. The scandal will rock Society back on its heels, I promise you. Particularly since I shan't follow the Marquess of Queensbury's rules." She patted her knee meaningfully, letting William recognize just exactly how she'd use it if need be.

From the corner of her eye, she watched Headleymoor pull on his shirt. In the midst of her exasperation, she still felt that annoying tingle as she caught the ripple of his chest and abdomen and the curl of his biceps. There was a graze on his cheek and his knuckles were raw, but otherwise he looked as fit as he had when she last saw him in the study.

He stepped close to her. Despite the fact that he didn't touch her, his large, graceful body felt protective. She smelled sweat and clean soap, and his scent, hot and musky, called to her like the Sirens had called Odysseus.

"Enough," Dev said.

William nodded. In a soft voice meant only for their ears,

William said, "I'll inform Mama that we have agreed. You will be wed within the week."

It was so unfair. To make Headleymoor pay with the humiliation of a public test of his manhood. And then, to force him to marry her.

Caroline's blood had cooled enough to remember the truth. Headleymoor wanted her in his bed. But he didn't really want her. He would never love her. And she was beginning to fear that she might well learn to love him. Marrying him would be like damning herself to purgatory here on earth.

"William, don't you dare!" Caroline said, and just like that, Headleymoor grabbed her arm and marched her into the house, past the whispering ladies at the French doors of the ballroom, up the stairs, and left, into her own study where all of this embarrassing nonsense had begun.

He shut the door and latched it behind them, then watched her, his face absolutely still and unreadable.

She skittered backward, then silently castigated herself for her cowardice.

"There is no other way, Caroline," he said firmly.

"It was my fault, my lord. I acted . . . shamelessly. However, I shall not be the woman who snared the great Marquess of Headleymoor with her own ruination."

He took another step toward her, graceful as a big, stalking cat. Oddly, he was smiling. She couldn't imagine how he could find any amusement from the predicament in which he found himself.

"Is that what I am in your eyes?" he asked. "A small, helpless rabbit with no control over my destiny?"

"Of course not! But you should not be punished for having saved me from Visigore's brutality. I can accept ostracism. I am used to it. If I'd wished to redeem myself in Society's eyes, I would have agreed to marry Nearing."

He stepped a foot closer. "Why did you not do so, then?"

Anger she'd kept in check sprang up inside, along with the memory of his rejection at Valoir. And now, here he was, requesting that she bare her soul.

How had the tables turned so completely? She should be demanding an explanation of him.

"I do not love Nearing and he did not love me. When it came down to that salient fact, there was no choice at all to make."

Oddly enough, his smile grew broader and he took another step. A slight sound rushed past his lips, almost as though he had been holding his breath.

Then he frowned. "And you refuse me, as well?"

She nodded. "For an even better reason."

His lips set.

"I do not mean to insult you," she explained quickly, holding back the hand that wished to trace the tense line and soothe it from his face. "But at least Nearing did not suggest that I live apart from him."

"We've already been through that. You know I only meant to give you freedom if *you* couldn't bear to be with *me*," he said hotly.

She wasn't going to sniffle all over him and tell him the truth. She wasn't going to whine that he wouldn't ever love her. She was going to attack, instead. "I never implied that I didn't want to be with you," she almost shouted. "Whereas you made it quite clear that spending the obligatory dinner hour with me was more than you could stomach."

"If I'd spent more time with you, I would have compromised you beyond redemption, woman!" He glared at her, hands on hips.

She shrugged, hiding hurt behind assumed indifference. "What difference would that have made if your intentions were honorable?" she scoffed. "We could just have wed earlier, by special license."

"I am a gentleman," he said through clenched teeth. "I wanted you to have a wedding night, not some rushed, painful introduction into lovemaking. By God, Caroline, you think I didn't suffer mightily for it? You think having to sit by you in the evening wasn't perdition?"

She nodded. "That is exactly what I think, and you've just confirmed my suspicions."

"You little fool." He took two steps toward her, his eyes burning with some unholy combination of fury and something else—something hot that made her blood race in her veins and her breath come fast and short. She had an embarrassing urge to press her body against his.

He did it for her in one masterful swoop of his arms. She was molded against him from her breasts to her toes. He took her hand in his and guided it between them, to the hard, full length of him. Dear God, he was huge.

"It hurts, Caroline, to want you this much. And this happened every time I was in the same room with you." He ground against her body, her hand there, on him, feeling the thrust and the heat and the strength of him. He groaned softly.

"I got to know that dining table very well. It was sturdy. It would take your small weight easily, and it would take the force of my thrusts after I threw up your skirts and came to you again and again, until I heard you scream for me, and come. Dear God. Come."

"That is vulgar!" She stared at him in shock. And then, in fascination. "I did that to you?"

"You have done it from the beginning Caroline. We have to wed now, so my guilt no longer serves a useful purpose, despite the fact that you could have done much better. It will be a very short engagement—I'll see to it. But don't you ever, ever say that I don't want you. I've spent most of my time desiring you. And the rest fighting that desire," he said with vehement, ironic satisfaction. "I get what I want and you get a bad bargain. But at least it's better than Visigore. And now, I'll excuse my sorry self and find some nice, freezing pond in the area to cure what ails me."

He let her go abruptly and turned toward the door. And in that moment, Caroline realized something quite liberating. As Society's outcast love child, she had considered a man's desire for her to be a bad thing. But Headleymoor obviously considered it to be a good thing. A powerful thing. Something that he couldn't live without.

It was a bald and coarse proposal he'd given her. Any other woman would slap his face for it. A fascinated grin spread across her face.

He didn't love her. But oh, he wanted her mightily! Perhaps that would be enough to keep him by her side.

"You'll give me children," she said to his back.

He laughed, a soft exhalation, and turned toward her. "As many as you wish. We shall get started on our nursery as soon as may be."

"I can expect passion, but not love from you, then," she said, wanting it all clear between them.

He came back to her, a haunted look on his face that made Caroline's heart wrench. "It's wise of you not to expect it. I don't think I'm capable of love. But I will want you until I'm eighty or in the grave—whichever comes first. That will never change."

He stood straight and tall before her, his eyes blazing as though he were a knight making a vow. "I shall stay with you. I shall be faithful, and believe me, that will be no sacrifice at all. I shall protect you from the Visigores of this world. I shall try my best to make you happy. I don't think I could bear it if you were not." On this last, his voice broke. "Will that be enough for you, Caroline? Will you marry me?"

He spoke of protecting her. Yet he looked so desolate, she felt the fiercest desire to take him in her arms and shield him from whatever storms threatened.

Filled with that need and determination, she put her hands in his, and said, "Yes. I shall marry you, Devlin Carmichael. And I shall do my best to protect you, as well."

"From what, pray?" he asked, his dark eyes crinkling at the corners.

But his hands grasped hers tightly. For the first time since they'd entered the study, Caroline felt something run through his hands to hers, as though a taut place inside him uncoiled and stretched like a shoot feeling the first rays of the summer sun.

She smiled back at him, wondering if she, like every other child, was sensing something only because she wished it so badly to be true.

"From yourself, perhaps," she whispered, and at the startled look in his eyes, slipped her two hands from his and cradled his face, pulling it closer to hers.

His mouth swept down upon her and for one moment there was no danger, no sorrow, no secrets. Just the sensation of two odd and multi-edged pieces of a puzzle coming together at last, in a perfect fit.

Dev felt the touch of her lips and almost forgot to breathe. Caroline felt . . . right in his arms. She was so soft against him, her sweet lips, still so unschooled and yet so eager to learn more, her arms, supple and strong, that slipped round his neck. Her fingers played through the hair at his nape and he wanted to shiver and stretch and purr like a cat. Instead, he murmured and slid his tongue over her lips, and she sighed, letting him inside as though it were the natural place for him to be.

She bent to him, yielding and pliant as a green shoot, and he tasted her. Dear God, her mouth was sweet and warm for him.

He had never been so glad, nor so afraid. With Caroline, it could be different. It could be more than desire. He had a terrible feeling that he would sink into that rapture, opening every part of his mind to her, his soul. What would she do with it— flay him with his flaws or accept him for what he was and was not?

He thought of the Tennyson poem, the one he always associated with his feelings when he was with Caroline.

" 'Now lies the Earth all Danae to the stars, and all thy heart lies open unto me.' "

That was what he wanted and feared. To have her so close that she would know him, in every sense. To meld with her, until there was no Caroline and no Devlin, but one being, whole and complete.

It would be a terrible risk bringing all the fear and the guilt into the light. Would she understand him even with his defects? Or would she stab at the tender, exposed heart of him, and leave him mortally wounded?

The lure to trust was there, in her open, totally honest gaze. He wanted a real home, and Caroline could either give or deny him that haven.

He shut his eyes and prayed for both of them. He held hard to her, the first, last, and only hope of solace in a world of storm and sorrow.

Gerard Visigore held the ice pack to his head and groaned as he lay on the chaise lounge in his London town house. He remembered nothing of the attack upon him in that forest, nor what might have happened afterward, but it was a damned bloody inhospitable thing for Eversleigh to do, shipping him off to his home rather than caring for him at the estate.

He assumed that whoever had hit him had done something to Lady Caroline, but there had been no word of her death or her abduction. He could only guess that she'd gotten away and summoned help. It would have been pleasant if Eversleigh had been gentleman enough to keep him there.

Caroline would have come to his room to ask him about his head, and perhaps stroke it for him. All sorts of interesting things could have happened in that room, just as he'd planned for them to happen in the forest. Things that would have compromised her beyond redemption unless she accepted his proposal.

Perhaps Eversleigh guessed, or perhaps one of the guests had been at school with him. Could someone have told Eversleigh about his activities? He cursed, long and low.

If he had been exposed, he'd be a pariah now, banned from every decent house in Society. It would be whispered throughout the ton, and he would have to leave England forever. The rumors might even follow him to India.

No, it could not have come out after all these years. He'd been so careful. He'd learned only to choose members of the lowest order or those whom he could blackmail. Those who would never dare tell a soul.

His head was pounding. He had to think, and he couldn't with this ache.

He needed to test the waters. Rising, he yanked the bellpull and his new valet scurried in like a small creature that hovered in the shadows.

"I'm going to the club," he said, and the man hastily got his clothing ready—a somber gray, perfectly cut frock coat and trousers, a maroon waistcoat, dove gray gloves.

When he arrived at White's, several of the men looked up from their papers and nodded acknowledgement. He breathed a sigh of relief. So far, he was safe. He'd go away for a while. France would be lovely this time of year.

When he returned, he'd go to Eversleigh, and make his bid for Caroline. He'd never met anyone quite like her. She was strong enough to be a fascinating challenge, but soft beneath. The sort who would take a while to break, building the pleasure past any point he'd known before.

Caroline remained at Eversleigh that week. Headleymoor had sent word that Gerard Visigore was gone from England. But as the United Band might still be operating in Britain, he again insisted that they marry within the week.

Mama was overset by the abrupt changes about to take place. "There's no time for the trousseau," she said fretfully, pacing across the maroon Turkey carpet in the rose drawing room. "You ought to be visiting glovers and modistes and milliners in London. But now, it's all I can do to find you a gown for the wedding."

"I should be heartily sick of the wedding preparations by the first day, and you know it, Mama," Caroline told her with a smile of reassurance that she wished she felt herself.

Headleymoor had expected to marry her the morning after his embarrassing contests. Mama's insistence that she would not be a party to such a havey-cavey wedding forced him to agree to wait the week.

"I've managed to cobble together an acceptable, if quiet, wedding," Mama said. "But I would have so looked forward to a grand event. If just to rub it in the faces of those cats who have plagued us for years. Still, with the guards Headleymoor has sent, it would have been grist for the gossip mills, so perhaps this is better."

Brawny men guarded the perimeter of the estate, while the tenants and residents of Upper Eversleigh, knowing of the situation, kept their eyes open for any strangers in the area. All of this was a constant reminder to Caroline that the sooner she left her home and family, the sooner they would be free from the jeopardy that she'd put them in.

It might have been easier to bear the tension had the marquess deigned to visit her, but since that afternoon at Eversleigh, he had not come by once.

She was in the rose drawing room the next day, glumly choosing monograms for the several dozens of new sheets when Munson announced that Lord Nearing had come to call.

"How very kind of you," she said with a smile, rising to take his hands in hers. "You must have known that this prisoner had a desperate desire to be set free today."

She motioned to the sheaves of paper and yards of linen crowding the study. "For all I care, Mama could have her pick of any and all of this, but I suppose I'll have to learn something about housekeeping, now that I must grow up."

He smiled back at her, looking every bit the dashing earl about town again, and quite recovered from his brief tendresse for her. "Take a ride with me," he said. "The fresh air will do you good."

"My hero," she said. "Give me a few moments and I'll meet you at the stable."

Her maid quickly helped Caroline into her riding habit, and Munson had sent word ahead to the stable master, so she was mounted on Firefly not fifteen minutes after Nearing had made the suggestion.

It was a bright spring afternoon, breezy enough for a good gallop down to the lake and back. As the wind cooled her cheeks, she laughed and let Firefly have his head. She and Nearing kept pace with each other, both riding full out, and she felt young and free again for those few precious moments.

In the last days, the reality of the commitment she'd made

had begun to sink in. She was going to marry a man she might already love. She was going to marry a man who didn't love her. It seemed the worst prison into which she could have placed herself.

"I heard there was a bit of a fracas down here last week," Nearing said as they slowed to a trot near the lake.

She shook her head, smiling. "I have never been so furious with my brother as I was that day." She told him what William had put Headleymoor through, and the utter humiliation she'd felt for both of them.

"How many did Dev have to fight before William accepted his request to marry you?"

"Five," she said. "I fear there would have been more, but the rest looked decidedly uneasy about the prospect of getting into the ring with him."

"Good God. That must have stirred up some unpleasant memories," Nearing said with a frown.

"Whatever do you mean?" Caroline asked him, staring at his thunderous expression.

"Oh, come, Caroline," Nearing said with a dark glance. "You're not a foolish woman. You must have guessed what it was like for him at Harrington."

"I never thought . . . He seems so clever and strong."

Nearing sighed. "Two cultures, Caroline. Surely I needn't spell it out for you?"

She stared at him. "But everyone wants to know him."

"Now," Nearing corrected, one finger pointed at her, professor to her rather slow-witted student. "Now when he's got the dukedom coming someday, and a fortune to boot. Suddenly the Zaranbadian blood isn't so distasteful. But boys at school can be very cruel to one who is different. And Dev was more than a little different. Besides, there was a reason for what happened to him."

"What do you mean?"

"Visigore. He was the bane of Dev's existence for two years. Visigore had hurt a boy." Nearing looked sick, the same way she had felt when she'd heard Visigore using his whip on Peeps. "He hurt him badly, and Dev went to the headmaster. He was naïve, you see. He thought that the powerful must protect the weak. But Visigore was the son of an earl, and the boy who'd been hurt was only the son of a country gentleman. They hushed the incident up. Shortly after that, Visigore discovered that Dev had tried to have him sent down. He was a piece of work, with a gang of followers almost as vile as he. They lay in wait for Dev quite often. Aubrey and I tried to stand with him and get our own back, but sometimes we could not be there. At those times, the beatings were brutal."

"Dear Lord." Her heart twisted at the thought of that young boy, so noble and caring, being beaten to a pulp on a regular basis by boys older and stronger than he. "How long did this continue?"

"For two years."

"Two years!" She imagined him at the start of each new term, a young boy traveling alone in a big, empty coach, knowing that he was about to face more of that brutality and helpless to stop it from happening. A thought occurred. "Couldn't he tell his papa?"

Nearing shook his head. His brows drew together and he gazed bleakly across the lake, not seeming to see how the trees bent down to meet their reflections in the water. "The duke traveled for those years. He mourned his wife, you see, and left England for Europe and the East. Dev had to manage it all himself. And finally, he did." Nearing smiled, a fierce, satisfied look in his eyes. "Visigore had an essay to write—Shakespeare's *Henry V,* as I recall. It's still one of my favorite plays. The master who assigned his class the essay had been at school himself, years ago, and had written a rather fine essay on the play. Dev found it in a dusty book in the library that year, pushed back behind others. Thank God they so rarely changed the work they gave us, for he knew Visigore would have the assignment that spring.

"He forged Visigore's handwriting. It was a delicate matter to creep into the Master's study and switch Visigore's paper for his forgery, but Dev managed it. I've always thought Dev discovered on that day that there were other ways in which he could get the justice that should have come swiftly from those in charge. You see, Caroline, they would not have sent Visigore down for the sins he'd committed. But they booted him out for cheating. Not what that bastard deserved, but at least Dev succeeded in getting rid of him."

"Oh, I am glad," she said, thinking of those small boys and how brave they had all been. And how Headleymoor had been so clever, even then.

"Yes," she said, as understanding came. "Yes. I do see." And so she did—beyond the glittering champion, the marquess to whom everyone bowed and simpered, the sensual, beautiful man who frightened her and lured her at the same time.

She thought of their first meeting. His aloofness became uncertainty, his silences self-consciousness, his few smiles precious pauses from a life spent apart and alone. Was it possible? In a shameful moment, she wished it were. For if Nearing was right, and Headleymoor had been a boy who'd suffered a great deal, then perhaps, if she tried very hard to be kind and understanding, he might someday be glad for more than the passion they would share. Gladness wasn't the same thing as love, but it was better than indifference.

Chapter Thirteen:
Pagan Rites, or the Lack Thereof

Felix Kendall stood in the darkness outside the tavern where Headleymoor had sent him. Tom Jarvis stood to his left. Several other men who worked for the Home Office were at his back, pistols at the ready.

Headleymoor had ordered him to come to this den where the United Band lay in hiding. Kendall hadn't known that Headleymoor had scouted the place out earlier. Nor had he known that there would be so many men in the group tonight. He'd thought there would only be three of them, and that he and Tom would get out alive. Headleymoor was meant to die here, but no one else. Now he wasn't so sure what would happen.

A bead of sweat trickled down his back. Headleymoor was so clever, he always seemed to land on his feet. But Tom . . . He hated that Tom was here. He'd just dined with the young recruit and his wife Wednesday last, and he'd met their two children for a moment—a toddler who looked at him with such trusting eyes and a brand-new baby.

What would Tom's wife do if he got shot? It might well happen, with the surprise of the added numbers and Headleymoor's disguise. Kendall had not known that when he'd gone to warn the Zaranbadians of the raid. He'd have to watch out for the lad and keep him well behind his back.

Headleymoor stepped out into the dim lantern light, dressed in a dock man's stained work shirt and breeches. His hair was a greasy shade of brown and he had a disfiguring scar slit across his forehead.

He gave the silent signal. What he didn't know was that the remaining members of the United Band were all armed and ready to do battle to reclaim their honor after so many frustrations.

Kendall rushed in with the rest of the men, into a hell of gunfire and smoke and shouts of furious surprise from his own countrymen. Death was waiting in this room. Death and agony.

Zaranbadian and English curses filled the air as men grappled, one on one. A lantern fell and flame glowed, first on the floor and then on the jodhpurs of a Zaranbadian. Screams erupted, curses and shouts. Knives glittered in the flames, and men grunted, locked together in combat.

Kendall looked around wildly for Tom. A Zaranbadian ran up behind the lad, knife flashing in the wavering light of the rising flames.

"No!" Kendall shouted and leaped a table, mad to get to Tom in time. He reached the thug, shoved hard with his shoulder, hit ribs that broke. But the man sliced downward and Kendall couldn't stop the heavy arm, the cold stab of steel, the blood. He crumpled to the floor, staring at his side.

There was blood. So much blood seeping out of him. His head rang, a tinny sound, and the rising flames, the shouts, the dark, struggling figures all seemed suddenly faraway, and slow, as though the men battled beneath a raging red sea.

Suddenly, there was quiet. So still and silent was the room, with only the flames hissing as the men poured water on them.

A figure bent over him and lifted him onto a table. Headleymoor.

"Let me see, Felix," Headleymoor said, and then, to Tom, "Give me your cravat and shirt. Mine are filthy." He calmly ripped and bound the rags from Tom's shirt around Kendall's ribs. "Get my bag out of the carriage," he added, without glancing up from the wound. "You'll be all right, Felix. You have to hold on for me. Do you understand, old fellow? You have to hold on."

Headleymoor's voice was so calm, so gentle, that Kendall gave a sigh. He was safe. Headleymoor would keep him safe.

"Call the carriage," Headleymoor said to one of the men.

"Don't let go," Kendall said. He could hear his voice shake, and he tried to hold on to Headleymoor's hand like a drowning man holds on to a spar.

Headleymoor said, "I shan't let you go. Drink this."

Kendall sipped something mixed in wine that Headleymoor held to his lips. The pain and the fear slipped away.

"Rest, and hang on," Headleymoor said. "You're going to live, do you hear? That's an order."

Kendall stared up at the man he'd been paid to kill tonight, and then at the men who stood respectfully around him, waiting for their next orders. Headleymoor had an intent look on his face. He was getting something out of the bag, pouring it on a piece of cotton wool. For the wound, Kendall supposed. Headleymoor was going to clean him up and stitch the wound right here in the tavern where Kendall had arranged for his death.

He'd never really noticed before how very . . . extraordinary Headleymoor was. How good. With a shock of horror, he realized what he had almost destroyed.

The day after Nearing's visit to Eversleigh, Mrs. Henley, the village modiste, had bustled in to measure and cluck, and Mama had come down with her old wedding gown, wrapped in blue muslin to preserve it.

"Oh, milady, just beautiful. And look at those stitches. Not a one irregular, and so tiny," Mrs. Henley said in a voice filled with awe.

"Troper's in London might still carry the same fabric. If you like it, Caroline, I shall send a messenger at once to bring more of it back for the skirt. But only if you like it," Mama said reddening and giving her a quick glance.

"I think it's beautiful, Mama." Caroline hugged her, and all the times her mother had listened to her dreams and absurd imaginings came back to her. She felt wetness on her mother's cheek and realized that she was a little teary, too.

"Oh, dear," Mama said, sniffling into her handkerchief. "Look how odd those old waistlines were, almost beneath the bosom! Can you make something of this, Mrs. Henley?"

"Indeed I can, milady. A little snipping here, and the lace trim on the bottom can be brought up to the top, and there I can use the new silk, and we'll order plenty of both fabrics so there'll be more than enough left for the veil. My two daughters are excellent seamstresses. If the man will be back by tomorrow noon, we shall have it all done in a thrice."

"Well," said Mama with a sigh. "It's quite a good thing we live in Kent instead of Northumberland. I shall send a man immediately." In a flurry of skirts, she was off like the Turkish whirling dervishes Headleymoor had told Caroline about at Valoir. Caroline heard Mama speaking to the messenger, then running off to meet with Cook and the gardeners and the footmen.

But while her mother was happily preparing the house for this impromptu wedding, Caroline was beginning to entertain visions of sailing for America.

Late that afternoon, she paced her study, wringing her hands. It wasn't so much that she didn't wish to marry Headleymoor. It was the risk to her heart and her happiness. She'd been halfway to loving him before Maxim had told her of his childhood demons. And now she feared her heart belonged to him entirely.

Was there even a ghost of a chance that with time his feelings might deepen? If she were strong enough to accept what he could give her with a smile and not wish for more from him, would it make him more comfortable with the arrangement, more prone to care?

Was it worth the risk of a broken heart to win Headleymoor's love? Was she brave enough to take the chance? At that moment, she knew. She was not going to America. She was going to marry Headleymoor and be the best wife he could have ever wanted.

The knocker sounded downstairs and she heard Munson's voice at the door, then a low voice like dark velvet in answer. The study door opened and Headleymoor walked in.

"Your mother and brother are out today?" he asked as he came toward her.

She nodded as he bent over her hand. Tension rose in her throat so that she could barely greet him without fearing her voice would croak. "They're seeing to the details, I suppose," she said.

"I am glad I could see you, before business keeps me away."

"What sort of business?"

His gave her a thin smile. "The sort I shall dislike remembering."

Dear Heaven, she thought. *I truly am marrying a spy.*

"I cannot tell you much, but one thing is important and must be shared now," he said. "I believe that soon it will be safe again for us, for Ari and Janighar. But not yet."

He spoke in such a formal manner. Good God, they were talking about life and death, like two business partners discussing a merger. She wished to shove him in the chest. To shout at him: *Aren't you scared? Angry? What are you really thinking? Say something to show how you feel.*

She'd seen him with blood on his hands, with it seeping over his whole body. For one horrible moment, she'd thought it was his blood. They had been touched by terrible events. And now he was back to the same old stiff-rumped, secretive lord she'd first met. The doubts, silenced only a moment ago, screamed at her.

"I wanted to give you this," he said. His hand slipped into his waistcoat pocket and pulled out a small box. "I looked for something that you might like, and hope it will do. I thought of you when I saw it, and it seemed the right thing."

He opened the box and took her hand in his. She stared, not at her hand, but at his face. So solemn was his countenance, so beautiful with the light shining on his golden hair. The ring slipped on her finger as she gazed up at him. He turned her hand in his, bent his head, and kissed her palm, closing her fingers over the kiss. Then he looked into her eyes, a question in his.

"Will it do?" he said, and it seemed he was asking about more than the ring.

She broke from the trance and turned her hand to look at his ring. A large, glowing ruby, surrounded by diamonds, glittered on her finger.

"It's beautiful," she said, her breath catching.

"You like it. I am very glad," he said, and smiled. His face was transformed by it. No stuffy prig here now, but Headley-moor.

She smiled back, feeling happiness enter her heart and refusing to push it away in fear. He'd remembered to give her a betrothal ring. Even better, he cared whether she liked it. Oh, that he would smile like that, so sweetly, so tentatively.

Munson knocked and came into the drawing room. He set down the tea tray. Caroline and Headleymoor parted quickly, and when she darted a look at him, she saw that he was watching her, as well. When Munson bowed and left them, he cleared his throat.

"I should like you to know where we shall go, after," he said. "After the ceremony, I mean."

She thought for a moment. "It isn't safe to go to Valoir, is it?"

His eyebrows rose in question. "I should have thought that you would never wish to see the place again. It can't hold any fond memories for you."

"Mostly not," she said. "But I think it does for you. And I was happy there, before the end. I began to know you a little. Perhaps at Valoir, I might come to know you a little better. After all, you are the man to whom I have pledged my life."

If a family of elephants had just strolled into the room, trunk to tail, he could not have looked more dumbfounded.

After a moment of stunned silence, he said, "The food's good, at any rate. We cannot go there, but I shall see what I can do."

I am happy (no, slash that) *delighted* (no again) *pleased to tell you that by the time you receive this letter*

Caroline sighed and wondered how she could announce the news of her upcoming wedding to Janighar with honesty. It was a problem when someone else would be reading the letter— probably Headleymoor's brother, King Ari.

Tomorrow was her wedding day. Her wedding dress was lying on her bed in the next chamber, all that ivory lace and silk softly shimmering in the candlelight. It was a frightening gown, far too beautiful for the likes of her. A princess should wear such a gown, not a lady saved from the brink of ostracism by a handsome prince who also happened to be an agent for Her Majesty's government. Actually, a true princess, rather than she, should be marrying that princely spy.

At the knock on her study door, she pushed the letter into her desk and half turned in her chair toward the door.

Mama stuck her head into the room, looking very solemn. "Darling, is this a good time for a chat?"

Caroline nodded and rose from the desk. Her mother had been unusually quiet the last two nights. Oh my, she thought. Mama was probably going to give her "the talk." She wondered if her mother would mention the riding astride problem. And whether that would give Headleymoor a disgust of her. Well, at least she would learn what it was all about, now.

"Of course," Caroline said in a voice that revealed not a whit of anticipation. "Come sit with me. It's been a while since we had a chance to talk together."

Mama walked into the study, carrying a large portfolio crammed with papers. Caroline looked up in question. They sat side by side on the sofa and Mama put her hand in Caroline's.

"I wanted you to see these and then I have a question for you."

"Mama, are you well?" Caroline asked, hearing the urgency in her voice.

Her mother smiled at her and nodded, squeezing her hand. "I am quite well, my love. But you are grown now, and tomorrow you will be a bride. I have a serious subject to discuss with you. That is all this little talk concerns."

Her mother opened the portfolio, and to her surprise, Caroline spotted a child's painting that looked very familiar. A line of chicks pecked for worms in the yard. All but one, that is. The one chick, in the center of the row, looked up in interest at a spider spinning her web from a branch right above the chick.

"I loved this watercolor," Mama said, brushing a tear from her eye. "It was just like you to paint something so original—and I already knew that you were the chick in the middle. The one who observed much more than the others. The one who looked for and treasured interesting differences."

She sniffled a bit into her handkerchief, then hugged Caroline. "You got that from your father. Both the ability to understand what to observe and the gift to express yourself in art."

Caroline went very still.

Mama took a deep breath. "The Earl of Eversleigh was a very good man, Caroline. He loved me, and I did my best to love him back. But we could only have one child. He became ill after that, with a disease that would kill me, too, if I shared his bed. I shall not name it, nor blame him for it. He had been young, and foolish. In the end, he suffered mightily, but he never lost his reason, and for that I thank God."

Mama pressed her lips together, swallowed, and continued, her voice only quavering a little. "When he knew that he would die within the next months, he called for me. I was shocked to find Robert already standing beside the earl's bed, holding his hand. The earl greeted me with these words: 'My dear Margery, I have known that you and Robert loved each other from the day you first met, at your come out.' I was shocked. I don't know how he knew, but he must have quietly watched me at the balls and the soirees enough to realize that both Robert and I loved each other, that it was a love to last our lifetimes.

"It hadn't mattered, of course, what we felt for each other. Our marriages had been arranged. At that time, duty to family and the ties that would bring more wealth and position were everything. So we'd only looked, and stolen a few moments together, all of them public, to quietly express our love. And after that, I married the earl, and Robert married a lady of great wealth and prominence. He was the unlucky one. His bride suffered from melancholia that degenerated into lunacy. Robert kept her at home, with knowledgeable servants and nurses. She died last year, never having known anything but her distorted world and the imagined, frightening voices that plagued her."

Mama took a deep breath. "But I digress," she said. "There was Robert, standing beside the earl's bed. And there was the earl, looking from Robert to me with such love in his thin, worn face. 'I wish to thank you both,' the earl said. 'Your devotion to duty has protected my honor throughout the years. Margery always wanted another child and I could never give her one. Robert, I am asking you to give her a child for me. It would ease my heart to know that what she so longed for could finally be hers. I could die without the guilt I have carried for the sin I have committed that led to this disease. I would know that at least, in this way, I did something to make her happy. Please. Please help me. Give her your child. I wish you both to go away together. I wish you to have these last months of my life to love each other as you should have done all those years. The babe will, of course, be considered my child, and you will be the only ones who will ever know.' "

"And you did that? You left your dying husband and went with the duke to . . . to . . . to make a child? To make me?" Caroline felt like a brimming cup of some roiling liquid, about to spill over with emotions she couldn't even identify.

"I argued at first, and Robert did as well. We felt it was wrong—wrong to leave him, wrong to take that precious time together when my duty demanded that I spend it by the earl's bedside. 'You have lived for duty all your lives,' the earl said, and he sounded just like a scolding schoolmaster when a pupil refuses to understand a lesson. He argued for a good half hour, and we could see he was flagging. 'You will do this for me, so my conscience is clear when I go to meet my God,' he said."

Mama paused to brush a tear from her cheek. The silence was broken only by the ticking of the ormolu clock over the mantel.

"In the end, he wore us down. We agreed and set off a week later, not for months but for a few weeks. It was the most joyous time of my life, Caroline. And you were the child of that joy, that love."

She clutched Caroline's hand. Caroline had no choice but to hold on, while shivers went up and down her spine, of confusion, of helpless understanding, of dawning compassion—for the earl, for the duke, for her mother, all caught in a vise of family expectations and duty.

"We returned and the earl lived for another three months. We thought we were safe. That you would be safe. But as most things happen, all did not work out as we believed it would. You have so much of your father in you that you suffered for our deed."

Caroline realized with shock that her mother said "*you* suffered," without any mention of her own isolation and ostracism.

Mama put the portfolio into her lap. "These are the paintings and the letters regarding you that your father has held close to his heart for all these years. Please look at them. He has known you far better than you ever knew him. My dear, we shall marry very soon, with or without your blessing. But we hope that you will understand and accept him into your heart as much as is possible. I shall leave you to look through these pages and make up your mind." She walked to the door and opened it.

Caroline watched her walk from the room, and then lifted the next paper in the portfolio. It was a letter from her mother to the duke, describing Caroline's first smile. Then came her first step and her first birthday. Only this was a portrait, done beautifully in charcoal, the hand firm and masterful. Caroline sat in a high chair, grinning, with a piece of cake crumbling in her fist and icing all over her face.

There was a portrait of her on her pony, again a charcoal, hastily drawn from a distance, as she took a small fence. And another, a group of studies from Scotland, she saw, one of her as she raised a pistol and shot at a target, and one of her gathering berries in the wood beyond her grandfather's castle. And vaguely, she remembered an auburn-haired stranger stopping for a day or two, dining downstairs with her grandfather, as she got ready for bed in her nursery.

With a shock, she realized she still had the small picture he'd given her then, a detailed watercolor of a lake in winter, and people skating over it, and others selling warm chestnuts and hot chocolate. She'd looked at that picture every day through her youth, always finding another fascinating detail, learning from it. Her style was very much the same as his, she realized— bright jewel tones of color and detailed lines.

The portfolio was full of such stuff. Finally, she came to the last painting. This was a small oil, done this year. A portrait of Caroline in a rose-colored gown, smiling up at a young, golden marquess as they danced. She looked . . . beautiful. With a shock, she realized that her father saw her as beautiful.

But he saw more than beauty. Her gaze, fixed on Headleymoor was free, and open, and full of—of . . . Dear God, her father recognized what she felt for Headleymoor. He recognized it because it was what he felt for her mother.

It was love. Love, shining in her. But only the chick who spotted the spider would recognize that look. The rest were too busy looking for what they could gain in the lower sphere of lucre and power.

This was the duke who wished to marry her mother. The artist, the devoted lover, the man who crept from the shadows into her life, to see as much as he dared of it. There was really no question, was there?

Her mother was waiting for her in the countess's bedchamber, sitting on a bench by the window and twisting her handkerchief in her hand. Caroline closed the door gently and crossed the room to kneel before her. She took her mother's hands in hers and kissed them.

"Thank you," she whispered. "For giving me such a father."

It wasn't until late that night, while Caroline tossed and

turned in a bed suddenly too lumpy, that she realized Mama had not given her "the talk." Oh, Lord. There would never be enough time for her to remember to give it before the wedding. How was she ever to explain about that riding astride business? Whatever that had to do with it.

Too soon it was morning. Caroline hadn't slept very well, and stood now, staring at herself in the mirror. She felt nothing but disappointment. Even in ivory satin and lace, she didn't look much like a blushing bride.

She looked a bit agitated and bug-eyed. She looked like a woman who'd agreed to do something that she'd never thought would happen, only to find it wasn't some strange dream but reality. A knock sounded and she turned to the door.

"Hallo, Caroline!" a familiar and dear voice called softly from the other side of the door.

Caroline whirled and threw the door open. Lilias Drelincourt, Lady Breme, stood outside the door, her dark brown eyes lit with a smile, a golden-haired angel sleeping in her arms. She swirled into the room, a flurry of skirts and ribbons, gently placed the little bundle of a six-month-old son in the middle of Caroline's bed, and threw her arms around Caroline.

"Oh, it's been too long. Let me look at you. How beautiful you are. Headleymoor is going to be over the moon when he sees you! And to know that I sensed this months and months ago!"

"Months ago? Sensed what?" Caroline asked. A treacherous spark of hope thrilled through her.

Lilias had a most decidedly guilty look on her face. "He has told you about his, ahem, work, has he not?"

"A man like Headleymoor? Of course not. I surmised that he led a double life on my own."

"Oh, dear." Lilias gave her hand a sympathetic squeeze. "You must have been furious. I know I would have been."

Caroline thought about that for a moment and then grinned. "I was for quite a while, until I realized that as Ram Dass, he advised me to marry himself—well, himself as Headleymoor. I haven't told him I know yet, and I don't wish to."

Caroline had thought long and hard about Headleymoor's secret identity. She didn't want to confront him with it. Somehow, it was terribly important that he trust her enough to tell her.

"Well, it's no wonder that he wooed you, even in that underhanded manner. The man was mad about you last year. You should have heard the scolding he gave me when we put ourselves in danger!"

"Oh, that." Caroline batted Lilias's comments away with a negligent wave of her hand. "That was nothing compared to what's been happening recently. I'm so glad you're safe out of it." She stopped stock still as she realized that Lilias and her husband were, indeed, in the thick of it now.

"Why in heaven's name are you here, Lilias? Do you not know how dangerous it is to have anything to do with us?"

Lilias narrowed her eyes and stuck her hands on her hips. "Did you think that would stop us? You and Headleymoor are our dearest friends. I would go anywhere to see you wed, particularly to him. Besides," she said, her brown curls swinging over her shoulder with the toss of her head, "we're perfectly safe. We came in a gypsy caravan. They're very quick, for they know all the back roads."

Caroline's shoulders relaxed and she let out a sigh as she gazed down at the sleeping cherub on her bed. "I am so very, very glad that you've good friends in low places," she said. "And that you brought little Alex!"

"I couldn't very well leave him at home," Lilias said. "He needs me."

At those words, Alex opened his eyes, and Caroline gazed down into blue as pure as a brilliant summer sky. "He looks just like his papa," she said, holding out a finger and laughing with delight as the baby grasped it.

"Yes, he does. Handsomer every day, too. Aubrey hopes the next baby will look a bit like me."

"Are you already . . . ?"

Lilias shook her head. "Not for a while—not until Alex is old enough to drink milk from a cup, rather than me, at any rate."

"Goodness," Caroline murmured. The fascinating things she still did not know were piling up.

Alex stuffed his fist into his mouth and started to fuss. "I'd better get to him," Lilias said, and took the baby, turning her back to Caroline and fumbling one-handed with the buttons on her traveling dress.

Caroline walked to the mirror and fussed with her hair. The contented sounds of a baby suckling and the sweet soft voice of his mother singing cut through the silence.

Caroline's reflection seemed to shimmer back at her. The first tear slipped down her cheek. Hurriedly, she grabbed a handkerchief and blotted her eyes, but Lilias must have heard the resulting sniffle. For presently, when Caroline had regained her poise, Lilias asked, quite matter-of-factly, "Are you concerned at all about tonight?"

Caroline started. What concerned her was far more upsetting than a maiden's fears of her wedding night. But it was too humiliating to confess that her bridegroom was marrying her only to save her reputation.

She turned away from the mirror. "You are referring to this mating business, no doubt. I've spoken to the Queen of Zaranbad. You would like her very much, Lily. And," Caroline added for good measure, "I've seen a good many animals mating here at Eversleigh."

Lilias lifted the baby to half hang, replete, over her shoulder while she gently patted his back. "The only thing that I can tell you is this. It can be—oh, so wonderful, Caroline. I'm sure it will be all it can be. Between you and Ram, that is." Her eyes held a devilish twinkle. "Or Dev, I should say. You're the only lady I know who may commit bigamy with impunity."

How could Lilias speak of Headleymoor so casually? Caroline couldn't imagine ever calling him Dev. And the thought of waking up next to him on the morrow and saying "Good morning, Ram," sent shivers of horrified amusement up her spine.

The church was not very crowded, Dev noted. Besides the surprise of Aubrey and Lilias Drelincourt, there was just his father, Caroline's mother, and beside her, the Duke of Welsingham. Dev took his place at the front of the little stone church beside Maxim to await his bride. His bride, who wished to have children. With him.

It was all he could think about for the last week. He'd never made love to a virgin before, and he had to admit, the prospect was daunting. Would he be gentle enough? How could one possibly make the act of love enjoyable for a virgin? What would she take away from it, other than the shock and pain of that first time?

The organ sounded a chord. The doors to the back of the church swung open and the small group rose. She came to him on her brother's arm, dressed in ivory, the new style since Queen Victoria had worn white at her wedding, a gown of ivory silk and lace, tight in the sleeves and the waist, while the skirt billowed about her like a cloud. She had chosen not to wear a bonnet. Rather, a filmy veil and a wreath of roses circled her hair—rose and gold. Their roses, he thought with fierce, possessive pleasure. The first flowers he'd given her. She'd remembered.

Her bright gaze found his, and clung like a vine that sought the support of a trellis before it collapsed to the ground.

Oh, Cara, he thought with a possessive wrenching inside. Her brother led her the rest of the way to him and stopped, and he took her hand, holding it tightly, holding her up beside him, so that she would know that they went through this together.

Suddenly, his own fear vanished. Right now, at least, he had enough strength to keep both of them upright. His greatest desire was to protect her from anything that might harm her. Please God.

Caroline felt Headleymoor's hand supporting her and without a shred of pride, she leaned on him. Beneath the formal black frock coat, his arm was steady and secure.

Mr. Remington, the vicar she'd known from childhood, smiled at them. He was a kind, portly sort of man with long, fluffy white sideburns and a cloud of white hair on his head. His voice was very reassuring as he went on about marriage and all that.

His wife, Mrs. Remington, had been the one playing Handel at the organ, and Caroline had seen their young daughters waving and grinning at her from one of the rows at the back of the church.

Mr. Remington began to speak, but Caroline's thoughts were on the duke, her father, who sat in the first row with Mama. He'd handed her a handkerchief as Caroline came down the aisle, and Mama had sniffled and smiled up at him with such a look of tenderness that Caroline thought she might begin to cry herself. And William had squeezed her hand as he gave her over to Headleymoor. She vaguely remembered that, too.

"Do you, Devlin Francis Ramsay Dassam Carmichael, take this woman . . ."

Aha! Ramsay Dassam. Ram Dass. Not the wisest alias, Caroline thought. Anyone who'd known his full name might have guessed. Perhaps Achmed or Sanjay would be less obvious—

Now what was Mr. Remington saying? Headleymoor looked down at her, his brow wrinkled. People murmured behind her. Drat. Headleymoor looked worried.

Mr. Remington cleared his throat and said, it seemed perhaps for the second time, "Will you, Caroline Rose Lavinia Berring, take this man—"

"Yes, yes. Of course I will," she said, and gulped.

A sigh rippled through the small gathering. One, she realized in horror, of relief. She'd apparently been wool gathering, hiding from her own wedding. While Mr. Remington intoned some more, she grabbed Headleymoor's hand harder.

After a moment, he pried her fingers from his and straightened them, one by one. As he looked down at them, his lips quirked upward a bit.

Then, very gently, he slipped a ring on her third finger. "With this ring, I thee wed. With my body, I thee worship . . ."

"With my body I thee worship"? When Headleymoor spoke of the act, it was not in terms of worship. It sounded more like a lust-driven, sweaty, marvelous romp. The language he had used! The pictures he painted heated her cheeks even now, and she felt a traitorous, melting thrill at the juncture of her thighs. In the middle of church!

How many children would he give her? As many as she wished, he'd said. How many times would it take to beget a child? Should she have asked that a week ago during the negotiations?

Somehow, it was time for the kiss part. Headleymoor lifted her veil and placed it carefully over the wreath of roses—had he noticed that they were his roses? He very gently pressed his lips against hers, a formal acceptance of the pact they'd made, and not at all like those other kisses, the ones that made her melt against him and make strange noises deep in her throat and feel pure, sensual joy seeping through every nerve of her body.

Then, carefully, he turned with her and strode back down the aisle, his arm a bulwark, his whole body warm and strong beside her. Protection, he'd said. He wished to protect her from the evil that had crept into their lives—to conquer it so she would not have anything to fear. That was a good thing, wasn't it? Perhaps it spoke of more than lust.

Of course, he wished to protect his valet, too. And Peeps, whom he'd taken into his service. And Valoir's tenants and inhabitants. So, aside from his desire for her, she was at least as important to him as they were.

Well, it was someplace to start.

Caroline noted that their journey was not at all like the one before to France. For one thing, she sat in comfort, in a smart closed carriage without a crest, a coachman and three footmen atop. Headleymoor had doffed his wedding garb and wore a plain, dark green frock coat, waistcoat and trousers. Caroline, too, wore a fine but serviceable gray gown of light wool and a bonnet that covered her hair. They looked to be a wealthy but untitled man and wife traveling through the countryside. The United Band would not have looked twice at them driving by.

Almost immediately after the cake was cut and the toasts given, Headleymoor had bundled her off into the coach and they'd rolled through villages full of rushing streams and further, past Salisbury plain. "I have a small country estate quite close to Eversleigh," he explained. "It is but a four-hour drive away."

They would arrive in the late afternoon. She cast a glance at him. He looked edgy, and heated. That little pang that had throbbed in her belly in church began to throb again.

Headleymoor rapped the coach roof and the coachman stopped at a field holding a great circle of standing stones silhouetted against the deep blue summer sky.

"Come, Caroline. You must see this." Headleymoor handed her out of the coach and led her into the sacred circle. She stood close to the center of the circle beside him, gazing out at the massive stones and the wide green space surrounding it. If ever there were a symbol of eternity, it was Stonehenge.

Headleymoor had her wedding wreath of roses in his hand. When they'd left Eversleigh, he had come to her chamber and taken it to the carriage. She'd wondered why at the time, for surely they would fade soon. Their scent had kept them company, a small reassurance. She looked from the circle of stones to the circle of roses—both symbols of forever. Did Headleymoor believe in that image? It was so poetic, so out of keeping with his self-protective secretiveness. If he did, oh, if only he did!

"In India and Zaranbad, there are very old monuments like these, built for the gods." He touched the stones reverently. "People leave offerings for luck. And now, for the first time I wonder. Perhaps the old Celtic gods still listen here. Do you think?"

"I suppose I believe that people make their own luck," she said.

"Well," he said and sent her a glance beneath his lashes. "Just in case." He walked to the center of the circle, knelt and placed the wreath on the ground. When he turned back toward her, he was smiling and red-faced, like an adolescent who had just made an utterly moving gesture that embarrassed him mightily.

She looked up at her husband standing tall and straight, his graceful, strong hand so gentle against the great stone beside him. She wanted those hands on her. Of the two of them, was she the only one thinking of tonight?

Headleymoor spent the following half hour gazing out the coach window. What a mass of contradictions he was—eloquent in gesture and word one moment, raw and lusty the next, silent and withdrawn the next. She spent the following half hour pondering how she would ever come to know him.

Outside a village of small stone houses glowing gold in the afternoon sunlight, the coach gave a lurch and slowly tipped sideways. Headleymoor leaped to the door, threw it open, and grabbed her hand. He lifted her out the door and jumped down beside her before the vehicle landed with a crunch upon its rear axle.

People slowly emerged from their houses to stare at the skewed coach, some of the spokes on its rear wheel broken and the rim buckled in one spot. The coachman was on the ground too, with his hand at the head of the lead horse, while the footmen freed all six from the traces. Headleymoor grabbed the halter of the lead horse and walked him to quiet him down.

"Is there a smithy in the village?" he asked a stocky man, one of the villagers who had come up to the coach to help him.

"Aye, sir. I be him," the man said, hunkering down and squinting at the mangled wheel.

"How long to fix the wheel?"

"It'll be done by mid-morning."

"That late?"

"Aye. With the light I've got left today. Can't hurry a job like this. There's an inn up at the next crossroads. Not the finest, but decent food and beds and a fine room for you and your wife."

Headleymoor frowned, seemed lost in thought for a moment, although what alternatives he pondered, Caroline couldn't imagine. There was a blacksmith and the wheel would be fixed by morning. They were together, both of them unhurt. There was an inn with a fine room to share. She shivered, felt the ache and that liquid warmth again, there, where he'd touched her the day he'd asked her to marry him.

What was the hurry, anyway?

How the devil had he ended in a room apart from his bride? Dev wondered as he lay back against the rim of the copper tub in his separate chamber at the inn. They were supposed to be at Austin Heath. This was the one catastrophe he hadn't prepared for.

The garden should be in violent bloom, the lake stocked for fishing. Or swimming, he thought. The image of Caroline's sweet body rising above the water had him instantly so hard he hurt. Oh, yes, definitely swimming.

But here they were in a modest inn, and he hadn't even thought to bring clean sheets. How could he possibly take his wife in a small, plain chamber, without his own clean linens scented with lavender on the bed?

She was a virgin, for God's sake. She needed to have all the comforts around her—freshly ironed sheets, a warm bath to get into afterward. She would be sore and shy and here they were in the middle of nowhere, and some cheeky chambermaid would give her a knowing look and snicker when she asked for water to wash in a second time that night. He couldn't possibly impose upon her tonight. He had to wait.

"Bloody, bloody hell," he said through clenched teeth.

He rose from the bath, roughly toweled himself off, and strode to the window overlooking the inn yard. Caroline was right next door, in an adjoining chamber. All he had to do was walk to the door and open it. All he had to do was throw off the towel and take her down with him into the feather mattress. She would be soft and yielding and his. He was her husband. He had the right.

His blood beat hard, beat *mine*. Then he heard it through his window, a sweet, gurgling sound, laughter and then song. She was singing in her bath. Happy. Somehow, he'd made her happy.

But he was a gentleman. A gentleman didn't "take" a lady. He carefully, gently seduced her in a place where she could call for anything she might need to comfort her nerves, and rest the next day with familiar servants aiding her.

He was hard and aching. He'd been that way since they'd started off in the carriage. How was he ever going to walk into that chamber and sit with her and sup on mediocre food and pretend that all was well? Her wildflower scent would serve as a goad to his already unbridled lust, and she would end beneath him, on that bed with inferior sheets.

He went into himself as Dr. Gupta had taught him all those years ago. Deep, below the needs of flesh and emotion, where there was nothing but breath and existence. Where there was peace.

By the time he'd surfaced, it was dark and he was late for dinner.

Headleymoor had been so late for dinner, that they'd taken the food back to the kitchen to warm. Caroline sat across from him in their private dining chamber in The Wild Swan. She fought down the flood of humiliation and took a sip of fish soup. With its warm, crusty bread and pungent sauce, it smelled delicious, but she found herself choking it down without tasting it.

He'd taken a separate chamber.

Was he already regretting this marriage? Had he lied to her out of some absurd sense of chivalry? Did duty force him into a match he couldn't tolerate? Had it moved him to pretend desire? How much dissemblance did a spy learn in his work?

Certainly enough to fool a fool in love. The rest of the long courses were torture, with a man who now sat politely, but strangely distant, during the interminable meal.

Well, she'd done it, and there was nothing for it now but to find some way to live with it. Or without. America, she thought, and sipped her wine in a silent toast to alternatives.

The staff finally arrived to clear the table. She held on to her glass of wine. Unusual as it was for her to have drunk three glasses in one night, she didn't really care. She'd hoped to drift through the evening, only to find that she still felt quite sober.

Headleymoor had fixed his gaze upon her for a great deal of this interminable meal, in a broody sort of way that left her wondering just how much he resented this match.

She was tired of the unremitting tension that left her shoulders so stiff she thought they might crack if she moved them. She was herself, first and foremost. If Headleymoor were a sham in every way, she would refuse to remain with him. It was part of their agreement, after all. Although it would be a shame, given William's reaction to the match. She grinned.

"A penny," he said from where he brooded in shadow.

"I was just thinking of William and how absolutely flummoxed he looked today. He truly didn't know whether he was relieved or horrified that you'd gone through with it."

"You speak as though I were facing a firing squad, Caroline. Was it that bad for you?" Those winged brows drew together.

"This morning? Oh, no," she said, gesturing with the glass, deliberately nonchalant. "Almost painless, I'd say."

"I see," he said rather curtly, and rose from the table. "I shall call your maid." Halfway across the room, he turned toward her. In an expressionless voice, he said, "And why would William be either relieved or horrified?"

She rose and moved to the far window. "Because now there are two members of his family who can outshoot him."

Headleymoor stared at her for a moment and then gave a sharp burst of laughter. At least he could laugh, she thought. If not, it truly would have been hopeless. His gaze metamorphosed into warmth and amusement, and something stirring beneath that. Her heart hammered while a million thoughts raced through her mind.

Perhaps I was wrong. He's always moody. He might come tonight, after all. Will he open that door and cross this floor? Will he knock before he comes in? If he does knock, how loudly will I need to call? What if I shout and wake sleeping travelers? What if I'm too nervous and he doesn't hear me at all? Should I be in my bed? Should I wear the scandalous gown Lilias gave me? Will he slip beneath the quilt without a word?

"Caroline . . ." his deep voice interrupted her thoughts. He bowed. "Until the morning, my dear," he said. "Have a sweet rest."

She could almost hear a clunk as her expectations dropped and smashed at her feet. Thus, as the clock struck midnight, Caroline lay in her big, empty bed, reliving the sound of that final click of the door as Headleymoor left her alone in the dining chamber. There had been no sound since but that of the grandfather clock at the bottom of the stairs, tolling off the quarter hours.

She was alone and very sober with her thoughts.

It was her wedding night. She was a bride, for pity's sake.

Exactly.

Married for the sake of pity.

"It can be wonderful," Lilias had said.

Caroline rolled over to her side and plumped her pillows with her fist. Apparently not. She sighed. "I suppose it's America for me, after all."

CHAPTER FOURTEEN:
AUSTIN HEATH

At dusk the following day, they entered the iron gates of Austin Heath. Of course, in the matter of all fiascos, this one had been prolonged today. The blacksmith had needed more time with the wheel. Headleymoor had grown more and more silent as the hours dragged by. She could feel the impatience and tension inside him. She simply refused to contemplate another night with the same incomprehensible bear of a man. She'd walk to Austin Heath if necessary. But at last, the carriage was ready and the horses hitched, and now here they were about to spend another night in separate bedrooms, no doubt.

The long, silent drive had left Caroline nursing a headache. Hmm, she thought staring out the coach window. Left at the altar or left in the bedchamber—which was worse?

A man who looked somewhat familiar tugged at his forelock and shut the gates after them. The carriage rolled up a long gravel drive and crunched to a halt, rocking on its springs before a large manor house made of Cotswald stone.

A very familiar Antoine, his face wreathed in a broad smile, took down the steps as soon as the horses halted. Headleymoor jumped from the carriage and handed her out himself. They walked together up the granite stairway and through the open double doors to greet the servants lined up in the hall. Looking at them with a flush of gratification, Caroline realized that Headleymoor had brought the staff of Valoir to England for her.

Marcel, the butler, bowed low.

Remy, resplendent in a sparkling white coat, removed his chef's hat and bowed over her hand. "My lady, it is so very good to see you again, and now that you take your proper place as chatelaine, I hope you will see fit to look at my ideas for the serious subject of dinner each day. If you would be so kind as to give me a bit of time."

She smiled, so happy to see him again, with his broad cheeks, his twinkling eyes, his stocky frame that spoke of lifting heavy implements and tasting meals fit for the gods.

"Tonight I have put together several of my dishes for your superior palate to judge. If you can spare me some time, I shall be happy to hear your suggestions. I wish to only prepare the meals you would like," he told her.

"For now, we welcome our lady to her home," Marcel said gravely.

The line of servants applauded and said, "Hear, hear!"

"And *voilà*," Marcel said. "You remember Mimi? She is eager to take you up to your new chambers. I have taken the liberty of ordering hot water for you and m'lord to bathe. Francois is seeing to it now, so you will be refreshed from your long journey before you enjoy Remy's many courses tonight."

"That was very thoughtful of you, Marcel," Headleymoor said, and Caroline realized that he was gazing at her with that dark, edgy look that she'd foolishly thought she understood.

He took her arm and led her to the winding marble stairs. "I should like the pleasure of showing you to your chambers," he whispered, leaning close to her. He was doing it again—changing before her eyes from aloof to seductive. It was blasted unfair, and at the earliest moment she would tell him so. Despite her best efforts at remaining cheerful but unaffected, she felt a traitorous tingle that left her breathless.

As they climbed the stairs together, his body so close to hers, Caroline felt wrapped in strength and warmth.

She was afraid to hope. This might be yet another stutter start and stop in this strange courtship. There had been so many.

He opened the door onto a set of rooms. She was surrounded with sky blue and light. She walked into the first chamber. It was a sitting room of delicate gilt armchairs from the last century, upholstered in blue velvet. Leather-bound books in English and French stood on a shelf that also held stretched frames of canvass and paints. Across the room, on a mahogany desk, lay a ream of her new stationery, complete with Headleymoor's crest, a hawk soaring above a lion rampant.

"It's beautiful," she said.

"I am glad," he said simply, and took her hand to lead her into the second chamber, where she found a large, intricately carved four-poster bed with deep blue velvet curtains.

"I hope that you will be comfortable here," Headleymoor said as she took in the silken wall hangings and the mullioned windows, where curtains of the same deep blue velvet hung. She turned her head to find Headleymoor's intent gaze upon her. His nostrils flared, his cheeks were tinged with a glow of heat. He looked—he looked ravenous. His hot gaze moved slowly from her face to her breasts, and her breasts ached and swelled with need.

Oh, God, he could see it. He would understand how badly she wanted his touch. She quickly turned, hiding her face, her treacherous body, and bent to examine a small painting on the table beside the bed. "Sixteenth century?" she asked with a quaver in her voice.

"Yes." His tone was a growl. He cleared his throat and shifted his gaze to an open door so quickly that she wondered if she had mistaken what she'd seen on his face just seconds before. "In there is a dressing room," he said to her back. "You will find Mimi there, with all you will need to be made comfortable."

"Thank you."

"Until dinner," he said. Then, without another word, he turned abruptly and walked out through the doorway, into the sitting room, and out to the hall. She peered after him, biting her lip. It was happening again. She didn't understand him. She would never understand him.

"Milady?"

Caroline turned to see Mimi, smiling and curtseying from the dressing-room doorway, and she sighed, walking toward the large copper tub that steamed with water scented like the roses in her bridal wreath.

She'd turned from him in disgust. Seeing her in that bedchamber after he'd so carefully chosen the colors for her, even to the smooth sheets upon which he'd envisioned her, he could no longer hide his naked lust. It was so strong she'd seen it in his face. And turned her back on him.

She didn't want him.

Francois shaved him quickly. After that, Dev dismissed him. He threw off his clothing and left it where it lay. Hurrying into the dressing room that adjoined Caroline's, he stepped into the tub. From the connecting door, he could hear water splashing and the soft voice of his bride answering a question from Mimi. Now he understood her behavior last night.

After Caroline had hastily downed her third glass of wine, he'd wondered if she was, indeed, beset by absolute terror. And then in the coach she'd been unusually silent. The doctor in him suggested the obvious—a hangover. However, upon seeing the servants, she'd perked up considerably.

Now, hearing her laughter, he realized that she was enjoying Mimi far more than she'd enjoyed his company last night. He admitted to himself that he hadn't been charming. Hell, he'd been downright laconic. He'd been waiting for this moment for too long and the interminable delays had made him into a growling mass of frustration. No wonder she didn't want him.

She wanted Ram Dass.

She wishes to have children, he thought, grimly soaping his arms and chest. How'd she think that would happen if she dismissed him so abruptly? He sloughed water over his head and shook out the droplets as he pondered the puzzle.

No. It didn't make sense. When he kissed Caroline, when he'd touched her before, she seemed to enjoy it. Had someone told her that the marriage act was a distasteful and hurtful necessity? Could she be terrified?

God, what was he to do?

She was his wife, damn it. She'd agreed. She wanted children. They had to get through the first time, and there was only one way to handle it. He must be the very picture of an English gentleman caring for his new bride.

Damn. He didn't feel like a proper English gentleman. He felt like a raging Zaranbadian.

He heard a splash and then a soft laugh, and then he realized that she must be stepping out of her bath. Mimi would be wrapping the linen towel around Caroline now. Mimi would help Caroline into her stockings and her chemise in just a moment. Her skin beneath was no doubt as luminescent as the sweet curves he'd touched when he'd unbuttoned her gown.

He swallowed hard and fought against the tight pull of his groin. They would discuss this as doctor and patient. It would be like a class in anatomy. They could get through this. Now.

Without conscious volition, he rose from the bath. Water sluiced all over the floor. He took the towel from the stool beside the bath and quickly rubbed himself. As he pulled on the silk dressing gown and tied it round his waist, he could feel the water drops running into his neck and wetting the gown. It clung to him, damp and cool, but heat sizzled through him.

Yes, he told himself with gritted teeth. He was the doctor. This was just like surgery. The sooner done, the sooner the healing could begin.

He threw the lock on the dressing room door and lifted the latch, walking barefoot into Caroline's chambers. The scent of roses filled his nostrils. Caroline sat at the dressing table, in dishabille, a blue silk gown falling from her shoulder. Her back was to him. A large cheval glass stood slightly to her left, and he saw that the dressing gown, tied at the waist, had opened, to reveal a glimpse of one long, smooth leg, clad in a white silk stocking.

In that moment, all of Dev's logical plans went straight to hell. He moved forward, as in a dream of pure, unadulterated lust, not thinking, not preparing his lecture, just feeling.

Mimi noticed him, and the brush she held stopped halfway down the length of Caroline's glorious auburn hair, glowing like a sunset in the lamplight.

The maid gave him a questioning look and he nodded toward the outer door. She curtsied and stepped away from Caroline. He took the brush from Mimi's hand and laid it down on the dressing table.

Caroline's face turned up to him, eyes wide with surprise. "How quietly you move," she said, and her voice was merely a breath. She was looking at him, following a drop of water that slid down his neck to his chest and disappeared beneath the lapel of the dressing gown.

His heart leaped in his chest. That was not fear on her face. That was bold, unvarnished fascination.

He lifted a lock of her hair to his face, inhaling the sweet scent of wildflowers. "Your hair is like flame, the way it catches the light."

It was too late. Had been too late when he'd unlatched the

door between their chambers. He bent, swooped her up into his arms, and carried her to the bed.

Now? Caroline thought in mixed panic and eagerness as Headleymoor bent over her, one knee on the bed, his hands braced on either side of her shoulders. She scooted up into a sitting position, backing against the headboard until the carving dug into her back.

"What are you doing?" she asked in a breathless voice. "I feel as though a different person has just walked into the room. Of course, with you it could be any number of different people."

He shook his head, drew a finger down her cheek, her throat, the gaping opening of her gown. She shut her eyes and arched, helpless against that touch. "I can't help it, Caroline. I don't know what's happening to me, but I can't seem to stop."

Her heart leaped at the ragged sound of his voice. She put her hand against his cheek, feeling the hard contours of his face. "Don't stop. I don't want stuffy Lord Headleymoor. I don't like him."

"Thank God." He bent to her, took her lips in deep, penetrating possession, ravaging them, his tongue playing with hers in a dance that had her heart racing madly and her body going limp and pliant beneath his hand.

His head lifted and he gazed into her eyes. "I have to feel you, all over."

"This is it, isn't it?"

"Yes," he said, "to my infinite relief."

"But I have a lovely night rail. It—it's very flattering. I was supposed to be dressed in it."

"Wear it tomorrow," he said, and with clever fingers, parted the gown further above the tie at the waist.

"Dear Lord." She watched him stare down at her breasts and her belly and down, down there, where the silk caressed her legs and the place between them. His searing gaze followed his hands, and he was breathing deeply, staring at everything.

"You're not undressed, either," she said.

"One would hope to rectify both situations as quickly as possible."

He loosed the tie and opened her gown, his gaze making a slow sweep from head to toe, like a gourmand at a feast, not quite knowing which dish to begin first. She lay there, feeling that odd tingle in her belly and slick warmth between her thighs. Dear Lord, could he see? The silk felt positively wicked at her back as Headleymoor bent over her.

His fingers caressed her cheek, then lower, her throat and neck, her collarbone, and down, down, and all she could do was stare back at him. His dressing gown had fallen open at his chest. She took him in, the muscled wall of his chest, the sheen of golden skin in the candlelight.

His lips followed the movement of his fingers, down, down, and then he was kissing her there. On the swell of her breast. She shut her eyes and moaned.

Oh heaven, he could see everything—even to the rose of her nipple. Her breath was coming in short, shallow pants. His thumb brushed across her nipple, and ripples of flame shot through her. She heard her soft cry of need and felt her legs sliding along the silk, trying find purchase in what was now a world swirling in new sensations.

"God, I love you like this. You are so beautiful," he whispered.

She opened her eyes to catch his gaze, a curious mix of awe and hunger.

She gained courage with that look, from the words that seemed wrenched from him. Besides, she was dreadfully curious.

Her hand came up to his chest and she touched him, stroked him. "How different you are from me," she said with a laugh that turned into a gasp as he gently squeezed and rubbed. She could feel her breast swell in his hands, heavy and ripe, while deep within her the flame blazed higher.

She touched him where he was touching her. Her hands parted the dressing gown further so she could see the damp shining curls on his chest. His hair was darker here, a soft furring of brown on the contours of muscle.

He was warm, so warm. Beneath her palm, his heart beat hard and fast and steady. Then she lost all thought as he bent, his head close to what he held and caressed, and blew a warm breath on her nipple. That was all it took to make her cry out, shock and pleasure streaming through her nerves.

"I want you, Caroline. Every bit of you," he said fiercely. "Don't be afraid."

It was a plea, she thought vaguely. "I'm not afraid."

"Good," he said. The bed shifted, sank, and he was lying beside her, and all the while his hands kept up their teasing, sending more fire through her body. He kissed her hard and she heard a moan. It was her moan, a small animal sound from deep in her throat.

His leg came up between hers and she squirmed, trying to get closer to the urgent need he was engendering with his thigh pressed up against her—there. It was heavenly and she whimpered, wanting something, wanting more.

He must have known what it was, for his hands moved beneath the bottom of the silken cloth. The next she knew, he was stroking up her leg, over the blue velvet garter at her thigh, and above, above, oh, so close to the ache in her. She thrust her head from side to side and moved her hips up to that hand, a silent plea for something more.

He found her in that moment. Found the curls that hid her private places. Bent his head and—God!—blew on them, his breath even hotter than it had been on her nipple. Would he?

No, it couldn't be done. She reeled in shock at herself. At what she was anticipating. No decent Englishman would do that.

But he did. He lowered his head and first he breathed deep, and groaned, as though the scent of her made him delirious.

She felt his tongue, tasting, savoring it seemed. Swirls of color burst behind her shut eyes, and she couldn't hold on much longer to sanity.

"Headleymoor!" she cried, as though he could anchor her in this whirlwind of aching delight.

He raised his head and she moaned in dismay for the loss of him and the wicked things he was doing to her.

"Look at me," he said in a tight voice.

It would be cowardly not to open her eyes, she thought through the haze and the need. She was his wife. She belonged to him. How odd. She'd never belonged properly to anyone before, other than her mother.

She peeked, and with an acute twinge of embarrassment and heat, awakened to her position. He was there, between her open legs, the deep eyes heavy-lidded now with the dark, dangerous sensuality she'd sensed in him before.

"Shall I stop?" he whispered. His sensual lips curved in a smile of absolute dominion. As though he knew every secret longing, every crazed wish she hid even from herself. She realized that this had drawn her to him, as much as his courage and his beauty and his mystery.

"Please," she said.

"Tell me you want this, Cara. Tell me you like what I'm doing to you."

If she didn't admit to these dark secrets, he would stop. It was too much to ask. Yet she couldn't hold back. "Don't stop. God, Devlin. Don't stop!"

She writhed, and beseeching sounds came from her. In contrast, he was a mystery again, covered while she lay wanton, completely revealed to him, so exposed. Her hand slipped toward her breasts to cover what she could.

His hand covered hers, holding it before she could hide from him.

"I am your husband. Give me my name," he said fiercely. And lowered his head slowly, holding her gaze, letting her know his intent, until she gasped when he kissed her there, and closed her eyes again. This time, it was faster and harder to resist. The dark pleasure swirled up, driving, pushing her toward something, and it was frightening how she wanted it, without knowing what it would be to lose herself so completely.

He lifted his head, and she lay panting, wanting, whimpering.

"Give in to it," he whispered, brushing his lips against the curls. "Call me by my name!" Hearing that plea on those wicked, clever lips, she had to follow his command and the mad, magnificent torment, up, up and out and crashing against the universe, in colors that sparked and flung themselves against the darkness.

"Devlin!" she screamed and flew.

A few moments later, her body was filled with thrilling little aftershocks and her mind reeled. Who was this golden sensualist, and where was her distant husband? And how was she ever to deny the ardent need he roused in her with one devilish glint of a smile?

Dev found himself smiling against the soft skin of her thigh. His wife, unafraid, joyful, melting in his arms.

His.

From where his cheek rested, he could feel little shudders of pleasure ripple through her as she lay beneath him, her beautiful body limp and pliant. Her hand was in his hair, stroking through the damp curls he hadn't even taken time to comb out before he rushed to her from the bath. And all the while his blood beat, triumphant.

He moved up in the bed and took her in his arms. He'd got it all wrong. His luscious bride didn't care about the sheets. She just wanted him.

She stroked his cheek, his neck, his chest, like a child learning to play a wonderful new game. He had to keep her like this, free and unencumbered by guilt or self-consciousness.

It amazed and humbled him that he had found the one woman who could feel so much.

If the raging demand of his body didn't beset him right now, he would have called this moment perfect.

She snuggled into him sleepily, her back to him, her rounded bottom pressed against his rock hard erection, maddeningly provocative.

He wanted her now. But he wanted her always willing. She moved against him and he stifled a groan of pure frustration. He stroked the long flame of her hair and kissed the back of her neck, holding himself still against the urgency to press into her from behind, to take her now, when she was wet and soft and willing.

Perhaps they needed a short intermission. With dinner and some wine and some brandy. He'd give her a scientific lecture on coitus. That was it. Knowledge would triumph over her maidenly fears.

He gritted his teeth against the demands of his body. "It grows late. Remy will be very unhappy if we do not dress and go down to dinner."

She looked off into the shadows filling the bedchamber now, and he realized it was full night.

"I don't quite understand how we're to have those children if you cannot bring yourself to bed me," she said in a fierce little voice.

He shot up beside her. "Bring myself! I've spent the last two days in a lather of heat for you. Did you not realize how out of sorts I was?"

She nodded, her eyes wide and a hint of a smile on her lips. "It was difficult to miss it."

"And you had no idea that it was brought about by unrequited lust?"

She shrugged. "If that was so, why did you not come to me last night? Why would you wish to stop now?"

"An English gentleman worries about such things."

"What things?"

He threw his hands up in frustration. "The sheets, damn it!"

"The sheets at the inn were perfectly clean," she said.

"They wouldn't have been for long," he huffed. "With an innocent, there's the probability of blood."

She stared at him, a thoughtful look in her eyes. "That's the way Englishmen handle the consummation of marriage? Everything clean and pure?"

He nodded.

"What about Zaranbadian gentlemen? Would they do the same?"

He shook his head, not daring to breathe.

She smiled, a lush, delighted tilt of her lips. "Well, then. As much as I appreciate your consideration, it's already made for some uncomfortable misunderstandings."

She leaned toward him. Her small hands wandered from his shoulders to his chest, and then toward the sheet that covered his rampant erection.

"If you please, Devlin," she said, "be a Zaranbadian gentleman tonight."

He felt a slow, answering grin spread on his face. His own bride, liberating him to act upon every secret, rakish desire he'd experienced in the last weeks of celibacy.

With deliberation he rose from the bed and began lighting

every candle and every lamp in the room.

"A gentleman from Zaranbad is a selfish swine. He wouldn't give a damn if his young bride was shy. If he wanted to see her in all her beauty, she would have no recourse but to stand before him naked as the day she was born." He held out his hand and helped her to rise from the bed. And then he slid her robe from her shoulders. In a whisper of silk it drifted to the ground at her feet.

She was blushing, of course. He could see the rose tint from the tips of her breasts to the top of her head. He twirled his finger imperiously at her and she lowered her gaze, obediently turning so he could see all of her in the bright light of the candles. Her white silk stockings caressed the contours of her slim calves, and the blue velvet garters that held them up emphasized the rounded beauty of her thighs.

"Naked but for those stockings, Caroline. They're quite alluring. You may keep them on."

He picked up a small bottle from the dressing table and pulled out the stopper. "The bride's maid would have already anointed her with perfume," he said.

Caroline felt the heat of her blush cover her whole body. Devlin was walking toward her with the graceful, predatory gate of a jungle cat. He stood right in front of her, a tall, glorious figure of a man holding a delicate, etched glass perfume bottle. The intimate space between them was filled with the scent of jasmine.

Devlin tipped the bottle and a drop fell onto his finger. "In fitting with the customs of Zaranbad, she would have placed it everywhere her new husband would wish to kiss her."

His finger slid from the sensitive spot beneath her ear down the line of her neck. He tipped the bottle again and rubbed the center of her collarbone and down into the valley between her breasts.

Her breath hitched and she shut her eyes, shivering, as the scent rose to her nostrils. His damp finger stroked her nipple and he rubbed the perfume in with thumb and finger. She looked down to see the shine of the jasmine oil on the beaded crest as he applied the perfume to her other breast.

He turned her away from him and knelt silently at her feet. She couldn't see him. It sent a chill of excitement and anxiety through her. Where would he touch her next? What was he looking at?

She had never, ever seen herself naked in a mirror. Did he think she was too round? She hadn't ever paid much attention to her hips and thighs. And now he was looking at them—from a position where he could see everything! She gave a start as she felt his touch, slick from the perfumed oil, stroking the back of her knee.

"Do you want me to stop, Caroline?" His voice was sinful, dark, delicious.

"No," she whispered.

"Then as a Zaranbadian gentleman, I demand that my bride pretend to a sophistication she does not feel. As though we've done this many times. As though this is all solely for your pleasure and you are determined to take it."

She could actually hear the grin in his voice. "As you wish," she said, her heart thumping. It was a game, but it was a deadly serious one. His finger stroked again, this time the sensitive skin at the back of her other knee.

And then, before she could think, two damp fingers drifted up the backs of her thighs and outlined the low curve of her bottom. She felt the excitement mount, felt the answering dampness of arousal between her thighs. His finger came to her again, opening them. Then she felt his touch, sliding down the line between her buttocks. She gasped and wriggled. His finger stilled, right at the point where the folds hiding her womanhood throbbed, plump and aching. His other hand cupped one rounded nether cheek. He bit her there.

She suppressed a squeak of shock.

"Shall I stop?" he asked her softly. "Or do you enjoy this?"

How could she admit to liking this—his inappropriate touch? In full lamplight, rather than under the covers, as she'd heard proper husbands initiated their wives into the act? But he'd taken his hand away. If she didn't speak, she'd lose this amazing feeling.

"Don't stop!"

"You enjoy my touch there, so close to your private place? Tell me, Caroline."

She could barely manage a coherent sentence. Her heart was pounding, and her legs felt as though they could barely support her.

"If you want me, you must tell me," he said. "You are my obedient bride, and I shall do whatever shocking things I wish to you. But you must say yes." His finger slid into the wetness there, and she felt the warm jasmine oil anointing her folds and then the slow slide of it round the small, aching nubbin that she had never known existed until tonight.

"Yes!" she cried out.

"Go to the bed, Caroline. Lie upon it and open your thighs to me. I want to see you glistening with perfume and ardor."

Somehow, she managed to walk to the bed and arrange herself as he'd directed. He rose from the floor and followed, dropping his dressing gown as he came. She peeked at his face. His nostrils flared, his eyes burned, and the color was high on his sculpted cheeks. To her, he looked the god of love, sensuality incarnate.

Her gaze dropped to his hard chest, the slim hips and taut belly, and below, to the powerful evidence of his arousal. He was larger than she'd even thought. She rose on one elbow, holding out her hand to touch him. He shook his head and smiled down at her. His hands came to her thighs and spread them even farther apart.

"You're very wet," he said as he gazed at her there, an arrogant Zaranbadian husband doing as he pleased. She wanted to squeeze her legs together. She wanted to pull him down to cover her and to enter that aching, pulsing place.

"I've changed my mind," he said, kneeling between her spread thighs, running his fingers through her curls, and then around and around that bud, rousing a need in her that made her cry out in rising anticipation and anxiety. He'd changed his mind. Would he stop? Leave her hanging this way? Now?

But his chest was lightly beaded with sweat and heaving as though he'd run up a mountain. She decided that she was not the only one hanging.

He grinned, still playing lightly with that spot that caused such pleasure and frustration. "I shall not kiss you—yet. I shall enter and slake my lust, like any proper man from Zaranbad."

He stroked her again, where she ached. A moan escaped her throat and she rocked against his hand.

"An obedient Zaranbadian bride does not move. Not if she wants her husband to continue."

She stopped, her legs trembling with the effort to remain still. "You are a wicked man, Devlin Carmichael."

"I am," he agreed. "I hope that pleases you."

One finger entered, testing. She felt her muscles squeeze around it, and cried out softly.

"Yes," he said. "Oh, yes. Just like that." Two fingers entered, and stroked slowly back and forth. She rose with them, clenching, her hips thrusting.

"I—I have to . . ."

"Say it, Cara. You must say what you want."

She was hot with need and embarrassment. But she had to

tell him or he wouldn't continue. "I need to move. Against you. Please."

"All right. Soon." He came to her then. Slowly, inch by inch he filled her.

Her passage strained to take all of him, but he was very large. He gave her time to adjust, to become used to him, and then he pushed into her more. The oil and the juices of her desire eased his way. She whimpered once, when he pressed against something—a barrier. He gritted his teeth, looking tortured, as though this hurt him, too.

"Cara, hold onto me."

She raised her arms and wrapped them around his neck. His hands came beneath her buttocks, and squeezed, lifting her up against him. And he thrust, swiftly, and certainly, all the way in to the hilt.

"Ow!" She bit back another cry. He lowered his head to her breast, his breath coming in sharp gasps.

"It will feel better in a moment," he said. "I promise."

She waited. One moment passed. Then another.

The pain eased, leaving behind a fullness that stretched her.

"Cara? Is it any better?"

She nodded.

"Because I'm the one who has to move. I simply have to."

She nodded again. He pulled out, slowly, and then came back to her. Again. And again. It began to feel better. Then it began to feel really good. Something was building. Something different from the first time—fuller, rising from deep inside, until she had to move with him.

"Open your eyes, Devlin," she said.

For his part, Dev hadn't realized he'd screwed them shut so he wouldn't see the disappointment on her face.

And she was smiling up at him, and she said in a hopeful voice, "We can keep doing this?"

And his chest filled to bursting with a deep, thrumming gong of joy that came from the earth and the sky and the oceans. Fire soared through him and he moved, gently at first.

And she said, "Oh. Oh, my."

So he did it again, and again, and the fever caught at him, and not once did he look away from her, so free and glad and passionate she looked. He heard the soft slap of slick bodies coming together at that place where they joined, felt the welcoming, silken tightness of her, the way she clenched around him as he thrust and slowly retreated. He heard his voice, his exclamations of wonder as he said her name, over and over again.

She was moving with him now, in a dance as old as time, and her breath was a soft sob in his ear as he bent to her neck and buried his face in it, moving, moving, loving the feel of it, free of worry about not being an English gentleman, free of everything but connection. Connection to her, his wife, his own, spirit to spirit and all of it joy.

She cried out, a surprised, sweet gasp in his ear, and he felt her contract and clench around him. He plunged, deep and strong, and whole, and took her, and took her, and took her, and fell, touching life as he gave it, deep inside her.

He lay stunned for a while before he recovered sufficiently to realize his weight was probably squeezing the breath out of her. He rolled and took her with him, so she lay atop him, resting against his chest in utter trust.

Never in his life had he forgotten himself so completely. Actually, now that he thought of it, never had he forgotten himself at all.

And he realized that with Caroline, the loss of his vaunted self-control was as seductive as the act itself.

He kissed the top of her head, then gazed down at her as

amusement tugged his lips. "This business of innocence, Cara. I should have known that of all women you would have faced this experience with no fear."

She glanced up and shrugged, a half-apologetic, half-embarrassed gesture. "I can't take credit for courage. I thought it would be easy . . . well, you see . . . Janighar's mother . . . it had to do with riding astride." She blushed and stared down at her hands.

"Caroline," Dev said sternly. "Janighar's mother is not particularly the best source for such information."

"Obviously," she said. "But she was the only source." Caroline stole a look at him as an idea seemed to strike her. "Perhaps it was lovely in the end because of riding astride," she said. "I mean, because there was little pain and a great deal of pleasure."

Dev manufactured a disgruntled look for her. "You might have massaged my masculine pride by telling me that was due to my expertise."

"That too," she said. "But of course, I haven't enough experience to make a scientific comparison."

"Nor will you," he said fiercely. He pulled her into his arms and kissed her. "You are mine," he said. "Mine."

"Well, then, it follows that you are mine," she said. And kissed him right back, little kisses like butterflies, brushing his lips, his cheeks, his neck. "I like the way you taste," she whispered, and he felt the heat begin again, almost painful as she brushed her lips against his chest. Her tongue licked across his nipples. He realized as his groin tightened that Caroline was experimenting, with all the careful intent of scientific exploration. Without thought, he rolled her over, took her face in his hands, and lowered his mouth to hers.

When he pulled back to turn her in his arms and force his unruly blood to cool, she smiled up at him.

"Oh, yes. Again," she said.

"No. You'll be sorry tomorrow."

"I don't care," she said, and lifted her hips to him, sweet and pliant and strong. Strong enough to meet his passion with the innocent joy and curiosity of a child in a new, magical world.

He shut his eyes and let her joy wash over him, smiling as the old, painful sense of isolation melted away.

"Rest now," he whispered. The doctor in him knew it was too soon. He could not take her. But he could hold her. His arms wrapped around her, hanging on to the pure pleasure of her in his arms. For now, it was enough to steal a little joy from this miracle he'd made his own.

For her part, Caroline lay within the circle of his arms, smiling. Her husband was a new Devlin Carmichael. A man who had thrown off his aloofness as one would toss an old cloak aside when coming in from a storm.

How curious marriage was, she thought, as he pulled her close and wrapped his arms around her. How wondrous.

The excitement of the last days, and, she realized, the tension, had worn her out. Or perhaps relief had made her suddenly exhausted. She began the slow, soft slide into sleep.

In the last waking moment, at the edges of her consciousness, a hand stroked her from shoulder to waist to hip, and a voice deep as velvet whispered, " 'Now lies the Earth all Danae to the stars.' "

Tennyson's *The Princess*, she thought, or dreamed.

" 'And all thy heart lies open,' " she murmured.

No longer alone. It was a hope, not a statement of fact. The wings of caution hovered above her, but she was warm and safe and at peace. It was enough. She let the darkness take her.

"Jonathan! Oh, God. Abdul!"

Caroline woke with a start. By the dim light of the fire in the grate she could see Devlin lying beside her. His eyes were wide open and he was shifting, restless, murmuring names of strangers.

"Devlin," she whispered. "What is it?"

He didn't appear to hear her. She shook him lightly, trying to pull him from the dream that held him in its claws.

He turned away on his side, his body curled in on itself, and he moaned, "Breathe. Breathe!"

She moved over, cautious now, and slowly, very slowly, put her arms around him. "Devlin, wake up," she said, stroking his arm, his back.

He jerked, came awake with a start, rolled over and stared at her.

"What is it?" he asked, but Caroline could see his gaze shift downward, away from hers.

"You had a dream."

"What did I say?" He was looking past her now, into the grate across the room.

"I couldn't make it out. Do you want to talk about it?"

His body relaxed. "I can't remember it. Just a dream. I'm sorry I woke you. Come. Let's go to sleep again." And he pulled her up against him, her back to his front, his arm around her, holding her like a shield against the night.

She lay very still, keeping her breathing even. For a long time she kept it up. Knowing he was still awake, too, and not the least inclined to confide in her about whatever demons made him cry out in his sleep.

The next days passed in a haze of sensual delights. Remy's supreme gastronomic artistry was on display every afternoon and evening. Rich Burgundies and Bordeaux accompanied dinner, and Caroline wafted up the stairs toward their bedroom in a decadent, wine-warmed haze of anticipation.

Her husband made love with a joyous sense of discovery. She

wondered what his past had been, and why, given his obvious skill, which pointed to a great deal of practice, he could exhibit such fascination in one female body.

The weather was unseasonably warm and Remy had packed them a picnic basket. They'd dressed informally, Devlin in a shirt and breeches. The shirt was open at the neck and rolled up at the sleeves. Caroline had dispensed of her crinolines and wore a simple white gown that buttoned up the front.

Walking beside him, Caroline stole glances at the strong column of his neck, the glimpse of light brown hair where the shirt gaped, and the love bite she'd put there the night before. She touched her own neck where it met her shoulder, feeling the slight soreness of his love bite, and thought with a start about their behavior.

She couldn't necessarily say that it was Devlin's fault, as she'd matched him in shameless promiscuity. The things they did . . . she could feel the blush heat her cheeks, and up even farther. Her whole face was in flame.

Devlin must have felt her glance and guessed from her heightened color what she was thinking, for he looked beneath his lashes at her and a grin of intense male satisfaction spread on his face.

Caroline thought back over all the times she'd spent in ballrooms with nothing much to do but observe. Aubrey, Lord Breme, was the only man she knew who gave his wife that look. And Lilias had also blushed, and looked down, hiding the smile that tugged at her lips. Well, at least Devlin and she weren't the first couple to engage in such depraved sensuality.

The lake lay before them, past the grassy slope where they walked. As they drew closer, Caroline saw that the bank dropped off abruptly.

"This is the best spot," Devlin said, as he stopped and placed the basket on the grass beneath a venerable oak. The dappled leaves of its far-flung branches cooled Caroline after the warmth of the walk and her speculations.

"If my lady wishes," he said with a flourishing bow, and spread a blanket for her.

Caroline settled on it and lay back on her elbows, watching the sun glint on the little waves rippling in the breeze coming off the lake.

"This is heaven," she said.

"The lake?"

"This house, the lake, this week," she said, gathering courage. After all the stutter starts and stops between them, it took boldness to say what she meant. "I wish . . ."

"What?" he asked, easing down beside her and turning on his side to look at her.

"That we could stay here forever."

He kissed her shoulder. "Good."

They lay back on the blanket, watching the clouds drift by, little fluffs like lamb's wool. Devlin made a lazy roll toward the basket and unearthed a bottle of Muscadet, the white wine from Normandy Remy had packed for them. Caroline turned her head to watch, goggle-eyed, as he pulled the cork with his teeth and handed her the bottle.

It was deliciously cold in her hand. In her imagination, her mother stared at her in shock. She sat up and gave him a questioning glance. "I'm to drink from the bottle?"

He grinned. "A new first," he said.

"Too much of a slacker to hand me a glass, are you?" She grinned back at him and raised the bottle to her lips. The wine was tart and clean going down. A few drops spilled onto her lips and chin. All those years of obeying the rules caught up with her and, self-conscious, she turned her face away from him, raising her hand to wipe the drops off.

"Leave it," he said, taking the bottle from her hand and placing it in a silver bucket. He leaned forward, and delicately as a cat, licked the drops from her lips, and the few on her chin, and then his tongue trailed back again, to her mouth.

Wet kisses, full, rich, deep, his fingers deft on her buttons. Even with corset, chemise and petticoats, this man could undress a woman in record time. He had her simple gown off her within a moment or two, and when she protested, he left her with the questionable protection of her translucent shift.

He pulled back to shed his shirt and trousers and she surfaced from the hazy delight. Only his small clothes remained. As he rolled over on his side again, facing her, she was torn between taking her fill of marvelously muscled thighs and chest and shoulders, or stiffening in self-conscious embarrassment.

Embarrassment won out. "Wait," she whispered, glancing around. The lake was open to fields on either side.

"Why?" His fingers walked up her leg, on a hunting trip for the garter holding her stocking.

"Anyone could come." She pushed his hand away and hid her head against his chest.

He smiled down at her. "I gave orders."

Her eyes narrowed. "That means they all know what we're doing!"

"Not all. Jem Baker's too young to know."

"The stable boy's the only one?"

He rolled to his feet. There was a devil dancing in his dark eyes. And he was grinning as he took a swig of the wine, set it down, then hands on hips, feet wide apart, he stared down at her. She scrambled to her feet, caution warring with the heady excitement flowing through her. A game, she thought. A game like none she'd ever played in her solitary life.

"I'm very disappointed in you, Caroline," he said in mock solemnity. "You promised—in the holy ceremony of matrimony, I might add—to *obey*, and within the first week, you are proving extremely disobedient. As your husband, it is my duty to punish you for such disregard to your vows."

"Oh, ho! Just give it a try, won't you?" she said, and took flight. Forgetting she was clad only in shift, stockings and shoes, she raced for the wood behind them, a gurgle of laughter rolling up within her as she sped.

He was on her in ten strides, lifting her by her waist from behind and holding her, a soft breath of laughter on her shoulder. "Now you're really in for it," he said, his shoulders shaking in silent glee as he swung around and swept her up in his arms, a golden-haired Apollo to her Daphne, now kicking madly in mock battle.

As they reached the grassy bank, her slippers flew off.

"Excellent," Dev said, watching them arc and land near the picnic basket.

He strode with her to the lake's edge and then, with a wicked chuckle, leaped into the lake with her.

The icy water came up to her neck. She gasped and sputtered, then broke loose, walking backward deeper into the lake, feet dancing in slow motion through the sandy bottom, splashing for all she was worth. He shouted with laughter, splashing back, swimming after her. She grabbed a deep breath and jackknifed underwater to stroke quickly toward the center of the lake.

He'd be coming after her, she realized, but in the murk she'd kicked up, he'd not see her. She whipped about, swimming silently underwater toward him. And felt him moving above her, cutting swiftly through the water toward the spot where she'd disappeared. She reached out a hand and tickled his belly, inwardly laughing as he started at her touch. Immediately, she was grasped by two strong hands and pulled upward, to surface grinning into a face that wore a look of such agonized urgency, she stilled.

He pulled her to him, hard, and drew her back to the shore. He almost threw her up to the bank and then raised himself onto it and drew her close into the warm strength of his body. She could feel the beat of his heart, faster and stronger than any fit man's would have been after exercise. And Devlin, she knew, was very fit.

"God, Cara, don't ever do that to me again," he said into her neck. She could feel the tremors wracking him, hear the panic in his voice, the anguish.

"I can swim like anything aquatic," she said, stroking his back and his shoulders in a soothing motion.

"I realize that. Now. But the lake drops off there. And sometimes you're a little too adventuresome." He took a deep breath. "I don't wish to lose you. I can't."

She clung to him. "You won't! I'm not going anywhere."

"Not today, anyway," he said, and sighed. "Not today."

He pulled her down gently onto the blanket and held her. "You're cold," he said, his arms tight around her. "Let me warm you."

He was still shaking. It was he who was cold, she thought. Cold inside with some overwhelming chill she didn't understand.

"Oh, yes," she said and pulled his head down to hers. Her lips were within a breath of his when she whispered, "Make me warm."

They walked home through the wood, swinging hands. She remembered how, when she was a child, she'd sometimes seen the village children do so, and envied them. Now, to be the recipient of such a simple, affectionate gesture almost undid her.

"I think you should be quite pleased with yourself, Lady Headleymoor," Devlin said with a smile and a glance.

"And why is that, sir?"

"It's the third time you've made me beg."

That telltale blush heated her cheeks again, and she ducked her head, hiding it as best she could. After a moment of silence, curiosity mixed with a liberal dose of feminine vanity and made her bold.

"When were the first and second times?" she asked.

Devlin stopped and tipped Caroline's face up, examining her hot cheeks. From the slight curve of his lips, she had a sneaking suspicion that he enjoyed making her blush. It occurred to her that she had never blushed before she met him.

"You do remember that I proposed twice, do you not?" he said.

"Actually, it was three times, if we are to keep count," she said, and then her eyes grew wide in alarm at what she'd just blurted. He held his secrets so dearly. There were things about him that he didn't wish her to know, and this might well be one of them. She gulped in air and felt her cheeks burning even hotter.

"I don't recall three times. When was the third?" he asked her, puzzled, his eyes narrowing on her cheeks.

It was so tempting to lie. She gave him a long look of resignation, then shrugged. "In your incarnation as Ram Dass, of course. You didn't beg, but you certainly advised."

She watched him carefully enough to see the way his jaw tensed. "When did you know?"

"William said that you did certain 'work' for the Home Office. Don't worry," she said hastily. "He was loath to tell me, and only did so to soothe my wounded feelings. He's been keeping your secret for years now, and he extracted a solemn promise from me to keep mum about it."

"How did you get from the Home Office to Ram Dass?"

She waved her hand in dismissal. "Once I knew about the

313

Home Office, it was rather easy to put two and two together and get one."

He stared straight ahead, stiff again, aloof. "I never wanted that part of my life to touch you. The danger . . ." He broke off, and took a step toward home.

She grabbed his arm. "Either we have a marriage or we don't, Devlin."

He sighed, staring down at the ground rather than at her. "You don't understand. I've never talked to anyone about this. I've lived my life in the shadows."

"Well," she said, forcing a smile. "You're lucky now. I'm here, and willing to share the shadows as well as the sunlight."

"Seeing how cleverly you put together the pieces, I suppose it's rather a good thing you're on my side, and not the enemy's."

In the long pause that ensued, Caroline noted with surprise that her husband had just accepted her, despite her solving of that puzzle. How far would he permit her to delve into his secrets? "I take it you have gathered information for England as well as Zaranbad?" she finally asked.

He nodded. "I have," he said. No recriminations.

"Will you have to—ah—silence me now or can you tell me something about that?"

His lips curved and he glanced at her. "I can't possibly kill you, Cara. No one else could satisfy this overwhelming lust I feel for you."

A tingle of pleasure flowed through her, mixed with a twinge of disappointment. It was good that he wanted her. But how wonderful it would be to hear a word or two of affection from him.

"I know you were gone from England early last year. Can you tell me about that?"

He was silent for a long, long moment. "Afghanistan? I worked for Lord Ellenborough there." There was a white shade about his lips. He looked like a man suffering from a mortal wound and using all the strength he had left to keep from crying out.

"Did it have something to do with the terrible fate of the British hostages?" she asked softly, hoping against hope that he would tell her and let some of the poison that pained him out.

His eyes looked bleak as he stared past her. "I want to share myself with you, Caroline. But this is very hard for me."

Afghanistan! Such a dangerous, strange country, full of factions and bitter war, and Russian spies. Lord Ellenborough had saved the few British men, women and children who had not perished in that horror-filled death march from one end of the country to the other and back again through snow and ice. Caroline had strong suspicions that Devlin's work had somehow gotten Ellenborough the information he needed to rescue them.

Something very bad had happened at that time, she just knew it. Something that he still carried with him. *How alone he is,* she thought, *carrying all the responsibility for foolish commands that others had given, leaving him to mop up the mess they'd made.* The pain of his isolation wrenched her heart.

Someone had to help him. There had to be a way.

And then, easily as a fish sliding through the lake, the solution came to her.

"Devlin," she said eagerly. "It will be all right. I've just had a smashing idea!"

He gave her a look tinged with unease. "It is not that I don't appreciate your ideas, Cara. But they have sometimes ended with you in grave danger."

"I promise you, this will work. As long as the Home Office would accept a lady working for them."

Dev stared at Caroline in horror. He'd had a taste of what it would be like if he lost her today, and he couldn't bear it. He could see it now—Caroline blithely risking her neck in Russia, or India, or Afghanistan, while he stood by, a wreck of a man, probably driven to drink.

"No!" His fist struck a tree as he strode away from her toward the house. "Absolutely not. I'll have waking nightmares for the next week, imagining you in danger again. I can't do this."

She caught up with him as they reached the front doors and held on to his arm with both hands as they walked into the hall, the very image of a wifely supplicant if he ever saw one.

"Oh, but Devlin, just think of it," she said, her voice wielding that most powerful of feminine weapons, a sweet, pleading note. "We could be twice as effective together. I'm an excellent observer and very quiet, as you well know. Brown seems to make me almost invisible in a ballroom, and I would have entrée into places you would never be able to penetrate."

"Indeed," he said in as cool a tone as he could muster, given the terror that gripped him even thinking about it. He pulled her from the hall and took the first door into the library. "Where would that be?"

She gave him an exasperated look. "The ladies' retiring room, of course. Women tend to talk a great deal, even if most of it is nonsense. The wife of a—what would you call him, a person of interest?—might have heard something she didn't quite understand. That wife might, in a moment of shared conversation while her maid repairs her coiffure, reveal something you could not have discovered otherwise."

Half horrified, half fascinated, he stared at her. His reckless wife had the mind of a Lucretia Borgia. The Home Office would be delighted to have her.

Never, never, never, Dev vowed to himself.

"And if I would agree to such a foolish scheme, which," he said, raising a hand palm out to stop the eager rejoinder he saw about to form on her lips, "I shall never do, you must realize that you would be involved in some very sticky situations. Situations that would require perfect timing and nerves of steel."

She smiled. "Such as that night when we were set upon by those villains. I did rather well, at that, if I do say so myself." She went silent for a moment, but that silence didn't reassure him. He reckoned it simply meant she was thinking, and that was dangerous.

"I suppose you have code words for your comrades," she went on. "Words to let them know you'd learned something, or where to meet, or that you are in danger."

"Do sit down, Caroline." She dutifully sat on a dainty yellow sofa, her hands folded in her lap, an innocent seraph of a woman hiding the mind of a scheming Amazon. "This is absurd, and I forbid it."

Her posture was meant to reassure—head bent, hands clasped in her lap, a veritable study in false meekness. Dev released a sigh and sat beside her. He tipped her face up to him and stared down at her suspiciously. From the intent expression on her face, she seemed to be thinking so hard she was not even conscious of the fact that she'd trustingly begun to pat his arm in affection. He felt the warmth of that realization all the way down to his toes.

"We could arrange different codes for all sorts of things," she mused aloud. "For instance, if we were at a ball and you were speaking with a group of men and I'd learned something important, I could sail up to you and say, 'Darling, Aunt Celia sent us an invitation to visit. Isn't that grand?' And you would agree and soon after, we'd slip out and I'd tell you."

She was having much too much fun. It was time to inject a dampening note into this conversation.

"Life is never that smooth. What if we were both captured by murderous villains, and we had only one very small chance to escape? Would you even remember the code word? Would I, being so terribly frightened for you?"

She wrinkled her brow, actually deep in thought, dammit. Why could she not be horrified by the hellish picture he painted?

"I suppose for one thing," she said, "I would be carrying a pistol."

He began to pace, picturing her facing off with five Afghan tribesmen armed with a pistol and determination. "Suppose there are five villains and I'm unarmed?" he said grimly.

"Then I should be carrying at least three pistols." She brightened. "And perhaps two knives. You could teach me how to throw them the way you do."

Dear God, she'd been watching that business! Why the hell had William demanded he do a bit of knife throwing?

"They would search you," he said.

She shook her head. "I'm a weak, frightened woman, and a lady at that. They wouldn't dream I'm armed to the teeth."

"All right," he said. "What code word could we possibly remember with us both out of our minds with worry for the other?"

She smiled, all the mischief in the world in her sky blue eyes. "Ballocks!"

And then she ran out the library door, laughing over her shoulder, but slowly enough that he knew she wasn't giving it her very best. She wished to be caught.

My woman, he thought. *Mine.* He sprinted after her, feeling his lips quirk and his heart lighten. After all, he'd made his feelings on the subject very plain. He'd said no, clearly and concisely. They were only playing a game. He might as well relax. None of this would ever happen.

CHAPTER FIFTEEN:
FURTHER COMPLICATIONS

Gerard Visigore scanned the Society notes in the daily paper for the usual purposes. He'd been gone for two weeks, basking in the sun of southern France, enjoying the wine and the occasional willing demimondaine. He wasn't up to his full panoply of sensual tricks, mind. The headaches still bothered him on and off. But it was time to return to England and see what he could do, and where he could take advantage.

The Society pages were one of his greatest sources of information. They revealed more hints about the nobility than other sources, be it in business or in his own brand of pleasure.

There were the usual announcements of marriages and deaths, he noted. Perhaps a young widow known to him might desire a bit of company. An unusual bit of entertainment, perhaps. He had to be careful with such women. He couldn't mark them, for they might well go to their families, preferring disclosure and ruin to the continued danger of his blackmail.

One or two of them had actually wished for the humiliation and pain. Had begged for more. But he never really enjoyed those sorts of women. The ones who gave him satisfaction were the ones who would never forget him, whose dreams he would haunt forever.

Caroline Berring had been different from all the rest. Something in her called to him—her pride, her courage, her beauty. It was destined to be. They were made for each other. She was like an exquisite blood horse—the perfect creature to control. He didn't want to hurt her—not too much, anyway. He wanted her to love everything he did to her. To understand the glory of giving in to that darkness.

Soon, when the damned headaches left him, he would pursue her and win her trust, and then he would have the joy of taming her to his hand and showing her how good it could be.

His eyes moved steadily downward, noting the familiar names and what he knew about each family. Lord Wisely, for instance, had bad gaming debts and a fine piece of land that was not entailed. He might pick it up for a song.

A particular piece caught his eye.

"By Special license, Lady Caroline Berring to Devlin Ramsay Carmichael, Marquess of Headleymoor."

No. That wasn't right. His Caroline? No. His heart thudded in his chest, and he could feel the sweat break out on his brow. This could not be true. She was his perfect mate, meant only for him, not for that half-breed who'd flouted him so long ago.

He read the words again. Married from home, it said. Eversleigh.

He shook his head again and again, but the words didn't change. Headleymoor—a thorn in his side since school days.

A cold, black rage rose slowly, and then his mind took over, and the cunning that had kept him free to do as he wished for his whole life. He knew how he would repay Headleymoor. He'd chain him, make him watch what he did to Caroline. It would only add to the pleasure. No. There was too much danger in capturing them both. Headleymoor knew how to fight. He must first dispose of Headleymoor. Then there would be time to woo his widow.

He needed Kendall for this. He needed him now.

An hour after he sent for Kendall, a knock on the door sounded. The butler opened it to reveal Kendall standing in the doorway, his face pale and white, his eyes shadowed, his mouth strained.

Visigore waved him in and the butler shut the door behind him.

"I don't understand," Kendall said, looking about the chamber. "I was told to meet someone here."

Visigore smiled. "You have. Come now, Kendall. You hadn't guessed by now?"

"You're Wolf?"

Visigore felt nothing but disdain for the man who'd had contact with him so many times before. Headleymoor would never have been so slow.

"Of course I am." Quickly, he told Kendall what his orders were. But Kendall just stood there, a stubborn tilt to his jaw, his gaze full of that disgusting self-righteousness that had no place on the face of a traitor.

"I was glad when you summoned me, Wolf," Kendall said in a grim voice. "I wanted to tell you that I can't go on with it. There's been too much blood, too many men dead. I won't tell a soul," he added. "I'm in too deep to do that, and you know it. But I cannot put good men at risk. And I cannot kill one of the best men I have ever known."

Visigore stood up and pounded the desk, and his head pounded almost as hard as it had that day when he'd been attacked at Eversleigh. "Do you have any idea what your refusal will cost me?"

"I don't give a damn whether the Company wants to annex Zaranbad and rule it as it does India. I don't bloody care if it means you personally don't get the spoils you've been counting on, either. I can't do it. I won't do it. And if you push me too hard, I'll go to the authorities and to hell with my freedom. By God, I swear I shall."

Rage, black and bloody flamed before Visgore's eyes. His

head rang and pounded from it. "I can't deal with you now," he said. "Go."

He had to think, to get the pain under control. But sometime soon, Kendall would understand before he died just whom he had betrayed.

Caroline stood in front of the cheval glass, smiling at her image, or more correctly at the diamond necklace she wore. She'd found it on her pillow this morning when she'd awakened, and she had run into the library to thank Devlin for it as soon as she'd dressed. He'd looked up from his work, a report prepared by his steward at Headleymoor, then out the window at the rain.

At which he'd given her a smile so carefree and audacious that she'd caught her breath. Devlin had taken her hand and tugged her up the stairs to her bedchamber, where he quickly divested her of all she wore but the necklace.

And she . . . Well, the things she'd done with him. The things she'd done to him. Only a woman totally besotted with love would have so little sense of shame.

Caroline dropped to her knees and covered her face with her hands. She loved her husband.

A jolt of overwhelming fear struck her. She'd given her heart into Devlin's keeping little by little until now it was all his. There was no turning back from what she felt for him.

"Oh, dear God," she whispered. "I'm madly in love with a man who puts himself in danger all the time."

How had this happened? She was usually a strong, pragmatic person, a woman who knew that life was not particularly fair, that one must do without certain things. Like this deep, forever sort of love that had taken up residence in her soul, and would never, ever leave her now.

My whole being hinges on him, she thought. Now she understood why, in the early hours before dawn she would awaken and turn toward him, watching him as he slept, seeming so free of all care.

She'd touch him, holding her breath, afraid to wake him. But he would sleep on, deeply, in a kind of peace she envied. She understood now why the old devils had returned to haunt her, whispering: *You'll never keep him. If you cling, he'll tire of you.*

Devlin was a man used to excitement, to action, to duty. These days, so precious to her, weren't the normal days their lives would entail. They were an interlude before he left her for the secret, deadly work he did so well.

He would leave her soon for another assignment. She knew how she would feel—an empty husk, a ghost of herself, crying into the wind each night. Alone and frightened for him. She would pace through the long nights. And chafe, for he would never permit her to accompany him, and that was the only way she could face the fear.

Why would he not recognize the weapon he had in her? The disappointment that he'd not taken her offer to help frustrated her to the point of irrational terror. She would never be able to control the most important part of her life, and it could be snatched from her at any moment.

She had been strong until now. Until love made her weak.

Footsteps ran lightly up the stairs. Footsteps so familiar now, and so unbearably dear. Devlin knocked perfunctorily and flung open the door. His smile lit his whole face, and the light from the wall sconce in the hall behind him gilded his hair into a nimbus. Her beautiful husband.

He waved a piece of vellum in front of her.

"It's safe, now. We can go home."

Tears pricked her eyes, but she held them back and smiled. She smiled so he wouldn't know of her terror. Of her love.

"That's wonderful," she said. "When do we leave?"

The air in London seemed heavy and odor-laden after the fresh-ness of late May in the Cotswolds. As Dev led Caroline into the large front hall at Wimbley House, Ari and Janighar walked across the marble floor to greet them, followed by Dev's father, whose grin spread ear to ear.

The duke bent and kissed Caroline on the cheek. "Welcome to your home, my dear. I wish you to be very happy here."

Janighar was next as Ari took Dev aside, speaking quietly to him. She threw her arms around Caroline, hugging her with such strength that Caroline gasped a little and laughed.

"You've been honing your boxing skills I think," she said, putting Janighar back from her a little to look her over. "Oh, you look splendid. Was your retreat in the country pleasant?"

Before she could answer, King Ari called to them over his shoulder. "I wish to consult my brother on many plans I have thought of concerning Zaranbad's security. Perhaps the queen will take Lady Caroline to her chambers where they can enjoy a tête-à-tête."

As usual, with Ari, this was not a suggestion but a command. However, Caroline forgave him when she saw the light of surprise and joy in Devlin's eyes.

"Yes, thank you, Ari. That would be just as I wished," Jan-ighar said, her face aglow at the prospect.

A few moments later, seated in Janighar's pretty chambers and sipping tea, Caroline admitted that there were some secrets only friends shared with each other.

"You asked about our time at Wimbley," Janighar said. "It was the first time ever that I had Ari to myself. It was wonder-ful." Her lips turned down a bit in a moue. "And it was not so wonderful, too. You may remember that Ari can be quite protec-tive of me. With his mind no longer occupied with matters of government, it focused upon me. Why did I not have a shawl before I walked out with him? Why did I not finish my enormous breakfast? It did no good to ask how much of his plate was empty. My health, apparently, depended upon a full English breakfast, when I was used to a cup of yoghurt and cucumbers and a piece of flatbread. I do not know how to explain to him that I am blind but not an invalid."

Janighar sighed. "On the other hand, it was my greatest joy to be with him. He says that we must do this each year for a few weeks—just the two of us together, with no courtiers or ministers to take us away from each other." Her smile seemed rueful. "I veer from delight and anticipation to horror at the idea. But I shall not desist from finding a way to make Ari see that I am a healthy, independent woman, just as you are."

"That is a great compliment," Caroline said. "I hope that I can live up to it."

Janighar waved a hand, dismissing that comment. "You are what you are, dear Caroline. You cannot help but be brave and strong. And so shall I be, one of these days. Now, back to you. Are you happy?"

"Oh, yes. Very."

And not so brave. Scared, actually. All the time, now. But she couldn't share what she feared with Janighar. She could hardly bear to face it herself. Their return was not only to London but also to reality.

She must realize that she was not the center of Devlin's universe—far from it. Devlin was free again to resume what mattered most to him—his secret missions. And he would be dealing with the same sorts of men who had plotted against Zaranbad.

She just knew that one day she would hear a knock on the door, and a grave-faced man from the Home Office would come in to tell her that her life was over. She wondered if she'd sense he was gone before she was informed. Doubtless she would not. She was too pragmatic to have second sight. She wouldn't know until the worst happened.

At Eversleigh House, William held a ball, to which all of Devlin's and her relatives had been invited, as well as select members of the ton. Her mother and the duke—her father, she supposed she might call him soon—rode up from Eversleigh with William. Lady Farraday was there, with her cane. Its only use, as far as Caroline could see, was as a banging accompaniment to Lady Farraday's comments.

"I can see you've come out of your shell, my dear," she said, and kissed Caroline on the cheek. "Perhaps it's the gown," she added, raising her lorgnette and surveying Caroline from head to toe. "Green suits your coloring, as did the lovely blue gown you wore to Lady Breadley's soiree last night. I was getting quite weary of brown and ivory. Hmm, either the gown or the last weeks have done you a world of good. I shall insist upon the latter, I believe. I would so prefer to see that my suspicions were justified."

"And what suspicions would those be?" Caroline asked in mock horror, despite the blush she felt heating her cheeks. Only Lady Farraday could get away with mentioning one's honeymoon in public.

"That you and that young rogue you married were headed in that direction when last I saw you at the Queen's ball."

Caroline's blush grew even hotter. She had no quick rejoinder, but hovered mortifyingly between a gasp and a giggle. "I believe Headleymoor and I shall suit," she said, finally getting her voice under control.

"That's one way of putting it," Lady Farraday said. "Another would be that you're both head over ears for each other." She patted Caroline's cheek. "No reason to be embarrassed, my dear. I heartily approve. And I was beginning to believe I'd never see another love match in Society. Hoy there, my man," she called out to the butler who stood stoically nearby. "Where are you keeping that champagne punch?"

Devlin caught Caroline's eye and, easing himself from the group of men surrounding him, walked toward her, a private smile in his dark eyes.

A love match, Lady Farraday had said. Caroline watched him come for her, her heart quickening. And he was there, taking her hand and placing it on his arm, his body strong and tall beside her, warm with the life and heat of him drawing her closer, forming a circle where hurt and loneliness could not enter. It was enough for now. She hugged the happiness to her, every crumb of it, committing it to memory. Just in case.

Two mornings after their welcome home, Dev received a message in Kendall's handwriting. It was terribly short.

"Come to my chambers. Midnight tonight."

He didn't like this. Supposedly, the danger to Zaranbad was over. Ari had signed a workable treaty with the queen and planned to set sail for home within the next week. But was it really over? Dev remembered that one moment when he'd caught Kendall exchanging glances with the killer who had almost sliced his knife through Caroline. He couldn't really trust the man.

Dev sent messages to several of his men. They'd go with him to Kendall's set of rooms, just in case. He planned to get to the bottom of this plot tonight. It would be the last thing he accomplished for the Home Office before he resigned.

A man with a wife and potential offspring had obligations to stay alive, he thought with a curious mixture of relief and anticipation.

Perhaps tomorrow at the latest, he could tell Caroline what was in his heart. That he loved her. That she had brought a part of him, dead for years, back to flowering life. She was so sweet, so honest in her reactions to their lovemaking. But he wished more from her. He wished her to open her heart to him. The only way to convince her to do so was to be brave enough to open his heart to her.

Soon. He would tell her soon, when he would be around long enough for her to learn to love him back.

By half-eleven, when Dev's carriage pulled up to Curzon Street, he was full of impatience to be done with Kendall and the plot against Ari. Kendall had moved his belongings into the fashionable neighborhood about a month ago, just after the failed attempt to kidnap Janighar from Buckingham Palace. Dev had checked into Kendall's affairs and had found that several large gaming debts had also been paid at the same time.

Dev's men waited in the shadows. And with them, Tom, just on the mend from the last incident, standing tall.

Dev shook his head. "Go home," he told Tom. "You're not ready for this."

"No," Tom said. "The doctor told me I'm well enough, and you need someone you know at your back. Kendall may be the man behind this plot to steal the throne from King Ari."

Even in the half light from a nearby streetlamp, Dev could see that Tom's round eyes were crinkled in worry. Dev made a mental note to recommend Tom for desk work. Brave, honorable and bright as he was, Tom's face really did show his every thought.

"I doubt that he's the puppeteer pulling the strings," Dev said. "As I see it, there could be two reasons for his note. He could wish me dead, or he could have finally found his conscience. Either way, we shall see, shall we not? And Tom, whatever happens, Kendall must be caught alive."

Now, Dev looked back at the rest of his group—seasoned veterans from the Home Office who'd served with him in India. A cloud covered the moon, hiding them all from prying eyes. He motioned to the men and they slipped into a garden behind the row of town houses, walking on cats' feet down the street toward Kendall's lodgings. With soundless steps, they followed Dev to the back door. Carefully, he slid a lock pick into the lock and twisted once, sharply. The lock gave with a quiet click, and after checking the corridor, Dev motioned them into the darkened house.

It was a substantial home, with three floors. Dev and his men stopped at the doors of a darkened library, a drawing room, an office and a small sitting room to ensure that no surprises awaited them on the first floor.

The house was preternaturally silent. The servants all slept. Dev could sense nothing of Kendall's presence, even though the man was supposedly waiting to meet him on the second floor.

Dev's men crept up the stairs. He could feel their silent excitement surrounding him. As for himself, he felt nothing but cold, clear thought and instinct. It was on nights like these that his control was at its strongest, and for that he was grateful.

He silently jerked his head upward and the men followed to the stairway. It was as dark and empty as a tomb. The plush wool carpet muffled a stumble by one of the men behind him. Dev stopped, letting the man recover his balance and his confidence, then continued.

As he reached the landing, Dev felt something beneath the scent of beeswax and polish of a fine, well-staffed domicile. Something . . . wrong. The hairs on the back of his neck stood up and a shiver ran down his back. He motioned to his men and they slowed their paces down the second-floor hallway. Gas lamps placed several feet apart lit the hall. As they passed each, they turned the knob, extinguishing the lamps.

Having placed a man across from the house after the incident at Buckingham Palace, Dev knew that the third chamber on the right was Kendall's. He opened two other doors to ascertain that those bedchambers were empty and then, with a finger to his lips, threw open the third.

Silence again, and the low glow of dying embers from a fire some servant had lit before retiring, delineating Kendall's inner sanctum—a sitting room filled with expensive new art. Dev walked past a comfortable sofa beside a table with a bottle of brandy and two glasses set out. He silently lifted the latch of another door and stole through a dressing room in dim shadow. Only a bit of light came through the open door from the study. The door to the large bedchamber beyond stood open. He walked through.

Silence and stygian darkness here. Dev's senses screamed a warning, but he stood still, waiting, his men behind him. He held a hand out in front of him, feeling blindly for any obstacles and took another step, his nostrils flaring. There was something wrong with the very air in the room.

At that moment, he felt a breeze through an open window and heard a faint creak above him. The breeze blew harder, freeing the moon from the cloud that had covered it. Above him, a silhouette appeared. His heart raced.

"Light the lamp," he said, and Tom struck tinder to the lamp beside Kendall's bed. The room sprang to life.

But not the figure hanging from the rope affixed to the ceiling.

"Christ," one man muttered.

Kendall's limp, dead body swayed above. But by the look of terror on his face, Dev was certain he had seen hell before he died.

Standing where he was, Dev fought the nausea and the fiendish memories. He struggled to hold on.

"Sir?" Dev heard Tom's anxious voice through the roaring in his ears.

"Sir?" Tom said again. "Shall I cut him down?"

"Not yet," Dev said. He walked around Kendall's body, swung himself up on a sturdy table that stood right behind the body swinging softly in the wind from the open window, and stared at the knots in the rope. Knots he'd seen in nightmares from the time he was eight years old.

"Sir?" Tom's voice again, anxious and pleading.

"Just like Jonathan Dinsmore," Dev whispered. "Oh, God."

He came down off the table and turned to Tom. "Yes, get him down."

Dev breathed, the clear air blowing into the room, saw the cool light flooding it.

"I know who did this," he said. "We have found the man behind the plot to murder my brother."

Sir Simon Walpoole's office in the Ministry was a large and comfortable one, with a window overlooking the front garden, deep leather armchairs facing the desk, and a plush maroon Turkey carpet. But sitting in one of those comfortable leather chairs, Dev's muscles were so tight that he wondered if his body would crack with the frustration.

Dev's superior was a tall, angular man, with a strong jaw and a long, straight nose. He sat behind his desk, his fingers pinching the bridge of that nose, his brow wrinkled in what looked to be a dreadful headache.

"I am sorry, Devlin," Sir Simon said, his own jaw clenched. "I do believe it's possible that Gerard Visigore killed Kendall. But my superiors—all the way up to the Prime Minister, I must tell you—do not believe that there's any concrete evidence to the theory. With Visigore a peer of the realm, they are loath to accuse him of murder without a reliable witness or a good deal of circumstantial evidence."

Dev snorted, remembering how his friend Aubrey Drelin-court, the eleventh Earl of Breme, had faced just such a hellish trial a short time ago. "The powers that be will now have the distinction of having been wrong two times in a row."

"They argue that Kendall must have taken his own life."

"He wished to see me that very night. Does that sound like a man who is about to take his life?"

Sir Simon steepled his hands and rested his chin atop them. His brown eyes looked weary. "Perhaps the guilt got to him. After all, he might well have been hanged as a traitor to his country. The Ministry has agreed to keep this quiet, for it will do no good to have anyone know of the circumstances sur-rounding his death. And after all, Kendall is no longer a problem, is he?"

"No. Now we face a far greater threat. Visigore is a poisonous snake, Sir Simon. If left unpunished for the crimes he's already committed, he will cause more harm than he has already done. I told you about the beating my wife witnessed. I believe he's mad, and that unchecked, he will only kill more helpless vic-tims."

"I cannot charge a man of such importance for beating a servant while in a rage. Look on the bright side of things, Dev-lin. There is no one left to expose him now. If you are correct in your suspicions, he has killed in the past because of that fear."

Dev shook his head and rose abruptly. "No, Sir Simon. In reality, Visigore kills because he enjoys it." Dev took a deep breath and tried one last time. "I shall continue to work and discover proof that he murdered Kendall. Sir Simon, I shall need a few men for this mission."

Sir Simon's face fell. "I cannot give you what you need. The Ministry refuses to countenance any more work concerning the viscount. I'm afraid that, for now, political considerations have forced them to declare this case closed."

The Ministry's doubts still resonated in Dev's brain as he walked the streets of London, deep in thought. He'd dismissed the carriage and strode for hours, battling himself all the way back to Wimbley House.

He could not do it, he knew. He could not let the case rest and leave Visigore to walk free, a mad killer loose among the unsuspecting populace.

Twilight fell as he neared Mayfair and home. Visigore must have known that Kendall was about to reveal his role in the plot against Ari. Visigore's reaction was not to flee. It was to murder the man who would have given Dev everything he needed to know about Visigore, his nemesis from the time he was eight years of age.

Dev straightened his shoulders. *I'm no longer a schoolboy,* he thought. *I hope I've grown into the man who can at last see justice done. I have to face him. God grant that I have the strength to bring him down at last.*

A dark flame seared his mind and soul as he remembered that day in the forest of Eversleigh, and how close his brave, idealistic Caroline had come to being a victim of Visigore's brutality.

There was no other way. To find the evidence he'd need to stop Visigore forever, Dev would have to battle his demons from the past and walk alone into the jaws of his own private hell.

The clock had just struck eleven. Caroline stood in her dressing gown, staring out the window into the darkness. London was unseasonably chilly tonight, and the fog swirled about the street, matching her mood and the ineffable anxiety that had clutched at her since Devlin had returned from some meeting the night before with a fiery sense of purpose shining in his eyes.

He had found her in the study with a book of Browning's

poems. Without a word, he had lifted her into his arms and carried her up the wide marble stairway past footmen who carefully looked right past them. Once in the room, he had taken her to the bed and loved her in silence and hunger. It wrenched her heart to watch him so driven, so filled with need.

"Devlin, what is it?" she'd asked him.

"It's nothing," he had told her, and devoured her mouth with his own.

In silence, he had stoked the fire within her, building it to a fever pitch, his flames joining hers, until the fear for him was consumed by the conflagration. In the end, he'd put his head down upon her breast and groaned, a jagged yearning sound in the darkness.

"For God's sake, Devlin," she'd said, stroking his hair as he lay against her breast. "Tell me what is wrong."

"Nothing," he had said again, holding tight to her for another moment. Then he had kissed her and pulled her into his arms, her back against his front.

"Sleep," he'd said.

When she awoke, he was gone. He had left no message for her. The worry had built all day and crested early this evening, when the coach had returned without her husband in it.

Twilight had turned to black night while she sat in the dining room with his family, and once free to return to her chambers, she had paced, tried to read, and paced some more. Now the chill rain slashed against the windowpane and the wind droned its sorrowful dirge.

Her imagination ran wild with lurid pictures—Devlin alone, fighting too many assailants, backing away from them as they stepped closer, forcing him over the edge of a dock into black waters that closed over him.

Devlin crossing a busy road. A coach charging out of nowhere, the horses wild and fast, too fast for him to get out of the way, hooves pounding over him, the wheels tearing at his helpless body. Devlin brought home, cold and still, because no one had fought beside him, protecting his back.

"Fustian," she whispered, chiding herself for her unruly fancies.

Behind her, the door to Devlin's bedchamber opened slowly. Caroline wheeled. He was there, whole and strong, with a gentle light shining in his eyes. The lines that she had seen on his face yesterday had smoothed out. He seemed to glow with conviction, as though he had truly vanquished the demons and come out on the other side to peace.

Relief rose like a cool, clear spring, and she gave him a smile full of everything she had never really had the courage to show him. Her heart which beat, it seemed, for him. Her joy, that grew each day, because of him. Her love, that she had not yet revealed to him.

She ran toward him, touching his cheek, feeling the rain's wetness on it. She peered into his face. Perhaps because she could hold nothing back from him, her senses were attuned completely with his. He kissed her tenderly and smiled at her, but there was something in his deep eyes that she couldn't interpret.

"Let me warm you." She pulled him close.

He put his head down into the hollow of her neck, and sighed like a child coming home.

"A long day, was it?" she asked him.

"Just difficult." His voice was muffled, but she could hear the tentative smile in it.

She stroked down his back. He sighed again, the tight muscles beneath his coat and waistcoat giving a bit. He lifted his head and looked down at her, silently, as though he were memorizing her face.

"Shall I call for a bath?" she asked.

"Yes, please."

He dismissed the servants immediately after they came in with hot water. She took his hand and led him into the bathing room. As she busied herself with towels and brushes, she felt like the chatelaine of a medieval castle, preparing to bathe her lord upon his return from a bruising campaign.

He stripped his wet clothing off and stood by the tub, rubbing his eyes with the heels of his hands. Whatever he'd faced today had exhausted him.

He stepped into the large copper tub and lowered himself against the back, resting his head on the rim and shutting his eyes.

"Is it over?" she asked him quietly.

He smiled. "By tomorrow, it will be done," he said.

"All done?"

"Completely."

Thank God, she thought, as her knees almost buckled from the relief that swamped her. "What will you wish to do then?"

"Perhaps we shall go to Paris, and purchase boxes and boxes of decadent unmentionables." He slid a teasing glance to her. "Would you like that?"

Hearing him joke in such a way made the last of the tightness loosen from round her heart. "I should love it," she said.

He grinned up at her and then quickly washed. She stared at the gleaming contours of his body in the soft light of the bathing chamber. He was magnificent in his lean strength. The flow of muscle beneath golden skin held her in thrall to the glorious essence of him. She felt warmth gather and throb between her thighs.

"Let me scrub your back," she said. The temptation was overwhelming to slide her hand down his broad shoulders, feeling the curve of biceps and forearms. Even his wrists were beautiful.

His smile turned wicked. "I'd rather you get in with me."

He held his hand out to her, a golden god coaxing a mere mortal with that look in his eyes, the one she had begun to know, hot and intense. She blushed and the muscles of her belly clenched with a delicious tingle.

"As my lord wishes," she said. The buttons to her silk dressing gown slipped easily from their loops. It opened, slid down her shoulders, drifted to the floor. She stepped from the froth of silk and walked to him, taking his hand.

He helped her in and settled her between his legs, her back to his front. She relaxed against his body, felt the warmth of him behind her, and the warmth of the water before.

His hands wrapped round her and worked the soap into a lather. "Shut your eyes," he whispered, a plea, a command.

She obeyed, as she customarily did in any situation that involved Devlin and their bodies, naked against each other.

She heard the soap drop onto the stool beside the tub and felt his large hands slide over her shoulders, her collarbone, her breasts. His lips caressed her neck as his slick thumb and fingers pinched her nipples, ever so lightly. She stifled a gasp and arched back into his chest, rising on her knees and grasping the sides of the tub.

"Lean forward," he said, pressing her shoulders down, and she did, her bottom arched to him, the thoughts of what he might do, and how much of her he could see exquisitely titillating. Silence behind her.

She turned, eager to see what happened next. Gently, he turned her back away. "Don't open your eyes, darling."

She heard a gentle splash of the warm water, and then the soft thud of the soap on the stool. His hands slid down her back, over her bottom in dreamy, lathered circles that had every nerve madly screaming for more. He gave it to her, rubbing downward, his fingers gently slipping between her buttocks, and down toward the part of her that ached to be touched.

He found it, cupped her, and trailed soapy, slick circles, each slow, gentle movement maddening, desperately arousing her. She lost all sense of propriety and decorum, making those mewing sounds deep in her throat, undulating with the rhythm of his lathered hands rubbing gently against her mons. Glorious heat throbbed there, causing her to arch toward him and thrust back into him, desperate for the feel of him inside her.

The sight of Caroline in the lamplight, the slope of her slender back curving into the round, perfect globes of her buttocks, her long, smooth legs above the water filled Dev so completely that all the darkness inside him dwindled, leaving only this night, this paradise he'd found in one woman, his perfect mate.

Whatever happened, he had this. Caroline, the sight of her, spread before him like a feast, the feel of her in his arms, the sound of her cries and joy-filled words of desire. He would carry these blessings with him, and in what was to come, she would shine before his eyes like a beacon.

He sluiced warm water over her body, rinsing the soap from her sweet curves. Then he rose, lifted her against him, smooth, warm, slick from the bath. Vaguely, he heard the water sloshing from the tub. It took but a moment to wrap her in a towel and slowly, slowly dry every inch of that soft skin. He felt her tensile strength beneath that softness.

These memories he would take as his shield. His Caroline, his own Valkyrie, so stalwart beside him through that long night of their flight. So new to childlike play, her face flushed with excitement as she rose from the water, free and totally engrossed in the games between them. And this night, this last night, the most joyful of all.

He let the delight he felt for her flow from him, hiding nothing as she looked up into his eyes, her own a deep, limpid blue as open to him as the sky on a clear, mid-summer's day. He could see almost into the core of her, feel her sweet wonder mixed with a heady anticipation. He lifted her into his arms and carried her to his bed—their bed. If God willed it, he would never again sleep without her.

But for now, they would play. They had played silly games in their lovemaking. Games like children, touching each other with their eyes shut, slowly moving until even the slightest nudge had sent them both over the edge. He wanted some of that lighthearted sensuality tonight—needed it to keep him from breaking down and laying his fear at her feet.

He put her down on the bed and lay beside her, his head braced on his bent elbow, his eyes gazing down at the beauty of her body.

"A new game, Cara," he told her. "You will like it, I think."

With one hand, he clasped both her wrists and held them over her head. Her eyes widened in surprise, but he merely smiled into the deep sky blue of them, and with his other hand stroked down, molding each curve, cupping her breast, bending to it. She arched into the warmth of his breath as he blew upon her nipple. It rose to his lips, pebbled and pointed already at that light stimulation.

"Stay very still," he whispered, as he rose over her and sat back on his knees. His thighs nudged her legs wider. "Or I shall have to stop."

The shock on her face was almost comical, as well as the stubborn tilt to her chin. She tugged against his hand, but he easily held her.

"Stay still," he said, and sat back, watching the emotions play over her lovely, open face, as she calculated the risks versus the rewards of this game. She relaxed into the bed, her legs gracefully extended beneath him, her expression one that would have done Aphrodite proud.

"For now," she said majestically. "As long as I wish it."

"You will," he said, and lowered his head to her nipple. He heard her gasp of pleasure and surprise, felt her hips rise in needy reaction.

He drew back. "You must not move and you must not touch me," he added. Her hips stilled, trembling. His fingers played with her breast, cupping it, and his lips closed over the taut nipple.

"You'll pay for this," she moaned, flexing her hips in tiny, tense motions. He watched, his blood racing, as she obeyed his commands, attempting to control her mounting urgency. Her eyes were shut tightly, her hands grasping the pillows in an attempt to hold herself still.

He stroked downward, over the white curve of her belly, still suckling her. She cried out, arching, her hands rising to his shoulders to pull him down. Immediately, he sat back on his heels and took her hands from his back, placing them over her head again. He eased her hips down to the bed, held them there with his hands, a gentle but inexorable hold.

"Disobedient Cara," he said with mock sorrow. "I fear we must stop."

"No!" she said, a demand, not a plea. He vowed he would hear her beg very soon, but as a reward, trailed kisses over her belly, and down, down to that perfect triangle of curls.

Caroline struggled between hot desire and curiosity. Devlin's games generally drove her out of her mind with lust, and her climax after his sensual teasing left her limp and satiated beyond belief.

His light kisses covered her there, in that most sensitive of all places. He offered her small licks that promised much but gave little to assuage her rampaging desire. She pulsed with it, clenched her teeth against the urge to press her hips upward, to pull his head down, to demand he give her what she needed.

The passion built and built. Her muscles trembled against the urge to writhe. Never had she been this eager, this mad with her need.

She wanted to laugh, to curse at the same time. He was so beautiful and so devilish, grinning down at her, rubbing that spot as he cupped her with his hand, pressing against it, listening to her gasps of pleasure and the rising sounds of her passion. It built, and built, until all she could see, all she could feel was the hunger and the pleasure that kept feeding it but did not satisfy. Oh, she would make him pay. But first, she would do anything, if only.

If only. Now.

"Please," she cried out. "Please, Devlin."

"Now," he said, bless him. And lowered his head to her, his tongue tracing her nether lips, then finding that small bud that held all the center of her pleasure. He slipped one finger inside her, then another, to fill her. Not as she longed to be filled, and then, she felt it—a small caress of his fingertips, a stroke up inside her, against something that she had never felt before, and the lapping of his tongue upon the nub at the same time. The exquisite torment urged her higher, higher, and he raised his head, his eyes no longer dancing with mischief, but hot, intent, the same glance he'd given her before they'd even been introduced—passion that she now recognized, blazing from him in a heat equaling her own.

"Move, darling," he commanded, and lowered his mouth to her.

She screamed, her hips thrusting at him, wild with the surging power of the climax that overtook her, bursting like a thousand lights behind her eyes, fragmenting in stars of color against the deep night. Brilliant, magnificent as a great aria, racing through her and from her and up to the very dome of heaven.

He laid his head upon her belly, his hands cradling her legs, as the aftershocks began. She could feel his smile, she thought weakly. And something else, farther down, nestled at her knees. Something hard and demanding. She grinned and wriggled over, gently dislodging his resting place. In a moment, he rolled over on his back, his eyes glazed with desire and, she could swear, delighted discovery. She glanced down his body and saw with satisfaction that he was more than ready.

She had him where she wanted him. She knelt over him, and he raised his hand to her breast.

"You liked that game," he said with immense satisfaction.

"I did. So much I wish to play it again." In a flurry of motion, she straddled his hips and lifted his hands over his head. "Your turn," she said with an evil grin, and bent to the task of driving him as mad as he'd driven her.

Hours later, after he'd made love to her again slowly and sweetly, she drifted in Devlin's arms, spooned against him, sleepily watching the coals glow in the grate.

Devlin began to recite *The Princess*, the shocking, glorious poem she knew by heart. The poem that wrenched her, enchanted her, gave voice to her deepest longings.

His voice was silk and velvet to her ears.

> " *'Now lies the Earth all Danae to the stars,*
> *And all thy heart lies open unto me.*
> *Now slides the silent meteor on, and leaves*
> *A shining furrow, as thy thoughts in me.*
> *Now folds the lily, all her sweetness up,*
> *And slips into the bosom of the lake.'* "

She felt his arm tighten around her, felt him curl closer, enfolding her in his warmth but seeking something from her, something deeper than he had ever seemed to ask from her before. Yet by the stealth of his movements, she thought he believed her to be asleep.

She turned in his arms and gazed up at him in the dying light of the fire.

> " 'So fold thyself, my dearest, thou, and slip
> Into my bosom and be lost in me.' "

She spoke the last lines of the poem, letting everything she felt for him glow from her like a lantern in the darkest night, and flow into him.

Finally she said, "I love you, Devlin. I love you," and rising to him, gave her lips, her heart, her soul into his keeping.

CHAPTER SIXTEEN:
INTO HELL

In the darkness before dawn, Dev stood beside the bed, gazing down at Caroline for what might be the last time.

I love you, Devlin. From the first moment he'd seen her, he'd thought of *The Princess* and the magical, otherworldly kingdom the poem envisioned. He'd wanted that kingdom, but only with Caroline. To be one so completely that nothing—not man nor God nor death could separate them from each other.

I love you. His soul held tightly to the words, repeating them like a silent mantra, too precious to even murmur aloud. He prayed that they had made a child last night. God knew he had never felt the same desire nor the same peace as he did holding her in the darkness. He'd longed to speak of his love, but held back.

If he returned, he would be free to open his heart to her. If.

His hand hovered over her hair, to stroke those silken, flame-streaked locks, to waken her and kiss her one more time. But he wished his last memory of her to be this—her face smooth, untroubled, the small tilt of her lips, as though he'd given her joy so great that she smiled even sleeping.

He slipped from the room like a wraith, a shadow man again, and prepared himself for hell.

Caroline awoke and stretched. A feeling of wicked decadence mixed with one of great joy. She had done shocking things to Devlin last night, but she couldn't elicit more than a tiny drop of embarrassment from the memory, along with a great ocean of pleasure.

She was a hussy, a loose woman, a strumpet. She grinned, reveling in the glory of all that unabashed sensuality. And then remembered Devlin's voice, the look he gave her as she recited the poem, the look that said "I love you" without words. It really didn't matter to her that she was the only one to say so out loud. Her love was so strong, and grew so each day, that she would have blurted it out sooner rather than later anyway.

The bedchamber was very quiet and she didn't hear voices in Devlin's dressing room, either. She checked the ormolu clock on the fireplace mantel and realized that it was only eight of the clock. Tugging on the fringed bellpull beside the bed, she stood and stepped into her slippers and wrapper.

Megan's knock sounded, and then she walked in carrying a large breakfast tray.

"Have you seen Lord Headleymoor up and about at this hour, Megan?" Caroline asked, accepting a cup of tea.

"Oh, much earlier, my lady. He was gone by six this morning."

By six? Where would he go and what would he be doing at that hour? "Did he leave a message for me?"

Megan gave her a quick look of surprise. "No, my lady."

Gone, she thought. Without waking her for a farewell kiss. After the most glorious night they'd spent together. She raised the cup to her lips and noticed that it trembled at bit. She took a long, careful sip and straightened her shoulders.

Ah, well, she thought. *He has work to do, no doubt, last-minute details of the case he was working on. I am sure this evening he will tell me whatever he can about it. And then we shall plan our wedding trip.*

But Devlin did not return that evening. Nor did he send word. She stifled the hurt and went down to dinner, but she could not escape the sidelong looks of the servants, nor the attempts of King Ari and the duke to cheer her up. And all the time, a telltale worry crept through her mind. She had told him she loved him, had bared her soul to him. Had he fled from the chains of that love?

That afternoon, in a fine town house just two miles away from Wimbley House, Gerard Visigore, Viscount Fortbras, frowned down at his boots. The shine just wasn't what it had been when Peeps had been in service to him. He regretted that he had punished the man at Eversleigh, and not waited until he got Peeps back to London, where he had nowhere to run after a whipping.

The sad truth of the matter was that none of his other servants had given him the original challenge of Peeps' pride and strength. They'd feared him after a day or so. But it had taken him weeks to put Peeps in his place, a good deal of physical pain mixed with mental humiliation that eventually wore the fellow down into the perfect servant.

A rap on the door to his study roused him from his wistful thoughts. "Enter," he called. One of his men came in, hat in hand. Dresher was a man as broad as he was tall, and all of it muscle. Visigore had found him down at the docks and immediately known him for the treasure he was. Visigore had hired him on the spot and had profited from Dresher's success in some of the more grisly assignments he'd been given. Now, Dresher gave him a smile that showed a mouth of rotting teeth and a great deal of evil satisfaction.

"That Lady Caroline rides every morn, m'lord, before the others take to the park, 'cause that other bird, Queen Janighar goes with 'er, ridin' astride. All we needs to do is disable the grooms. Do you wants the queen as well?"

"Just the one, Dresher. Grab only the marchioness."

"Oh, that'll be slick as grass from a goose, m'lord," Dresher said with a grin of anticipation. "Sosah an' me can do it. I needs a few days to make the plans is all."

"Excellent." Visigore waved the man out and sat behind the desk, his hands steepled beneath his chin as he contemplated the revenge he would wreak on that half-breed, Headleymoor. Just a few more days!

The man had been the bane of his existence for years, and now, finally, he'd take the prize Headleymoor had snatched from him and destroy his enemy in the process.

Another knock at the door, an unexpected one, pulled him from the exciting visions of what he would do to Caroline once he got her.

"What is it?" he barked, annoyed.

The door cracked. The butler slowly eased his head into the room, his face white with strain. "I beg your pardon, my lord. A man is here, seeking employment, and I thought perhaps you should see him. As you always wish to interview the servants before they are hired," he finished quickly, the fear shrieking silently from his eyes as Visigore rose and sighed. He did take pleasure in their fear. He only wished that more of them had begun by showing no fear at all. Like Peeps. The challenge was everything.

He motioned the butler inside the room. Then he froze, shocked into a startled laugh, as a man he recognized followed the butler into the room, straight-backed and proud as a prince, despite his lowly status in the world.

"Well, well," Visigore said, feeling the anticipation spreading through him and then evidence itself as his lips cracked into an excited grin. "Do come in, Ram Dass, and tell me what brings you here."

Ram Dass stood even straighter, just as Peeps had done in his first interview. Visigore had gone about breaking Peeps by small measures, but with Ram Dass, he must move more quickly. It was too serendipitous to wait. The reward would be having Headleymoor's wife and his trusted servant in his power at the same time.

"I am weary of serving both the House Dassam and the Duke of Wimbley," Ram Dass said. "However, I wish to remain in England. I heard that you have need of a valet. I have filled that position before, as you will see from my references, and I have papers that testify to my skills as a physician, if you should wish to use them."

Visigore yanked the bellpull and waited in silence, staring at the wog until the door opened. The man stared right back, with the pride of a prince.

Visigore hid his excitement by flipping through the papers Ram Dass laid on his desk. Here was a servant trusted by the very man he wished to destroy. What a weapon of steel he could create to wield against his nemesis. He might also know enough about Zaranbad for Visigore to recoup his losses in the debacle with the United Band. Adding spice to the mix was Ram Dass's inherent dignity. A dignity Visigore would have the pleasure of stripping, as a painter removes the layers he no longer wishes to see on his masterpiece. He couldn't wait to begin.

A moment later, Dresher and Sosah entered the room.

"Aye, m'lord?" Dresher said, staring Ram Dass up and down.

"Open the cabinet above the sofa, Dresher," Visigore said.

"Aye, m'lord." Dresher grinned, and did as he was told. "Look at this, Sosah," he said as he returned to his place beside Ram Dass.

Sosah, a tall, well-muscled brute, stepped forward to the Indian's other side. "A wog is it?" he said.

"Ye need us to give 'im a lesson, m'lord?"

"Just hold him for now," Visigore said, the anticipation gathering as Ram Dass glowered and struggled against the rough hands that clasped his arms. "I need to know that you will be absolutely loyal to me. Do you understand? No returning to Wimbley and telling tales to Headleymoor."

Ram Dass looked straight at him. "I do not wish to return to Wimbley again."

Visigore scowled. "You do not wish? And why is that? The family has given you your pay, has it not?"

"I have never had my rightful place in that family," Ram Dass replied.

"Ah," Visigore tapped his fingers on the desk. "Then the rumors are true, are they? You should by all rights be one of them, and yet you are nothing but a lowly servant, is that it?"

"The details of my birth are private, my lord. But you basically have the right of it."

"This is even more delicious than I had imagined. I shall expect certain things of you, Ram Dass. Absolute obedience. The ability to betray those you have worked for all these years. Did you guess that coming here would give you a chance to do those things?"

Ram Dass looked him square in the face. "Yes, my lord."

"Your pride has always offended me. But your anger at the duke and his son is encouraging. I will warn you, however, that your introduction into this household will not be an easy one. I cannot tolerate a man who thinks for himself, and you have always struck me as one of those sorts. Your blood also disgusts me. Only your abject humility and obedience can make up for that. And I shall make certain of your loyalty before I permit you to serve me. That loyalty will show itself in blood and tears. Do you understand?"

"I begin to, my lord." Visigore discerned the first glimmer of fear in Ram Dass's eyes. It was quite satisfying.

"Good," Visigore said. And nodded to Dresher. "Hoist him up," he said, and as his men affixed the rope they'd tied around

Ram Dass's wrists to a hook in the ceiling, he strolled around the desk, anticipation rising like a blood red tide. He took the whip from Dresher.

"Remove his shirt."

Dresher ripped the tunic from Ram Dass's body. The man really had lovely flesh, unblemished and smooth. It would be a pleasure to mark it.

"And his turban," Visigore said. "I shall have no heathen practices here in this house."

Dresher pulled the black length of material from the Indian's head, revealing a mane of dark, silken hair.

Visigore smiled. It would be good to see the sweat run down this man's back along with the blood.

Dev half fainted from the pain. They dragged him into a cold, dark room in what he supposed in his half-conscious state was the basement of the town house. Thank God he had been wise enough to dye his hair and apply a special ointment that could not wash off for a while. It might take that long to discover incriminating evidence that Visigore was the traitor who had financed the United Band.

"Why do you not wish to remain at Wimbley House?" Visigore had asked softly each time before raising the lash.

At last, he'd judged it time to give him what he wanted. "I hate them all," he'd whispered. "The old king who got me on a servant woman. The king who now rules Zaranbad. It should have been me."

And Visigore had smiled in triumph. After all, he was a man who would understand hatred and the need for revenge.

The cold congealed the blood weeping from Dev's wounds, and permeated the water they'd thrown on his back after the beating. It ran down his body along with his sweat. He'd known, from his interviews with Peeps, what to expect from Visigore, but the reality had been much worse than what he'd imagined.

Was Visigore satisfied, or would they beat him again? Dev raised his head and studied his prison. It was empty but for a scarred table holding a pitcher of water, a metal cup and a heel of bread. There was no cot, just a worn blanket on the ground. A chamber pot stood against the wall. He began to shiver uncontrollably, as the cold stones chilled his body.

How many days would Visigore take before he was satisfied that Ram Dass was broken to his hand?

He sipped the water slowly. He'd heard Visigore mumbling orders to Dresher and Sosah that would take them away from the town house. No one else but those two came near this rank, cold prison. The pitcher of water might have to last a long time.

Whatever happened, he must not despair. He must not fear. He must think. Dr. Gupta had taught him the slow, even breathing to hold his pain-wracked body together and give it time to heal from the inside. He knew the thought, the vision upon which he would meditate.

He curled his body into itself on the cold stone floor. Shutting his eyes, he found his mantra. "Cara," he whispered, and her face appeared, alight, her soul open to him. Slowly, the world receded, until all that was left was love.

Five days, gone, Caroline thought as she walked through the morning fog toward the stable. By now, everyone in the household was aware that her husband had left her without a word. She caught the pitying looks from the servants, overheard the dressing down Megan gave two of the chamber maids for whispering something to each other Caroline had not heard but could imagine. Even the duke awkwardly patted her hand and reassured her that Devlin often left for parts unknown on the spur of the moment, and that he always returned. Eventually.

She awoke, silently screaming from nightmares of Devlin,

bleeding in some squalid, freezing cell, unnoticed by the people walking by outside it. She pounded on the iron bars across his blind window until her arms could no longer raise her bleeding fists. Always, he sat isolated, suffering, utterly alone. No cry of hers could reach the heedless crowds, no tears soften the hearts that beat in that stream of humanity eddying by her like the unheeding sea.

If she had never known rejection, she would have sworn that he was in danger and in pain. That he might, at this very moment, be dying. That was the two-edged sword hanging over her existence. Either he had fled from her arms because she declared her love, or he had not trusted her enough to tell her the truth.

Her only outlet was to ride in the park early each morning with Janighar. It was the one time she escaped the worried glances everyone shot her way when they thought she was not looking.

The rides took place at dawn so Janighar could ride astride. It was the safest way for her, given her blindness, and the early hour at the park long before the ton arose kept Janighar free from disapproving eyes. Caroline envied her riding costume—a dark blue flowing gown, divided so that her legs could easily sit a boy's English saddle.

As Caroline mounted beside the young queen, she inwardly breathed a sigh of relief. Thank goodness Janighar had proposed this exercise. It was the only thing keeping her sane.

Even though the danger was over, Caroline still insisted that two of the ex–Bow Street Runners come along to guard them. She gave no reasons for her demand. How could she, like Caesar's wife, claim dreams and portents in this modern age?

Janighar was in her usual good spirits, Caroline saw. Her back was straight and her hands were steady on the reins of her horse, a fleet, faithful bay gelding that had been in the Wimbley stables for its whole life. The two guards riding behind were both strong and agile horsemen.

The queen urged her horse into a canter. Caroline squeezed her chestnut mare and it broke into the same loping stride alongside Janighar.

"Oh, feel the wind," Janighar called to Caroline over the hoofbeats. "What a wonderful time to ride out! The night air has left the park cool. What more could one wish?"

My husband, safe home. Caroline tried to think of something pleasant to say, but her heart was so heavy that she could not.

Halfway through their ride, Caroline decided that she could not stand another day like this one. She would take the coach to the Home Office with or without the duke's help, demand to know where her husband was at this moment, and tell the ministers of her misgivings. They would probably give her the same looks of pity she'd gotten these last days and dismiss her as a foolish female who had married above herself and now refused to face facts. Her husband, like so many others she'd known all her life, preferred to be anywhere but near her.

By God, she thought. *I'll insist, pester, prod and manipulate until someone gives me a hint that might lead to Devlin's whereabouts.*

A sound from behind broke into her thoughts. A pop and a whiz, but Janighar whose hearing was so sharp, was faster than she at halting her bay.

"It was a bullet!" she cried and there was terror in her voice. "What is happening?"

Caroline wheeled her chestnut back and looked. The grooms slumped in their saddles and slowly slid to the ground. Blood seeped from their coats.

"Someone just shot the grooms," Caroline whispered as sick horror surged inside.

"What will we do?"

Hoofbeats sounded behind them. Two figures, one tall and the other short and stocky, came out of the fog from the left of the riding path. Both looked like something one would find in a dark alley or one's worst nightmares.

"We must ride, hard, for home. Do you hear me?" she told Janighar. "Right now, before they get you. Trust the horse. He knows the way."

"Yes." Janighar kneed her bay into a gallop.

They ran on, madly for the gate. If they got out of the park, Caroline could lead the bay home. Janighar need only stay on top.

The park entrance was close. They might make it, after all.

The brigands gained on them. Caroline reached into her pocket and fumbled for the pistol she'd brought with her. She had it in her hand when her chestnut reared. Dropping the gun back into her pocket, she rapped the horse on the head and pushed him forward with her legs at the same time. Good God, what she'd give for a man's saddle today!

The chestnut came down hard on all fours. Caroline's heel beat a tattoo on the horse's flank, and they sprang after Janighar. She reached again into her pocket for the gun. Only a few more strides and they would be out in the streets of London, and could raise the alarm.

Suddenly, she was roughly plucked from her mount and shoved down over the neck of another horse. She could smell horse sweat and the reek of an unwashed human body holding her down. The other blackguard who'd accosted them slowed to a trot beside her captor. She raised her head to see Janighar racing from the park and into the cobbled street, crying out for help as she rode.

Dear God, she was blind. How could she make it home at that dangerous pace? A small lorry trotted across the street just as horse and rider reached the same spot. Gathering his haunches, the bay leaped over the impossible barrier.

Caroline's captor shoved her head down and laughed as he

wheeled his horse and cantered away from the terrifying scene toward a waiting carriage. "Visigore don't want 'er," he shouted over the horses' hoofbeats. "No need to worry about that'un anyways," he said to the ruffian beside him. "Blind as a bat. And dead for sure by now."

CHAPTER SEVENTEEN:
INTO THE BREACH

Very early on the fifth morning of his captivity, a servant entered Dev's prison and gave him new clothing to wear. English clothing, he realized. A black coat and trousers. White waistcoat, shirt, and tie. White gloves.

The footman brought him hot water and soap. The footman remained in the dimly lit room, standing quietly against the wall, his eyes shut. He did not seem very old, but deep grooves lined his face, making him look like a martyred saint.

"Shall I shave you?" he asked, his gaze carefully on the wall beyond where Dev stood.

Then he slowly approached, as though he expected an assault. Perhaps others that Visigore had tortured almost to madness had turned upon this servant before.

"Be at ease. I shan't hurt you," Dev said, running his hand across the bristles on his chin.

But as the footman grew closer, Dev realized with a start of horror that he had been so intent upon bringing Visigore to justice that he'd made a horrible mistake. He had forgotten the color of his beard, a slightly darker blond than his hair. It had only been blind luck that the beard grew slowly enough not to be visible before today.

"Give me the razor," he told the servant. "I'll do it myself."

The man glanced up and his eyes widened. Dev's muscles tightened in preparation. Dear God, must he take an innocent life to save his own?

The man must have noticed the menace in his stance. "I don't know why you're here," he said, and tears glistened in his eyes. "And I don't care, unless it can give me some hope. But I'll not betray you, sir. Not when I've been through the same thing you have."

Dev looked at him hard, assessing. *I can either strangle the man or trust him.*

In the silence that enveloped the two of them, Dev took a deep breath, nodded, and decided to risk all by dropping his Indian accent. "You, too, have been the subject of your master's tender mercies?"

The man gave him a look of despair that made Dev's heart wrench.

"I have," the man said with a shudder.

"Why haven't you left?"

"Where was I to go without a reference? And there's my mother and my sister. Who would see that they were fed were it not for me?"

"How long have you been here?"

"Two years. Feels like twenty."

"I imagine it does." Dev paused, then said in a voice almost too soft for even the footman to hear, "Were Visigore found guilty of a crime, you would not need a reference."

The footman's eyes grew wide. His face lit with something close to hope. "You're not a servant, are you, sir?"

"I am not."

"Someone decent would take me?"

Dev nodded. "The Duke of Wimbley would speak for you and the others. What are you called?"

"James Dobson."

Relief surged. The man wouldn't have given him his name if he wasn't prepared to trust him, and perhaps follow him. "Well, then, James, if you know of any place where Visigore keeps his important papers, I might be able to find something to implicate him." He let the thought sink in as Dobson shaved him, and did his best to help Dev bathe as much as he could in the washbowl.

The soapy water he sluiced down his back stung like fire, but he had no time to think of the lash wounds. If he was lucky, they'd only scar and not succumb to infection. He washed his face. It was battered, one eye half shut from yesterday's beating, bruises and a split lip from the day before. His torso bore deep purple bruises, as well. He dressed, covering them all. Perhaps they wouldn't beat him today, given that Visigore had obviously paid for this new clothing and would be loath to have it ruined.

As he tested his muscles to bring back whatever strength he could, the footman glanced furtively to his left and right. "I do know of a place, sir. For papers and things."

"Good. I need to go through those papers as soon as I may."

"Now, sir, please. His lordship's abed until ten, and those two snakes he keeps are out doing something for him. Now's the only chance."

"Then let's get to it, James."

Dobson took the key out of his pocket and unlocked the door to his prison.

Dev remembered his distaste yesterday, when he finally crawled across the carpet to Visigore. He'd groveled and begged for mercy, for a chance to prove his loyalty. Visigore had beamed at him like a father with a child who had learned his first lessons perfectly. Dev, after hearing about Visigore's customs from poor Peeps, had planned it so, but the urge to rise suddenly and strangle the bastard had nearly overwhelmed him.

He stepped out into the dark corridor. The household was beginning the morning routine while their master slept. Most were down in the kitchen, finishing their breakfast. Following the scent of bacon and scones, Dev entered the kitchen. There was a little light from a couple of lamps on the long table. But the servants were not seated there. They were huddled in groups of threes and fours, whispering to each other.

One of the maids gave him a sympathetic look, and pressed a mug of tea and a scone into his hands. He tried to smile, felt the sharp pain as the lip split again, and whispered his thanks.

Then he used his senses as he'd been taught so long ago. What Dr. Gupta would call the aura of the house was a dark purple and black swirling cloud of fear. The servants all looked at him with a mixture of what Dev would call pity and outraged wrath. He concentrated harder, and knew that the wrath was not directed at him, but at the men who'd done this to him.

On a naval ship once, he'd seen men about to mutiny looking just as these people looked. He and the captain had been able to avoid that problem, but he would do nothing to stop any uproar in this household. It would only aid him.

As he walked past some of the servants, they lowered their heads. But Dev could feel their eyes on his back, and he reckoned they were thinking of what he'd suffered, just as others had suffered in the years since they'd been imprisoned here.

They drifted away, muttering amongst themselves, but the footman remained, and so did Dev.

Visigore woke to the aroma of chocolate and a very gratifying message from below stairs. The servant Ram Dass was properly dressed and ready to perform his duties. Today's events would conclusively prove his abject loyalty to his new master.

At a rap on the door, Visigore motioned to the footman, James Dobson. "My dressing gown," he demanded. Once Dobson had helped him into it, Visigore gave the footman one of his more piercing looks, just to keep the man on his toes.

"Open the door," he said, sliding into his slippers.

The tough he'd hired, Dresher, strutted into the bedchamber, his beefy hands tucked into his braces. "We got 'er, m'lord.

What'll ye have us do with 'er?"

"I shall see her in an hour. Meanwhile, put her in the same chamber where the wog most recently slept." He scowled, remembering Caroline's effrontery in befriending Ram Dass. "Let her know a man whom I needed to punish occupied that cell for the last five days. Before she sees me, I wish her to realize what I do to those who have displeased me."

Caroline's gaze scanned the cold chamber where they had put her. It looked like the hellish prison of her nightmares, down to the chill and the barred, filthy window near the ceiling.

"*Visigore,*" the filthy brigand had said as he carried her away. She was in Visigore's house, surrounded by servants who would not or could not aid her, given their master's sick cruelty. She thought of Peeps and waited for the terror to overcome her, as it had that day at Eversleigh.

She looked down at her hands. They did not tremble. She must have become a different person in the last few months. She took in the bloody water in the basin, the rags on the floor, the crust of bread. Her heart wrenched for the poor soul who had been here so very recently. She had no fear for herself, however. Only a cold, clear purpose.

There was no hope of rescue. Janighar—dear, courageous Janighar was surely dead or wounded.

She must save herself, if only to see that Janighar was avenged. Or if she must die, she would at least take that vile madman with her.

"M'lord'll see you in an hour," the villain said and slammed the door.

She heard his heavy footsteps retreat down the corridor. In an hour she might be dead. She would never see Devlin again. Grief swamped her and threatened the small, shining flame of her outrage and conviction. She sank to the floor, covered her face with her hands, and wept.

In a very short time, she wiped her tears and began to pace. She didn't have time to grieve. She must think.

Visigore was a coward, but he would come close enough to her, she thought. Close enough, as long as she played one of two roles. One of those was the frightened, shy maiden. She personally despised that role, but she had often enough fooled others with it. The other was more like her. She would make the decision once she'd tallied the odds.

" 'E wants to see you," Dresher said, jerking his head upward.

So the charade with the warm water and the new clothing had been a ploy to make it that much more frightening when Dev faced his next beating. He picked up the tray he was to carry to Visigore's study, taking care that the china on it rattled.

"Watch what ye'r doin'," Dresher said over his shoulder. " 'E ain't goin' to 'ave you whipped today. 'E's got better fish to fry."

Who else had Visigore brought into his den? If Dev acted quickly, he might save the next victim. He followed Dresher meekly up the stairs, reviewing the plan he had conceived during the last few hours. All he had to do was wait for the opportunity.

One last thought filled his mind, adding strength to his mission, as it had from that first terrible day. He held fast to it. *Caroline.*

Dresher knocked and opened the study door. Dev had become very familiar with it in the last five days. He knew just where Visigore liked to stand to watch his victim. He knew just how many seconds it would take to get close enough.

As they had been for the last five days, the heavy drapes were drawn. Only a single lamp lit the room, plunging it into a world of shadows and menace.

As he entered, Dev lowered his head in a picture of abject

fear and obedience. "Your tea, my lord," he said in a voice that trembled.

"Ah, yes. Bring it to me, Ram Dass, and take care not to spill a drop."

Dev worked slowly, picked the cup and saucer up, let it rattle a bit, held it in both hands. He got it to Visigore's desk, and bent his back, setting it carefully down, as though it had taken all of his inner strength to accomplish that simple task.

He knelt before Visigore and bowed his head even more.

"Very good, Ram Dass." Visigore laid his hand on Dev's head. "You may rise and remain. I wish you to see how easily I can destroy anyone at any time. It will be a lesson to you. One in which you will take pleasure, I believe."

As Dev rose, bowed again, and backed slowly to the side of the desk, Visigore took to his feet in what looked like an attitude of expectation. Dev's hands itched to go for the man's neck immediately, but a sound outside the door stopped him.

"I am about to welcome a lady to my household," Visigore said, walking out of easy killing range. "She'll be here for only a short time, however. You will remain in the chamber to help me, along with Dresher and Sosah—ah, there you are Sosah, with the lovely Lady Headleymoor."

Dev's head shot up. He stared at the door while his heart filled with terror and love. Caroline stared back at him with the same look, and then her face smoothed of all expression.

She turned to face Visigore. "I demand to be released immediately," she said in a voice that might well freeze a lake in summer.

Visigore stood and walked round the desk, lifting her chin to smile down into her eyes. "My dear, how lovely you look today. I am delighted that Dresher could offer you transport to my home. I hope you enjoyed your accommodations. Too bad they were only temporary."

"Do not play this game with me, Visigore. Release me, or all of London will know of your villainy."

"No one will know. Your dear friend, the Queen of Zaranbad, is dead. Ram Dass, whom you recognize behind me, is my loyal servant now. He will aid me in the future to destroy the rest of the Dassam family. Your husband will soon meet his end, and after him, the King of Zaranbad. One by one, they will all fall to my sword."

Dev sent Caroline a look that screamed *caution.*

"Do you think that I will allow any man who has insulted me and robbed me of my intended bride—yes, my dear, you were to be *mine*—that I would allow him to live? That half-breed stole you from me and he will never get you back."

She nodded, but spoke again in that cool, stern voice. "Have you a sword, my lord? Do you intend to meet these men in a fair fight? Or is your method one used only by a coward? You pay or brutalize to destroy men's lives, do you not? Even now, word of your unhealthy proclivities is whispered throughout the ton. You will die before you can do more harm." She smiled.

Dev thought to himself that he would never wish to face an enemy who smiled at him like that.

Visigore was trembling now. But the flush on his face deepened to dark purple rage. He looked at Dev with burning eyes. "I need that length of rope behind the desk," he barked. "Get it!"

"Yes, my lord."

Apparently satisfied that his cowed servant would do anything he ordered, including stringing up a lady who had treated him with kindness, Visigore turned his back on Dev. Taking a step forward, he said to Sosah, "Hold her arms. I don't want her wriggling out of your grasp."

Sosah grasped her by the forearms. One of her hands was in her pocket, Dev saw.

Visigore turned to Dev with a glitter in his eyes that signified madness. "The rope, Ram Dass," he said, holding out his hand. Then he turned back to Caroline. "I had planned to keep you alive for some time, Caroline. I had hoped to convince you that we were meant to be together. I had much to teach you. But you have been unconscionably rude, and I cannot permit such treatment from anyone."

She smiled again, then shot a look at Dev.

"Ballocks!" she said in that same, clear voice.

Dev lunged forward, his hands tight on the rope. He threw it over Visigore's head, and wrenched it tight.

The crack of a pistol sounded loudly in the small study, along with Sosah's scream of pain. He lay on his back, rocking, his hands covering his bloody knee.

Visigore clawed at the rope round his neck as Caroline rolled to the side. Dresher had his pistol out, waving it at Dev, then Visigore, as the two struggled with each other. Caroline aimed the second pistol and shot. Dresher dropped to his knees, howling, holding his mashed and blood-soaked hand to his chest. Caroline took a brass figurine from the table beside her and smashed it over his head. Dresher lay like a felled tree.

The sudden silence was broken only by Sosah's sobs. Dev barely felt his hands pulling the rope taut around Visigore's throat. He thought of gentle Jonathan Dinsmore, abused and hanged when only eight years old. Of Kendall, swinging from a hook in the ceiling of his chamber. Of Peeps and all the other victims. His hand wrenched tighter. He could hear the gurgle of Visigore's last breath. Finally.

"Devlin." A quiet voice, full of love.

He stared at Caroline. She stood over Dresher and Sosah, her face lit like an avenging angel. His angel of light, who had killed no one, yet triumphed.

"I am not Visigore," he told her. His hands slackened.

"I know that," she said.

Visigore fell to the floor at Dev's feet and heaved a gasping breath.

Caroline was there beside Dev. Together they tied Visigore's hands and legs with the rope the bastard had planned to use on her. Then they worked on the two thugs, until all three were neatly trussed. It occurred to Dev that Caroline, constant, quick and steady, was better than any man he'd worked with.

A crash resounded from the front hall of Visigore's town house. Fists pounded on the library's closed door. Dev had only enough time to grab the still primed pistol from Dresher's side and pull Caroline down behind the desk.

"Just a minute," she said, wriggling her hand into her boot. A knife and a third small pistol emerged. "Here," she said, handing him the knife.

"Keep it," he said, trying to reckon the odds and how they were going to spring this next trap.

She shook her head. "You take it," she whispered. "I saw your excellent work at Eversleigh."

The door shuddered and held, then shuddered again. It fell open, half hanging drunkenly on the one hinge left to it.

"Where is my brother!" an enraged voice roared.

Dev breathed a sigh of relief, grinned, and rose from behind the desk, pulling Caroline up beside him. Ari and his guards stood with Tom Jarvis and several of Dev's men. On the floor between them, Sosah began to whimper.

Ari's eyes were imbued with astonishment and relief. His gaze perused the scene, scanning slowly from the trussed-up Visigore to the thugs on the floor, one still rolling and whimpering in pain.

"It took you long enough," Dev drawled.

Ari returned the grin that Dev felt cracking the split in his lip.

"It appears that you did quite well without me." Ari strode across the floor to Dev, opening his arms and pulling his brother hard into a bear hug. "Thank God. I couldn't bear it if I lost you."

Dev stood within his brother's rough embrace and felt the ancient weight of loneliness slide from his shoulders.

"Caroline?" a soft voice called from the doorway.

"Janighar?" Caroline's heart almost stopped beating in her chest. She turned and raced to the door, and then she and Janighar were in each other's arms, laughing and crying. Dev understood. He felt the same heady relief, the same happiness.

Caroline's voice was soft and filled with wonder. "They told me you were dead."

"Oh, those idiots," Janighar said, kicking Sosah in the ribs for good measure. "Too slipshod to check and make sure their victim had fallen. If they had been my palace guard, I should have given them the sack immediately." Janighar's mouth curled in disdain. "What fools, to think I could not manage a little jump like that."

"Janighar, that was not a jump. That was a lorry!"

"Was it? Well, I had a lovely horse beneath me. I knew after the first day up that he could take anything I threw him at."

Caroline cleared her throat. "You do realize that you are a hero?"

Janighar smiled. Her face turned toward the sound of Ari's voice as he spoke with Dev. "I always knew that," she said. "But now, my husband knows it, too."

Dev immediately took Caroline back to Wimbley Street, with orders to the men to imprison Visigore and his thugs in Newgate.

Ari, loath to leave Janighar's side even for a moment, helped her into their coach and quickly climbed in after her. He still didn't quite understand how all of his beliefs had suffered such a killing blow in the last few hours, but he knew he had a hard lesson to learn from all this. He would probably be learning it again and again for the rest of his life, if Janighar had anything to say of it.

When she had galloped back to Wimbley House all alone but for a lorry driver who followed close on her heels, his first act had been to lift her in his arms and carry her up the wide marble stair to her chambers.

His gentle wife had fought him, kicking, punching, Good God, she would have even used her teeth on him had he not had the good sense to carefully and quickly put her down on her own two feet.

She had grabbed his shoulders and shaken him, stamping her foot and screaming that he had better listen, by God, or she would never, ever speak to him again.

"They've got Caroline, you big oaf! We must save her! Send a message to the Home Office. Gather our guards. We must ride immediately to Visigore's town house. There's not a moment to waste. To the rescue, my lord king!"

The lorry driver was still standing in the front hall. As Ari gave orders and sent messages, he heard the driver talking to the duke about Janighar jumping his wagon, and how she'd raced like the wind away toward Wimbley House. To save her friend.

He sighed, remembering that moment of amazed realization shooting through him like an arrow.

She was a tigress, his wife. A blind tigress, he reminded himself as the guilt and sorrow sliced him yet again.

Ari rapped on the ceiling of the coach. He heard the crack of the coachman's whip and they rolled forward. His gaze shifted to Janighar's beloved face. A little frown played across her perfect features.

"I shall no longer live like I have lived this past year, Ari," she said.

He took her hand and kissed it. "Forgive me, dearest, for doubting your strength."

"I am strong, am I not?" she said with an incandescent smile. "So you will permit this subject of yours to ride and to walk where she will, and to learn all it is possible to know of this delightful world."

"I never meant to cage you," he said. "I just felt so . . ."

"You worried for me," she said, and squeezed his hand.

"No, Janighar," he said, trying to swallow the lump in his throat. "I felt so guilty."

She turned to him, surprise and a little impatience revealed in her expressive face. "You did not pull the trigger that blinded me, Ari. That lunatic did."

"The bullet you took was meant for me," he said in a voice that cracked. He blinked against the moisture in his eyes.

In a rustle of silk, she turned toward him. Her hands were soft and cool and inquisitive on his face. She found the tear that had escaped his efforts.

"And we are both of us alive. Do you know how lucky we are?" Her fingers poked softly into his chest. "The conspirators have been defeated and our kingdom is safe. For now."

"Yes," he said glumly. "For now."

"That is what it means to be king, especially in our part of the world. It is always 'for now.' And what will we do with our halcyon days, Ari? Shall I spend them imprisoned in my chambers because someday we will be fighting another United Band? Or shall we work for our people, and walk among them in gladness? Shall we enjoy the special music of our land, the food and the flowers of our garden? Shall we make children for us to hold and love?"

He held on to her as though she were his whole world. Which

she was. "Yes. That is what we shall do."

He felt Janighar's smile against his cheek. "Excellent," she said. "I cannot wait to begin."

CHAPTER EIGHTEEN:
A LADY'S REQUEST

Caroline gently washed Dev's back again with the softest cloth and the gentlest soap to be found in Wimbley House. He had not said a word to her on the carriage ride back, and she'd been afraid he would not allow her to see what they'd done to him. She was terribly surprised that he'd actually permitted her to tend him after he'd bathed. Now he sat with a towel draped around his hips, while she finished the careful job of making sure that each slash from the whips was completely clean. Perhaps his willingness to have her there was a sign that they could talk about what happened.

Sir Simon Walpoole was due in another hour. If she didn't allude to those past days in Visigore's clutches now, he would never give her another chance to find out just how bad it had been. He held his secrets so tightly inside that she feared she had only this moment to lure them from him. And somehow, she realized with a deep pang of anxiety, Devlin must free himself of these demons if he were ever to escape the shadows and break into the light.

"Your poor back," she said, patting it dry with a clean linen towel. She bit her lip, but then quite purposely let the words come out. "They put me in a terrible room. It was like a dungeon, with blood on the floor and on the rags of a shirt. It was your shirt, was it not?"

"Unfortunately, yes," he said with a throwaway smile. "I liked that shirt." But she saw the shadow beneath, the part of himself that he had always hidden from her.

"How badly were you hurt?"

He shrugged, then winced. "Badly enough."

She turned to the table beside the copper tub. "A brilliant doctor devised this salve," she told him. "It has made the deepest scars almost disappear from a man's face and chest. I believe we ought to rub some of it into your scars."

Dev turned his head, his color rising.

Good heavens, she thought. *I've made the mysterious marquess blush.*

"You think I'm brilliant?" he asked.

"I think you are a genius." She dabbed some of the black ointment on a lash mark and kissed the skin beside it. "An almost magical healer, a frightfully clever agent, a wise councilor. However . . ."

"Ah. There's always a but."

She took a deep breath. "I think you need some help when it comes to handling your wife."

"To whom should I turn for that help?"

"I might be able to give you some necessary insights into that."

"If you must, have at it then." His face wore its inscrutable mask again.

Her heart sank. Perhaps she ought not to have raised this subject at all. Perhaps they would go along as they had gone, with blissful nights and days. Until the time when he would leave again, a shadow slipping from the house. She would walk once more through the dark nights, never knowing whether she would ever see him alive again.

It would not suffice. She deliberately began on the next raw line sliced across his back.

"Your wife wishes you to trust her with your secrets. As you may have noticed on the last night you were together, she was quite willing to trust you with hers."

Dev sat very still, beneath the touch of Caroline's gentle hands. He was afraid to move, afraid that she would not, could not ever again tell him what lay in her heart if he said the wrong thing.

"It has been a very long time since I trusted myself to another person."

"Do you remember when you stopped?"

She was excellent at interrogation. Sir Simon would love to get his hands on her. That unwelcome thought filled him with enough dread to force him past the old reticence.

"I think I told my mother every thought that occurred to me," he said.

"And after that?"

"Unfortunately, I trusted the headmaster of my school once. That was a mistake."

Her voice was as gentle as her hands on his scars. "Will you tell me what happened?"

"I had a friend—my age. He was frail, and had an ability to tell the most amazing stories. He had a sweet nature, as well— the sort of lad who cared for all the creatures of the earth."

He needed to explain Jonathan's essence, to make her understand how precious that life would have been. In the pause, Caroline took his hand in hers.

"Do you know how, in a boys' school, the older boys will have a younger boy to do errands in the town, and sometimes toast bread and cheese for them over their fire?"

She nodded. William had told her all about the perquisites of age in that insular kingdom.

"Visigore chose Jonathan. For the first weeks, it was only . . . difficult. But after that, he would come back to our chamber with bruises on his face, or a split lip. The last time he returned thus from Visigore, I found him lying facedown upon his bed, sobbing. God, Caroline, he looked so fragile, so broken." Dev shut his eyes, remembering the tears, the blood. His breath hitched, and then he forced himself to go on.

"Slowly I got the full story out of him. I cannot tell you all, but Visigore's brutality was matched only by his twisted perversities."

Dev's heart beat faster. He stared down at their joined hands and realized that he was crushing hers. Loosening his grip, he closed his eyes and breathed deeply.

"I reported what I had discovered to the headmaster. After all, Father and Mother had told me that those with power must defend those who have none. The headmaster was shocked, of course. But he would not send Visigore down for the sins which he had committed."

Dev opened his eyes and looked into his wife's face. Her understanding gaze gave him the strength to finish it. "Visigore was, after all, the heir to an earldom. And Jonathan was only the son of a barrister."

He gulped air, like a drowning man.

"There's more, isn't there?" Caroline asked softly.

He nodded. "Official or not, news runs through a school like fire through silk curtains. Speculation was rampant as to what Visigore had done, but nobody knew for certain. And there was Visigore, sneering. I told Jonathan that he had the headmaster's promise that he needn't ever go near Visigore again. For two weeks I watched over him. Nothing happened. I relaxed a bit, went off to play cricket one afternoon. When I returned, I found Jon's body hanging from the ceiling."

He cleared his clogged throat, and forced himself to go on. "Until I saw Kendall's body, I thought Jonathan had killed himself. But it was the same with Kendall. The knots—the look on their faces. They had been through something terrible before they died. Oh, Cara." He buried his face in his hands. "Visigore would have hanged you, too."

"How old were you at the time?" she asked him.

"I'd just celebrated my eighth birthday."

"And that is why you wished to rid the school of Visigore. It was for your comrade Jonathan, wasn't it?"

Dev nodded, his hands covering his eyes. It was hard to speak of these things so directly. But good, too.

"You were very brave, Devlin. Very kind. You did everything you could. It was not your fault."

"I know," he said, and felt wetness on his cheeks.

"But do you really know?"

He looked straight at her and let her see the tears. "In here, I realize that," he said, pointing to his forehead. "But not in here." His hand covered his heart.

She rose and came round the stool, to kneel at his feet. Her hand covered his, where it lay over his heart. "Then I shall find a way to remind you every day, until you finally accept that you are the best man I have ever known."

He looked into deep blue eyes and caught the shimmer of her tears in the lamplight. But her smile, though a bit wobbly, warmed him.

"It's the secrecy, isn't it?" he said. "That's what my wife cannot bear."

She nodded. "Please trust me with your secrets, Devlin. Do not leave me to pace in the darkness, never knowing where you have gone or what terrible danger you are going through."

He went down on his knees before her and pulled her into his arms, holding her, both of them kneeling, her head on his chest. "I promise. No more secrets."

She sank against him, and he heard the first stifled sob.

"Cara?" He raised her chin with his finger so he could look into her face.

The tears had overflowed and trailed down her cheeks.

"Thank you," she whispered.

There was one last secret begging to be released. He opened his mouth to tell her, and then heard the knock on the door.

"My lord?" the footman's voice on the other side of the door. "Sir Simon Walpoole has arrived."

"Please take him to my study and offer him something to drink. The marchioness and I will be down shortly."

"Devlin?" Caroline stared at him.

"I wish you to be with me, Cara. In this and all things."

Sir Simon Walpoole was a tall, distinguished gentleman, who unrolled himself from the maroon wing chair in obvious surprise when Devlin entered with Caroline on his arm. He seemed, at first glance, a good man for whom to work.

Caroline felt a bit like a person learning to swim all at once. She was leaping into deep water for the first time—excited and a little frightened. But she knew she could do this. If she had Sir Simon's approval, then Devlin would be easier to convince.

Sir Simon came forward. He bowed over her hand.

"What a delightful . . . surprise, Lady Headleymoor. I had not thought to meet you this afternoon after your terrible ordeal."

"Actually, what happened to me was nothing compared to what happened to my husband. As you can see," she added severely. She stood very straight as Grandfather had taught her when facing a possible adversary, and looked him in the eye.

"My husband truly needed someone at his back for this work," she said, giving Sir Simon only a *mildly* censorious look. "Because he did not have another loyal person to help him, it will take a long time for him to heal from his wounds. It is a loss, both to him and to the valuable work he does for the Home Office."

Sir Simon sent a dire warning glance Devlin's way.

"Lord Headleymoor did not reveal this side of his life to me, Sir Simon," she said, rushing to reassure him. "I deduced it fairly easily, on my own. As others, I am certain, would do if given enough time to think of the doctor, Ram Dass, and his surprising resemblance to the Marquess of Headleymoor. I believe that a possible solution would be either Ram Dass's sudden demise, or his desire to travel back to his home in India and see the wife and children he left behind two years ago."

She paused, and then, as the excitement concerning her new project mounted, she began to outline it for Sir Simon.

"If Lord Headleymoor still wishes to give his all for England, he will need to play a new role. After you have spoken to my husband and learned of the day's work, I should like to discuss with both of you a particular persona that would admirably suit. However, it would include the presence of another trust-worthy agent working closely with him. That agent would be me."

She gave Devlin a saucy smile, then curtsied to Sir Simon. "I shall leave you now, to discuss this last case, and the happy outcome."

She smiled and took Devlin's arm for a moment. "Do please tell him all the details, Devlin," she whispered. "About the pistols and the code word and how very, very well it all went. I know I can do this." She squeezed his arm and slipped out the study door, eager to let them get on with it, hoping against hope that they would see the brilliance of the idea.

She strode out to the garden, knowing Devlin would find her there when his meeting ended. She was certain that he had understood the project to which she alluded. It was difficult to wait, but she supposed that every new recruit had to learn patience.

★ ★ ★ ★ ★

"What was that?" Sir Simon asked with a rather dazed look on his face.

Dev grimaced. "That was my wife, interviewing for a position as an agent for the Home Office."

Sir Simon's head snapped about to stare at him in shock. "Good God, man! We cannot have ladies engaged in such activities."

"The French have ladies. The Russians, as well. I've known some, and very nasty characters they are, too."

"Well, we've not got 'em. It just isn't done."

"Officially or unofficially, Lady Caroline will find her way into the thick of the fray. She has done so in this instance, and will do so again." He sighed. "She simply cannot refrain from protecting the people she loves. So we have a conundrum here. Either she must participate, or I must resign."

Sir Simon gave him a long look. "We need you. England needs you."

"Thank you, Sir Simon. I shall discuss all this with my wife, and tell you of our decision."

Dev walked his superior to the door. A footman quietly held it open as Sir Simon turned to Dev. "See if you can talk some sense into her, will you?"

Dev smiled as they shook hands. "Unfortunately, she makes a lot of sense. To me, at any rate."

As the door shut, Ari walked down the marble stairway. "Do you have a few moments for me?" he asked with unaccustomed gravity.

"Of course. Come into the study," Dev said.

Ari could not take his eyes from his brother's face. The livid bruises, the bloodied lip were just a small fraction of what Dev had gone through. For him.

He was so ashamed that he did not know where to begin.

It had taken Janighar to show him how wrong he'd been all these years. How he'd rejected the love of his only brother, who had meant him nothing but good. How he'd let jealousy and a terrible lack of confidence in himself build an impenetrable barrier between them, when he should have been building a bridge.

Dev poured two brandies and passed one to Ari. Then he slowly sank into a wing chair. His careful movements, Ari noticed with a wince of shame, were due to the bruises and the slashes on his back.

Ari took a sip and looked his brother in the eye. "I have been an ass," he said. "A mean-spirited, ungrateful and suspicious idiot. Three times now, you have saved my life, and the life of my beloved. You have saved Zaranbad. While you faced death and danger at each turn, I did nothing to help you. Instead, I upbraided you and blamed you for my own failures of judgment."

He shook his head. "I knew it at the time, but I couldn't stop. You see, Dev, I did it out of jealousy. Pure, base jealousy."

Dev gave him a stunned look. "How could you be jealous? You're everything that's brave and wily and strong. You can rule a difficult kingdom wisely. You can make men follow you just by saying the right thing at the right time. Despite the multitude of problems you face, you are bringing Zaranbad, kicking and screaming at times, into the nineteenth century. And best of all, you know who you are."

"You are mistaken. I do not know that at all." Ari looked down into the brandy glass as though all the answers in the world swirled in its depths. Questions he'd always silently asked himself battered at him now. The very questions that had tainted his relationship with Devlin burst out of him.

"Why did mother leave me behind?" he asked Dev, although he didn't think Dev could possibly have that information. "She could have taken me to England with her. Like she took you."

"I think she had to leave you, Ari. You could not be a strong king unless you grew up in Zaranbad and understood its culture and the people surrounding you. You needed Grandfather's help to learn all you needed to know."

Dev looked around at the study and the garden beyond its windows. For a moment, he was silent. "One day, I came upon her here," he said finally. "I was four years of age at the time, but I've never forgotten it. She was crying, Ari. She held your letter in her hands and she cried for the loss of you."

Ari's breath caught in his throat. He had believed that she had not cared at all for him. Else why would she have gone?

"She loved my father," Dev said as though he'd clearly heard Ari's silent question. "But it cost her so much to lose you. Why do you think I've looked up to you all these years? She told me all about you. About how strong you were and how much you were learning and what a great king you would make. She loved you deeply."

Ari shook his head. "I have been a fool, brother."

"You have been a man, intent upon saving what you were meant to save—a nation. You do not know me well, Ari, but I should like that to change."

"So should I like that. Will you come to us? You and Caroline? Will you help us as much as you can? I need you, Dev. Your guidance. Your courage. Your wise counsel."

"We will come." Dev smiled, and for the first time Ari clearly saw beneath the masks Dev wore. His brother had a loving heart, he mused. And Caroline had made it possible for him to reveal it.

As Dev left the study, his thoughts raced. Maybe the breach between Ari and him had been part of what had driven him so hard all his life. Maybe it had made him too careful, too secretive, too certain that he would always be alone. Shock, understanding, and love welled up in him. He had a brother. He had a family.

Where was Caroline? His compass, his center, his love. He needed to tell her. He needed, simply, to be where he could breathe the same air she breathed. Forever.

Caroline heard footsteps crunch on the gravel and wheeled to see Devlin walking toward her. She caught up her skirts and ran to meet him.

"What is it to be, then?" she asked, as he held her close. She breathed in his masculine warmth, and clung. It had been such a close thing this morning—her fear that she would not see him again in this life. Now, she wished to never let him go.

"You have flummoxed Sir Simon," he said, stroking her hair, his fingers smoothing through it.

"But what about the outcome?"

They walked together toward the shade of a venerable oak tree. His arm drew her into his side. "That is up to us. If we wish, we may do this work together. If we do not wish, I shall quit. I want you to know that I would rather quit, Caroline."

Beneath the tree, he turned to face her completely and took her hands. He cleared his throat against the emotion that welled up in it.

"For most of my life, I've lived in two worlds. I never felt I had a true home in either. I told myself it didn't matter, because I had my duty. It was ugly, it was dangerous. I didn't care much about what happened to me. But there were others whom I couldn't save, and innocents who got in the way."

He looked up, and the leaves glowing emerald green in the sun shimmered as though underwater. "But it was something I did well. And it was all I had.

"Until you came into my life, that is," he continued, despite the embarrassing way in which his voice broke. "With you, I found my home. I need to spend my days by your side. I need to spend my nights in our bed. I love you, Caroline. You are my home."

Caroline gazed into the dark eyes that held her by the greatest bond of all—clear, soul-deep love.

She, too, understood what he was talking about—the all-encompassing loneliness. She had lived a life of shame, where people who should have respected her barely tolerated her. It had made her so angry that she'd fought them all by becoming what she really wished to be—herself. But there had been no home for her, either.

It didn't matter where they went or what they did. As long as they had each other, they would always be home. She flung her arms around his neck and pressed her body as close to his as she could get. As though, like the princess in the poem, she could fold herself into his bosom.

"All I wish is to be with you," she whispered.

His arms were strong and warm around her. His body was a bastion, a fortress. "Then it is settled," he said. "We shall bid the Home Office farewell and find our own adventures."

Caroline's face brightened considerably, Dev noticed with a tiny frisson of alarm.

"Oh, yes," she said. "Perhaps we could go to India."

A laugh gurgled up inside him as he thought about pirates and tribal conflicts and Eastern intrigue and how an Englishman and his wife might find deadly adventure aplenty there.

"Could we please remain where we are for the next few months? I should like my heart to take a good rest before it leaps into my throat again."

She sighed. "Perhaps you're correct. After all, there's Hindi and Pashtu to learn, and remedies to pack, and guides to hire. But while we're in India, we might keep our eyes open for any Russians we meet."

"Ari needs us, Caroline," Dev said, and his heart brightened at the thought. "Zaranbad, thank God, is not now as interestingly deadly as Afghanistan, or as I suspect India will be in the near future. But there is much to do." He told her about his brother's invitation. He turned her in his arms, tucking her back against him, placing his hands gently on her abdomen.

"It's possible, you see, that you are carrying our child at this moment, and I would trust Zaranbad's physicians to help with the birth."

She nuzzled her head back against his shoulder. "Well," she said softly. "Having a child would be an adventure in itself, would it not?"

"Indeed." He laughed, swept her up in his arms, and carried her swiftly up the marble stairway, passing a gaping maid who turned swiftly away and plied her feather duster to some portraits on the wall. He carried her through the doorway to their bedchamber and laid her down on the bed, gazing his fill at this miracle that had come into his life one dismal night in a garden full of moonlight.

"For now, there is only one place where I should like to be. Here, with you. For where you are is peace and adventure and love."

He bent to her, cupping her face in his hands. "Come, Cara. Beloved. Take me home."

A WORD OR TWO ABOUT TENNYSON'S SHOCKING POEM (AND THE AUTHOR'S SHOCKING USE OF ANACHRONISM)

"Now Sleeps the Crimson Petal," Alfred, Lord Tennyson's lyrical and sensual poem, was written for a "serio-comic" book of poems called *The Princess,* the story of Princess Ida, an original feminist who founded an elite school for young women and refused to allow males near it—or her. Until, of course, true love came calling.

The book was published in 1847, to the sighs and blushes of Victorian matrons. I had the gall to pre-date the publication to 1843, the year that Caroline and Devlin meet and fall in love.

I had a sneaking suspicion that unwed daughters were not given the opportunity to read such material, and thus decided that it was the perfect poem at which Caroline would sneak a peek.

Modern women have argued over the imagery, especially the last two lines of the poem, suspecting Tennyson of writing male chauvinist tripe—that is, his plea for the beloved to lose herself in him.

But to me, it seems a universal desire of lovers. The need to become so close that each is a part of the other's soul is an ideal of love that has no gender. And for Dev and Caroline, both outsiders, both lonely, this yearning for a true merging of souls seemed the heart of their quest for meaning and fulfillment.

So with apologies to Lord Tennyson and you, I ask for pardon, if just for the few hours it takes to read this story.

ABOUT THE AUTHOR

Mary Lennox is an author of both fantasy and historical romance novels that have been received with critical acclaim.

She lives in southern Ohio and spends her time between a small, old, craftsman home in the city and a large farmhouse in the country which she and her husband built board by board. The wood floors of both houses are slightly uneven.

When not at the computer, Mary takes care of horses, a dog, two cats and a large garden. Or conversely, dabbles in politics. As with the wood floors, there are certain similarities in these country and city activities—namely the need for constant care and patient observation, be it in approaching farm animals, or city Donkeys and Elephants.

Half Hollow Hills Community Library
55 Vanderbilt Parkway
Dix Hills, New York

45